CW01430997

LEVIATHAN'S SONG

ELSIE WINTERS

LEVIATHAN'S SONG

Copyright © 2021 by Elsie Winters.

All rights reserved. Printed in the United States of America. No part of this book may be used or reproduced in any manner whatsoever without written permission except in the case of brief quotations in critical articles or reviews.

This book is a work of fiction. Names, characters, businesses, organizations, places, events and incidents either are the product of the author's imagination or are used fictitiously. Any resemblance to actual persons, living or dead, events, or locales is entirely coincidental.

For information contact: https://www.elsiewinters.com

ISBN: 978-1-7375355-0-8

ASIN: B098KL6V9H

First Edition: August 2021

10 9 8 7 6 5 4 3 2 1

Cover illustration by Girleyne Costa (GIIH) @GiihArt | @giih_costa20

Editing services provided by Kathleen Walker and Wolffe-Stoirm Publishing

CONTENTS

For Susan, without whom this book would never have been written.

CHAPTER 1

THE BELL RINGING over the door made me grit my teeth in frustration. All I wanted was to focus on the project at my fingertips and ignore the world outside for a little while longer. If I'd been paying attention, it wouldn't have caught me unaware, because the man entering had just enough magic for me to feel him coming from outside the shop.

I had a habit of blocking that extra perception out when I worked, since Sidney usually dealt with the customers. I preferred to hide away and lose myself in my projects. Today, that was impossible, so with resignation I set down my current piece, a jewel made to look like a wasp.

I couldn't get it working yet anyway.

"Elara! Just the person I wanted to see!"

I masked a grimace, wishing I could say the same.

Val Harrington stalked across the entrance of my shop and pressed his meaty hands to the glass case in front of me. He was a paunchy, mid-level professor of archeology and fancied himself some kind of Indiana Jones. His magical ability was dowsing—finding things underground like water or minerals or fossils—and gave me the faintest impression of a scavenger following a scent through subterranean caverns.

My magical gift, one of the two, allowed me to suss out the nature of people's magical abilities. My other magical gift, passed down by my father, allowed me to create magical objects, which was probably why he was here in my shop, Northern Charm.

"How can I help you, Mr. Harrington?" I plastered a smile on my face and braced myself for the inevitable conversation about how he had trapped and killed a dragon in the Boundlands... twenty years ago.

Never mind that it had been hibernating and, being over ten thousand years old, so decrepit that the majority of its scales were missing. It hadn't even had any teeth left, but Harrington was a hero in his own mind. Anyone who disagreed would be talked over with tales of his "trophy hunt of a lifetime," though it had been so large that Harrington and his men couldn't get it out of the mountain cave. They had taken only a single horn, and bringing it down the mountain had nearly cost one of the men's lives when the group fell during descent. The great beast's body had lain up in the mountain for the last twenty years, fouling up the passageway, while Harrington blathered on about it to anyone with ears.

"I have a fantastic business opportunity for you," he said. His voice was booming, too loud for the small indoor space. "I just saw Sidney, and I told her to put in an order with you. I killed a dragon, you know." *Here we go.* "I bet you could make a golem out of the bones still up in that cave!"

I choked. Technically, I *could* make a golem—an artificial construct magically animated with a heartstone—out of bones, but the idea turned my stomach. It was too close to necromancy.

"If you can't do that," he said, responding to my reaction, "I will take a stone golem instead. Sidney wasn't inclined to pass along my order, since I don't have a heartstone. I can't understand why you have someone like that working for you."

My expression hardened. I didn't like anyone disparaging my friends.

"I'm sorry you felt dismissed," I hedged, "but Sidney knows my policies. I insist clients provide certified heartstones up front because they are prohibitively expensive and difficult to procure." The only way to get one was to trade something of value to the little fairy-folk, unless you wanted to deal with the kelpies. And *no one* dealt with the kelpies.

The fairies themselves were nearly impossible to barter with, not to mention terrifying. The water fairies, or sprites as they were known, had huge, luminous eyes and needle-like teeth. They left vicious bites when angered and rarely came to the surface for trade anyway. The fire fairies were basically born of hot coals and seething rage. Bargaining with them was like trying to bargain with a nest of angry hornets. Sparks were said to have the shortest tempers of all the fae, and anyone known for trading with them was bound to be covered in disfiguring scars. In fact, the only fairies who resembled the cutesy darlings of folklore were the pixies from the woodlands, and even they could leave a nasty bite.

It was risky business to bargain with the fae. After one of them suggested bartering a human child in exchange for a heartstone, I'd cut off trading with them all together. Now I insisted on my clients producing their own heartstone first, *with* a certified receipt detailing exactly what it was traded for.

"Not to mention," I continued, "that a golem's entire *being* is designed around the type of heartstone that drives it. A spark's stone would need to power a creation of lava rock and fire. If a client wanted a fire golem, and then later was only able to procure a stone from a pixie, my work would be worthless, an empty husk. I'd have to start again. That's why I require a heartstone and a *substantial* down payment up front, and because of this, I don't make many golems. It's not really the type of work I'm interested in pursuing."

And that was fine with me. The task of building them was fraught with ethical quandaries and stacks of legal documents, and I tended to be suspicious of those requesting one anyway.

Especially Val Harrington.

"What is your purpose for needing a golem?" I asked.

"A down payment?" he sputtered, looking horrified. "This is an opportunity! Imagine how much interest you would get from people wanting to do business with you when I tell them you made it for me! You wouldn't have to waste your time peddling these little trinkets anymore."

He gestured to the cases of magical amulets, jewelry, and knives surrounding him that I'd poured hours of my time and energy into. I made a good living and got to work on new projects every day, so to have him dismiss my work as merely "trinkets" was incredibly insulting.

"For your information," he continued haughtily, "I need a golem to help care for my... father. He's ailing, you know."

My expression hardened further, and I chose to dismiss that last bit, as I knew his family. His father had passed away when I was a child.

"I like what I do, Mr. Harrington, and I'm truly not interested in creating golems, stone or otherwise."

"You elves are all the same, keeping your magic to yourselves and refusing to share it with other people." He whirled on his heel and stomped from the store, trying and failing to slam the door behind him, since it worked on a self-closing hinge.

I blew out an angry breath and shook my head, making the tiny chains woven into my hair jingle, then turned to sigh at my bejeweled insect. My groan was audible when the bell chimed again, but relief filled me when my best friend swept in.

Today her long blond hair was pulled back in its usual ponytail, with several braids woven in. She was stunning, with her high cheekbones, pointed chin, and darker eyebrows and dark blue eyes that contrasted against pale skin. She was muscular for a woman, and with her height and strong frame, she always reminded me of some kind of warrior princess reincarnated from eons past.

"Was that little weasel coming from here?" Sidney asked, pointing toward the door. "I told him to get lost when he tried to corner me at the warehouse. He must have slipped out while I was still haggling and come here to pester you instead."

We were opposites in both appearance and attitude. Sidney was a magpie-shifter and everything you might imagine a corvid's personality to be: coarse, gregarious, and fun. She was built like a Nordic warrior, generally flippant, and self-assured. I was absolutely none of those things. But once she'd seen me accidentally destroy half a building in college, well, she'd decided immediately that I was her new friend, and we'd become just that.

Because we both shared an interest in magical items—though

hers ran more to knives and weaponry—she'd come up with the idea to open a shop together in one of the less expensive districts in Seattle. We both procured supplies and items of interest, but Sidney spent most of her time dealing with customers and book-keeping. That left me free to tinker and build, supplying our shop with finished items. This morning she had an appointment with a dealer and had left me to cover the shop by myself.

"Sorry I took so long," Sidney grumbled, dropping her backpack with a loud thump and heading for the fridge in the back. "You know how Mason Gentry likes to talk. I did find some nice daggers though." Her voice became muffled as she scavenged.

Finally heading back my way with a carrot, she perched on the nearest counter with an odd expression. "Did you hear about the kelpie attacks?" she asked with her mouth full.

"No," I replied, distracted by my unfinished project. "Did you find my silver filament?"

"Sure did." She frowned, pulling a bundle from the pocket in the front of her hoodie and tossing it to me.

"What happened with the kelpies?" I ripped out the material I'd hoped to substitute for the silver, threaded the new filament through the back of the clasp on the tiny heartstone shard, then worked on attaching it to the wings.

"Gentry said he heard a lot of water sprites have gone missing from some of the trading outposts, and it turns out kelpies have been eating them."

I dropped my pliers. "*Eating* them? Sprites are sentient *people*. That's *disgusting!*" My stomach turned. That was one of the most disturbing things I'd heard in a long time.

Sidney nodded, clearly in agreement. Kelpies were known for using their magic to lure things and kill them, but the thought that they would be seeking out *people* to dine on regularly now was beyond the pale.

Forcing my attention back to my project, I clipped off the filament. I focused on the heartstone, pushing my energy into it, and perhaps some pent-up anger, willing it to 'life'. Immediately the wings began to flutter, and it rose as if flying. It was actually levitating, but the fluttering wings added a nice touch, and it really did resemble a large wasp. It didn't have a purpose yet, but

I'd think of something. I hadn't created something like it in a long time, and I was thrilled to get it off the ground.

Hearing a scream morph into a screech, I turned in time to see Sidney disappear, her clothes a clump on the floor, the lump of her avian form hidden within.

"Sidney! You *just* watched me build it! It's not even real!"

She fought her way free of the neck hole and flapped her wings angrily, squawking at me. Her sleek black and white form hopped to the countertop, and I scooped up her clothes and carried them to the back room so she'd have some privacy to dress once she calmed down. We really needed to work on her startle reflex.

<hr />

STEPPING OUT INTO THE CRISP, fall Seattle air, I scanned the street and made my way to the Golden Laurel Gate, heading home. Feeling the rings on my fingers and bracelets on my wrists, I made a mental tally of each magical item on my person, the way another girl might note the mace in her pocket or a whistle around her neck. I had amulets, charms, and talismans woven into my loose hair in tiny chains, draped from my neck, and clustered in my pockets. I wasn't quite five feet tall, certainly wasn't strong, and had no defensive or offensive magic, but I had enough energy to power my stones, and they had some built-in surprises.

I pulled my jacket a little tighter, thankful the weather where I lived in the Boundlands—known to some humans as Faery—matched up for now with the weather here in the Void—or the human realm.

North Seattle made a great location for our shop, thanks to being a relatively large magical crossroads. There were enough people coming and going between the Void and the Boundlands that we had three separate Gates in this neighborhood alone. Seattle itself wasn't a great draw, but it was an important hub with lots of magical traffic and cheap rent, at least compared to the Boundlands. It was a logical midpoint to set up shop.

As I neared the corner, I felt a spider web of sensation, a

tingle along the outer reaches of my perception. I focused on the tugging sensation. Most people might have given in to it, been pulled under by the feelings of joy and gratitude, but I recognized it as an enchantment. I had a ward against such things, and while it wasn't perfect, it did its job.

I continued forward, working my way through a gathering crowd and paying attention to the threads of enchantment. Sitting on a concrete ledge in front of the local coffee shop was a man playing guitar and singing about a January wedding. His guitar case was propped open and overflowing with bills from passersby and the gathered crowd. Tall and lanky, with a swimmer's build, he had loosely-curled, dark-blond hair and an angular jaw covered in light scruff. A tattoo sleeve of an ocean scene flowed up his left arm.

He was breathtaking.

As I came to a stop nearby, the man raised his eyes to meet mine, and a lazy grin spread across his face, making my heart race. He reminded me of seafoam and the joy of looking for little treasures washed up in the surf. I tried to get a better feel for his magic, but what I got didn't make any sense.

It felt like he was *singing* his enchantment, but the only spell singers I knew of were mermaids, and only the females were sirens. Male sirens didn't exist. Another oddity was that the regular run-of-the-mill humans around me appeared to be under his influence. Since they didn't have any magic of their own, *our* magic didn't usually affect them.

Although, there were stories in human folklore of sailors being lured by sirens.

Maybe they *could* be affected.

There was also the possibility that he was just a good singer. His voice was warm and slightly husky, drawing you in, making you feel wanted, cherished. Singing as he was, about weddings and love, about knowing his beloved even though she speaks so low that he could barely hear her... Yeah, it was easy to fantasize about being in love with this singer in another life, but looking at the small crowd, they all seemed... excessively cheerful for people in this area. It wasn't called the 'Seattle Freeze' for the weather after all. Even as I stood there, several people approached and threw large bills in his case. *People aren't this generous with buskers.*

There was more going on than just his singing ability.

I narrowed my gaze as he finished his song, and people began to blink off their confusion and disperse. I bristled at their dazed expressions. Just like the kelpies, this was one more example of seafolk using their lures to target vulnerable people.

"Hello, Empress." He continued looking at me with that impish smile. He might recognize me as being—very distantly—related to the currently ruling family within the Boundlands, but I'd never met this man before. I would have remembered him.

"Empress?" I asked, my voice flat.

He broke into a large grin, his teeth *just* this side of too sharp for a human. Merfolk supposedly had sharp teeth, similar to a water sprite, but I'd never met one myself.

"It seems fitting," he said, his light eyes assessing my form. "You're wearing enough jewelry to finance an empire." His eyes were warm as he said it, as if, perhaps, his teasing wasn't meant to be taken as mocking.

I didn't know how to respond, so I simply asked the question on my mind. "What are you doing?"

His smile dropped by a degree, and his eyes narrowed a fraction. "What does it look like I'm doing?" The crowd had dispersed, and being the focus of his attention made me feel as though a wave were crashing over me, pulling me toward him in a rising tide. A flush crept up my neck and into my cheeks.

"It looks like you're playing guitar on the sidewalk," I began, struggling to focus. "But it *feels* like you're enchanting people. That doesn't make any sense, though, because you're not a mermaid." The last bit was mostly muttered to myself.

"Last time I checked, that was correct," he replied with a smirk.

If I narrowed my eyes at him any further, they would shut. This guy could weaponize his charm.

He hesitated before seeming to catch himself, then leaned over, straightening the money in his case. Clearly a dismissal.

"Wouldn't that be stealing?" I asked, because I couldn't help myself. Everything about it just felt *wrong* to me.

"Why?" He sat back on his haunches and looked at me. "Everything here is freely given. Performing is an art, and art makes people feel things. I can't help it if the words I speak affect people more than someone else's words. I have bills to pay, so I use what gifts I have at my disposal to make a living." His eyes grew colder as he spoke, defensive and cautious. "I don't suppose someone who comes from old money would know much about that though."

I looked down at my clothing: a draping top, designer jeans, and a light peacoat. "Why would you think that?"

"Lots of things, Empress, but your accent screams Upper Golden Laurel." He stuffed his cash into a cubby in his case and gently placed his guitar inside, nestling it carefully before closing the case.

"I'm not an empress," I muttered.

"Not *yet.*" He stood, his grin returning, and picked up his case. "But if you work very hard, you might get there someday. Maybe this will help." He pulled something out of his pocket and flicked it to me as he walked away.

Catching the object out of the air, I opened my hand to reveal a quarter.

CHAPTER 2

I WAS SURPRISED, as the week went on, how many times the siren returned to my thoughts. While there were many men I found to be attractive, it was incredibly rare for me to feel *attracted to* someone, and I wondered if the frequency of my thoughts was simply that: attraction.

When we'd discussed the encounter the next day, Sidney had been nearly hysterical at my retelling.

"Lord, Elara, I can't believe he pegged your accent right down to the neighborhood," she'd said with a laugh. "Only you would question the ethics of a siren singing on the street. It's not like he was luring sailors to a watery grave."

She had asked me multiple times why he'd given me a non-magical quarter, not understanding why he thought I might want human money, not understanding that it was meant as a taunt, and a well-deserved one at that. My face heated at the memory. I was more embarrassed every time my conversation with him mentally resurfaced.

I jerked from my distraction when my name was called, stepping forward quickly to collect my coffee from the counter at the local Starbucks. Halfway to the door, I felt the siren's magic outside and froze.

I briefly contemplated living in a coffee shop for the rest of my life. That was assuming he wasn't planning to come inside.

The possibility of him finding me standing here like a deer in headlights had me glancing toward the bathroom. That was ridiculous, but I wasn't ready to see him again.

I recognized that I'd still been irritated about Harrington's behavior toward me in my shop that day and upset about the kelpie attacks on the water sprites, and it had been unfair to direct those feelings toward him. He'd also been right that I *didn't* know anything about struggling to pay bills. I'd been born to a wealthy family in a wealthy area, and thanks to my father's abilities as an artificer and golemancer, which he passed on to me, he'd never had difficulty securing contracts with the government in the Boundlands.

The siren provided entertainment, and people willingly paid him for that service. No one was harmed by his manipulation, and if perhaps they were a bit more generous than they would have been otherwise, who was I to say what he was doing was *wrong*? I used my own magic to make a living for myself. Admittedly, I still had some quibbles about the *way* he was using his magical talents, but I also had concerns about the morals of the contracts my father took to make the money he'd provided for our family as well. I came to the conclusion, while glaring into space, that I had indeed been too quick to judge him.

I knew I needed to apologize, but that didn't mean I wanted to do it *right now*. Unfortunately, there wasn't a reasonable way for me to get back to my shop without him seeing me.

I could feel him outside, impressions of sand and surf, high tide and clear, starry nights, rolling over me. Once I'd met someone and felt their magic, I could usually recognize them from a distance. Each person's unique combination of presence and magic stood apart to me from anyone else's, even if just slightly, like a scent or a taste. Feeling him out there and knowing I was only delaying the inevitable, I made myself move.

Forcing myself forward, I stepped out onto the patio, as the wind lifted loose strands of my dark brunette hair around my face. Moving slowly to keep from jingling, I did my best not to draw attention. I found him bent over a shaded table, writing on a sheet of paper with an empty cup near his hand.

I realized I could walk past him, pretend like I hadn't seen

him, but now that I *had* seen him, it felt inexplicably rude. While
I despised inviting confrontation, I knew I'd offended him, and
my conscience wouldn't allow me to escape from apologizing
now that I had the opportunity to do so.

I hated this. Sidney would never fret over a conversation.
She'd just stroll right up and say whatever she wanted to. I could
be brave. *Right?*

I stilled near his table, unsure how to approach. Should I
interrupt him? Wait for him to see me? I hadn't really thought
this part through. I was half a second from chickening out and
returning to hide in the store when he paused to brush his hair
back from his face, spotting me out of the corner of his eye.

Setting his pencil down, he turned toward me, eyebrows
pulling together, and one side of his lip quirked up. I probably
looked like a squirrel caught raiding the birdseed with my eyes
wide and my hands clutching my coffee beneath my chest. His
grin widened.

"Empress."

"Siren."

"Are you just going to stalk me, or would you like to sit?" he
asked, making me sputter. He laughed lightly, his eyes shining in
amusement.

"I'm not *stalking* you. I wanted to apologize," I said, mortified.

He gestured at the chair across from him, obviously seeing
my slight horror.

"I promise I don't bite," he murmured. My gaze jumped to
his slightly too sharp teeth, though I knew he meant it jokingly.

"You really want me to sit?" I asked, stalling. I looked toward
my shop, briefly wondering how awkward it would be for me to
simply dart away. *Pretty awkward.* Only my years of ingrained
composure training rooted me to the paving stones.

I didn't like how flustered looking at him made me feel. He
was too pretty to focus on. His angular jawline framed generous, soft looking lips, and high cheekbones highlighted a straight
nose. Full, sweeping eyelashes surrounded piercing, clear-blue
eyes. When factored in with his enchantments tugging at me
this way and that, I knew I was bound to embarrass myself
again.

"*Sit.*" He nodded at the chair and pushed it out with his foot, staring at me like he had guessed my plan to bolt.

I hesitated. "Can you turn it off?" I asked, creeping slowly around the table.

The curve of his mouth dipped down into a frown, his eyebrows drawing low. "Turn *what* off?"

"You know…" I waved my hand around in the air near my head.

He stared at me, obviously having no idea what I was talking about.

"The enchantments."

He blinked. "Ah, that." He gave a brittle smile that didn't reach his eyes. "No, I'm afraid I can't. That's a permanent feature."

My cheeks grew hot again. Apparently, I had pointed out something that bothered him. Maybe it was frustrating, constantly influencing the people around you, whether you wanted to or not.

"I'm sorry," I said in a rush, quickly pulling out the seat and lowering myself into it. "It's just a little disconcerting, that's all."

"Most people don't mind. In fact, they never even notice."

"Oh, I see. Yes, *that* doesn't turn off for me either, unfortunately," I said, eyeing the passersby. It was easier to talk to him if I didn't look at him.

"And how is it that you're able to feel them, yet you don't seem to be influenced by them?" he asked, sounding casual, though when I glanced at him his eyes betrayed his curiosity.

I tapped the manacle bracelet on my wrist, a wide silver cuff inlaid with labradorite and pale jade. It connected to several rings on my hand that were holding pale blue and green chalcedony gemstones via strands of thin, silver chains. It was an intricate piece and one of the more physically taxing to imbue and modify. I was immensely grateful I'd spent the time to get it right.

Every word he spoke felt like, if it could just get its hooks in me, it would be an overwhelming lure, dragging me toward him. Is this what everyone felt like around him? I found myself wondering what it would be like to kiss him.

My experience with men was nearly zero, unless you count my childhood friend Rafe, who was strictly an older brother figure anyway. *And he certainly doesn't look like the siren,* I thought, gazing at his flexing biceps as he set an arm on the table.

"Huh." The siren's eyebrows drew together. "Where'd you get that?" he asked, drawing me back to our conversation.

"I made it," I answered, focusing on my bracelet, suddenly self-conscious.

"You *made* it?" he asked, his eyebrows rising in shock. He actually looked impressed. His eyes skated over my body again, flickering from one piece of jewelry to the next, cataloging them. "You make amulets?"

"I do." I dug a card out of my small purse and set it on the table in front of him. "Do you need an enchantment ward?" I asked, a little confused by his interest.

"No, I'm good on that front," he muttered, inspecting my card. He dropped his forearm onto the table in front of me with a soft thump, his hand landing palm up. The tattoo sleeve started at his wrist and crawled up under the sleeve of his t-shirt. A large, detailed cephalopod I recognized as a kraken sprawled lazily across his skin, flanked by a predatory whale, while little fish flitted among coral arches and rocks. The piece was exquisite, but even more intriguing than the artwork was the feeling of fortification or even numbness radiating off his arm.

I set my coffee on the table and lifted my hand to let it hover a few inches above his skin, inspecting the artwork more closely. There, hidden among the seafoam and tentacles, were runes, expertly drawn and permanently embedded. Rune smiths were a rare find. Granted, so were golemancers and artificers, and I was sitting right here.

"Elara," he said, causing me to jerk my hand back. He was reading off my card. "I still think Empress is a better fit. I'm Levi," he smiled.

"Levi... like the jeans?"

"Short for Leviathan." He smirked like I was slow. I guess that did make more sense. I glanced down at the paper he'd been writing on, realizing it was sheet music. Which reminded me...

"I actually came over here because I wanted to apologize." I pursed my lips and winced.

"Oh?" He raised an eyebrow and leaned back, letting an arm hang limp over the back of his chair, the other hand reaching for his empty plastic cup. His long leg stretched forward into my space as he inspected the siren in the logo printed on the side.

"Yeah, I'm sorry about last week. I shouldn't have judged you or accused you of stealing just for using your gifts." I watched him out of the corner of my eye. My heart felt better just having said it, even though my cheeks felt hot with shame.

He considered me silently, his eyes shifting between mine. "We're good," he said with a secretive smile, my chest suddenly buffeted with a riot of butterflies.

My phone buzzed, startling me, and I dug it out of my purse to find a message from Sidney.

Sidney: I think I found a buyer for the daggers, but he needs a charisma and speed mod on them ASAP. Where are you anyway?

Charisma on a ceremonial dagger… *Must be a performer.* I rolled my eyes; I hated rush orders. "It was nice to meet you, Levi, but my empire needs me," I said, rising from my chair.

He tapped my card on the table and smiled. "I'll see you around, Empress."

I grinned to myself as I walked away, wondering what he'd think when he noticed the quarter on the table. A muffled shout as I rounded the corner told me he'd taken the bait. It might not have been magical when he gave it to me, but it sure was now.

<hr>

THAT EVENING I locked up the shop and made my way home. As I passed the coffee shop, I found myself gazing at the empty tables, only to find that the siren, Levi, wasn't there. I was slightly uncomfortable with the realization that I'd hoped to see him again. It obviously wasn't the first time I'd ever seen an attractive man before, but for some reason, this one made me a mess.

Maybe I needed to figure out a way to strengthen my ward.

I was, by nature, an introverted, shy, and reserved person. An only child, I'd grown up on a large estate without any children my age to play with and had spent much of my time tinkering with scraps and cast offs in my father's shop, under his watchful eye.

I'd attended the Golden Laurel Girl's School of the Arcane growing up, only coming home on long weekends and holidays. When I did come home, if my father wasn't explaining his latest idea for a project in his workshop, then I was either playing with our pack of mastiffs or exploring with Rafe.

Thinking about Rafe made my heart beat a little painfully. He was a dryad, and his people migrated often, though they'd made their home in the woods near my family's estate for a number of years in between migrations. I'd first met him when I was six years old, and he'd been tickled by my assumption that he must be a golem like one of my father's constructs. I smiled at the memory.

He was gracious with me, returning often to keep me company when he knew I'd be home from boarding school. Though he was about thirty or forty years old (they didn't bother to keep track of time the way most people do), his people lived an average of around six hundred years, so he was about the equivalent of an eighteen-year-old. I laughed at the thought that I was now "older" than him.

Even though I would probably live much longer than the average pureblooded human (thanks to my mixed elvish blood-lines and the fact that I spent most of my time in the Bound-lands), I was twenty-four and was treated like an adult by the rest of society. Poor Rafe had at least a decade left before his people would treat him like an autonomous adult.

It'd been a while since I'd last seen him, though we kept in touch through my parents very occasionally. Last I'd heard, he was out in the foothills of the Ardac mountains, where it wasn't safe for me—or any creature made of flesh—to visit him. Sometimes I missed his gentle presence and his slow, thoughtful approach to life.

In college I'd been thoroughly absorbed in my studies and hadn't had much time for friends. My teachers, upon learning of my talents and my parentage, had pushed me *hard* in my school-ing. This had resulted in what Sidney refers to delightedly as "The Year of Destruction". I'd gotten a little too big for my britches and tried to animate a golem that was a *little* beyond my abilities at the time. After that, most people—which included all the boys—steered clear of me.

Thankfully, Sidney wasn't so easily frightened. She'd been impressed by all the carnage and had shoehorned herself into a friendship with me, which I quietly appreciated.

Looking back over all this, it made sense that I'd go all swoony over an absurdly handsome siren who gave flirty smiles and distracted me by trying to tug at my feelings. I sighed as the Golden Laurel Gate came into view. I'd have to do a better job of keeping my wits about myself in the future.

As I approached the Gate, I felt the magic of the guard on duty wash over me: vague impressions of crushing strength and brute force. I wondered idly if he was part orc, looking surrepti-tiously for a hint of tusks as I dug my ID out of my wallet and handed it to him.

The signs behind him looked like they would fit better along a highway than in a community park. *Golden Laurel Gate*: *Magical creatures only. Enter at your own risk*. The guard returned my ID without looking at it. He wasn't here to keep non-magical people out of the Boundlands; the Gate did that on its own.

Pureblooded humans couldn't pass through the Gate—a shimmering hazy plane surrounded by a stone archway. If they tried, they simply fell through the other side, dead. It wasn't that we *wanted* to keep them out, they just weren't capable of passing through.

The familiar painful prickling sensation swept through my body as I entered, and I shivered, my jewelry rattling as I shook the pins-and-needles out of my limbs. Dodging around a lumbering man reeking of decay and dark magic—a necro-mancer for sure—I made my way toward the skyscrapers ahead. After spending the day in the magical desert of the Void, it always took a few moments for my senses to come to grips with the magic inundating me in the Boundlands.

Not only did every person around me reach out to me

without noticing, their magic curling around me and whispering its secrets, but the Boundlands itself carried its own special kind of magic, which every life here depended on.

It was an important part of the ecosystem, stronger in some areas than others. Places where the magic was strongest tended to be more densely populated with creatures that depended on it more urgently to survive: the purebred-races of the Boundlands, especially merfolk, dryads, fairies, and the like.

They couldn't even survive in the Void due to the lack of magic. They could cross the Gate, and they'd exit alive, but within a matter of minutes, they'd be dead if they didn't make it back through. Elves could last much longer—in fact, the mixed races wouldn't exist if they couldn't—but their health suffered if they spent *too* much time in the Void. It was really only those of mixed-race—and we were many—who could cross back and forth unharmed.

Even so, our lifespans were greatly reduced if we spent too much time in the Void, so most of us commuted. We lived in the Boundlands but worked in the Void.

The Boundlands gave us a healthier environment to live in, but the Void gave us access to not only humans, but travelers from all over the Boundlands coming through the many Gates who we wouldn't have access to in a single city otherwise. In my north Seattle neighborhood, I had access to not only buyers in Golden Laurel, but Oar's Rest and Dry Gulch as well, thanks to the other Gates. Both were far-flung cities on the coast and in the desert, respectively.

There was a seat open on the railcar next to a man who was an electric conjurer (probably employed by the city and quite possibly this very rail line), so I gratefully sat for the short commute. Across from me was an elvish lady who stared straight ahead, unmoving, completely unaffected by the jostling of the train car. Next to her was an elder dwarvish man, covered in dust with his toolbox between his feet, swaying in his seat.

Blue lights, provided by light benders or conjurers, flickered by outside the cars, and we rode in silence until I departed to walk the final two blocks home. I didn't live in Upper Golden

Laurel with my parents anymore, instead choosing a cozy town-house in the trendy, hilltop Crown District, closer to downtown.

I climbed the short flight to my stoop, kicked a pile of white feathers onto the lawn, and let myself in. Desperate for some tea, I dug through my cabinets, which were full of gifts from Bette, my neighbor to the left. She was an apothecary and loved to leave me tea, but I was too scared to drink any of it. I felt too guilty to part with it, though. I found my favorite stash in the back and just as I put the kettle on, I heard a knock at the door and a cheerful greeting. I grabbed a second mug and set it on the counter as my neighbor Bette, the tea-gifter, let herself in.

"Evening, Elara. Oh, no, I can't stay. No tea for me, dear, but thank you." Bette's coppery brown curls were tied up in a scarf, her wide brown eyes tired and blinking as she slumped into the chair at my kitchen table. She was older than me and often stayed up too late working on things that caused something smelling vaguely of sulfur to waft onto the front lawn. If I asked what she was making, she would hem and haw and change the subject.

"I heard you come in," she said, "and I just wanted to make sure you saw the notice to vacate in the mail before I head to my sister's for the week."

"What!?" I turned, shocked, and trotted to the entryway to grab the mail.

"Oh, it's just for one night. No need to fret. I've been wanting to visit family anyway, so I'm going to head out early. Old Man Higgins down in unit 6 is having problems with banshees again, and management had to call in eradication."

I found the notice she referred to and quickly scanned it. I had to be out of the unit next Tuesday night.

"We have to clear out the whole block in case things go side-ways with the banshees," she said.

"Great," I muttered, tossing it down.

"Yeah, I know. Frustrating." She propped her chin on her hand. "I'm not actually convinced there *are* any banshees," she groused. "I certainly haven't heard any. You can stay with your parents in the Upper District, right?"

I blew out a breath. "My dad's off on a contract at the

moment, and I'm not sure if my mom is back from visiting him yet or not. I could stay at the house anyway. I'd rather spend the night in Dry Gulch with my friend Sidney and her brother, though," I answered absently, already making plans to talk to Sidney. That sounded more fun than staying in a large, empty house with a rock-golem butler and the new maid for company. I had a week to figure it out.

Bette narrowed her eyes. "*Dry* Gulch," she said, a little scandalized. "I don't know how I feel about someone like you spending time in Dry Gulch."

I shot her a look out of the corner of my eye. "Someone like me," I repeated flatly.

"Now, don't get *huffy*. You're just so... dainty. Bunch of bandits down in that town. Doesn't seem safe."

She wasn't wrong. "Sidney doesn't live in a seedy area. Plus, her brother would be with us." I didn't mention that Sidney would be fully capable of sticking a knife in an assailant on her own... or the fact that I'd spent some time in Dry Gulch by myself, trading for supplies for my shop. No need to worry the lady. "Are you sure about the tea?" I asked as the kettle whistled.

"No, I'm heading out. I can't," she replied absently, frowning. "Be careful, whatever you decide. I'll be back the Wednesday after the eradication. I'm taking the cats with me. That way I'll know they're safe from the banshees... and the harpy."

The neighbor who lived on the other side of me was a harpy named Isadora. While Bette had lost a few cats to unknown circumstances, I didn't think it was fair to pin that on the harpy.

I waved absently as she left and finished making my tea, carrying the mug to my table to finish looking through the mail. As I finished my drink and was rising to make another, I heard a firm knock at the door. Confused, because Bette always just waltzed in, I wandered to the door and opened it, still trying to finish reading the last piece of mail in my hand.

A throat clearing had me looking up... and *up*. I took a step back, startled, because this man was enormous and I had no idea who he was. I swallowed. If I'd been paying attention, his magic would have tipped me off. Some kind of blood magic.

"May I help you?"

The man on my porch had buzzed hair, shiny skin, and a wide mouth, which he'd curled into an amused smirk, like he knew something I didn't. People who are very large never realize how it feels to be someone who is very small when they loom over you. I looked at his cold eyes and smile, which had grown into a predatory grin, and wondered if, perhaps, this man knew *exactly* how he was making me feel. I narrowed my gaze at him, trying to ignore the prickling feeling at the back of my neck so I could focus.

His wide smile showed jagged, yellow teeth. "Elara Hawthorne, aren't you?" he asked, leaning even closer. "I've heard you have some special abilities for sale, and my boss is very interested in having you make something for us."

"Make something," I repeated dully. "You're welcome to tell him to come down to my shop. I don't do business from my house. If he wants to buy something, he can come to north Seattle, or if he can't enter the Void himself, he can always have someone pick up his order for him."

I'd feel safer dealing with this guy at my shop, where Sidney could keep an eye on him. The creeping dread in my gut was edging toward slight panic as I noted that Bette would be long gone by now, and while I had some defense in my jewels, I didn't think I could fight this guy off for long if he got into my house. Something about his stance and the gleam in his eyes set off my alarm bells. "What did you say your name was?"

He smiled, a quick, indulgent smirk that didn't reach his eyes. "They call me Bones. My boss prefers a certain level of discretion, you see. We weren't aware you sold constructs out of your shop, only your little trinkets."

Constructs. These people wanted a golem. *Of course they do.* Who *didn't* want a silent, obedient slave that never questioned what you told it to do and could do any job from light housekeeping to club bouncer to mech-warrior? I felt myself frown. "I'm not interested in selling constructs."

"Is that so? I heard you were making a stone golem for someone else. My boss would be very disappointed to hear you're not interested in his offer. I don't think you would want to disappoint such an important person. I've heard suppliers don't like to sell to shops that disappoint people like him. Sometimes things even happen to them." His voice was soft, beseeching, a sharp contrast to the menacing look in his eyes and the implication of his words.

This creep was threatening me! For some crag-faced rock-golem! The only person I knew of who had asked about a stone golem was Harrington. So, now I had this guy's attention thanks to that pompous, slack-jawed, cretin, *Val Harrington?* Maybe I'd build one for myself just to stomp the two of them! It looked like I needed a sentry of my own anyway.

Raising my chin and mentally seizing the gems I wore capable of inflicting any kind of damage, I answered in a voice that was steady enough to surprise me.

"I wouldn't make a golem for Harrington for all the gold in South Danton. I'm *not interested* in selling constructs. Have a good night, sir." I tried to shut my door, but he was faster than me and got his arm against it, forcing it open.

Sheer panic blasted through my body as I poured more energy into a ring on my right hand, but before I could use it a piercing, deafening shriek had us both stumbling back.

Above us and to the left, a loud thump sounded as a blur of white feathers and claws landed on the edge of my roof. The harpy was large enough that, when she leaned down to scream again, she was right in the man's face. He shouted and tumbled down the three stairs to my front walk before scrambling up and darting off into the early dusk. My neighbor dropped heavily from the roof to the brick railing of my porch, never taking her eyes off the retreating figure of the man.

I took a shuddering breath, trying to calm my nerves, but my heart was pounding, and my ears were ringing.

"Thank you, Isadora," I said faintly. She didn't turn to look at me, still hunched forward, with her wings slightly raised like she might leap into flight and chase the man down. I didn't think I could possibly be more grateful for her as a neighbor in that moment. *She can eat all the cats she wants.*

CHAPTER 3

"I'm gonna *kill* that asshole, Harrington. Just stick a knife right in him and gut him stem to sternum."

I flinched. "I don't think that's how that saying goes," I muttered.

As soon as I'd calmed down enough to deadbolt the door, I'd sent for Sidney. She'd made it to my house in twenty minutes. From the state of her glistening skin and overheated cheeks, she'd flown most of the way. It was a good thing she had the foresight to stash extra sets of clothes at my house, because there's no way she'd fit in mine.

She ignored my muttering. "So, was he running his ignorant mouth about golems in public, or did he feed that info to other people specifically? Does that blowhard think at all?" After her arrival, I'd filled her in on my visitor and subsequent rescue by Isadora. She'd been stomping around my kitchen, making threats about Harrington and the man at my door ever since.

I was trying to distract myself by being productive and was seated at the table with my materials spread out in front of me, working on a gem set that doubled as a hex against people wielding blood magic. Needle-nosed pliers in one hand and silver findings in the other, I busied myself with my work while her anger worked itself out.

Was I angry? Yes. Was I scared? Absolutely. But I couldn't

concentrate on it or I'd panic, and panicking didn't help. I'd called in reinforcements; I knew when I was out of my depth.

"I kind of want to send Isadora a gift basket," I grumbled, mostly to myself. "What kind of gift basket does someone send a harpy?"

Sidney stumbled, apparently startled. "Um... fancy rats? I don't have any idea." Her anger evaporated in the face of her confusion. She covered her forehead with her palm and leaned back against my kitchen counter.

"Describe him again. Bald head and looming stature aren't a lot to go on. Did he have any tattoos? On his face or hands? Crossbones on his bottom lip or a windrose on his left hand?"

I shook my head. "I would have noticed a facial tattoo, I think. I didn't look at his hands though." I raised one shoulder apologetically, and she sighed.

"Okay, let's think this through. We've got anything from possible mobsters to general grifters sniffing around, wanting giant melee weapons for whatever little schemes. We've got a soft target who has zero street smarts—"

"Hey," I frowned.

"—and no protection. They didn't want to come to the shop, either because they'd draw too much attention, or they thought you were too protected there. So, they came to feel you out here, at your house, where you're more vulnerable. We need to remove your vulnerability."

I held up my gem set. "Working on it."

"Okay, but that's just against blood magic," she huffed. "What if they send a different guy next time? Or a number of different guys?"

I frowned, ceding the point.

"Do you have any extra heartstones?" she asked.

"What, like full blown heartstones? No. I've got some chips and shards but nothing big. I can't go walking around north Seattle with a golem stomping along behind me! Are you crazy? Like four people in known *history* can animate a golem that can function in the Void, and I'm one of them. Do you realize how much attention that would attract?" I looked at her incredulously.

"What about an actual guard?"

I gave her my crazy eyes. That sounded delightful: a living, breathing stranger following me around everywhere I went. Every introvert's dream come true. Not to mention the cost. I *hated* that idea.

"Talk to me about the shards," she said.

My eyebrows drew together. "I just keep the chips and shards leftover from heartstones on previous constructs, or my dad gives me his so I can have more chances to experiment. They aren't large enough to create anything big. I just use them for little stuff I want to tinker with."

I watched her eyes brighten with evil delight. "Like your wasp?"

⁓⁕⁓

THE NEXT DAY we closed the shop early and headed down to the Gate for Dry Gulch. We were currently sitting on the bus looking a little worse for the wear. After I'd finished the blood magic hex and we'd binged on cheap takeout for dinner, we stayed up way too late discussing Sidney's ideas for my wasp construct.

She'd decided we needed some kind of drug or venom for the wasp to carry, since it was small, discrete, and easy for me to keep with me. I'd declared her idea absurd and highly unethical, and we'd argued about it for hours.

Eventually, we'd fallen asleep in my bed—I wasn't going to let her sleep on my too-small couch and she refused to leave me alone in my house—and spent the night trying not to elbow each other in the face. Sidney was a wild sleeper.

After I'd attached a stinger to the wasp this morning, she'd convinced me to let her pick up a venom sample she knew of that would "simply knock a person out". I'd asked her if it was a legal substance and her response had been to shrug one shoulder and mutter something along the lines of, "Everything's legal until you get caught. It's fine." So, you know, super reassuring.

So here we were, looking a little wrecked, with Sidney glued to her phone watching an eBay auction for a small sword and me wondering how I'd gotten to this place in my life, when I felt a familiar magic.

The bus pulled to a stop, the front doors opened, and Levi stepped on. The siren's magic wrapped me up in seafoam and the gentle crash of waves without him even knowing, because he never looked up as he grabbed the standing rail and leaned his face against the back of his hand.

I took advantage of the fact that he couldn't see me to watch him as he swayed gently with the motion of the bus. His eyes had dark circles under them, and he looked as tired as I felt, but with the sun backlighting his blond hair, he looked positively ethereal. My heart dropped a little to realize he looked a little sad or run down. Both times I'd seen him previously, he'd had a brilliant smile or mischievous smirk on his face nearly the whole time we'd interacted. I wondered what his life was like.

Three stops later it was our turn to get off, and I turned to tap Sidney and stood. I looked back to find Levi staring at me. The sadness on his face melted into what I could only describe as utter devastation before he turned and disappeared into the crowd. I stood in place, blinking and trying to make sense of his reaction, until Sidney grabbed my arm and pulled me bodily from the bus.

We made our way into Dry Gulch, with me worrying all the while what Levi's look had been about, until I finally shook myself free of it and resolved to puzzle it out later.

Though the Gate was relatively close to the Golden Laurel Gate, the cities themselves were nowhere near each other within the Boundlands. Traveling via Gateways could be a little confusing because the Gateways had been created as there was need for them, organically, and not necessarily with the best foresight and planning.

But if you knew the right combination of Gates to take through both the Void and the Boundlands, you could travel from, say, Seattle to Brazil in a matter of a few hours, with just a pit stop in London, Morocco, and a few cities in the Boundlands along the way.

I tried to focus on keeping up with Sidney, which was proving difficult because she'd apparently forgotten I had little legs. "Slow down, you absolute giant! I can't walk that fast."

She gave an amused bark of laughter. "I'm not a giant, you're just a fairy. Keep up, pixie. We've got to make it to the warehouse district by nightfall."

I wasn't quite *that* small, and we were a long way off from nightfall yet. "Brat," I grumbled, earning another chuckle.

Dry Gulch spread out around us, not particularly attractive but certainly thriving. The city used to be an old watering hole, which had long since dried up, but eventually became the sprawling, grungy metropolis it was today. Boasting swarming crowds and more heat than most places in the Boundlands, it wasn't my favorite place, but the street markets and warehouses were full of any kind of supplies you could imagine, which meant I visited occasionally to pick up something or other.

Sidney and her younger brother, Josh, both felt perfectly at home here, and they'd found an apartment to rent as soon as we'd graduated from school. She'd offered to find a three-bedroom so I could join them, but even though I occasionally found myself enjoying bartering in the street markets here, the general feel of the city was too rowdy for me to want to live here.

As we wove through the crowded streets, she filled me in on the plan. "Alright, when we get up here, I'm gonna have to leave you behind for a bit. Don't... don't look that guy in the eye. Get behind me." I dodged behind her as a towering lich with an aura of... plague bending strolled past me. *What on earth?* I shot a look over my shoulder at him as I struggled to catch back up.

"My guy is in a warehouse down on 11th Ave.," she continued, "and I don't really feel safe taking you in with me. There's this market here on 9th you can shop in while you wait, lots of people around, and I should only be a few minutes tops. Sound okay to you?"

I glanced around as we came to a stop among street stalls spilling out into the road, each one draped in fabric to block out the glaring sun. Hawkers called out their wares and tried to catch my eye.

"Uh, yeah, sure. Sounds good." I'd shopped alone in Dry

Gulch street markets before. Of course I'd be fine. "Since when are you such a mother hen?"

Sidney came to a dead stop and turned to look at me. "Since my best friend had some creep try to force his way into her *house* last night. Just... stay here." She motioned to the general area. "Don't talk to people. Don't go anywhere with anyone." I gave her my crazy eyes. It might become my permanent expression.

"Right. Okay. Fifteen minutes. I'll be right back." She turned and darted off, her magic fading into the crowd and finally disappearing to my senses as the distance between us grew.

With a sigh, I turned to the nearest booth. I might as well get some shopping done and see if I could find anything interesting. As I browsed the booths in the first row, I was immediately disappointed. Some cheaply made clothing, assorted soaps, and random dishes were displayed haphazardly on vendor tables. I picked up a plate and looked at the back, doing a double take. *Made in China.* I... what? What a bizarre thing to smuggle into the Boundlands. The vendor gave my side-eye a dispassionate shrug.

I passed a booth selling questionable potions stored in what appeared to be old plastic Gatorade bottles labeled with marker. Another booth had wall hangings and hastily made talismans boasting poorly drawn runes. I wondered at the state of the population that kept these vendors in business. I'd never shopped in this particular district before, but I hadn't missed much of value.

The last booth in the row sold finely woven linen scarves, hand dyed in a variety of beautiful patterns and colors. Many of the women in the streets wore them around their heads to keep the sun from beating down on them during the hottest parts of the day.

I reached out to touch one, noting its softness as the vendor engaged me, telling me about his different varieties and showing me how thin the fabric was. He was a sweet-looking older man, with dark skin like my father and an impression of elemental earth magic, a low level of alchemy perhaps. I wondered if he used it to help dye his scarves somehow.

As I was looking through a stack of fabric to my left, and

simultaneously trying to pay attention to the chatter from the vendor, I heard voices to my right.

"Hey! That's her! Grab her! That's the tink with all the gems that Bones was after." I stiffened, ducking my head as I tried to rein in my sudden panic.

Tink or tinker was a common name for an artificer, or someone who made small magical objects, among poorer populations. I whirled to face them, taking stock of the situation. There were lots of people around as witnesses, so they probably couldn't actually drag me away right here. I cast out my magical feelers for Sidney but didn't feel her nearby.

The men in front of me weren't overly large, but looked wiry, like they were probably stronger than their size would indicate. The man closest to me had a similar sort of magic to my ability to feel out other's magical abilities. The one catching up to him had a *very* low level of healing magic, almost unnoticeable. They were large enough physically to overpower me, but at least they didn't have any magic they could use against me.

"Did you change your mind about coming for a chat, then?" the man in front asked, indicating toward the building behind him. The one behind him held a knife low, close to his body. I swallowed and took a step back, bumping into the vendor's table and raising my hands slightly.

"I don't know what you're talking about," I said, stalling. "I'm just here doing some shopping." My voice shook slightly. The man's eyes were calculating, and his lips twitched up as he reached back and pulled out his own knife, holding it low like his buddy to hide it from view in the broad daylight. Both of them had a windrose tattooed on the ring finger of their left hand.

"It's such a lucky day that you came down to visit," he said, flicking his knife toward the building behind him to indicate I should move that way.

The vendor behind me got involved, yelling at them to leave me alone and get away, that they had no right to harass his customers. The man in the back told him to shut up, that this was Phantom business and to stay out of it. I couldn't take my eyes off the knife held by the man closest to me to see the vendor's response.

ELSIE WINTERS

A block of ice formed in my gut at his claim of "Phantom business". A loosely organized separatist group who occasionally leaned toward anarchy, the Phantom Council had spread all over the Boundlands and had been cropping up sporadically in the Void. I'd never noticed any kind of gang presence in Golden Laurel and only knew about them from what I'd heard on the news or through the rumor mill.

Now they wanted to snatch me off the streets so I would supply them with weapons? My mind flickered to the riots they'd been behind two years ago, which had left New Gradstein littered with dead. I could just imagine some twenty-foot stone golem stomping through the streets along with the rioters. *Over my dead body.*

The rest of the milling crowd glanced our way when the vendor raised his voice, and a few even paused. They kept back from us, making no move to intervene. From the uneasy looks on their faces, the bystander-effect was running strong.

I focused on the ring on the third finger of my right hand, obsidian and silver, pushing all of my excess energy and adrenaline into it, ready to let loose if anyone touched me. It wouldn't help me any if he stuck his knife in my guts, though.

When the man stepped around me and leaned forward, trying to herd me toward the alleyway, I tried to dart in the other direction, only to be blocked again. My heart was pounding in my ears, and the other man was blocking the only other way out but the alley. *Please come back, Sidney,* I begged internally. These men were so much bolder than we'd imagined.

"Help!" I shouted, trying futilely to attract attention. A crowd was gathering, though no one other than my elderly vendor-champion (who was still shouting at them from his stall) was making any move to help. I'd never been in a situation like this before, and I knew it was going downhill fast.

"*Get away from her!*" Sheer terror and the urge to flee struck like a tidal wave as enchantments rolled over me and entangled my mind.

Levi.

I noted peripherally that his enchantment was having the opposite effect than it normally did, pushing—*shoving*—away instead of drawing toward. I could only imagine what the enchantment felt like to someone without a ward against it, and it was certainly effective in startling my assailants.

As the man with the knife in front of me took a slight step back and turned to look at Levi, I took advantage of his distraction to duck around and run past him. I'd only managed to take the first step when he recovered and reached out with his free hand to grip my wrist. The charge I'd been holding in my ring released instantaneously, and I felt his fingers clench involuntarily before he released me and threw his arm back, shrieking as he fell on his backside.

Levi darted in between us, his arm held in front of me protectively, but I was already on the move. I scrambled back farther along the table just as I felt the clear open skies and beguiling updrafts of Sidney's magic advancing at a furious pace.

Suddenly, she was *there*, airborne and almost completely sideways, knives clutched in both fists as she caught the second man in the shoulder with her boot, sending him to the ground. She stumbled as she landed, but immediately launched after the first man who'd tried to grab me when he stood and bolted away. The second man scrambled to his feet and lurched back down the alleyway they'd come from.

Everyone stared, frozen for a long minute, including Levi. His jaw was hanging a little loose as he stared off in the direction Sidney had run.

"Miss? Miss, are you okay?" The vendor's quiet voice eventually snapped us out of our daze. I turned, working to find my voice. The entire ordeal had probably taken only thirty seconds.

"I'm fine, thank you," I said, though it came out noticeably shaky.

Levi turned to look at me, his eyes still wide. "What did you do to that guy to knock him down?"

Guy? Oh. "I... the same thing I did to your quarter."

"You shocked him?" he asked, still confused.

"Yeah. I dialed it up a bit." He raised his eyebrow. "A lot," I conceded.

.

CHAPTER 4

SIDNEY JOGGED BACK around the corner toward us, and Levi stepped closer, moving to tuck me behind him. I touched his arm to reassure him, grateful for his presence. "She's with me," I murmured. He took a slight step away but left his arm in contact with my hand. His skin felt warm and soft, his arm muscular and sturdy.

Sidney stopped a few feet in front of me, panting, and doubled over with her hands on her knees to catch her breath. Her knuckles were reddened and smeared with spots of blood. She raised her head and squinted at me. "You alright? I heard you scream."

"Are *you* okay? Your hands are bloody."

She wiped them on her pants. "It's not mine. Oh, hey, it's the mermaid." She straightened to look at him, brushing some loose hair out of her face and pulling out her hair tie. She gripped it between her clamped lips to redo her ponytail.

"Mer... *maid*..." Levi repeated drily.

Sidney frowned as she finished pulling back her hair. "Sorry... mer*man*. Mer... dude?" She cringed. "I'll be honest, I have no idea what to call you."

"Well, I'm not a mer, so let's stick with Levi, I guess," he muttered.

"Levi, then." She nodded and puffed out a breath. "I'm Sid," she replied, before turning to me. "What happened?"

People had scattered when Levi's first enchantment rolled through, but as his voice had returned to its usual siren lure, some had edged back in and were watching us, completely failing to be inconspicuous about it. I eyed the crowd and leaned toward Sidney, coming distractingly close to Levi. "They were Phantoms, and they're *here*," I hissed quietly. "Like right there." I pointed toward the warehouse next to us. She jerked her head around to look at it. "They knew the guy from my house."

She turned back to face me with widened eyes and a somewhat amused expression, then started forward. "Yeah, I saw their tattoos, but w*hoopsies*... I wasn't aware of that when I left you here." She waved us ahead of her. "Less talk, more walk. I got what we needed."

I faltered, scrambling my way back to the moment, then started back the way we had come as Sidney clutched my upper arm and began to tow me along. Levi followed closely, hovering protectively as I turned to catch the vendor's eye and thanked him again. He gave a small wave and watched me leave with obvious concern on his face.

"Should we file something with Enforcement about that?" Levi asked, throwing his thumb over his shoulder.

Sidney's eyebrows shot up, and her laugh bordered on hysteria. "Uh, no. *Nope.* Enforcers have way bigger fish to fry down here than those guys, and if they took them in, I'd get tossed in along with them for sure." She rubbed a thumb absently over her first knuckle while scanning the streets around us.

Levi huffed an incredulous laugh, and his blue eyes danced with amusement. His laughter made my heart stutter and pulled at me even more than his words did, and I wondered again at his reaction on the bus.

I glanced at Sidney to make sure she was wearing the new ear cuff I'd made into an enchantment ward for her. She didn't typically wear jewelry, because every time she shifted, it just fell on the floor, but she'd made an exception for this one.

"I've seen some *wild* stuff go down out here, but I gotta say, that was pretty incredible."

He looked appropriately impressed. I smiled, grateful for my friend. She'd always been rough and tumble. Her middle brother had started doing mixed martial arts with her in early high school, but she'd joined all her siblings in more intense training when she moved to Dry Gulch. It was well known for its higher crime rate, though most of that reputation was for pickpockets and petty theft. At least, I'd thought…

Sidney preened, turning her cheek into her shoulder with a coy smile and sketching a sarcastic curtsy, making me smile despite my nerves. It was the right thing to say to her. Complimenting her appearance usually made her uncomfortable, but nice comments about her fighting skills would always light her up.

"Why, *thank* you," she said in a sing-song tone with a little more bounce in her step. After a few more steps, she paused, then rushed to catch back up. "Wait, you're really not a mer?" she asked, the previous conversation having caught up with her.

"Nope." He let the "P" sound pop on the end of the word.

Sidney screwed up her face. "But you're a siren, so where did you come from?"

Levi stared ahead with a bored expression on his face. "Well, you see, when a man and a woman love each other very much, they go and take a *special nap*—"

"Whoa, hey, whoa," Sidney blustered, hands up and eyes wide. "I don't need details. I just don't understand how all this works." She circled her arms in his general direction.

He smirked at her bluster and then rolled his eyes, obviously having heard this line of questioning before. "It works just fine. Thank you for your concern," he said, giving a flirty smile.

Sidney squinted at him and fought a smile, obviously both amused and a little annoyed at his evasiveness. I just shrugged. He didn't owe her an explanation of his heritage.

Levi laughed at her expression. "There's nothing to explain, darlin'." He held out his arms. "What you see is what you get. Are you two going to be okay? Can I walk you back to the Gate? I was gonna meet a guy about a gig next week, but I got a little distracted with screaming and dudes with knives and flying ninjas and the damsel in distress."

Even as the effect of his words swept over me, kept at bay by my ward, I wanted to bristle about being referred to as a damsel in distress. Unfortunately, it was a legitimate description of the situation I'd been in. Without their intervention, I wouldn't have been able to save myself. If I was honest with myself, it wasn't the reference that chafed, but the fact that it was true.

We paused on the sidewalk once we'd made it enough blocks that I didn't feel like I had Phantom eyes staring holes in my back. When I turned to thank Levi for helping me, I found him already staring at me with an intense expression I couldn't really make sense of.

"Thank you for helping me, for distracting them…" I shifted a little uncomfortably as he searched my eyes for a long minute. His hair was mussed, and his brow wrinkled in thought.

Finally, he frowned, and all the humor drained from his face as he murmured, "That scared me half to death, Empress."

It almost felt like a confession, something he didn't want to admit, and I felt skitters of his enchantment through my ward, lightly drawing me toward him. It felt trancelike, caught in the pull of his magic as he studied me. I was completely unable to look away from him.

Eventually, Sidney cleared her throat, breaking the moment. Levi's eyes snapped to her, releasing me from his gaze. Then, glancing back and forth between us, he said, "I can stay here with you if you'd like. I really don't like leaving you here."

Sidney huffed a dismissive laugh. "Dude, I *live* here. Miss me with that bird shit."

Levi's mouth gaped, but then his teeth clicked shut and his jaw clenched. I guess that wasn't the reassurance he was looking for. He looked back and forth between us a few times, and I wondered briefly what he thought of the stark contrast he would undoubtedly find between us.

I felt wholly inadequate under his gaze, a miniature, dark-haired nobody being weighed by a dark-blond titan who could seemingly direct the world with his voice. Whatever he found didn't seem to please him as his lips pursed and his eyes grew guarded and shuttered.

"Right," he said to Sidney. "Well, someone like her probably shouldn't be down here in the first place, but you should do a better job of protecting her anyway."

Even as he said the words, he cast his eyes around the crowd, presumably looking for trouble. I took a step back, stung by both his words and the feeling of their enchantment suddenly pushing me away. Then he glanced toward me with hardened eyes, turned, and disappeared once again into the crowd.

I stood there for a moment, stunned, before I glanced at Sidney. She was still staring after Levi, her expression strangely skeptical. His words rang in my ears.

"Someone *like her*," I gritted out. "What does *that* mean?"

Sidney pressed her lips into a duckbill and glanced over at me, her eyes considering but with a spark of mischief. I could already tell I wasn't going to like this.

"Tiny. Puny. Human." She said it totally deadpan.

Yep, I didn't like it.

"I'm not *that* human." I whirled and stomped forward toward the Gate.

She barked a laugh, easily catching up with me. "Yeah, you kind of are," she chuckled. "I thought you'd object to the puny part, not the human part."

I glowered. Someone like her.

Sidney was quiet for a long moment, and when I looked over at her, she was lost in thought, her eyes shrewd. She caught me looking and asked, "That was weird, right? You guys were totally having eye-sex—"

I sputtered, mortified. *What was eye-sex?*

"—and then all of a sudden he's being snotty and shoving me away with whatever he was doing with his enchantments."

My heart sank. "I don't think that was meant for you," I said.

"What do you mean?" she asked.

"His spells don't seem to be targeted." For whatever reason, I was sure it had been meant for me.

"OBVIOUSLY, the guy you went after had a magical discernment ability similar to mine, but I'm not the only artificer around," I said to Sidney as we made our way home. "I could have been anybody just standing there in the market. Does the entirety of the Phantom Order have my image and orders to track me down?"

Sidney's eyes were sharp as she scanned our surroundings. "I doubt it's anything that complicated, or you would have had more than just one goon show up on your doorstep last night. He's probably based with those guys in Dry Gulch, and we were spectacularly unlucky in our destination today." She cringed visibly. "My fault."

We climbed my front steps and I let us in the door. "Even so, tinkers aren't *that* uncommon. How would he have known it was me?"

Sidney dropped her bag with a thump on the floor and launched herself onto the couch, sprawling on the multitude of blankets and throw pillows. I had a problem with collecting things that made me feel cozy, and I would fully admit it when accused.

"Mercy, I feel like such a princess on your couch," Sidney sighed. "There might be other tinks, but you're pretty distinctive looking." She opened one eye and gave me a once over. "You might be able to pass for human in the Void where nobody knows any better, but you're too perfect looking to be human. You've got those delicate little elvish features and a perfect little heart-shaped face. I'm honestly surprised your dad didn't pass on the pointed ears," she muttered absently.

"Anyway, combine the heightened beauty with the fact that you're tiny, have long, dark hair, and are constantly dripping jewelry, and I don't think they'd even need to pass around a photo. A simple description would do." She said it matter-of-factly. Beauty didn't impress Sidney, but I still felt my cheeks heat at her compliment, even if she hadn't meant it as one.

"Should I try to change how I look? Take off the charms?"

She frowned slightly and shook her head. "No, I don't think so. The charms make you stronger and add some defense. Everything you wear has a purpose. I'd focus on finishing that wasp and making yourself less of an easy target. If you're just a passing interest to them, that might be enough to make them back off. If not, we'll involve Enforcement, or maybe even call in your dad."

I winced at that. My father was a very busy man and bothering him while he was away on a contract was the last thing I wanted to do, even though I knew he'd want to be the first to know if I was in trouble. I sighed and bumped her legs with my thigh. She drew them up to make room for me on the couch, and I slumped into the open seat, facing her.

"Thanks for rescuing me today." I felt the back of my eyes start to burn as everything from the day caught back up with me. "I never thought someone would attack in broad daylight with all those people watching. If you and Levi hadn't come, they would have taken me." My voice shook a little, but I was valiant in fighting my tears.

Sidney sat up and scooted back, her legs crossed between us. She leaned forward and took my shoulders in her hands. "Elara, you are my ride-or-die. No one else other than my brothers would put up with me, and you are *not allowed* to kick-off and leave me with them. You are my *best* friend, and I will always take care of you the way I can, just like you take care of me the way you can." She tapped the enchantment ward cuffed on her ear and the hilts of her knives, which I'd altered with various runes and gems.

I lost the fight with a few tears, and she pulled me into a tight hug. She gave the best hugs.

After a few deep breaths, I sat up, and she announced, "Come on, time for some hot tea." She made her way to my tea cabinet and stopped to pull a vial from her pocket. She set it on the kitchen table and started the process of making tea as I picked up the vial and inspected it. The liquid inside was a light amber color and viscous looking.

"This is the venom?" At her nod, I popped the top and took a cautious sniff. The smell was faint but acrid. It was supposedly from a beetle that lived in the dunes around Dry Gulch. In ancient times, it had been used as a sedative for medical work but had eventually fallen out of favor for more modern drugs. I replaced the cap and went to retrieve my wasp construct.

Sidney huffed while staring into my tea cabinet. "Are you ever actually going to drink all this tea?"

"Probably not, no. How much of this is a dose?"

"Ten grams should do. Is the stuff in the white packages from the neighbor lady?"

"Yeah." I got out my scale and some bottles and began measuring out the venom.

Sidney grumbled and started tossing my neighbor's tea into the compost. She knew my quirks. I felt too guilty to get rid of the presents myself, but she had no such qualms. A small smile tugged at my lips.

Sidney brought me tea and left to get ready for bed, while I filled the chamber inside the wasp that I'd retrofitted for the venom, then stored the rest. Placing the wasp on the table in front of me and taking its abdomen in my fingers, I focused on its heartstone and modified the intent I'd originally given it.

I instructed it to defend me upon request, to administer its venom via the newly added stinger, and to keep the venom chamber magically chilled. I wasn't terribly skilled in elemental modifications, but for something as small as the venom chamber, I could make do.

Alone with my thoughts, Levi's words came back to me, and I gritted my teeth. *Someone like her.* I never wanted to be defenseless again.

I was going to make an *entire army* of wasps.

～⬥～

THE NEXT NIGHT Sidney talked me out of making dinner in favor of dropping in on Hyrak, a mutual acquaintance from college. He ran the bar in an upscale establishment in my neighborhood called The Silver Tongue Brewing Co., along with his little sister Sabine.

We made our way through the small, swanky eatery, past a cozy fireplace and intimate tables for two, heading back toward the bar. Sidney perched easily on the towering barstool, though for me, it took a little climbing to get myself situated, earning a few glances from the older gentleman next to me.

Why is everything made for giants? I frowned to myself as my legs swung free in the air like a child in an oversized chair and turned to gaze longingly at the specialized dwarvish seating near the end of the bar. Sidney would never fit.

"Sid! Elara!" Hyrak called as he came out of a door in the back and leaned on the bar top, wiping his hands in a perfectly white cloth. "What can I get for you ladies?" His voice was deep and rumbling, a good fit for his large bulky frame and friendly disposition.

Both he and his sister were very large people, having some orc ancestry, though he was considerably taller than Sabine. They shared the enlarged lower canines, tusk-like bottom teeth common among orc peoples as well as the slightly luminescent green eyes, and their skin was the much darker shade of the lowlands orcs, but that was where their similarities ended.

Where Hyrak was calm and laid back, Sabine was feisty and gregarious. While she also had dark green, nearly black skin, Hyrak had a condition called vitiligo, which caused patches of his skin to lose its pigment. When I'd met him at the start of college, he'd only had a few small patches of white on his hands and face, but now there was a large patch on his right cheek that spread up over his eye, and most of his body was covered in piebald-like patches.

In many places where the pigment had gone missing, he'd had tattoos of various ancient orcish texts placed. His skin was a riotous cacophony of texture and contrast. He kept the sides of his head shaved, and the rest of his hair in a top knot.

Sidney air-kissed his cheek and then took the drink list, humming slightly as she browsed. He cast me a smile, which I shyly returned. "I just want a Flaming Pearl," I told him while we waited, catching a glimpse of a ring on his hand I'd once made for him. I was pleased to see it still looked great, even though I suspected it took a beating here at his job.

"Evil Pecker, just for the name," Sidney ordered abruptly, slapping the menu down.

Hyrak chuckled, taking the menu. "Pearl and a Pecker, coming right up. Try not to blow the place up while I make them okay, El?"

"That was *one time*," I called to his retreating back, immediately forgetting my shyness. "I blew up the lab *one* time!"

"Technically it was two or three," Sidney replied lightly, drumming her nails on the counter, "and that isn't even counting the Great Golem Catastrophe."

"You're supposed to be my friend," I grumbled, my cheeks flaming. "I don't even have a golem here."

"I *am* your friend. I didn't say it wasn't awesome. And you've got your wasps. Those are golems."

"I can't bring the place down with rogue wasps." Sidney's eyes widened as she stared into the distance and the corner of her mouth dropped into a frown as if the thought of my wasps going rogue had only just occurred to her. I smacked her arm lightly with the back of my hand. "That hasn't happened in years."

Hyrak returned, and I felt his elemental magic climb a bit, rising from vague impressions of a chilly morning to biting frost-covered tundra, as he chilled the drinks in his hands to the exact temperature he wanted. He could freeze or chill things simply by touching them. He set them in front of us, mine a smoking rum and liqueur cocktail with a tiny ball of white suspended in the middle.

"Take it easy on that one." He nodded toward Sidney's. "It sneaks up on ya."

"Thanks, Hy. You're a doll." She flashed a smile at him, earning a wink in return.

A familiar shivery sensation of animalistic magic brushed over me.

I glanced over my shoulder to see Bane, one of Sidney's acquaintances, duck his large frame through the entrance of the bar and saunter to the back counter. His swagger and grace belied his bulky, muscular frame, and paired with the feelings of intense predatory focus, I could never mistake him for anything but the panther shifter he was.

Sidney raised an eyebrow as a Cheshire grin spread across his face. "Bane," she greeted.

"Sidney," he returned, still grinning. He had a broad jaw, golden brown skin, hair as dark as mine, and lively chestnut-colored eyes under heavy eyebrows. "How are you lovely ladies doing today?" His voice always sounded flirty.

"Just peachy," she answered idly. "What's new?" she asked, focusing on her drink. Bane seemed like a shoo-in for Sidney's 'type' but for reasons even she couldn't explain, she'd never been interested in him. It didn't deter him from his constant flirting, but then, he flirted with everyone. I bit my lip to try to contain my smile.

He spread his large hands on the countertop beside her and bounced on his arms a little before setting his elbow on it and resting his weight on his forearm. "Was down at the Salty Wench a few nights ago and heard some gossip you all might be interested in."

"Uh-huh." Sidney looked like she was half listening.

"This old guy was runnin' his mouth. You know that old doofus that's always talkin' about that dragon he claims he killed way back when?"

That had Sidney's attention.

"Harrington," she muttered, setting her drink down.

"Yeah, him. So, he got a little sloppy on the sauce and starts tellin' the whole bar he's getting a stone golem from little Miss Elara here." He points a meaty finger at me. *'Little Miss'*, like I'm a child. I gave him a slow blink. *Come on, dude.* "Anyway, I didn't personally think that was true, but regardless whether it was or not, I didn't think you ladies would want that kind of attention."

"Uh-huh." Sidney took another sip, not looking at him. "And why didn't you come find me a few nights ago when you first heard it?"

He lifted a shoulder lazily and dropped it as his smile dimmed a little. "Was it urgent?"

"Seeing as *Little Miss* here has had some Phantoms after her over it, yeah, I'd say it was. But I guess we probably couldn't have expected that, even if we'd known at the time," she groused, leaning back farther in her chair.

His smile dropped completely. "Phantoms?" He glanced at me.

Sidney waved a hand dismissively, still not looking at him. "Don't worry about it, we've got it."

Bane's smile returned as his eyes scanned up and down her figure. Maybe her disinterest felt like a challenge to him? I shook my head slightly at their antics. "You know," he said absently, "while I've got your ears, I wouldn't mind putting in an order for a speed boost." He gave a winning smile.

"Don't think you're getting some kind of discount in exchange for your gossip. *A fool too late bewares when the peril is passed*," she said, quoting some dead queen from the Void. One side of his smile fell.

"Is it passed?" I asked her.

Sidney glanced at me and sat forward in her chair. "If it's not, it will be soon. Any idea where I can find Harrington?" she asked Bane.

"Well…" He paused to think, rubbing his thumb along the stubble of his jaw. "I dunno about tonight, but he usually starts day-drinking at the Wench on Friday afternoons and stays there for the rest of the evening, I think. At least whenever I'm there on a Friday he's always around." Today was Thursday, so it would have to wait until tomorrow.

Sidney stared at him for a minute while he gave a small but hopeful smile. "What do you want your boost on?" she asked. I laughed as he crowed in triumph and ignored their haggling to flag down Sabine. I needed to get some food in my friend if the way her drink was disappearing was anything to go by.

"Evening, lovelies! What can I get for you tonight?" Sabine was friendly and warm, and anyone could tell by her features that she and Hyrak were siblings. She wore her long hair with bits of colorful cloth woven in, and they fluttered when she walked.

"Excuse me, Ma'am. Can we have the news?" the man to my left interrupted before she disappeared with our orders.

"Sure thing." Sabine dug in her pocket and tossed some tiny calling stones onto a raised dais in the corner behind the bar.

As soon as they landed, tiny celestial spirits appeared, fluttering about the dais like little spectral butterflies. These spirits, which had many names but were often referred to simply as messengers, fed eagerly on the energy people left behind in the little pebbles we called 'calling stones'. In return, they would absorb information and present it to the desired party. People in media could present them a story and send them along to various locations.

The first spectrals to land took turns delivering their stories, ghostly images flickering above the dais, informing viewers that a trade agreement between far-off kingdoms had fallen through or that the mountain village of Thurim's Reach had been isolated again due to an avalanche.

By the time Sabine arrived with our order, we had finished our drinks and were engrossed in the latest celebrity scandal. It involved two major political rivals who had been discovered to not only be having an intimate relationship, but to have been hiding a lovechild as well. Their political parties were in an absolute uproar, but romantics everywhere were hoping for a summer wedding.

Sabine laughed as she approached. Sidney had her glass clutched to her chest and an enraptured expression on her face. "Sid, I always knew you were a giant softy! You've got the biggest heart-eyes I ever saw."

Sidney slid a happy, glassy glance to Sabine. Okay, maybe that drink had hit her a little harder than she'd expected, too. I wondered what was in it—she usually had a pretty high tolerance. I half listened as they gushed about the rumors that the rivals were planning to wed now that the secret was out in the open, and watched as the next spectral began a piece detailing an attack on one of the sprite strongholds, a city named The Deep.

I placed my hand on one of Sidney's hoping to quiet her so I could listen as images of kelpies ransacking the underwater city and journalists detailing decimated family lineages flickered and swam in the air in front of us. The numbers of dead and injured were high, mostly young and elderly sprites. They had the hardest time fleeing, and youth were often drawn to kelpies before they attacked, lying in wait in one of their various harmless-looking forms.

Silence fell around us as people listened with interest, and we learned that the attacks were still ongoing. Kelpies had a reputation for treachery, and speculation was rife that they were after the sprite's stores of heartstones.

The problem was that, even if the surface governments wanted to help, the oceanic pressure was so great at the depths the city was located that even the mer people couldn't venture down that far.

Well, if I hadn't already made the decision to stay out of the golem trade, this would have been the decision made for me. I couldn't imagine the prices of heartstones would recover from something like this during my lifetime.

CHAPTER 5

FRIDAY MORNING HADN'T BEEN KIND to Sidney. She'd spent most of it bleary-eyed and grouchy after indulging in a few more drinks the night before. She swore she was never drinking anything with the word 'evil' in the name ever again.

I wasn't sure I believed that, but I was more concerned with clarifying our plans.

"What are we going to do about Harrington?"

"Gonna head over to the Salty Wench and deal with him," she answered, obviously dodging my real question.

I frowned, not sure what "deal with him" entailed. "We're just going to waltz in and yell at him or what?" I asked as I finished connecting the silver filament to the heartstone of a new wasp and clipped it off. When she didn't answer, I set aside my tool and glanced at her.

Sidney rubbed her forehead with a sigh. "*We're* not going anywhere, El. I'm gonna go find that windbag, and you need to stay here and close up the shop."

My jaw clenched. I turned to face her as I felt the heat rising in the back of my neck. "This has nothing to do with me needing to close up the shop and everything to do with me being the 'damsel in distress'," I said, keeping my voice as calm as I could in my irritation. "I'm not going to sit here and have you go risk yourself for me. *Again.*"

Sidney pursed her lips and gave me a considering look before sighing again and redoing her braid. "You know I don't see you that way, but we have to be reasonable here. The Wench is back down in the warehouse district, and we have no idea who's gonna be in there. Nobody's after me," she continued, tugging her braid over her shoulder to reach the bottom. "I can be in and out of there and no one's gonna bat an eye. You're the one they want, and if a bunch of guys caught wind you were over there and tried to haul you out, I'm not strong enough to take more than one or two at a time. I am realistic about my limitations. Why make this more difficult than it needs to be?"

She finished her plait and wrapped the hair tie around the end, fixing me with a meaningful stare. "And you know as well as anyone that I *utterly despise* admitting when I'm wrong, but that siren was right the other day. I shouldn't have been so reckless with you over there," she said softly. "I knew the place was seedy, and I didn't think it through." Sidney tossed her braid back over her shoulder. "Things like this can't be about your pride, Elara. They need to be about being realistic and knowing when you're out of your depth and being safe. You don't have the *years* of training I do."

I chewed on my lip, knowing she was right and still hating it.

"Plus, this goes back to what we were talking about the other night, right?" she asked, cajoling. "You have your ways of taking care of me, and this is my way of taking care of you. Sometimes that means I gotta kill a guy," she joked with a little shrug.

At least I hoped she was joking. *Was that another quote?* "Is that from a movie?"

Sidney's eyes narrowed, and she slid them to me, looking decidedly shifty. "Of course."

While releasing a large breath, I slid my hand down my face, trying to figure out where my patience had gone today. "Sidney" —I tried to keep my voice reasonable—"you can't kill Harrington."

She rolled her eyes. "Okay, mom."

"Sid—"

"Good grief, Elara, I'm not going to *kill* him."

I stared at her.

"Yet," she muttered.

There it is.

I frowned at her, but she didn't notice, busily tucking knives into her boots and various places about her person. A small handgun went into a holster under her sweatshirt. "Are you going to need all that? Should we call one of your brothers to go with you? Why are you going so early?" It was only two-thirty in the afternoon.

Sidney adjusted a strap on her side and checked the mirror to make sure everything was inconspicuous. I walked around her, double checking, but even so, I couldn't help wringing my hands a bit. She rolled her eyes as I readjusted her equipment, but waited patiently for me to finish.

"No, I'm not going to need it all, but I'd rather have it and not need it than need it and not have it," she said. "Josh has to work today, and the other two are doing who knows what. I'll let them know if I need them, which I won't. Don't worry so much, okay?" Sidney gave me a quick hug and pulled back to look me in the eye. "And I'm going early since I'm only allowed to *talk* to him. I'd rather have this conversation early before he gets too sloshed to remember any of it." She trudged into the back room to grab an apple and took a huge bite on her way back, chewing for a second before continuing to talk with her mouth full.

"It'll be fine. I'm just gonna go find out if he's working with the Phantoms and tell him, in no uncertain terms, that we are not making golems. Then I'm going to tell him that, if he can't watch his tongue, I'll cut it out." She said it so lightly and offhandedly that I was pretty sure she was joking.

"If I'm not back by the time you close up here, just wait for me, or if you want, call one of the boys." I couldn't call her brothers from the Void if they were in the Boundlands, but I'd be fine walking a few blocks to the Gate.

"Okay, just don't get into any trouble. Have someone come get me if you need bail money. Maybe we should just close the shop, and I can go home so you can call me more easily if you need me."

Sidney rolled her eyes and took another bite. "You're fretting. Stop it. I'll be back soon." With one final weapons check, she blew me a kiss, waved, and was out the door. I really hoped her hangover didn't affect any of her decision making today.

I blew out a big breath, hoping to clear some of the nervous feeling in my gut, and tried to remind myself she'd fought for sport on the weekends for years.

After I'd settled into my work for a few minutes, I felt magic at the edge of my senses: ocean mist and warm sand. I fought down the butterflies in my stomach and turned, expecting to see Levi walk by, but the feeling faded to nothing, was gone for a few moments, then came back again. The door swung open, and Levi stalked in with his jaw set and a determined look on his face.

I sat quietly, a little confused by his mood as his eyes flickered over me, unsure of whether or not I was still irritated with him. He opened his mouth to speak, paused, and then abruptly snapped it shut and glared at the ground, frustrated.

"What's wrong?" I asked.

He huffed. "You said my enchantments were 'disconcerting', but I can't speak without making them, and I don't want to make you uncomfortable. I guess I could write, but my penmanship is terrible." Even as he said it, I felt the magic in his words roll over me, crashing waves and sea foam, full of life and tiny creatures burrowing in the surf. It tugged at my soul, just barely kept at bay by my bracelet.

I laughed at his words despite myself. "I'm sure your penmanship is fine. Can I help you with something?" I noticed he had my card tucked between the fingers of his left hand and was flicking his thumb across the edge over and over again.

"I wanted to check on you," he answered, gazing around absently at the items in the glass cabinets. "I would have come yesterday, but my dad needed me… and then I was down the street and saw your guard leaving without you *again*."

My guard? "What guard?" I stood and walked to the counter, feeling my brows draw together in confusion.

He shot me a look like I was crazy. "The girl, Sid, with the blond hair and the kicking and the knives who just stomped out of here murdering an apple." He gestured behind him.

"Oh. No, Sidney's not a guard. She's just my friend. I don't have guards."

That took the wind out of his sails. He dropped his hands, and his face blanked. "You don't have guards."

I shook my head.

"You were attacked by Phantoms, you don't have guards, and you don't want to report them, because apparently, it's no big deal."

"It does sound a bit crazy when you phrase it like that, yes." I gritted my teeth and stared at my hands fisted on the counter. Even though he was clearly exasperated and doubting my mental competence, his magic was still a lure, a caress. I had to focus on trying to ignore what I felt and listen to his words because the tone of his words and magic were at odds with each other.

He looked to the ceiling like he was pleading for help, or maybe sanity. "Okay. I thought she was your guard. Do you mind if I ask why those men attacked you?"

I glanced at the glass case to his left and shrugged, feeling a little uncomfortable. I didn't want to bring up the golems with anyone new and risk more talk getting around. "They want me to make weapons."

His gaze followed mine to the case—which happened to contain knives—and his shoulders relaxed, as if that scenario wasn't as bad as what he'd come up with in his mind.

He pursed his lips in thought. "So, this is where you work?" He approached the counter slowly, his eyes scanning some of the pieces on the shelves below. "I had to come and find it. I didn't have any other way to get ahold of you."

We didn't bother with a shop phone, since most of our customers were in the Boundlands and couldn't contact us from there anyway. We'd had one for a few weeks in the beginning and the only calls we'd gotten were from curious humans. Sidney had canceled it without asking me, and frankly, I'd been relieved.

Hating myself just a little for being flattered he wanted to check on me, I reached under the back of the counter, grabbed a small pair of scissors, and snipped off a tiny lock of my hair. In the Boundlands, where technology was more limited than in the Void, we'd found a multitude of ways to make use of the spectral messengers. You could present them with a lock of hair that belonged to your desired recipient, and they would travel through the Mahajarem—a celestial river of energy—using rifts in space to locate that person's life force and deliver your message.

Levi watched with a small smile as I located a locket, closed my hair neatly inside, and held it out for him. We didn't give out our hair as easily as humans handed out phone numbers— usually only gifting it to family and close friends—so my gesture felt a little vulnerable. I was essentially telling him he was important to me. His eyes were soft as he plucked the locket from my hand and closed his fingers around it.

"Thank you," he said, his voice gentle. His eyes held my own, then dropped to my lips, making my neck heat. "I would actually need your phone number, though, if you have one. I live here in the Void."

I realized I'd been in a daze and blinked, feeling confused. "Why did you take my hair then, if you only needed my cell?" I asked, a little embarrassed. I looked at his closed fist that held my locket.

A large, mischievous grin spread across his face. "I like it. It was sweet." He clenched his fist tighter and held it to his chest. "It's mine now. Don't try to take it back." His smile was winsome and boyish. He thumbed open the clasp and hooked it onto a thin leather bracelet around his left wrist.

His smirk stayed as his gaze returned to mine and then dropped to my neck. It was probably flushed bright pink at this point. I covered it with my hand and ducked my head a little, making him blink and shake his head.

He placed his hands on the edge of the counter and took a step back, bending to look closer at the items shelved underneath. The tattoos on his left arm drew my eye, and I followed the line of his arm up his shoulder to the muscles flexing in his back.

Levi blew out a breath and straightened, stepping away again as he did. "Would you have any interest in mer artifacts or amulets? Do you buy things that are already magical?" he asked, crossing his arms and continuing to stare at the shelves. He looked a little unsure of himself, and I felt the lure of his enchantments lessen substantially.

He glanced up, and I realized I'd taken too long to answer. "Oh, sure. Yes. Sometimes. Are you looking for something specific or do you have something to sell?" I asked.

He pursed his lips and glanced down at the shelves again. "I have some things I wouldn't mind parting with."

"Oh, well, sure. I can take a look. Would you like to bring them in? Or are they very large?" I made my tone more business-like, which seemed to put him a little more at ease.

He uncrossed his arms and stuck my card in his back pocket. "They aren't particularly big, but there are a few of them, and I'd prefer not to handle them myself if possible. You're welcome to stop by my place whenever you're not busy, it's not far from here," he shrugged.

The pull of his enchantment returned, and I had to work to block it out this time. It felt too inviting, too comforting, like hiding under a warm blanket on a cold morning, like coming home. I shook it off and thought back to what he said about contacting him. *I live here in the Void.*

What? "Did you say you live here in the Void?" He nodded and I felt my eyes widen. "Why? Why would you do that?" *He's going to die.* Okay, that was dramatic, so I tried to rein it in. He was obviously part human so he wouldn't die immediately.

But even those of us with mixed human heritage could lose decades from our lifespan if we spent all our time in the Void. In addition to being cut off from the life-giving effects of the magic in the Boundlands, human governments as a whole didn't place a high priority on limiting pollution. Since lived, on average, two to six times as long as humans, depending on one's genetic mix, we had a lot more time for pollution to build up in our systems. Because of this, technology was much more limited in the Boundlands, with the burden of safety resting on developers. It was simply a healthier environment overall.

Okay, so he probably wasn't going to die tomorrow, or even next week, but I still felt the urge to grab him by the scruff of his neck and drag him to the nearest Gate so he could *breathe*. The side of his mouth quirked up, and I wondered how much of my internal panic was showing on my face.

"I get back into the Boundlands often enough, and my roommates aren't terribly concerned about the whole 'shortened lifespan' spiel. We each have our own reasons." His smile turned a bit brittle.

I wondered what the story was there. "Well, I don't have any plans after work. Since you're close by, I could stop by when I'm done here. I'm not sure when Sidney will be back, but I should probably wait for her in case any of those guys are lurking around."

He frowned and cast a glance behind him out the plate-glass windows to the street.

"How about I give you my number and you can text me when you're done? I'll come to walk you over. No one would dream of messing with you at my place. It's quite safe."

At my nod, he took a receipt from the counter and scrawled his number on the back. I smiled. His penmanship wasn't great, but it certainly wasn't terrible.

We made our goodbyes, and he left, pausing on the sidewalk in front of my shop to look around. He looked a little predatory as he cast his gaze around, jaw set, arms loose, and fingers clenching and unclenching.

I expected him to leave, but he didn't quite disappear, instead stalking down the street past my field of vision and settling just at the edge of my magical perception. Was he… guarding me?

I tried to focus on finishing my third wasp, but by the time four o'clock rolled around, I felt like I was coming out of my skin. I was too wound up, antsy from being able to feel his magic just down the block, nervous at the idea of spending more time with him, getting to learn more about him, see where he lived. I was definitely in crush territory.

The afternoon had been slow with no customers, so I reasoned it wouldn't hurt to close things up a little early. It was one of the perks of being self-employed. Besides, I was still being productive, scouting for resale items. My heart thrilled a little bit at the thought of genuine mer articles, and I wondered what he had squirreled away.

Mind made up, I hurriedly closed down the shop. I left a note for Sidney and texted Levi that I was done. Feeling impatient, I donned my jacket, quickly glanced in the mirror to make sure all my amulets were in place, grabbed my purse, and stepped outside to lock up the front door. I restrained myself from sprinting down the block like a dork. Barely.

I looked up to find him strolling toward me with his thumbs in his pockets, apparently uncaring about the fine mist landing on his bare arms and thin t-shirt. His smile was genuine, if a little dim.

"I would have come to get you," he said gently. His words were a caress, an embrace, his stance aloof. Did everyone feel this confused by him?

"I couldn't wait. I was too excited," I admitted.

His smile warmed. "Don't get too excited. You might think it's all a bunch of junk," he said, thankfully misconstruing my meaning. I followed him as we passed the turnoff to the coffee shop and approached one of the large, blocky, vinyl-sided buildings so popular in north Seattle.

Levi let us into the lobby of the building, and we mounted the stairs before I froze mid-step. I felt the most powerful, deadly, all-consuming magic I'd ever encountered in my life. It was dark and ancient, not necessarily evil, but harrowing in the way one might feel when standing on the edge of a deep, black abyss. He made it to the landing before he noticed I was no longer behind him, and when he turned to find me, I scrambled to catch up.

My heart was pounding in my ears as we left the stairs and made our way down the hall. Maybe the magic was coming from somewhere else in the building? *Please let the magic be coming from somewhere else in the building.* We stopped in front of a door on the left with a simple black doormat and no other adornments. The magic was definitely coming from his apartment.

Levi unlocked the front door and cast me an odd look as he turned the knob and pushed it in. I realized my breaths were coming in little gasping pants. He probably thought I was exceptionally out of shape and climbing the stairs had done me in, but I couldn't help it. I'd never been confronted by magic of this type or magnitude before, and I had no idea what was behind that door.

He stepped inside and held the door open for me, giving me a confused smile as I followed him in. "Here, let me take your jacket," I heard him say. As soon as I was in, instinct took over and I backed up against the wall by his door. *What in the world am I doing!?*

CHAPTER 6

"Dude, *could you not?* I don't know what you're doing but I feel like I'm choking." My attention snapped to a man sitting on a barstool, hunched over a kitchen island with a bowl of something and a pained expression. I noticed belatedly that he was coughing, very pale, and exuding blood magic.

A vampire, then.

Oh.

"Oh, no! I'm sorry!" I snatched the gem set from my hair responsible for his troubles and quickly rifled through my purse, dropping it in a leaded pouch just to be on the safe side. "I'm so sorry. Levi didn't tell me there were vampires here." I felt as though I were trying to melt into the wall already pressed at my back.

"I didn't realize you were covered in hexes," Levi murmured, his attention returning to taking my jacket, tugging me gently away from the wall.

"I'm covered in *everything*," I babbled.

"Noted. Jordan, what are you doing eating food? Aren't you just going to have to barf those back up later?" Levi sounded distracted as he hung my coat on a hook near the door.

Jordan frowned into his bowl and clicked the chopsticks he held in his hand. "I just really miss dumplings. Don't ruin this for me."

I'd already shifted my attention back to the pulsing, suffocating magic emanating from farther back in the apartment. From the corner of my eye, I noticed Levi's cheerful expression begin to slip.

"Elara? What's wrong?" I'd migrated back to the wall by the door and was now entirely flattened against it, my eyes probably as wide as saucers. "Jordan won't hurt you. He's never even bitten anyone."

"It's true," Jordan muttered. "I prefer to pretend my food comes from the store just like everybody else."

"Just think of him as the weirdo guy with the special diet and severe sun allergy who lives in my apartment." Levi gave a sarcastic grin and did jazz hands. "He's kind of like a strange pet cat."

"Thanks, *ass*," Jordan grumbled, rolling his eyes. I opened my mouth but, unable to produce more than a squeak, settled for shaking my head slightly and pointing toward the back of the apartment. The magic was growing by the second, rolling over me again and again. It felt like a current dragging me into the yawning mouth of a cold, dark chasm in the bottom of the ocean.

Levi's eyebrows pulled together as he stared at me, and he glanced toward where I was pointing before I saw recognition dawn in his eyes. "Oh, hold on." He walked to a bedroom door at the entrance of the hallway in the back and raised a fist to pound on it.

"Yo, Eeyore! Knock it off! You're scaring the guest!" he hollered.

After a few seconds, the door opened, and I felt my face blanch. The man was tall and lanky, probably more than seven feet, with lean muscle and shaggy black hair. He had deep-set eyes, which were stark white with no pupils or irises, and strong, masculine features. His skin was alabaster, paler even than the vampire's, and this man was *not* human. Not even a little bit. I had no idea how he could survive outside of the Boundlands.

As I watched, shadows swirled up around his feet and began to gather around him like a cloak. The denser they got, the harder it was to focus on him. It was like my eyes tried to slide away from him, even though I could tell *exactly* where he was because I could feel his magic with my extra perception.

"Oh, dang. Grim's got a job. No point in talking to him when he gets like this. Sorry, I'll have to introduce you later. Come this way. I'll show you what I've got." He turned and strode down the hall like what we were seeing was the most natural thing in the world.

Grim, if that was his name, started forward, crossing the room and coming toward me. When he drew near, he raised his head and turned it to look me square in the face, the shadows of his cloak trailing out around him like spider webs into the ether.

I raised my hand and gave a halting finger wave, unsure of what to do as he grabbed the handle of the front door and left.

When I heard it click shut, I bolted, barely hearing Jordan's "Nice to meet you" as I streaked past him after Levi. I blew right past him and rounded on him, wanting to put him between me and whatever that guy was. He caught me by the upper arms to keep from stumbling into me.

"Who was that!?" I gasped.

"Whoa, you okay? That's Grim. Have you never met a reaper?" he asked as he steadied me.

"You have a reaper in your house?" I asked incredulously. A grim reaper? Who collected souls of the dead? Just hanging out in someone's house?

"Well, yeah, I mean, he lives here. Pays rent and everything. You don't need to be afraid of ol' Eeyore. It's not like he kills people, he just collects the ones who are already dead." Levi chuckled and wrapped an arm around me, tugging me the rest of the way down the hallway to the last door on the end.

"So how did *I* get the 'weirdo' label?" I heard Jordan call from the kitchen.

"That's a legitimate question," Levi mumbled under his breath, entering what I assumed was his room.

Now that the reaper's magic had finally faded away to nothing, I felt like I could actually think. I looked at the small room around me and found it rather spartan, but adequate. The navy bedding was rumpled, but everything was otherwise tidy and comfortable if a little bare. His guitar case was propped in the corner and a desk covered in sheet music sat to one side.

I tried to blink away my confusion. "Is his name Eeyore? Or Grim?"

Levi barked a laugh. "Neither. His name is Victor, but only his parents call him that. Everyone else calls him Grim." He leaned against the edge of his bed. "I've just called him Eeyore since… well, at least middle school. It really used to get his goat."

I felt like I'd just stepped into an alternate universe. Granted, I probably did that every day when I stepped through a Gate, but this was different. I didn't know what to think.

Levi laughed at my expression. "Did I just rock your world?"

"Maybe?"

He chuckled. "I'll introduce you when he gets back. He's basically running on instinct right now, so social interactions are a little beyond him." His eyes sparkled with his amusement, and his general comfort with the situation put me a little more at ease.

It finally dawned on me that we were alone together in his bedroom, and I felt myself blush. Watching him at ease in his own space, and feeling the warmth of his enchantments, especially from his laughter, left me with a delicious, happy feeling.

Levi cleared his throat and pushed away from his bed. "Everything's in the chest in there," he said, gesturing to a small, tidy walk-in closet.

Right. The artifacts.

I took a cleansing breath and tried to clear my mind as I approached and knelt at the chest he had indicated. I didn't usually go digging through people's closets when I scouted for items for the shop. Normally, I'd be poking through a warehouse or another store, but sometimes people brought me old relics they wanted to sell.

The clasp on the chest was a little stiff as if it wasn't used regularly, and the hinges creaked as I opened it. A light flicked on overhead, and I glanced over my shoulder to see Levi back up and lean against the wall outside of his closet. He stuffed his thumbs in his back pockets, looking oddly uncomfortable. He always seemed so at ease within himself.

I gave him what I hoped was a reassuring smile. Usually, people were talking up whatever items they were presenting me with, extolling all of their virtues and exaggerating what they were capable of, if not outright lying about their abilities. He said nothing, just raised a hand and picked at his thumbnail.

I turned back to the objects in the chest and began pulling them out carefully, examining them one at a time before laying them on the carpet beside me and moving on to the next one. I felt all kinds of magic as I moved my hands over them—wells, amplifiers, echoes—but most of the objects were geared toward a siren. There was a broken necklace, inlaid with mother-of-pearl, that had something to do with water breathing and a coral scepter that magnified only enchantments.

I realized I'd been absorbed for a while when my legs began to ache from kneeling on them. I stood with a groan and turned to find Levi sitting at his desk, working on a piece of his music. I carried the coral scepter in my hands as I approached him.

"Why do you want to get rid of these?" I asked. "It seems like some of them are perfectly geared to your magic."

He frowned as he glanced at the object in my hands, and when he raised his eyes to mine, they looked a little guarded. "They remind me of someone I don't like to think about," he said as he went back to writing. His magic held no lure now, and instead, I picked up a slight rebuff.

"Mm." I glanced down at the scepter and then at the chest in the closet, unable to come up with an appropriate response. "How much would you want for them?" I asked, expecting to haggle and pick and choose which objects would sell the best in my shop.

"Whatever you think is appropriate is fine," he replied.

I blinked and looked back at the chest, considering for a moment. "Do you want drahk or dollars?" I asked. Drahk was the currency we used in our area of the Boundlands.

"Either one is fine, but if you don't care either way, I'll take drahk." So, he lived in the Void, but preferred payment in drahk. My curiosity was growing by the minute, but I kept it under wraps. This was clearly a touchy topic for him.

"How about three thousand drahk for the lot?" It was a

more-than-generous offer. Not everything he had was immedi-ately sellable, and a few items would have to be deconstructed and repurposed, but I didn't like the idea of leaving him with items that clearly caused him pain. My heart was too soft for that.

His jaw dropped a little as his eyes shot to mine. "That can't be right. I was expecting a few hundred drahk at most." He was a little low. They were worth more than that.

"Don't worry, I'll still make money on them," I lied. I might break even at best. I knew from our first interaction that he needed money, and money was something I didn't have to worry about. I didn't like the way his countenance changed in regard to the artifacts, so if I could remove this burden from him and help him a bit with his bills at the same time, so much the better.

His brows pulled down a little in confusion, but the relief on his face was evident. "Oh, okay. If you're sure." He set his pencil down. "I can find some paper or bubble wrap and a box for them. I think Grim just got a package yesterday," he said, straightening and heading for the door.

I realized I could feel Grim's magic again, but the level of it was so much lower that, absorbed in going through the artifacts, I hadn't noticed him come back. When Levi returned with a box, I carefully wrapped each item and set it inside. Then I closed up the box and followed Levi as he carried it into the living room.

"Let's do Super Smash. I get Princess Peach this time," Jordan said from the couch as we entered. He was sprawled on one end with a console controller in his hands, and Grim sat forward on the other end with his elbows on his knees as he navi-gated a character selection screen on the TV.

He pressed a button to make his selection, causing Jordan to curse at him. "You can't always take Peach, you selfish... Fine. I'll take Kirby." Jordan selected a character that looked like a wad of pink bubble gum, and they loaded their characters into a cutesy cartoon arena where they proceeded to beat the absolute stuffing out of each other.

I noticed, as I peeked around Levi's back, that Grim's eyes were different now, with normal, pale-blue irises instead of the solid white they had been earlier. He wore a white short-sleeved button-up shirt and blue jeans. His shadow cloak was nowhere to be found. His magic had the same general feel—a dark abyss and general feelings of doom—but at a much lower level.

Once I took a good look at Jordan, I saw he was of average height, with a trim build, and he had black hair with dark eyes. He had the hallmark pale skin of a vampire and a sharp jawline, but overall, he still somehow managed to appear boyish and young. He was probably about my age, or at least had been when he was turned. My eyes flitted back to Grim. It was hard to tell exactly how old he was, but he was definitely youngish. If Levi had gone to school with him, he was probably about our age too.

Jordan appeared to be losing their game, since he kept up a string of curses that would have left my mother apoplectic. He cut off abruptly when Levi bent to set the box down and he noticed I was huddled behind him.

"Oh, shhh—oot," he said. "Sorry."

I gave him a small smile.

"Yeah, watch your mouth, Fangs." Levi straightened and lightly tapped the back of Jordan's head with the back of his hand.

"Shut up about my fangs." Jordan ducked in an exaggerated movement and froze. "Sorry, Miss." I realized that, layered underneath the blood magic he produced as part of his vampirism, there was something that reminded me of crackling embers and woodsmoke. *Could he create fire?*

I tried to swallow my shyness as Levi introduced me to his housemates officially. "She runs a charm shop down the street," he said, placing his hand below my elbow. I ducked my head a little as Grim made eye contact and nodded in greeting. His eyes dropped to where Levi's hand rested on my arm. I felt my neck heat.

"It's nice to meet you both. Jordan, sorry again, about the blood-magic hex." Maybe I shouldn't make hexes for specific magic types. At least I knew it worked.

"I'm going to walk Elara back down to her shop," Levi said. "When I get back, I want Princess Peach." We left the apartment to the sound of Jordan grousing and complete silence from Grim. I realized I'd never heard him speak.

Levi carried the box for me, and we made our way back to the shop. It was now around five-thirty in the evening, and the front door was unlocked when I checked it. I felt Sidney somewhere in the back, and my note was gone. An empty takeout cup was in its place, so I tossed it in the trash as Levi set the box on the counter.

"Hellooo," I called. "Sidney?" I turned to Levi. "Let me grab your money for you. Drahk, right?" I'd have to open the safe in the back. I didn't keep that much in the register.

"Hey, I'm here!" Sidney called from the back room. "Sorry I took so long, I got distracted." She stalked into the front, pulling knives out of her boots and tossing them in the bag by her chair.

I turned to look at her just as she noticed Levi was with me, exploded out of her skin, and disappeared. Her clothes hit the floor with a heavy *thunk*, probably because her gun was still in her holster. She struggled for a second before I realized the holster was keeping her from crawling out of her shirt. She was probably *so pissed* right now.

I jogged over and jerked the shirt off the top of the pile, only to be greeted with an angry squawk. I sighed and scooped up my friend, settling her black and white form on my shoulder and gathering up her clothing in my arms. I turned back to Levi to tell him to hold on just a minute while I put Sidney's stuff in the back room for her and made sure I had enough cash in our safe, only to find him staring at us with the most excited, gleeful expression on his face.

"What. Just. Happened?" He had stars in his eyes and looked like an excited puppy. Sidney screeched and flapped her wings, obviously irritated at his amusement. I dropped my face into her pile of clothes and muttered that I'd be back in just a moment. For being so tough in every other aspect of her life, Sidney sure was easy to startle.

CHAPTER 7

"I JUST WASN'T EXPECTING anyone else to be there!"

"I get that, Sidney. I do, but I don't understand how changing into a bird would help if Levi had actually been someone dangerous." I took my time pulling apart the last of my pastry. It was Saturday morning, and we were seated on a covered patio at a quaint eatery in downtown Golden Laurel.

Last night, as soon as Sidney had pulled herself together and Levi had gone home, I'd made her spill about Harrington. She told me she'd found him easily enough in the bar and questioned him about the Phantom showing up on my doorstep. He swore he had 'no idea' what she was talking about, that he'd never met a Phantom in his life. Sidney informed him that his 'loose lips' were creating problems for us and that I would not make *anyone* a golem. Ever.

She was incredibly dodgy about the rest of their interaction, so I had to take her at her word that Harrington was alive and unharmed. I made a mental note to ask Bane about him when he came in to pick up his finished weapons. She assured me she'd talked to him nicely, and she very well may have, but knowing Sidney it had been with a knife between them.

We'd spent way too long at the shop last night because, after that, she'd wanted to see all the items I'd bought from Levi. Mermaid culture was fascinating to a lot of people because they were particularly insular, and Sidney wasn't immune. Eventually, we'd dragged ourselves home, made dinner, and collapsed into bed.

Now we were out having 'brunch', even though it was a little past noon and Sidney was finishing her third coffee. She'd said she had plans for us today, and if we were going to need that much caffeine, I was... concerned.

"Reflexes don't always make sense," she grumbled, drawing me back into our conversation, "but if I was startled by something dangerous, it would make sense for me to fly away from it. If you could change into an animal with flight reflexes, you'd do it all the time too." That was probably one-hundred percent true. I would never be a person at all, and I'd just live in the treetops for the rest of my life.

"That doesn't help, though, if you're swaddled in clothing and weighed down by a handgun," I pointed out. "What are we doing today?" I asked, for the third time.

"*We*, my sweet, beautiful, lovely, dearest Elara—" She stood and tossed her cup in the trash. "—are going costume shopping."

I was instantly suspicious, both from her tone and her flattery. I stood and threw away my napkin, staring at her out of the corner of my eye. "Why?" I drew the word out.

I was usually the one who liked clothing and fashion. More often than not, Sidney settled for hoodies stolen from her brother Josh. Costumes were her main exception. This girl would go all out for a costume party, which would be fun except for the fact that parties pushed all my introvert buttons.

"It's not for us, sadly." She started and waved me along with her. "I stopped by my place on the way back from the Salty Wench, and Josh was home. He said Sam and Aaron heard about an underground rave coming up in a few days."

That sounded like my version of hell.

"Josh asked if I could pick something cool for the three of them, and unfortunately for you, I have to drag you along with me today because I'm not comfortable leaving you alone yet."

Ugh, I was being babysat. "Why aren't you going?" I asked curiously. This sounded like it would be right up Sidney's alley. "If you're worried about leaving me behind, you can just deadbolt me in my house. I'll make sure Isadora and Bette are going to be around to keep an eye out."

She sighed. "It's this Tuesday. You have to be out of the house that night. Banshee eradication, remember?"

Guilt swamped me. It was bad enough that Sidney felt the need to babysit me like some wayward child. Now she was missing out on stuff I *knew* she would have loved to do.

"As much as you know I'd rather have my teeth pulled, I'll go with you so you can go, too. Who throws a rave on a Tuesday, anyway?"

"People who don't want Enforcement to bust it," she said matter-of-factly. "They're usually expecting that kind of thing on a weekend." Yeah, I would be too.

"I'd honestly be dragging you, kicking and screaming, to this party if it weren't for the fact that it was down in the warehouse district in Dry Gulch. Mostly because the main event is a siren in the DJ line up. A *male* siren," she said with a sly grin. It took a moment for her words to register, and then she laughed at my expression.

"Levi is the main attraction? Are you serious?" I asked.

She nodded, looking impressed. "Sounds like it. Josh said he's heard of him and he's a popular draw in certain circles."

I chewed on my lip for a moment as we approached The Velvet Cloak Masquerade and Costumery and stopped to think. "I kind of want to go."

Sidney laughed and pulled the door open, holding it for me to enter. She wrinkled her nose at me as she said, "No, you don't. It's okay though, there will be other parties."

I stepped through the entry and eyed the racks of clothing. Seeing Levi in an environment like that, getting to watch him perform and interact with his magic in a way that was such a core part of who he was? That sounded... really attractive.

"No, I do. I want to go," I told her.

She paused, flipping through the clothing on the rack, and glanced at me. "Did you not hear the part where I said it was down in the warehouse district?"

I thought for a moment, because that did seem sketchy, but eventually shrugged. "You'd be there, and I'll have my wasps."

Not that I actually ever wanted to have to use the things, but now that I had them, I should try to live my life, right? "Plus, you said your brothers would all be there. I can't imagine someone messing with Aaron, let alone all of you."

She stared at me for a moment, considering. "You never ask to do stuff like this."

I just stared at her, knowing I had her. A slow grin crept over her face until suddenly she was beaming. "I'm going to be a valkyrie, and for you, I'm thinking... eighth-century elvish royalty meets moon goddess," she announced, ecstatic.

I didn't have any idea what that meant, but Mistress Adereth, the older, elvish woman who worked in the store, sure did. She wore a high-necked dress and a permanent frown and had some very minor artificer abilities, which leaned toward object enchantment.

We were ushered into a changing area where she quickly took our measurements and began bringing us costume pieces, frowning all the while. Maybe it was just her face.

Everything Sidney approved of looked really skimpy. When I pointed this out, she told me I could wear something more modest if I wanted, but to be prepared to sweat my make-up off.

By the time our assistant was done with me, I was wearing a white wrap top that left my midriff bare and a heavy collar necklace that dangled thin chains down my front and back. I had on gauzy, billowy white pants that gathered at the knee, and they would require shorts underneath them to keep them from being indecent by today's standards.

Sidney took one look at the gladiator style sandals Adereth brought out and vetoed them. "If you get stepped on in those, our night will be over." She turned to the assistant. "She'll need real boots." I finally settled on some cute ankle boots, and Sidney was satisfied.

She had gone full valkyrie with the winged headpiece, a molded corset that looked like armor, and a belted bottom piece that left her legs bare, save for small red cloth panels hanging down the sides. She was going to wear her own boots since they already had knife sheaths built in.

When Mistress Adereth walked up behind Sidney, I felt her

magic build a split second before she touched the corset and it cinched tight on Sidney's waist. Her breath gusted out, and I cackled when she wheezed. "Holy mercy, lady! Warn a girl!"

We found something simple and mysterious looking for the boys, and Sidney bounced on her toes while I paid. "You're like my fairy godmother. This is way nicer than anything I would have bought for myself." She slid me a sly look and wiggled her eyebrows.

"You're the one who decided our salaries," I muttered. Also, the trust fund didn't hurt. Buying some costumes was the least I could do, considering all she put up with for the last week.

***

By the time Tuesday rolled around, I'd finished six wasps in total and armed them. I was sick of looking at them, tired of working on them, and physically and magically drained from powering up that many shards in quick succession. Large heart-stones took more magical energy to work with, but even small ones took their toll in quantity.

I tried to wear them as jewelry pieces as much as possible, but since they were a bit large, most of the time they ended up simply nestled in my loose clothing or in my pockets or purse. Even tucked away, they were still easily summoned if I needed them, but at least Sidney wasn't complaining about my "creepy devil bugs."

Even though she didn't care for them, she still verified I was wearing them every time we left the house, especially after she swore she saw a glimpse of the two Phantoms from the market while picking up breakfast Sunday morning.

On Tuesday morning we packed up our costumes, and I packed some makeup for us to use for the rave, and a night bag to stay at Sidney's place. She was a little more skittish about us going, but I felt more confident with my wasps and her family there.

In the end, I had to remind Sidney six times that there was no point in closing shop early to go to the rave because it didn't start until after dark anyway. Thankfully we did brisk business most of the day and it passed relatively quickly. By the time we packed up and locked the doors, my friend's excitement was palpable.

We made our way through Dry Gulch and arrived at Sidney's apartment to get ready for the evening. I noticed before even entering that I couldn't feel her brother's magic nearby. "Where's Josh?"

"The guys will swing by and pick us up when it's time to go," she said as she unlocked the door, and we dumped our bags on the living room floor.

Her apartment was outfitted mostly with hand-me-down furniture from her parents or other family, and it was worn, scratched, and threadbare. Even so, or perhaps because of this, I'd always found it to have a welcoming and homey atmosphere. Scuffed hardwood floors and paint chipping from the kitchen cabinets didn't detract from the feeling of family and togetherness that permeated her home.

We piled into her small, shared bathroom, and I worked on my makeup while she stepped into her costume. Her corset eventually had me cry-laughing and her cursing, because even though it was pre-fitted to her form, I still had to close up the back. No easy task, that. We ended up with her braced against the bathroom wall, and I felt like I needed a crowbar by the end of it.

While I got dressed Sidney stepped out to the kitchen, coming back with some goblets. "I know you prefer your tea warm but it's already sweltering in here, so I made it iced," she said as she handed one to me.

I took a sip without paying much attention and choked on it. "Oh, and I added vodka, we're pre-gaming," she said as I coughed. She brushed her hair out and started plaiting it into intricate braids.

"You look phenomenal in that outfit, Elara," she said as I snapped the collar of the heavy necklace shut. The necklace with the skinny chains and the gauzy, gathered pants were definitely reminiscent of ancient elvish royalty. The light-colored fabric served to highlight the dark skin most royal elves had back then, but it still looked nice against my more medium-colored complexion.

She eyed me as she said, "We should go to a real ball some-day. Couldn't your dad get us an invitation to one?"

"Prime Minister Pertoris is only my fourth cousin," I hedged. "We're not that close." In reality, my parents got invitations to all kinds of government functions, but the thought of attending something of that magnitude shifted my nerves into high gear. "Do you want me to do your makeup?"

"Does this outfit say makeup to you? It does not. It says wear war paint." She grabbed a pot of white, iridescent, cream-based eyeshadow and drew two slashes under each eye and a streak starting in the center of her bottom lip and disappearing under her chin.

On the middle of her forehead, she placed three white dots in a vertical line, the middle one smaller than the other two. She'd told me before that it was the same style the Magpie Clan of Shifters, the Warbirds, had used in ancient times. We were quite the mashup of ancient clothing styles and mythology tonight.

"Will you know anyone else at the rave?" I asked, feeling my nerves start to climb a bit.

"Not that I know of. Other than your merman." She replaced the lid on the pot of eyeshadow and took a swig of her drink.

I knew she was teasing me, but I couldn't help grumbling my retort. "He's not mine, and he's said he's not a mer. At least I'll know you guys." I clipped a wasp on the gathered fabric of my wrap top where it crossed each shoulder and clipped two onto the center chain hanging down my back.

"I guess it's possible he might bring his roommates," I muttered. "How can that reaper cross the Gates and live in the Void, anyway? He didn't feel like he had a single drop of human blood in him." I'd filled her in on my meeting with Levi's house-mates when we'd gone through the box of Levi's items. She'd never met a reaper either, hadn't even known of anyone who had met one.

Sidney shrugged. "I guess it doesn't matter if you go some-where that should normally kill you if you're immortal to start with." I hadn't thought of that. I supposed that would also explain why the vampire wasn't concerned about living outside of the Boundlands.

I felt her brothers at the edge of my periphery and took a deep pull of my drink to steel myself. Their magic was mischief, soaring flight, and raucous laughter. "Your brothers are here."

"More drinks!" Sidney declared as she made her way back to the kitchen.

I listened to their boisterous banter as I gave up on my extra wasps and packed away the rest of my supplies. When I entered the kitchen, Sidney had set out drinks for her brothers and plates of sausage, smoked fish, and dilled cheeses. Josh dug out a roll of crusty bread.

All the boys were taller than Sidney and heavily muscled. Josh looked like he still hadn't filled out completely, whereas the older two could easily be described as hulking or burly. Sam and Josh, the eldest and youngest, both had Sidney's blond hair, cropped short. Aaron, the middle brother, was the only one with dark hair and was the largest of all of them. They all shared the same cornflower blue eyes and brash, jovial nature, and of course the ability to shift into birds.

They were all donning the loose headscarves in earthen or ashy colors we'd found for them. Ragged or pieced clothing reminiscent of the style of clothing tribal shifters had worn back when they were nomadic warrior clans made up the rest of their costumes. Josh was asking Sidney to paint his face like hers, and Aaron was horsing around with Sam when they noticed me standing by the door jamb.

Aaron gave a piercing wolf howl before taking two giant steps toward me and dropping to his knees on the dingy kitchen tile with a flirty grin. "A queen beautiful enough to start wars! Sidney, why didn't you tell me we were in the presence of royalty?" I laughed at his dramatics as he clutched his chest and mocked a bow of fealty.

He flinched when Sidney cracked him on the head with a slotted spoon. "Elara's off limits. Eat some food. I don't want you goons eating or drinking anything at the rave tonight. Last thing I need is your drunk ass thinking you can fly to the moon again."

Sam groused as Josh put Aaron in a headlock and jostled his

drink. As an only child I felt entirely out of my element in the midst of their roughhousing, but Sidney barely seemed to notice as they grunted and rattled the cabinets. Sam tipped his glass up and grabbed a hunk of bread. "Time's up ladies! Let's move this party out of here."

Sidney shrieked as he hauled her up under his arm like a newspaper. "Put me down, you giant oaf! I still need my boots and my headpiece." I grinned at them when she squealed like a little girl as he swung her around and set her on her feet. He gave us to the count of ten before they tossed us over their shoulders and physically hauled us out, with Sidney accusing them of acting like wildlings and Josh trying to chug the last of his drink as we left.

I had a feeling we were actually bringing the wild to the party.

CHAPTER 8

THIS PARTY DIDN'T NEED any help getting wild.

I'd had a moment of false security while we were in line to get into the warehouse. I could feel that the building was cloaked in some kind of auditory dampening barrier, but I hadn't realized the full extent of it until we'd stepped into the dimly lit, body-rumbling interior.

The heavy, rhythmic bass felt trance-inducing, even without the effect of the mind-altering drugs some of the occupants were obviously partaking of, if their thousand-yard stares and awkward swaying were anything to go by. Sam walked in front of us as we weaved through the crush of bodies, with Sidney in front of me and Josh and Aaron behind us.

We'd made it maybe twenty steps from the door when Sidney jerked an arm back and decked a guy. He dropped like a sack of rocks, and she leaned over him. "Just because you can see it doesn't mean you can touch it!" I barely heard her yell over the thumping of the music, and I hadn't even seen what had happened to start it.

She was pushing through the crowd again before I could piece together the interaction, and Josh and Aaron pressed in a little closer to my back. Flickering lights pulsed over the crowd, and the sheer number of magic users operating around me made it impossible for me to follow all the threads of energy and magical intent roaring through the revelers.

We passed a djinn breathing fire, arcing it high up into the rafters where spark fairies darted in and out of the flames. A man on stilts had glowing neon-turquoise tattoos. I noticed most of the girls in the crowd were more naked than not, and face-obscuring masks were popular among the guys.

I felt a prickle of fear when I considered the sea of masks and the fact that any of them could be hiding a Phantom. I pressed still closer to Aaron, wishing I could turn into a little barnacle on his side.

When we stopped in a small opening in the crowd, I could see a DJ in a crow's nest high up near the rafters, but his skin looked too dark to be Levi. It was hard to make out any distinct features from this distance, with all the flashing lights and smoke in the air. Sidney leaned in close to my ear, but she still had to yell to be heard. "Josh says there are still a few more sets in the line-up before it's Levi's turn!"

I was a little unsure what to do with myself other than simply following the rhythm of the music with my body, like everyone around me seemed to be doing. Sam had already ingratiated himself with a group of girls in iridescent body suits and pigtail-buns, but he kept darting a watchful eye back over to me and Sidney.

The girls opened their circle to include us and cast us friendly smiles while they danced, cheering and waving us into their group. I couldn't tell if they were just super friendly or if trav-eling with hot guys had perks. Probably both. There was defi-nitely a free-love type vibe among many of the dancers. I didn't know what to do with that, so I just smiled back and waved a little.

Josh leaned over my shoulder from behind me. "Can you actually see anything down here? You can sit on my shoulders so you can see!" When I tried to look up at him, he was already hoisting me into the air. I expected him to seat me around his neck, but he was big enough that he just perched me on one shoulder and kept dancing.

"Wouldn't it be easier to hide from the Phantoms down

below?" I asked in his ear. I felt safer down below, where I was more hidden from view. Being exposed like this gave me anxiety.

He shrugged and shook his head. "Nobody's gonna touch you. Sam would put anybody who tried anything in a dumpster somewhere, I promise. Have fun and enjoy the show!" His confidence relaxed me a little, and I sat up to take in the party.

Music hammered around us with stuttering, drumming beats and people gathered in tight groups, dancing and stomping and passing people up to crowd surf over the surging horde.

An illusionist off to my right created a light show as he danced, shimmering orbs spinning into planetary systems that morphed into galaxies before disintegrating and becoming something else entirely. The hot press of bodies swayed and shook and waved and sang as one DJ after another entertained from high above us.

Eventually, another DJ, in a headscarf that glowed bright green, took the crow's nest, and I recognized Levi immediately as he spoke, amplifying his voice with an amulet. His enchantment rolled over the screaming crowd, but I couldn't pick out its effects since it was blocked by my ward and there was so much other magical distraction flying around me. That is, until he boosted it with another amulet, and I began to feel surges of elation and glee paired with his usual siren lure.

The crowd roared around us, screaming and jumping in time with the music so that the floor shook dangerously, and I ducked a bit, feeling a little concerned about the stability of the warehouse as everything pounded and rattled deafeningly. Someone shot streams of water into the air nearby and a water bender turned it into mist, a welcome respite to the hot bodies dancing below. She didn't even open her eyes or pause in her dancing. If I hadn't felt how strong her magic was, I wouldn't have known how it was done.

As the volume of the music dipped momentarily, Sidney leaned over and yelled, "I don't know how he found you, but he's staring at you!" She pointed up at the crow's nest.

I craned my neck to look up and sure enough, the hood of Levi's glowing scarf was pointed in our direction. I shivered despite the heat in the room, unsure how I felt about being so easily spotted. To be the focus of his singular attention among a crowd of slathering groupies felt heady, and I fully acknowledged that I was in full-blown crush territory now. However, it didn't speak well for my safety that he'd seen me so easily.

After another song with his stare unwavering, it looked like he raised his arm and beckoned, but I couldn't be sure I was seeing it correctly. Even if I was, I didn't know if he was directing it at me or even how to get up there.

"I think he wants you to go up there," Sidney yelled next to me.

I gave her a deer-in-the-headlights expression and shrugged my shoulders. Then I almost lost my balance and Josh had to grab my waist to keep me from pitching backward when a wisp swooped too close to my face. I glanced at Sidney to see that she'd managed to keep her composure by not noticing at all.

I wondered briefly if anyone would even notice her turning into a bird, then a naked woman, and then getting dressed in this chaos. Probably not, but I shuddered to think how easily a magpie could get crushed in a crowd like this. Sidney shook my arm, pulling me out of my thoughts.

"Tall, dark, and death! Twelve o'clock!" she yelled. I raised my head as Grim pushed through the crowd toward us. "Man, you weren't kidding about that guy being menacing. Yeesh." She cringed back just a hair. When he reached us, he shot Sidney a look like he wasn't amused, but I had a hard time imagining he'd heard her.

My eyes snapped open. *HOLY CRAP*, what if her dressing as a Valkyrie was some kind of grim reaper cultural appropriation? I knew my expression was a bizarre mixture of absolute horror and inappropriately absurd amusement when he made eye contact with me and arched an eyebrow. I slapped my hand over my gaping mouth and just shook my head. I'd have to try to ask him later.

His eyebrows drew together in confusion as he held my gaze, and then he glanced up at the crow's nest and back at me with a question in his eyes and shrugged. He turned his body toward Levi, but looked back at me like he was waiting for an answer.

Did he want me to come with him? Did the man ever actually talk?

I looked to Sidney, and she clapped her hands like an excited child. "Go if you want!" She leaned toward Grim, and I heard her yell, "You'll keep her safe?"

He nodded without taking his eyes off mine, and I shrugged. The man still made me nervous, but it was in the way a person might respect a calm but vicious-looking guard dog. My fear felt deeply embedded but at the same time logically irrational.

I patted Josh's neck, and he hefted me off of his shoulder and set me lightly on the floor. He glanced at Sidney with a concerned expression, and she waved him off.

"We'll go closer so we can keep an eye on her," she yelled to him. I still had my wasps on me, but I tried not to bristle at their kid-glove treatment. This felt like being inside a blender and a riot all at once. Wild was an understatement.

I moved toward Grim, and he put an arm around me, not actually touching me but hovering a bit as if to shield me from the crowd. He walked half a step ahead of me, and I noticed the crowd parted slightly, always moving just before he touched a person. I wondered if others could feel his magical aura.

A glance behind me showed Sidney with a hand around Josh and Aaron's wrists, dragging them along in our wake. I laughed as I heard Sam whine loudly in the back about having to leave behind the pretty girls.

Flashing lights reflected off of an ogre's jagged teeth, making him look particularly gruesome, though he danced with great care for those around him as we passed by.

When we got to the wall near the crow's nest, I saw a recessed groove that had a built-in ladder going up the side. Metal rungs stuck out of the side of the groove, but the bottom rung was up above my head. Before I could puzzle out if I was supposed to jump for the ladder, Grim startled me by wrapping his long hands around my waist and hoisting me up so that my feet touched the bottom rung.

He waited until I grabbed onto a higher rung with my hands before he turned and gazed out over the crowd with a bored expression. I guess he was acting as Levi's bouncer tonight.

Feeling a little self-conscious, I glanced over my shoulder to see if people were staring, but the groove was so deeply shadowed that it would have been hard to see me, so I began my slow ascent.

When I reached the top, Levi leaned over and took my hand, hauling me onto the small metal platform that made up the crow's nest. There were metal pipes running this way and that, and levers and dials that must have been used for some kind of maintenance. A small ledge served as a table where he had amulets laid out with an entire handful of calling stones. It was barely enough room for both of us.

He kept ahold of my hand and pulled me close so he could speak directly against my ear without yelling. "What in the world are you doing here?" I shivered a little despite the oppressive heat this high up in the rafters.

"Having... fun?" I was a little surprised to find the statement was true. I was overstimulated and still felt like I was in a washing machine spin cycle, but as long as I wasn't actually down amidst the swaying, shaking, and jiggling mass of hot bodies I was willing to admit this was more fun than I would have expected. I'd have to thank Josh for letting me ride on him like a camel all night.

Levi glared over the meager handrail. "Is one of those your boyfriend?" he asked as he tapped on various calling stones, shifting them from one spot on the ledge to another with his free hand while he worked.

I glanced down into the crowd and quickly spotted Sidney and Sam, but it took a little longer to find Josh and Aaron, who had moved into a seething, boiling section off to my left. People were slamming their bodies into each other and pulling back to do it again and again. I frowned. I didn't understand that kind of dance, it looked painful.

I turned my attention back to Levi. "No, they're my guards," I said with false petulance. I resisted the urge to stick my tongue out at him but cracked a smile when he laughed.

"As much as I want to be irritated that you're down here in Dry Gulch again, the bouncers here are *very* good," he said.

His eyes dropped down to my costume, and I realized he was still holding my hand when he gave it a deep, slow squeeze.

"Not an empress, huh, little queen?" he asked with a boyish smirk and a teasing glint in his eye. "Come join me. It always feels weird sitting up here by myself. You can survey your empire."

He took his seat again, on some pipes traveling along the wall, and tugged me gently into his lap, wrapping his arms around me loosely and releasing a shuddering breath. I didn't know how he could stand to be touching me—his skin was obviously flushed from the heat—but I couldn't find it in me to ask or remove myself. He took three red pebbles from an out of the way pile and slid them across the ledge, aligning them with some stones already in use.

"Check this out." An illusionary ball of flame lit on each of the large walls opposite us and to the sides. It began splitting into writing, which flickered and morphed into images that told a story of the Bound's three moons and how they'd been placed in the sky—an ancient legend from the mer.

Levi moved the pebbles into a different pattern, leaning around me as he worked, and added a blue one to the mix. The flames took on a sickly green tint and coalesced into a single giant form in the center of the room, the image spinning and morphing as it went. It settled on an ethereal image of a leviathan, one of our world's mega-behemoths—in miniature size, though still large enough to reach the rafters—swimming through the crowd. Only a few behemoths had survived in the deep waters of the Void, but the Boundlands still had behemoths in spades.

As I watched the ghostly creature begin to disintegrate, I was startled to see Sidney climbing the ladder beside me. She leaned over the railing toward me with an exasperated expression on her face.

"So, I've got bad news," she yelled. "Josh thinks he broke his foot in the mosh pit, but I'm also pretty sure Aaron has a concussion, so we're gonna have to bail early and take them to the healer."

I glanced down to the area I had seen them, where people had been throwing themselves into one another like mountain goats in rut. I nodded to Sidney.

"Okay, climb down, and I'll come down after you." Did I imagine Levi's arm around my waist holding me a little tighter?

"No, no. You guys look cozy," she said with a little grin and mischief in her eyes. "We're going to the medic across town, since they have more experience with shifters, and they won't let you into the back with a patient if you're not family. You'd have to wait outside, and one of us would have to stay out and guard you. Can you stay here with Levi and his reaper buddy?" She twisted to look at Grim. "I'll call when we're done to find out where you are." She tapped the top of her 'chest plate' where her necklace was nestled with her lockets.

Levi's arm pulled me more firmly against him. "We'll take care of you," he said against my ear. I nodded to Sidney. I felt safe with Levi, and I had my wasps. I couldn't imagine anyone ever crossing Grim—just the thought of doing so made my skin crawl.

"Tell the boys I'm sorry that happened, and I hope they're okay."

She waved me off as she started her descent back down. "You play stupid games; you win stupid prizes. I'll check you later." She climbed down the ladder, gave a sloppy salute to Grim, and plunged back into the crowd. Levi shook his head and shifted several pebbles out of the smaller pile, making the last bits of the behemoth disappear.

As a new song started, I realized I was starting to get light-headed from the heat, but after a few more minutes, I was dizzy enough to feel sick and told him I needed to climb down for a bit to cool off. He nodded and gave my back a soft pat, releasing me from his lap.

"I only have two more songs, and then my set is up. I need out of this hotbox too. Stay behind Grim, please. The crowd can be pretty rough."

He helped me over to the ladder, and I had to focus on not missing a rung. The last thing I needed was to slip and make a spectacle of myself in front of hundreds of people. When I got to the bottom Grim lifted me down with the smallest smile on his face. *Yes, yes, so funny.* I pouted, remembering that Sidney had simply jumped and not required any help at all. I noticed his eyes were beginning to cloud with the faintest white haze.

When he set me on the floor, he kept himself between me and the crowd as much as possible, making sure I had enough space and didn't get trampled on. I heard Levi's sultry voice enter the mix of music and didn't recognize the language, but those in the crowd with any kind of ocean-related magic began cheering at a deafening pitch. I looked up to see him staring out over the crowd, his cowl pulled up to obscure his face, and felt his enchantment roll over us.

His voice was husky and ragged in some places, strong and resolute in others, and all the while I felt the pull of his magic wrapping me up and dragging me toward him. Some of the people nearby looked nearly rapturous, like they were waiting on orders from a beloved king. Grim looked mildly bored, only focused on making sure those closest to us kept their distance.

By the time Levi's replacement took to the ladder and he had climbed down, the feeling of Grim's magic had grown strong enough to drown out all the other magic users around us. He still had a faint impression of his pupils showing through the white haze, and there was no sign of his shadow cloak yet, but Levi took one look at him and clasped Grim's forearm in an embrace, leaning close to his ear to say something I couldn't hear. Grim gave me a curt nod and turned, melting into the crowd. They parted and closed back in around him as he left.

"I wish he could stay but he can't fight his magic more than he already has." Levi's fingers brushed down my forearm as he stepped closer to me and leaned in to speak close to my ear. "You're killing me with this outfit, Empress," he said with a groan. "Dance with me?"

He kept his eyes locked on mine as he took my hand and backed through the crowd, pulling me away from the wall a bit. When he stopped, he kept tugging me forward until I collided with his chest and then wrapped his arms around me loosely with his hands resting on my back.

"Is this alright?" he asked into my ear so low I could barely make out the words.

I nodded my forehead against his chest as we began to move

slightly in time with the music, and I marveled in the feel of his enchantments wrapping me up as much as his arms did. I gripped the front of his shirt gently in my fingers and noticed the hard muscles underneath flexing against the backs of my knuckles as he danced.

Peripherally, I noted that his skin felt cooler than mine and that he moved with a primal kind of grace. Where many of the men around us danced in a way that felt tribal or carnal at its roots, Levi's movements struck me as almost sinuous and fluid, with a kind of infectious sensuality. His hips guided mine in a deliberate, skilled dance that reminded me of ocean waves rolling gently but relentlessly against an ever-changing shore.

He was confident in his movements and in his body, expertly navigating the rhythm of the song like it was second nature to him. I felt myself relaxing in his grip as our bodies swayed and bounced with the music through several songs. I found myself melting into him as the party roiled and pounded around us, one song after another.

I felt a little in awe of him as I pulled back to gaze up at his striking features, like I was seeing a new piece of him, like he was speaking to me in his native language with his body. His face looked pleased but fatigued as he gazed down at me with an almost imperceptible smile in his eyes. I noticed his cheeks were rosy, giving him an adorable flush, but something about how slowly his eyes blinked struck me as off.

When I reached up and touched his cheek to feel his temperature, he hissed quietly and snapped his head back in a way that seemed reflexive. I gripped the front of his shirt and tried to tug him down closer to me, suddenly feeling a little alarmed at the way his eyes cast about in confusion. He blinked, trying to reorient himself.

"Levi?" I heard panic in my voice. "Are you okay?"

His eyes focused on mine and then closed for a second. "I think I'm too hot," he said after a moment. There was no draw in his enchantment that I could feel this time. His hand lifted to his thin headscarf—still emitting a faint green glow from before —which was draped loosely around his shoulders and tried without success to pull it free. I hurriedly pulled it free from his neck and gathered it in my arms.

"Can we get out of here for a bit and cool down? Where can we get you some water to drink?"

He was nodding his head before I finished my last question. "There's a back way out," he said, slurring a bit as he spoke. He hooked an arm through one of mine and turned, but I walked in front of him this time, pushing through the crowd as best I could and yelling or patting to get people's attention when they didn't notice me. 'Aura of the reaper' I did not have.

With his direction I found a metal door in the back corner and asked the intimidating looking bouncer posted beside it if he knew where we could get water for Levi. He slid his eyes over to my companion and I saw recognition there before he nodded and started to wave us through.

Before he could get the door open, a large sweaty man with a bald head tried to block our path, and I froze, but the bouncer's hand was on his chest pushing him away immediately. I looked at his face, thinking he was the man who had come to my house, but he was just a stranger from the crowd trying to tell Levi how much he loved his work as the bouncer pushed him away.

"Give them space," the bouncer yelled, and then waited to make sure the other man turned and walked away. "I'll be right back," the bouncer said to Levi. "Try to steer clear of the damned groupies." He stepped away, going back the way we'd come from.

I opened the door and shivered as we stepped outside into the relatively cooler night air. The cool, quiet alleyway felt miles away from the riotous interior of the warehouse, and I tried to breathe out my nervous energy. At any other time, this would have felt like a warm, balmy evening, but after the sweltering heat from inside, the air felt chilly against my damp skin.

Levi slumped back against the metal wall of the building and began tugging the collar of his shirt loose, opening the three buttons that held it closed, and then dropped his hand while his eyes found mine.

The bouncer from beside the door returned with a green glass bottle, commonly used to hold water for sale, and he held it out for us. "Thanks, Ramar," Levi mumbled as he took it and broke the cap.

"Don't mention it," Ramar said in a deeply scratchy voice that spoke of years of heavy smoking. "Like, *at all*, 'cause I stole it. Management needs to take better care of the talent. Cheap little pricks."

Levi coughed and choked on his water before clearing his throat for a proper laugh as Ramar walked back inside and let the door swing shut. He finished half the bottle before letting his head thump back and offering me a drink. I took a few small sips and then—realizing how desperately thirsty I actually was—took some longer pulls before returning the bottle. He was in much worse shape than me.

"Sorry about that," he said with his head still tipped back against the wall. "I'm not built for this stuff."

"What do you mean?" I studied his face carefully and noticed that the redness in his cheeks was beginning to fade, if only just a bit.

"Well," he said with a huff. "I may not be an *actual* mer—not enough that they'd claim me anyway—but I have enough in me to make me more susceptible to the heat than most people." I couldn't tell if he sounded a little bitter when he said that. "Deep ocean being what it is, mer folk are built for cooler temperatures, generally." He raised his head and leveled his eyes at me. He was definitely looking a little perkier.

"Does that bother you? That you're not an, as you say, 'actual mer'?"

"Pffft. No." He took another swig from the bottle. "Hell, no. Nothing like hauling a ninety-pound tail with you to class because it started to rain… or your jerk friend threw a cup of water on you." He narrowed his eyes while staring at the ground, presumably at a memory.

I blinked. "That sounds oddly specific."

"Grim didn't believe that I couldn't transform and thought he'd test me on it one time, right after we met. We both got detention because I tackled him."

I huffed a startled laugh, having a difficult time reconciling the friend Levi described and the silent man who reaped the souls of the dead.

"Thank you," he said quietly. He raised the bottle of water and touched the hooded scarf in my arms when he noticed my confused expression. "Most people think it would be great to not be able to sweat, but turns out it's not really ideal for landwalkers."

"Oh." That made sense. "Pour some of that over your head." I nodded to the bottle. He bent away from me and poured some water in his hair, shaking it out before straightening. As he did, a spectral appeared in front of his face, wispy and glowing faintly in the night.

He reached in his pocket, activating a calling stone, and a man's harried voice groused, "We got incoming! Try to clear them out!"

Levi gave a low curse as the light winked out and turned to jerk the door open.

I felt his magic swell as he pushed some of his energy into two amulets, one on his chest—probably on a necklace—and one in a pocket. His voice boomed out even louder than when he'd been singing above the crowd. "Everybody, get out! Enforcement is on its way! *Godspeed!*" On the last word, his enchantment gave such a firm emotional shove that I actually stumbled a step backward.

CHAPTER 9

HE CLUTCHED at my arm as people began pouring out of the exit, and I followed him down the dark alleyway into a labyrinth of tiny streets.

"Ditch that." He snatched the glowing scarf from my arms and wrapped his glass bottle in it, tossing the package into a dumpster with a low thud as we ran. Our largest moon was full tonight, providing just enough light to keep me from turning an ankle as we navigated narrow passageways and tight turns.

I spied an Enforcement uniform between a gap in the buildings and felt the strength-boosting and defensive magics they were known for hiring into their ranks. We climbed a few steps to a higher level and made our way to the next street as quietly as we could.

Most people must have been leaving through the front entrances, but there were still others crashing around through the alleyways behind us. Levi peeked around the corner before we darted out across the street and into the next alley.

It hadn't really occurred to me we'd be in trouble for attending a rave, but the thought of an Enforcer chasing me down a dark alleyway made my adrenaline spike. For a split second, I considered that I still had my wasps on me, and then was instantly flooded with guilt that I would consider using them against people just doing their jobs, especially people just enforcing the law when I was breaking it. *Ugh.* This was one of the reasons I didn't like making golems—you never knew what people might be tempted to do.

"How much trouble will we be in?" I whispered quietly while he pulled me around another bend. I moved as smoothly as I could to avoid jingling any of my decorative chains, but I had a lot of practice with that.

He threw a glance back at me and grinned. "None, really," he said quietly. "They're out here because the rave didn't have permits, breaking fire codes, illegal drug usage, stuff like that. I might get a slap on the wrist for being paid to help, but I don't want to spend the night sleeping on concrete while they process everybody. They might make us pay a fine. But there were so many people rolling in there that I don't think we have to worry about them catching us. We don't have to be fast, just faster than the others."

He broke into a wide grin before I felt the previous Enforcer's magic quickly edging toward us from behind. My eyes widened, and I pointed behind me. His focus flickered behind me before he grabbed my hand and pulled me up a flight of stairs and into a dark loading bay. As we crept farther into the shadows, Levi looked like he was trying to suppress laughter at our antics.

A man's voice became audible, "… need another drunk tank and some medics with hydro kits at the Wilkerson warehouse down on…" and then faded into the night. We slid behind a wooden crate as he jogged past. Levi opened his mouth to say something when he was out of sight, and I shook my head slightly. I could still feel the Enforcer's magic.

As I felt it fade, I realized Levi and I were standing very close together in our hiding place. We were huddled against one another in the dark, his breath skimming over my cheek when he exhaled. His eyes were deep in shadow, but his face appeared vaguely amused.

He stared at me for a long moment, possibly listening for more footsteps, but I only felt people moving around in the distance. He leaned closer in, and lightly, ever so gently, brushed his lips against mine. I heard myself gasp over the pounding in my ears. When I stiffened, he retreated slightly, moving back an inch or two before I clutched at his shirt collar and pulled him back.

He gave me a small grin and appeased me, leaning back in and whispering against my cheek, "May I kiss you?" His lips grazed against my skin as he spoke, his enchantment powerful, alluring. *Compelling.*

I nodded, my mouth suddenly too dry to answer. He shifted and pressed a light kiss against my temple, and I felt his grin widen against my skin. He placed his hands gently on my elbows and slid them up to my shoulders, then my neck, finally cradling my jaw like a baby bird. I knew my eyes were wide, but he wasn't looking at them. He was staring at my mouth.

He approached slowly, hesitating as if he was giving me time to prepare myself, but it only served to make my blood roar louder in my ears. I couldn't breathe. He pressed his lips gently to mine, freezing my mind and stilling my panic. When I responded in kind, he pulled back slightly and returned again with another soft kiss. Slowly, he began plying my lips with his own, little nips and tugs in between more soft presses. It felt like he was savoring me, taking minuscule little sips that left my chest aching and my breathing ragged. My fingers tightened in his shirt.

I gradually began to move with him, enjoying the feel of him against me and trying to catch his lips in mine the way he did to me. Levi slid one hand farther back into my hair, and his fingers tangled lightly with it as he kissed me sweetly, tenderly, over and over again. His softness, his gentleness, made my heart hurt in a way I didn't understand. I felt hungry for him, wanted to consume him—all of him. My only thought was that I wanted *more.*

He must have felt some of my frantic need building as I moved my grip to his shoulders—thick, rounded caps of muscle that emphasized his swimmer's build—because he slid one arm around my back and gathered me against his chest. Our kisses became deeper, less gentle, and I was startled to feel the wet heat of his tongue slide across my bottom lip.

Voices of fellow revelers seeped into my consciousness as a large group of partiers made their way down the nearest street. We broke our kiss and Levi rested his forehead against mine as we struggled to quiet our breathing. I focused on his face and found his eyes intense and searching, and I quietly returned his stare as we waited for the voices to fade into the distance.

"You are quite possibly the most beautiful little creature I've ever seen," he whispered when all was quiet again. His voice was low and reverent. I was grateful for the cover of darkness because if my face wasn't already flushed by his kisses, it certainly was now.

Even as my heart thrilled at his praise, I felt clumsy, unsure how to respond. I'd always been awkward with compliments.

I slid my hands down to his waist and buried my face against his chest, feeling shy but unwilling to remove myself from physical contact with him. Everything about him felt steadfast and sure, firm muscles and strong bones, like a fortress against the dark unknown. He smoothed his hands up and down my back and toyed with the ends of my hair.

I wanted his mouth back on mine. I wanted more of his hitching breaths. I wanted to climb him like a tree, but I didn't know how to ask for that.

"What is this?" He tugged on a lump buried in the swath of cloth wrapped around my side. A wasp.

"Don't prick your finger on that. It might knock you out."

"What? What is it?" He craned his neck over my shoulder to get a better look and tried to tug at the cloth without touching the lump.

"My *actual* guards," I muttered.

"A true empress," he teased.

"Why do you still call me that?" I wrinkled my nose against his chest.

"Because you can be my queen anytime you want," he murmured against my hair with amusement in his voice. I didn't know what that was supposed to mean, but the mental images it conjured felt a little shocking.

I pulled back to look at his face. He had a wicked grin.

"You look magnificent in this outfit, by the way." His eyes trailed appreciatively down my torso to my legs and back to my face. He shook his head as if he were trying to clear it and huffed a breath.

"We should get you home," he said, sounding a little rough. It occurred to me that Sidney had forgotten to leave her key with me when she left. What a mess. Horrible banshees. Ridiculous brothers. I let out an irritated huff.

"I can't. I'm supposed to bunk with Sidney tonight, and she forgot to leave her key. I'll have to go find her and pick it up, since she hasn't called to let me know that they're done yet." I began digging through a hidden pouch for one of my calling stones.

"Didn't she say she lives here in the Gulch?" His mouth pressed into a frown as he shook his head slightly. "I can walk you back to your own house."

I sighed. "My block has been evacuated for the night due to *banshees*, of all things. That's why I'm staying with her." His frown deepened.

"Why don't you come stay with me?" he asked, quickly adding, "I can sleep on the couch."

If I was honest, I was a little unsure how I felt about staying at Sidney's apartment alone until she came home. It would probably be fine, but knowing what I did about the crime rate in the city put me on edge. Staying with Levi came with its own set of problems, however.

"I don't have any clothes though," I said, glancing down at my costume.

Levi broke into a deep, teasing grin. "I'm sure we can think of something."

While we made our way back to the Void, I sent a spectral to Sidney with a message that she should take her time with her brother and that I'd be staying with Levi for the night.

I dreaded the interrogation this was going to earn me tomorrow, but I'd deal with that when it came to it. My stomach was churning with butterflies, both over Sidney's potentially aggressive enthusiasm about my time spent with a guy she knew I liked, and because I felt skittish just thinking about staying with him.

Levi startled me out of my inner turmoil after we passed through the Gate into the Void. "There's going to be a vampire inside my apartment again, just in case you decide you don't want to choke him out this time." I cast a guilty glance at Levi as we paced up the sidewalk, only to find him wearing an entertained grin.

"I'm not wearing that gem set tonight. I didn't want to risk hurting someone by accident in a crowd full of unknown magical traits. I didn't see him at the party. Was he there?" I asked, more out of politeness than real curiosity. Maybe he was just a roommate and they weren't truly friends.

"He said he would think about coming when I invited him, but he never actually comes to anything. Jordan doesn't really leave the house unless he has to. The Vampire Advocacy Committee leaves him a cooler full of blood bags on the doorstep every few nights, and his classes are online, so other than his meetings with his mentor he doesn't really have any reason to leave. He's had a rough couple of years from what I can tell, but he won't talk about it. Not that I'd have much of an idea what to do with him if he did talk to me. That's probably why we all get along so well. Deep down, we're all a bunch of touchy Eeyores."

I pushed through the enticement of his voice to focus on his words. I didn't entirely know what to make of all that, but the implications made my heart sink. Did he mean they were all depressed in some way? Levi always seemed to have some innate cheerfulness about him, a teasing smile or a playful glint in his eye—but then I remembered his downcast expression when I saw him on the bus last week and his gruffness about the items he'd sold me.

The apartment was quiet when we arrived, though I could feel both Grim's and Jordan's magic through their closed doors. I toed off my boots and followed Levi back to his room, where he set to digging through his dresser. He pulled out some clothes, a t-shirt and a pair of soft looking shorts, and set them on the bed.

"These are probably the only things I have that have a chance of fitting you. I hope you don't mind if they're baggy." He opened the door next to his writing desk and showed me to his bathroom, pulling an unopened toothbrush out of his cabinets and setting it next to the sink for me.

He turned on the hot water for the shower and brushed his knuckles down the back of my arm as he passed behind me toward his bedroom. "Towels and washcloths are under the sink.

I'll be in the living room, just call for me if you need anything."
He pulled the door to his bedroom quietly shut as I retrieved his
spare clothing from his bed.

The water in the shower was still cold when I returned, so I
brushed my teeth and grabbed a washcloth and set about
removing my makeup as well as I could without makeup
remover. After my face was red with my efforts, I began my
nightly ritual of removing all my amulets and charms from my
hair, my neck, my wrists, and all the little hidden places tucked
about my clothing, setting them on the countertop in neat little
rows as I went.

By the time I was finished, the water was warm, so I
stepped in and tried to make sense of his washing supplies. The
shampoo was obvious, but the little pot of sea salt and a bottle
full of floating seaweed raised some questions. I washed quickly,
trying to save him some hot water, and was done in record
time.

He was right about the clothing being baggy. I had to cinch
the soft shorts as tight as I could get them and then fold the
waistband over a few times, in hopes they would stay put. His
shirt hung loose and smelled like him, fresh ocean breezes and a
hint of oak (which I now knew came from his shampoo). I
toweled my hair and hovered over my amulets for a moment,
ultimately deciding to replace the thick manacle bracelet that
provided my ward against enchantments.

I padded quietly out of the bathroom, opened Levi's
bedroom door to let him know I was done, and took a seat on his
bed. The clock on the small nightstand beside his bed said it was
just before midnight. The party hadn't even really had a chance
to get going, but I was going to be dragging at work tomorrow
anyway. I cherished my sleep and needed a lot of it.

As I scooted back toward his pillows, the smell of popcorn
drifted in, and Levi came in shaking a steaming bag and carrying
bottles of water. He smiled when he saw me perched on his bed
and passed me the popcorn and a bottle. "I figured you might be
hungry, and we could both probably use some more water. Do
you mind if I use the shower? Or I can use the one Grim and
Jordan share if you need to sleep right away." His magic beck-

oned gently, and I was glad for my foresight to put my ward back on.

I shook my head. "Please go use your own shower. I'm fine. Thank you for everything tonight."

He shot me a look like I was silly and lifted his arms out to his sides a little. "Yeah, I'm really going out of my way here," he said sarcastically. "What guy doesn't want a beautiful girl sitting in his bed wearing his favorite sleep shirt?" He flashed me a grin and winked before he snagged some clothes out of his dresser and walked into his bathroom.

"Elara, what the *hell?*" He stumbled back out of the doorway immediately and grabbed the door frame. He wasn't looking at me but, unfortunately, I'd just taken a bite of popcorn, so after a beat of confused silence, he shot me a harried glance before returning his attention to the bathroom.

"What?" I asked, trying to choke down my food and swallow some water.

He looked at me like I was crazy. "What are these *giant insects* doing in my bathroom?"

Oh. I laughed. "They're not real," I explained. "But don't touch them. Like I said, they might knock you out." I took another bite of popcorn.

He hadn't moved, and his expression was still incredulous.

"I can move them if they bother you," I said after I swallowed. "I use them for protection."

He blinked, but otherwise didn't move. It was like his brain was trying to put together puzzle pieces that just wouldn't fit, and I bit back a grin.

"How about I just move them out here with me instead?" I grabbed ahold of the wasp heartstones with my mind and called them to me, a simple task to control all of them at once after I'd spent some time practicing with the full group of six. They responded perfectly, levitating quickly and fluttering their wings as they darted past Levi and settled next to me on the bed.

Levi jerked back with wild eyes, and his mouth dropped open. He cursed loudly and reached under his bed to snatch up a bat before jerking back upright against the wall. "You just said they're not real!" His voice was accusing, his enchantment repelling.

I blinked at him. My wasps were made of metal and gemstones, but I supposed if you didn't look very closely, they probably looked pretty intimidating. It occurred to me he might not know what a golem was or didn't recognize them as one. I picked one up carefully.

"Have you never seen a golem?" I asked gently. Their prices were such that, generally, only the very wealthy or the very lucky could afford to own one privately. It was entirely possible for someone from a less affluent area to go their entire life never having laid eyes on one.

He narrowed his eyes at me. "I know what a golem is," he hedged, "but they don't work here in the Void, and they can't fly." He gestured at the wasp in my hand with the end of his bat while eying it warily. His suspicion was kind of adorable. I bit my bottom lip.

"They're not really flying. They're levitating, which is pretty common among golem, really. We don't actually make them support their own weight, so often their torsos and other body parts are floating instead of truly being attached." I clicked my teeth shut because I was getting off in the weeds, answering questions he hadn't asked.

He shifted his wary eyes to my face.

"Most constructs can't function in the Void, that's true. It just depends on the amount of magic and skill that a golemancer has," I said, studying the shimmer of the heartstone mine carried. I lifted my eyes from the wasp in my hands to find him staring at me with something akin to fascination and could see the mental puzzle pieces finally snap into place.

"You made Void functioning golems!?"

"Sssssshh," I chided him, glancing at his open doorway. "You're going to wake your roommates." And I didn't really want knowledge of that skill set getting around.

"Jordan is a *vampire*, and I'm not convinced Grim actually sleeps," he hissed, but lowered his voice anyway. "You *made* those?" He covered his mouth with his hand, but a spark danced in his eyes like he was trying not to laugh. I didn't understand his reaction. His magic had shifted back to its natural lure, but this time it startled me with its intensity.

"Are you… upset?" I asked, eyeing the bat he'd seemed to have forgotten he was pointing at my little creation. Realizing he was still clutching it, he quickly dropped the bat and kicked it back under the bed, and then shook his head. He dragged his palm roughly down his mouth and chin, then glanced up at the ceiling and down at the floor, as if looking for answers.

"No, no. I'm just… kind of weirdly turned on right now, and I don't even entirely understand it myself," he said with laughter in his voice, before turning and closing himself in the bathroom.

I felt my eyebrows draw together in confusion as I looked down at the little magical device I held. Sometimes I wondered if I would ever understand people at all. I sighed to myself, set the constructs and popcorn on the nightstand, then pulled back the sheets and burrowed into Levi's bedding. His bed smelled like his shirt, but with an added undertone of warm skin that seemed unique to him, and it made my heart stutter a little bit.

As I settled into his pillow, I fanned my damp hair out to dry and began to wonder if I'd made the right choice staying here tonight instead of chasing down Sidney. It was the kind of impulsive decision I would have shunned normally, but I blamed Levi's constantly enchanted voice and charming kiss. I also admitted to myself that I felt safer here with Levi than I would alone in Sidney's apartment.

I tried not to fret about how weird I felt being in someone else's apartment, or how this was my first night away from my best friend in a week and I didn't even know where she was.

Despite my best efforts, by the time Levi emerged from the bathroom, I'd talked myself around in circles multiple times. He emerged with his blond hair damp and tousled wildly, wearing loose shorts with his chest bare. He wasn't overly cut or bulky, but his muscles looked strong and functional. The tattoo on his arm continued up to his shoulder and part of the way down his left pectoral, tentacles from the mighty kraken curling onto his chest.

When he turned to flip the light switch, I caught a glimpse of markings on his lower back, horizontal bars of a slightly darker color that faded to nothing across his sides. They reminded me of camouflage markings I'd seen on the fish that often hid among the reeds in streams back home.

"Can I get you anything?" he asked, stepping closer to the bed. His silhouette was dark against the lighted hallway. His hand twitched toward me, like he wanted to touch me, before he closed it and stuffed it in a pocket. I shook my head against the pillow before I realized he couldn't see me in the dark, only he was already answering me before I could correct myself. "Okay, I'll be on the couch if you need anything alright?"

This time he did touch me, reaching out and brushing his fingers through my damp hair to push a wayward strand off my face. Before he could turn to leave, I had a momentary flare of panic at the idea of sleeping in here by myself, and if I were honest with myself, him being down the hall just felt... *wrong.* I caught the tips of his fingers before he turned away.

"You don't have to go." If anyone should be sleeping on the couch it should be me, but I couldn't bring myself to offer that with two other guys in the house who were barely acquaintances.

I heard him swallow, and he glanced toward the doorway again before turning back to face me. "Yeah, sure, if that's what you want." He seemed vaguely uneasy about it, but before I could tell him not to worry about it, he was already lifting the sheets and sliding into the double bed next to me, forcing me to skitter back closer to his wall.

While he got settled, I found an errant thread on his sheet to pick at. "I'm sorry. Should I not have said that? You don't have to stay. I just feel a little strange about all this." And even without touching him, I enjoyed the feel of his presence next to me.

Levi was on his side facing me, and he grabbed my busy hand and pulled it to his chest. "Shhh, you're fine," he murmured. His hand and the skin on his chest were startlingly chilly. I reached out with my other hand and felt his forehead and face, which felt cool but not cold, but when I moved my hand down to his neck and shoulder, his body was cold. I could feel his eyes on my face in the dark.

"Why are you so cold? Are you okay? Is something wrong?"

"Does it bother you?" His voice sounded sleepy, but his lure still beckoned.

"No?" I raised the end of the word like a question.

"Cold shower," he mumbled into his pillow.

I gasped. "Did I use up all the hot water? I tried to be so fast!"

"You didn't. Don't worry so much. Hot water feels uncomfortable. I always prefer them cold." His words were slurring together, but his enchantment stayed strong, beguiling and enticing. I couldn't turn my mind off. This was one of our problems when Sidney stayed with me and didn't shift into a bird. We stayed up way too late talking.

"Well, that's got to be some kind of sacrilege," I muttered. "What kind of weirdo doesn't like hot showers?" I made a face in the dark.

He chuckled into his pillow, low and husky, and then wrapped his arms around me and pulled me against his chest. He tucked my head under his chin, completely uncaring about my damp hair, and I shivered slightly against his cool skin.

"This kind of weirdo doesn't. Now go to sleep, little Empress." We laid quietly for a beat before I heard him murmur, "The cold water feels like… home." Then he was quiet again. His breathing became slow and even, and his arms loosened slightly around my shoulders.

Instead of pulling away like I thought I probably should have, I burrowed deeper under his covers and against his chest. I reveled in the feel of his heavy arm over me, his broad chest against my cheek. Could he feel me tucked against him in his sleep? Could he feel the care and affection I was beginning to feel for him, overtaking even the attraction I felt toward him?

I lay in his arms, feeling my heartbeat slow and my mind begin to quiet with one thought echoing around inside me and taking vicious, sorrowful bites from my soul. What would it feel like to be drawn to the cold, dark depths of the ocean, to feel like it was *home*, but not actually be able to survive there?

CHAPTER 10

Sometime during the night, I felt Levi stir next to me. He draped an arm back over me and squeezed me against him, and I smiled against his skin in my sleepy haze. In the next second his body tensed, and he gave a startled curse and lurched backward off the bed with a thud. Another muffled curse, and then a whispered, "Damn, I'm such an idiot."

I blinked myself awake and drew his covers around me as he stood and left the room in the dark. I sat up in the bed trying to make sense of where I was and what had just happened. Had I done something wrong? I looked down at myself to check that all my clothing was still in place.

No errant boobs: Check.

Shorts still present: Check.

No giant puddle of drool: Check.

Feeling confused, I stood and wrapped my arms around myself, then made my way down the hall, where I found him lying on the couch in the living room with his arm thrown over his face. I stood at the mouth of the hallway for a moment, trying to shake off the fog of sleep.

"Levi?" My voice was small and tentative. I cleared my throat and tried to make it stronger. "Are you okay?"

I saw him wince and sit up slightly, propping himself up on a forearm. "Elara, sorry. I didn't mean to wake you."

"Did I do something wrong?" I hugged myself tighter.

"No! No, you're fine." He scrubbed his hand down his face. "Everything's fine. I just had a bad dream. Go back to sleep, we'll talk tomorrow, okay?"

I took a step back and frowned to myself before turning and retreating back down the hall to his bedroom. As I began to quietly shut the door to his room, I heard another door click open and saw Grim lean out toward the living room. It sounded like he said, "You're *definitely* an idiot, just not for the reasons you think you are," before pulling back and closing the door again, but I couldn't be sure. As I finished closing the door, Levi's muffled reply from the living room sounded frustrated.

I climbed into the bed and huddled under Levi's blankets in the dark, but I couldn't go back to sleep for a long time.

WHEN I WOKE up the next morning, it was still early, and I didn't hear any movement in the apartment. I was too restless and uneasy to sleep any longer. Maybe it shouldn't have, but Levi's behavior last night had felt like a rejection, and I felt a little wounded by it.

I made my way to the bathroom to change my clothes and brush my teeth because all I really wanted at the moment was to escape, even if it was just to my little shop by myself. I frowned at my rave costume before sighing and putting it on. This was going to be the weirdest walk to work ever. Not only was I going to be strutting to work in a costume, but it was going to look like a bizarre walk-of-shame. Whatever. I just hoped Sidney remembered to bring my overnight bag with her when she came in today.

I felt silly for my feelings, like I didn't have the right to feel rejected by him. After all, we'd only shared one kiss. Maybe it meant more to me than it had to him. Maybe it meant more to me than it should have. Maybe I was making something out of nothing, but *I liked him, dang it*, and I couldn't change how I felt about it.

So, my brain said the best course of action was to just disappear into the shadows and not hash through it or have some awkward "it's not you, it's me" talk. I could take a hint. I'd had crushes in the past (minor ones… from afar) and I wasn't going to get all clingy on the first one to even barely reciprocate my feelings. I felt like maybe I was trying to convince myself of that last part, but I was doing the best I could right now. I couldn't shake the hollow feeling in my gut.

After I brushed my teeth and got my amulets and wasps situated and tucked away, I straightened his bed and left Levi a note on a scrap of paper left out on his desk, thanking him for a place to stay for the night. I padded down the hallway in the dark, thanks to the heavy blackout curtains that must have been hung over the windows for Jordan's benefit, and found Levi still asleep on the couch.

I was mistaken, however, when I thought I could make a clean escape. I heard him stir as I zipped up my boots and cursed my luck. I should have zipped them up outside.

"Elara, hey. What time is it?" He sat up looking confused and, though I hated to admit it, absolutely, wretchedly adorable. His hair was a mess, and he had that dopey 'still half asleep' look, which made my heart pinch and made me curse myself internally. I mentally slapped away the little claws his enchantments tried to hook into my heart and focused on his question.

"It's early," I answered. It wasn't even six-thirty yet. "I'm just going to head into work," I said as I pulled the front door open quietly.

"Oh." He frowned. "Can I make you some coffee first?" He stood up, still a little unsteady on his feet. "If you'll give me a minute to get some clothes on, I'll walk you down there."

Nope. No. Not happening. My heart was already too tangled up in this guy and the last thing I wanted was to suffer through some kind of pity escort.

"I'll just get a latte at Starbucks on the way. I'll be fine. I've got my wasps, remember? Thank you for letting me stay last night," I said quietly, slipping out the door while he was still opening his mouth to say something. I was done being escorted around. I had my own defenses now. I needed some me-time, anyway. I closed my eyes and swallowed. This was fine.

I did not stop by Starbucks on the way, because *hello, rave costume*. I also didn't get any me-time because Sidney was already there taking apart an old amulet chain for repair. She glanced up at my face when I walked through the door and went back to prying apart the chain link. "You don't want to talk about it," she muttered. It was a statement, not a question, and in that moment my heart overflowed with love for her.

"No, I really don't." I sighed with relief when I spotted my overnight bag on my desk. "Bless you for this," I said as I jerked it open and started pulling out my change of clothes. "What are you doing here so early? How are your brothers?"

"Josh is fine." She was growling as she spoke. "His foot wasn't even broken." She set down her pliers with a little more force than necessary and reached for her cutters.

"We took him to the clinic, waited hours for him to be seen, only to find out that the chucklehead had just sprained it. Which means he could have shifted just fine and we wouldn't have had to drag his whiny, human-sized ass across town. They told him to stay off it for a few days and he'd be good as new." Shifters didn't heal as fast as, say, vampires were rumored to, but they healed incredibly quickly. "Aaron probably has a concussion, but Sam took him home and kept an eye on him."

"Well, that's good news. How come you're here so early?" I asked again. "Aren't you tired?"

"*Yes.*" She thumped her cutters onto the counter and went back to her pliers. "I was pissed at Josh for acting like an idiot and making us leave early and stressed out about not knowing where you were. I just couldn't sleep so I gave up. I didn't think we'd be gone so long last night, and I don't know where Levi lives so I couldn't kick his door down if I needed to." I was pretty sure Sidney couldn't kick a door down at all, but I was touched that she would want to.

"Aww. You were worried about me." I clutched my clothes to my chest. "You looooovvee meee."

"Shut up. The shop would go under if you died." She didn't

look at me, but I saw the side of her cheek lift like she was grinning.

"I was fine. I had my wasps." I saw her shudder out of the corner of my eye as I dragged myself to the back room to put on clean clothes. I was thankful for my snug jeans and a wrap sweater. The walk here had been exceptionally chilly in the gauzy clothes from last night. I dressed quickly and was beginning to look at an inventory list when I heard the doorbell chime. I groaned; we weren't even open yet.

"Elara..." Sidney dragged my name out. "You've got a visitor."

Drat.

I felt impressions of cold salty mist and smooth sea stones swirl around me.

Double drat.

My shoulders slumped, and I immediately straightened them. When I stepped into the store front, I locked eyes with Levi, who had his jaw set and was glaring at me. He stood in front of the register counter with two cups of Starbucks coffee set in front of him. Sidney was studiously ignoring us both.

"Can we talk for a minute?" he said.

I sighed. So much for running away. I guess we were doing this 'it's not you, it's me' conversation anyway. If I lock myself in the back bathroom, he'll have to go away, right?

Cursing at myself internally, I heard myself say, "Sure." It sounded like a retort.

"One word from her, and I'll cut your balls right off," Sidney muttered dryly without bothering to look up from her work. Levi pursed his lips and slid his eyes over to her, looking decidedly unimpressed. I rolled my eyes. Levi hadn't done anything remotely deserving of that kind of warning. So he didn't like me the same way I liked him. I could be a big girl, even if I didn't feel like sitting patiently while he told me that explicitly.

"Down, girl," I muttered back and walked around the counter toward the front door. Levi handed me a warm cup of coffee and moved to open the door for me.

"Thanks." We stepped down onto the sidewalk in the cool Seattle morning and I focused on the sound of the grit crunching under my boots instead of my heart pounding in my chest. I hated confrontation with the fire of a thousand suns. I followed him down a few blocks to a small neighborhood park with a picnic table I'd never noticed before.

"Were you running away this morning?"

Yes. "Maybe."

"I'm sorry," he said before we reached the table. "I should have talked to you last night, but I was so damn tired, and it's hard to have a conversation when both of my roommates have preternatural hearing. Like being immortal isn't enough for them, they have to go and be able to hear a pin drop from anywhere in the apartment too." He sighed as he sat on the edge of the table, and his hand twitched toward me before he clenched it tightly shut. He gripped his shorts with both of his hands, the same loosely fitting athletic shorts he'd worn to bed last night. My throat felt tight thinking about how good it had felt just to be held by him.

"Look, thanks for the coffee," I managed. I watched a breeze move gently through the branches of the nearby trees so I didn't have to look at his face. "I get it. You just don't like me as much as I like you. That's okay." It wasn't okay, but I could act like it was. "We don't need to hash through it all." I swallowed thickly. Now the conversation was through, and I could go finish my work in peace.

"Elara, I wasn't... I don't—" He raised his hand toward me when I took a slight step back. "That's not true. It's just a lot more complicated for me. Can we please talk? I'm sorry I hurt your feelings. I know I must have."

His enchantment rolled over me, more intense than I had ever felt it. It almost felt like it was close to breaking through my ward. I raised my eyes to meet his and found his expression regretful, his eyes soft. He opened his mouth and closed it a few times, as if unsure how to start.

"How much do you really know about merpeople?" Levi rested the side of his head on his hand and propped his elbow on his knee. He looked as exhausted as I felt.

"Not much," I answered honestly. I took a sip of my coffee (a latte apparently), hoping it would wake me up, and tried to remember what I knew or had heard.

"I know that it's usually the females that have the siren ability. They can shift into a human form with legs when they're dry enough. They're a pretty insular people, rather private, which is probably compounded by the fact that they keep their cities underwater."

He grimaced but nodded along as I ticked off each point, taking a sip of his own coffee.

"That's about it, honestly."

"Politics? Biology? Relationships? Culture?" I shook my head at each question, and he sighed heavily. "I really need more functioning brain cells than I have at the moment for all of this," he said, rubbing at his eyes with his free hand. "So, I'm just going to be as plain as I can be, and you'll have to forgive my lack of subtlety here. I like you a lot. Probably more than I should at this point, Elara."

What? My first reaction was to assume he was placating me out of pity, but my heart wanted to thrill at his words. Between my emotional upheaval and his lure skittering across the edges of my consciousness constantly, it was through sheer force of will that I was able to follow what he was trying to impart to me. I tried desperately to focus.

"Mer have areas where we are very instinctively driven, biologically and somewhat culturally. Again, there's a lot more nuance here than I'm going to be able to get out right now." He paused for a few minutes to gather his thoughts.

"There's a very strong drive for females to birth as many babies as possible, probably because the pureblood birth rate is rather low and so many children are lost to predation. And males…" He hesitated and swallowed loudly. "Males get attached to their partners very easily. For pureblooded mer, that attachment transfers to the child when the mom inevitably leaves them. Mermaids usually start the process by enchanting whatever guy it is she chooses so he'll stick around long enough to get attached, physically bonded. One of the major drivers in that attachment, that bonding, is physical contact. The process isn't as fast in the Void as it is in the Boundlands, but it's still there."

I met his eyes, and somehow, they looked both earnest and guarded at the same time.

"I've spent my whole life wanting things I couldn't have," he said. I thought back to his statement last night that cold water felt like home. "I've watched my dad become a virtual shell of a man over the years because my mom left as soon as I was weaned, and because he's part human, he's still been bonded to her all this time. He can't *un*-attach."

Levi visibly tensed, taking a slow breath before continuing. "I can already feel myself getting attached to you. I should have just explained that it would be better for me to sleep separately last night, but I did what I wanted in the moment instead of what I should have done." He raised his hand and gently laced our fingers together before releasing a tremulous breath.

"Is that why you live in the Void?" I asked, feeling some of the pieces of the puzzle click into place. "You're afraid you'll get attached to someone in the Boundlands because the attachment happens faster there?" I studied his face and thought I saw a trace of bitterness there. He removed his fingers from mine and picked up his coffee from the table next to him.

"I don't want to be trapped." His voice took on a defensive edge. "I won't be trapped by someone who isn't just as trapped with me as I am with her." He stopped and took a swallow of his drink, and when he spoke again, he sounded detached.

"Mer folk just live such a different life, culturally, and it's not something I want for myself. But it's what I was raised around, and it's what I've known for most of my life. Mermaids don't want a mate, they want a father for their child, and they trap him with their voices. But *they're* not trapped with *him*. Once they're bored, they're off to have another baby with someone else, and *he's* still trapped. Stuck with a baby with no mother and a broken heart, longing for the one who enchanted him. I don't want that. I won't do it."

I looked at his tattoo, with the hidden runes, permanent protection against such enchantment. "Couldn't you just enchant them back?" I asked, curious. His mouth pressed into a flat line, his eyes on the horizon.

"I'm not strong enough for that. I don't have that kind of power. Even if I could, I'm not... I don't want to do that."

"What do you want?" I asked gently.

He raised his eyes to meet mine for just a moment and the intensity flustered me even as it made my chest feel tight. "I want someone who wants me for who I am and not for how my magic makes them feel, and I want that person to want me as much as I want them." His gaze drifted down to the manacle on my wrist, my ward. "What do you want?" he returned quietly, earnestly.

Just *him*. He was beautiful and thoughtful and fascinating, and he made me laugh. Levi had a light-hearted levity about him most of the time that seemed like it could balance out my serious side in a similar way that Sidney often did. He was strong and confident, and he made me feel safe just by holding me.

He had kissed me like he wanted me, too.

My heart ached for his wounds and his longing, and my eyes stung as he watched me process. I couldn't say the words out loud, but his expression softened, as if he could read it in my eyes. He set his cup down to reach for me, gently taking my arms in his hands, and pulled me forward to press a light kiss against my forehead. "Can we just... take things slow?" he asked.

I nodded.

<hr>

When I walked back into the shop, Sidney's eyes flickered over my face again before she bent back over her work. "Now can we talk about it?"

"Please, no." I slumped into my chair.

"When you guys get married, I want to be your flower girl. You're going to make beautiful babies."

I turned to give her my crazy eyes—because what else was I supposed to do when she said insane things like that—but she was still looking at the broken amulet she'd been working on. "He literally just asked me if we could take things slow. You sound insane."

She turned slowly with a smug grin on her face to let me

know she'd won something, and I realized she had just baited the information she wanted out of me.

"You are such a brat."

She laughed at me, sounding quite pleased with herself.

The workday passed torturously slowly because we were both so exhausted. Sidney alternated between teasing me good-naturedly about Levi and begging to go home and sleep. Eventually, I caved, and we locked the doors an hour early. After a quick squabble—wherein I insisted on going home alone, and told her that Josh needed her and I needed a break from people in general—she relented, and we went our separate ways.

As I came up the walkway toward our row of townhouses, I found Bette on the front lawn, raking up a flurry of familiar white feathers.

"Welcome back, Bette," I called to her.

She paused and waved. "Hello, dear. Yes, it's good to be back. Quite a mess out here though." The word "cat-eater" was distinct as she grumbled under her breath.

"Isadora must be going through a molt again," I surmised.

"Mmm, yes, that was my first thought too, but, you know, I also found some pieces of men's Underoos strewn about the grass as well." She dug around in her feather pile with her rake and pulled a shredded and bloody-looking pair of men's boxers out, holding them up by the waistband from a rake tine.

"They look like they've been ripped clean off the poor soul. You don't think something happened during the banshee removal last night, do you?" She frowned. "Or maybe someone with an odd kink got lucky."

I gasped and grabbed her wrist to shake the offending garment back into the pile. I couldn't be sure, of course, but I had a sneaking suspicion Isadora might have run off another Phantom. I could totally picture her grabbing for a guy by the back of his pants and ripping the band of his boxers out in the process. I glanced around to see if anyone was nearby but didn't feel any magic that seemed out of place.

"Come inside with me."

Once we were settled at my table, I filled her in on the man who'd tried to push his way into my house after she'd left last week, and then been chased off by Isadora, and the Phantoms who'd cornered me in the market. Her eyes were wide as she digested my story and she sat with her mouth pressed into an unhappy line.

"Do you think we should go check on Isadora?" I asked. If she'd lost that many feathers in a scuffle, maybe she was hurt.

"I haven't seen her come home yet," Bette said, "but it's not quite time for her to come home." Sometimes having a nosy neighbor who knew everything about everyone in the neighborhood had its perks.

"I'll keep an eye out for her, and if I don't see her come home soon, I'll come to get you and we can go knock on her door together. I'm a little frightened of her myself. I bet she could be more vicious than an orc with a missing baby." She shuffled slightly, eyeing Isadora's house.

"No," she continued, "I'm more concerned about miscreants still lurking around. I'll be another set of eyes now that I'm home. I may not have enormous talons or a deafening harpy scream, but I've got some *very* unpleasant potions, should the need arise." She sounded so sure of herself that I didn't doubt her for a moment. I wondered if those particular potions had anything to do with the occasional sulfur smell.

"Oh, that reminds me," I started. "Do you happen to know of any potions that can break a longstanding enchantment bond?"

Bette eyed me curiously. "How long are we talking about here?"

I shrugged. "I'm not sure exactly. Twenty-five, thirty years, maybe?"

Her curiosity dimmed. "That's a tough one. Enchantments are better blocked than broken, as I'm sure you're aware." She gestured to my amulets. "Permanent enchantments or enchanted bondings, those are quite difficult. I might be able to figure something out." She chewed on her bottom lip and drummed her nails on the tabletop while she thought. "I'd imagine, if it's possible, it is probably incredibly expensive to make, but if you give me some time, I can probably come up with something helpful or find someone who can."

"Thank you," I said with a sigh. "That would be lovely. I'll pay whatever necessary."

She waved me off dismissively. "I'm sure we can work something out. I can always use another amulet for something or another. I'm honestly not even sure if it's possible yet, so let's not get ahead of ourselves." She winked and slapped the table lightly. "Alright, I'm going to go dispose of the mess out front. I'll keep an eye out for your neighbor. Lock this door behind me."

CHAPTER 11

THURSDAY MORNING HAD BEEN BUSIER than we were used to, with several people stopping by through the morning to place orders or pick things up. I kept hoping I'd see Levi stop in, but it had been so hectic there wouldn't have been time to chat even if he had.

We'd finally gotten a break a bit after lunch, and I was working on a ring for a little girl named Avery. Her father had brought her in from Golden Laurel this morning because she was beginning to show an aptitude for conjuring lightning, and he was afraid she was going to hurt herself or someone else.

After a brief assessment, I'd agreed with him that it was a concern at her age and had agreed to produce a small power limiter for her to wear until she was able to control her abilities. I didn't want to muzzle her power completely, because that would limit her ability to learn to use it. Instead, I had created a small ring that could be sized with her as she grew and that would hopefully constrict the flow of power to something less likely to singe her mother's arm hair off. Orders like this I always rushed without an extra fee, because I considered it a safety issue.

I finished the tiny ring quickly and handed it off to Sidney for paperwork and storage in the back. As I picked up my checklist to start on my next project, I felt a magic with strong impressions of sea squalls and cresting waves crashing on jagged rocks.

I turned, excited to see Levi, but he wasn't there. In retrospect, I should have known it wasn't him because his magic was warm and mellow, sea mist and rolling tide. Sea crabs frolicking in a gentle surf. This was violent and cold, raging tempests and ships being crushed.

I felt the magic coming from directly in front of the shop, but I couldn't see anyone when I looked out the front glass.

"Sidney?" I called, feeling uneasy.

"Yeah, just a minute."

I heard a strange noise near the front door and went to get a better look through the glass. My heart seized in my chest, and I flung open the door. There, on the filthy, gravel-strewn sidewalk, was a tiny sprite no bigger than my hand, beautiful and wild-looking, sprawled out and lying in a dark puddle of her own water. I gathered her in my hand as carefully as I could, hearing her gasping breaths beginning a death rattle in her chest.

"Take it." Her words were a thin breath, but I couldn't stop to think about her meaning.

"SIDNEY!"

Sidney raced from the back room, war written on her face, only to see the tiny sprite laid out in my cupped hands.

She skidded to a halt next to me. "*What on earth?* What is she *doing* here!?"

"She's dying. You have to get her back through a Gate." My voice shook. Her skin wept more water into my hands, the scent sharp and metallic as it dripped out between my fingers to the floor. Her labored breaths had too much space in between them, and her eyes stared unseeing.

Sidney cursed profusely and began stripping her clothes off right in the front of the store. She knew exactly what I meant— running to a Gate would take too long. The sprite's best chance at survival was for Sidney to fly her there.

"She needs the tide pools," Sidney said, stripping off her pants. "Meet me at the ones south of the Gate into Oar's Rest. Open the door, and hold her out flat for me."

Heart pounding, I raised a prayer for the little sprite and backed out the front door, lifting my hand up. Sidney's naked body collapsed in on itself with a muffled snapping sound. In a flurry of black and white shapes that my eyes could never make sense of, she shifted into her bird form and launched herself at me. She snatched the dripping sprite with both feet and rose into the air, sailing toward the Oar's Rest Gate.

I grabbed Sidney's bag, crammed her clothes inside it, and scrambled for my keys. With shaking fingers, I somehow managed to type out a quick message to Levi on my phone: *Emergency. Meet me @ tide pools S. of Oar's Rest Gate. Need help.* He was the only person I could think of who might know how to save her.

I locked the front door as fast as I could, but as I was about to step over the puddle of water on the walk, I spotted a small velvet bag. I hadn't noticed it in my haste to get to the sprite, but it must have belonged to her. I scooped the tiny bag into the pocket of my jacket and set off running. Whatever was in it must have been vitally important for her to carry into the Void, a place she knew beyond a shadow of a doubt would be her death.

None of the fairy species were remotely capable of surviving outside of the Boundlands. Sprites themselves were deeply tied to the magic that resided in the deep ocean, which is why they so rarely came to the surface to trade. I couldn't imagine what made her come here, but I was heartbroken for her. Nobody should meet an end like that. Nobody. But for the little fairies, so feral and free, the indignity of such a meaningless death felt like a weight on my soul.

I ran the eight blocks to the Gate with my heart in my throat. There was no guard at the entrance, but I plunged through the Gate anyway. Shaking out the stinging pinpricks and jumpy muscles in my arms as I ran, I headed south as fast as my legs would carry me. No amount of shaking removed the feeling of the sprite's water dripping through my fingers. My feet pounding down the sandy path echoed my heart racing in my chest. My own over-exerted breathing and the crashing of waves in the distance were the only things I heard.

I felt Sidney's familiar magic and followed it to where she crouched, naked, over a puddle in the rocks. I didn't need to see her grim expression to know the sprite hadn't survived.

The sprite's body floated lifelessly in the water below, with small polyps and miniature anemones waving lazily from the tiny crevices around her. Where before I'd felt the sharp, icy storms of the fairy's magic, now I felt... nothing.

A few steps away from us, a muscular man in a guard uniform—who felt like acrid, choking magic—was frantically relaying messages with some spectral messengers. Sidney saw me watching him as I dropped to my knees next to her and handed her the bag of clothes.

"He saw me fly in through the Gate and followed me in. I guess a bird carrying a dead sprite in from the Void is pursuit-worthy." Her face looked as weary as I'd ever seen it. "Sorry I didn't get her here in time."

I shook my head and pursed my lips, taking a shuddering breath to fight the burning sensation in the backs of my eyes. "You were faster than I could have been. We did the best we could." But I couldn't help thinking I could have done more. If I'd gone to the door a few seconds sooner, if I'd gotten my panic under control faster, given Sidney instructions more quickly, maybe we could have saved her.

I reached into the tide pool and let the sprite's body rest on my fingers as I straightened out her floating form with my other hand. While I found the little creatures beautiful, they probably couldn't be described as beautiful by human standards. She was delicate and feminine, with large eyes and dainty limbs, and her body was mostly translucent, with bioluminescent highlights in her eyes and scattered across her body.

There was a viciousness about these fairies though. Her tiny hands were tipped with claws, and I knew if I opened her mouth her teeth were long and needle sharp. The fact that she'd made it so far into the Void before succumbing spoke to her tenacity.

The guard cleared his throat behind us, and I sat back on my heels to turn toward him. He was carefully keeping his gaze locked right on mine, and I realized about the same time Sidney did that she was still stark naked. She unzipped her bag and began methodically dressing, as slow and uncaring as if she were getting ready in the morning with no one watching.

"The medics will be here shortly," the guard said, "although it doesn't look like much can be done other than returning the deceased to her family. I'm afraid I have to ask you two to step away from the body until Enforcement gets here. They'd like to take witness statements from everyone involved."

I felt Levi coming down the path behind us, and the guard turned to address him. "Sir, I need to ask you to stay back." He drew to a stop, but his gaze locked onto me, distress written on his features. Medics arrived right behind him, and I moved, making my way to Levi.

He was short of breath, and his cheeks were pink again. He gathered me up in his arms when I reached his side and tucked my head under his chin. "Are you okay? I was so afraid something had happened to you." His magic was heavy and forceful, crashing waves and surging tides.

My chin wobbled, and I took a shaky breath to steady myself. "No, I'm fine. I found a sprite outside my shop, but we weren't able to save her. I didn't mean to scare you. I was in a rush and thought maybe you would know a way to help her."

He cast a stunned look at the small group of medics packing up the tiny body and shook his head minutely. "Oh, no." He was quiet for a moment, processing. "Other than getting her back here as quickly as possible, I can't imagine what could have been done to save her."

I nodded, slightly comforted by his words. "Should you be holding me?" I asked. If physical contact would bond him to a partner even more quickly in the Boundlands, then this probably wasn't the best idea, even if I desperately wanted it right now. Levi groaned and held me tighter for a moment before letting out a heavy sigh and releasing me. His expression was regretful when I stepped away from him.

A single Enforcement Officer came down the sandy path and surveyed the medics, asking a few questions I couldn't hear. He stopped and talked to the guard next, who directed him to Sidney, propped in the grass nearby, and then gestured to me. The man nodded and strolled toward us with a casual gait. I couldn't be entirely sure of his magical abilities without him directing his energy into some of them, but I got the impression he could boost his speed or agility, or perhaps both.

He introduced himself as Officer Balcorte, gave us his card, and asked if he could take our statements. He decided to start with mine, since I was the one who found the sprite. As I was telling him what had happened, I remembered the small velvet bag I'd found on the sidewalk as I was leaving. When I dug into my pocket and pulled it out to hand it to him, a tiny shard-sized heartstone rolled out into my palm.

⌘

WE SPENT A WHILE ANSWERING QUESTIONS, dictating our separate witness statements, giving the officer our contact information, and then waiting around to be cleared for release. After I explained to the officer what a heartstone was, I handed over the one belonging to the sprite and it was collected as evidence.

By the time we were cleared to leave, I felt drained and hollow inside. I felt twitchy and shuddery, but I resolved to push it away and deal with it later. I would be fine. This was fine. People die every day.

While I drifted down the sandy path toward the Gate home, Sidney cast me odd looks I couldn't quite figure out. She seemed resigned almost, matter of fact about what had just happened, even as my mind was still in shambles. It felt like I had a million questions about the sprite coming into the Void with a heartstone but none of them could seem to gain any traction in my brain.

Levi was also acting unlike himself; his usual cheerfulness was subdued, and he was visibly agitated, frustrated with something. Maybe he was irritated that he'd just wasted a chunk of his day standing around watching a postmortem cleanup and preliminary investigation for no reason.

I felt guilty for texting him to meet us.

As we neared the Gate, Sidney grabbed my arm and pulled me slightly off the trail into a small copse of trees.

"Elara, stop. Stop. Just cry. It's okay." She wrapped her arms around me and held me against her, and I realized my face was wet and I was shaking. She held me for a long moment while I got myself together. "You did everything you could. She would have known coming in that she wasn't going to live through it," Sidney said consolingly, but it had the opposite effect.

Obviously, I didn't have a lot of experience with people practically dying in my hands, and Sidney wasn't the best at soothing emotionally fragile people. We were a hot mess. Worse, I could feel Levi standing behind my shoulder to the right, watching the whole exchange. I pulled away and swiped at my hot tears in embarrassment.

"I know I'm being ridiculous. I'm sorry." I couldn't even imagine how my poor, bewildered father would have reacted to my crying jag. My mother was the more emotionally demonstrative between them, and even then, I'd only seen her shed tears a few times in my entire life. My father had been entirely flummoxed when I hit puberty and began having mood swings. The memory made me huff a small laugh.

Sidney's concern morphed into vague disapproval, and her gaze sharpened on mine. "I don't want to hear that from you, Elle. There is nothing wrong with feeling strongly about people, and your compassion makes you who you are. It's one of your best features." She flinched slightly before admitting, "At least one of us has to care about things."

I scrubbed my arm across my cheek. That comment was pure bluff. More than once she'd brought orphaned baby animals into the shop with her to make sure they didn't miss a feeding time while she reared them for release into the wild. She shrugged at me as if she could read my thoughts.

"Alright, game plan: I'm gonna go back to the shop and shut it down properly. You two should chat or whatever it is you love birds do, 'cause it looks like Levi's about to blow a gasket over something or other."

I glanced over my shoulder to see him roll his eyes at Sidney, but she just narrowed her eyes at him and prodded me toward him. "Here, make yourself useful. She likes warm hugs. Coo at her and say nice things."

Is it possible to cringe so hard you turn yourself inside out? I feel like I'm about to find out.

"When I'm done at the shop, I'm gonna find a bar and get sloshed," she said cheerfully. "Call me if you feel like joining me. Otherwise, I'll see you in the morning." Sidney gave her signature dramatic, sloppy salute and stalked off down the path. I watched her pass through the Gate before taking a deep bracing breath and turning to face Levi.

His jaw was clenched, and I could see the muscles ticking in his cheek as his gaze skated over my face. We stared at each other in silence for a few moments before I finally made myself talk.

"I'm sorry I wasted so much of your time today." I couldn't think of any other reason for his ire. "I'm not sure why I thought you'd be able to help." My voice was scratchy, so I cleared my throat.

"My time was not *wasted*." He spoke through clenched teeth, but his enchanting lure battered against my ward. He gusted out a heavy breath, and when he spoke again, his voice was softer. "I'm frustrated with *myself*, Elara, not with you. Of course I'm glad you texted me. Can we talk about this in the Void, please? Feeling like I can't touch you right now is driving me insane."

I felt my forehead crease in confusion, but I allowed him to lead me from the Boundlands. A new guard was posted at the Gate. As soon as we were out of the park, he wrapped his arms around me and pulled me into his chest. I stiffened slightly. I wanted to relax into him, but his embrace felt forbidden even though he was the one giving it.

"Should you be touching me at all?" I asked glumly, trying to be responsible, even though I didn't truly want to be.

He huffed a laugh that held no humor. "Probably not, no, but at least the bonding effect is lessened out here." He tightened his arms around my shoulders and rested his chin on my head. "You have no idea how hard it is for me to watch your tears and see your anguish and feel like I can't comfort you. To have to stand and watch your friend do it because holding you could wreck me. So yeah, I'm a bit of a mess right now. I look at you and it pulls the breath from my lungs. I already feel like I'm too attached. I don't know what the right thing is anymore."

His magic whispered along my subconscious with his words, reminding me it was there as he spoke. What would it feel like without my ward? Would it be as dangerous to me as he feared my touch would be to him? The lack of control in allowing someone to meddle in your emotions and desires was scary to contemplate.

"I wouldn't wreck you," I said, more from hope than anything else.

"Wouldn't you?" he asked with a sad smile.

Our gazes held as he slowly released me, and his eyes seemed equal parts regretful and guarded. He wasn't able to let go of me completely, and his fingers hooked through my belt loops to hold me in place while he studied me.

"I'm glad you texted me," he reiterated. "Even if I couldn't help the sprite, at least I could be there with you." He pursed his lips and his eyes glazed over a bit as if he were thinking. "Can you come to my place tonight, let me make you dinner?"

I blinked rapidly, trying to realign myself to his abrupt change of topic. My knee-jerk reaction was to ask him if he could cook, but that seemed rude, so I refrained. Instead, I went with, "What will we be making?"

Levi seemed to hear the doubt in my voice anyway and gave me an amused smile. "I've got stuff for shrimp scampi or sushi. Do either of those sound okay to you? Is there anything you don't eat?" His eyes took on a slightly teasing glint.

I had been an extremely picky eater as a child—preferring simple elven dishes over everything else—and I was suddenly grateful my parents had insisted on me learning to eat a variety of foods, whether I liked it or not. I shook my head as he laced his fingers lightly with mine and tugged me in the direction of his apartment.

"I can eat most things." I wrinkled my nose at him. "You can make sushi? Are you going to make us sick?" So much for not being rude. He rolled his eyes good-naturedly but didn't deem my question worth a response.

CHAPTER 12

WE WANDERED toward his home in the darkening twilight, and I wondered at his ability to shrug off the chilly mist beginning to fall around us. He wore summer clothing—flip flops and shorts with a short-sleeved shirt—even though it was early fall in the Boundlands. Just looking at his bare legs made me shiver in my light coat, and I tried to chafe some warmth into his arm, drawing a chuckle from him.

"I'm not cold," he said as we entered his building.

"You *feel* cold." His arms and hands felt icy, but his cheeks and torso felt mildly cool when I pressed the backs of my wrists against him. He seemed to find humor in my fussing over him, smiling at me as we entered his apartment. He took my coat and hung it by the door before I followed him into the kitchen.

"What can I do to help?" I asked, watching him fill a large pot with water. He shut off the faucet and moved the pot to the stovetop.

"You could grab some ingredients out of the fridge," he replied over his shoulder. "There's some parsley and a lemon in the crisper, and a pack of shrimp in there somewhere."

I washed my hands and opened the fridge, noticing the drawer next to the crisper was packed with what looked like bags of blood. They were all marked as medical waste, and a post-it note on the front of the drawer stated, 'Don't eat my food, assholes. -J'.

I pulled the lemon and parsley from the crisper and located the shrimp on the top shelf. "Who is Jordan concerned will steal his blood?" I asked as I set the food on the counter next to Levi.

He huffed a laugh as he washed the lemon and parsley. "No one. He put that there as a joke, because who would want to steal medical waste? Nobody. I have to wear gloves to even be able to handle the bags for him. Go have a seat. I've got this."

I was growing so used to the feeling of his blocked enchantments skittering along the edges of my periphery that most of the time they barely registered as he spoke. I climbed up on a barstool at the kitchen island, toying with the manacle on my wrist as I watched him peel shrimp.

"I thought we were having sushi?" I asked curiously.

He cast me a wry look. "I figured we'd save the raw stuff until you have a little more faith in my culinary abilities," he said with a small grin. I couldn't help but return his smile.

I looked around, but the apartment was quiet. I could feel Jordan in his room, but not Grim, and a thought occurred to me.

"Did Grim come for the fairy today?"

Levi looked up to meet my eyes, then shook his head while refocusing on his shrimp. "No, he was still here when I left, and she had already passed before I got there, right? Grim usually only does collections in the Void, as far as I know." He glanced over his shoulder toward Grim's room, looking a little uncomfortable with the topic.

"He's not here," I said, assuming Levi's discomfort was probably based on Grim's hearing abilities. I didn't want to talk about it if the subject itself would make Grim or Levi uncomfortable, even though I had a million questions. It's not every day you have an opportunity to ask someone about the afterlife who actually knows something concrete because they've *seen it.*

Also, I couldn't decide if I felt a bit upset at the thought of Grim reaping someone I was trying to save, like he was dismissing my (and Sidney's) efforts to help someone. That didn't make any logical sense, but I never claimed to be entirely logical.

I realized Levi was staring at me.

"Who's not here?" he asked.

"Grim." Wouldn't he know where his roommates were?

But he dropped the shrimp he was holding back into the strainer and sidestepped over to Grim's closed door, knocking on it lightly with a knuckle. His forehead was creased in confusion.

"Yo, Eeyore, you in there?" No response. He opened the door and peeked in, then closed it and gave me a bizarre squint like I was strange. "How did you know he was gone?" Levi sounded a little suspicious. He returned to the sink and started back to work on the shrimp.

I gave a small shrug, feeling a little awkward. I guess we hadn't had this discussion yet. "When he's here, I can feel his magic. I can't feel anything of him in his room or anywhere else close by, so that means he's gone."

"You can feel his magic? Just him, or everyone?" He tossed some butter and a splash of oil in a skillet to warm and diced up some garlic to add in.

"Anyone, as far as I know, as long as they have magic." *And are alive*, I mentally added. My stomach twisted as I thought of the little sprite with no magic left in her.

I watched him add some white wine to the pan and drop the shrimp shells and some spices in it. "Do you eat the shells?" I asked.

He shot me an amused grin. "Sometimes, but these are just for flavor. What does magic feel like?"

I blinked and considered how to answer his question. "Everyone feels different, depending on what magic they possess," I said, "and how strong or weak it is. Sometimes I get vague impressions, other times I see very specific images in my mind. It's difficult to explain, but it feels like an extra sense or perception that's just always there. I tend to mentally note a person's magical impression, like I would their height or their tone of voice. It's usually one of the first things I notice about someone."

His face shone with curiosity, and he had to shake himself to remember to put the noodles in the large pot before he turned to chop the parsley and juice half of the lemon. "That's fascinating. How far away can you feel someone?" His hands were sure and quick with the knife as he chopped, and my cheeks heated with how attractive I found it.

"It's not an entirely uncommon magical ability. My mom has it, and I've passed people on the street here and there who have it. There are usually one or two people employed at universities who possess it."

Levi turned to scoop the simmering shells into the trash and added the shrimp meat to the pan, stirring it as I remembered his actual question. I always felt weirdly singled out when people were surprised by my magical perception.

"I don't have a set limit on how far away I can feel someone. If their magic is very weak, I would need to be close by. For your average person... I could probably feel them from thirty feet or so, if I focused on it and was familiar with the feel of their magic."

"What about really strong people?" He was enjoying this entirely too much. I wrinkled my nose at him, and he laughed.

"Grim probably has the strongest magic I've ever felt, at least when he left to go... reap someone... that first day I met him. When he gets like that..." I shuddered. "I could probably feel him from a block or two away."

"Don't tell him that. He'll be unbearable. Last thing he needs is an ego boost." Levi stirred in the parsley and lemon juice before flipping off the heat, straining the pasta, and plating it with the shrimp.

I slid off the stool and carried the plates over to a small dining table in their kitchen nook. It smelled amazing, and I couldn't wait to try it.

"Hey, Jordan!" He only raised his voice slightly. "You want me to heat you up a drink?"

"Ugh, what do I even have?" Jordan answered through his closed door.

Levi stepped over to the refrigerator and opened it, peering into the drawer full of blood bags. "Looks like it's mostly AB positive." He jostled the drawer a little. "And there's a bag of O negative."

Jordan's door burst open, and he wheeled around the corner on one foot, needing to grab the wall to keep from toppling over.

"I've got O neg? How did I miss that one?" He snatched it out of the drawer and danced around Levi to grab a plastic sport bottle out of a cabinet.

"Hey there... Elara, right?" He pointed at me with finger guns, then emptied some of the bag into his bottle when I smiled at him. He capped the bag and put it back in his drawer.

"I offered to do that for you," Levi said, pushing at him. "Get out of my kitchen, I'm working in here." Jordan held his bottle over his head while he capped it and then dodged around Levi to drop it in a cylindrical device on the counter and flip a switch.

"Stop it. No touching! I could make one wrong move and snap your puny little body like the twig that it is." He bent at the waist and shook his booty with his hands on the counter, humming a little song as he stared at the light on the appliance. In a lot of ways, he reminded me of Sidney's brothers.

Levi grabbed a kitchen towel from the oven handle, deftly twisting it and snapping Jordan on the rump before I even noticed what was happening. "That's rich," Levi said to him, "coming from the guy currently heating up his dinner in a baby bottle warmer." He filled some wine glasses for us and set one in front of me with a fork, giving me a quick peck on the mouth before returning for his own glass. I tried not to blush and failed.

The timer popped on the bottle warmer, and Jordan grabbed the bottle out, drying off the clinging water droplets with the towel. "If it's stupid and it works, then it isn't stupid," Jordan called over his shoulder as he headed back to his room. "I'm studying for a test. I might be out later."

Levi sat with a sigh and took a gulp of his wine. "I don't understand why he doesn't just heat it up himself," he muttered.

Jordan yelled through the door, "Melted plastic makes it taste weird! Let me study!"

"He's taking some online courses," he said, by way of explanation. I didn't really understand any of that, but I didn't want to bother Jordan by talking about him, so I let it go.

His pasta was delicious, and we talked for a while about everything he could think of to ask. Every time my mind would start to drift back to the sprite, he would pull me back to the present by asking me questions about things like my favorite flowers or what genre of music I preferred. I learned that he mostly ate seafood and was currently obsessed with some human music called K-pop.

By the time Grim came home with an armload of groceries, we had moved to the couch with our wine and were watching a documentary about the Boundlands and cringing at some of the wild inaccuracies it contained.

"How hard would it be to just ask someone who lived there if The Orc Wars had destroyed a whole country?" Levi muttered. "I've never heard about that in any of my history classes."

Jordan wandered out while Grim was unloading his groceries and stretched his arms in front of him. "Hey, now that Grim's back, we have four people. You guys want to play that settlers game?" Jordan asked. "I could use a break from studying." His face looked like a hopeful puppy's. Grim just shook his head slightly without looking up from the food he was pulling out of the bags.

Levi gave Jordan a slightly dirty look. "Last time we played we ended up having to replace the kitchen table, you moose."

"I said I was sorry."

I bit back a grin. Definitely like Sidney's brothers. "Maybe next time," I hedged, "I should probably be heading home actually."

Levi stood and took my glass. "Let me walk you out."

I put on my jacket and waved goodbye to his roommates. We walked silently side by side down the stairs to the front of his building, where I turned to say goodbye. "Thank you for dinner. It was lovely."

Levi's face brightened considerably when he smiled in return. "You're welcome. Can I walk you home?" He glanced down the darkened street, lit only by streetlamps making pools of bright light in the maritime haze.

I wrinkled my nose. "It's a long way, especially for you to just turn around and come back. I feel pretty safe now that I've got all my wasps with me."

His eyes roamed over my face, as if he were trying to discern my truthfulness. "To the Gate, at least? It would make me feel better." Did he notice that his luring enchantment pulled harder at my ward as he said that?

When I shrugged a shoulder in acceptance, he took my hand in his, and we walked the blocks down to the Golden Laurel Gate while I reveled in the simple luxury of getting to touch his hand. I had to push away the feeling of guilt that crept in when I thought about how much I'd enjoyed tonight and the little fairy who would never know an enjoyable night again. 'Life is for the living,' my mother had said to me once.

When we were just outside of the city park entrance, he pulled me gently to a stop and ducked his head to brush his lips faintly against mine, as if he were asking permission to kiss me again. Did he think I would refuse?

I met his mouth with mine and felt him smile briefly against my lips. His kiss was gentle, soft, and sweet, and he slipped his hands into my jacket pockets and tugged me closer to him. After a second, he pulled away slightly and looked down at his hand. "What do you—" He held up a tiny, folded paper in the dim light. "It poked me."

I didn't recognize it, so I plucked it from his fingers and unfolded it. It came to about an inch and a half square, with tiny letters in a language I couldn't read. My mind darted back to the sprite. This was the same pocket I'd carried her pouch in. Had a note fallen out?

I turned it to Levi. "Can you read this?"

His eyebrows drew together as he took the tiny note and held it at a normal reading distance.

"Do you need more light?" I asked.

He shook his head but kept his eyes on the note as he scanned it. "I can see fine in the dark," he said absently. "It's from the sprite."

My breath caught in my throat. "What does it say?"

Levi closed his eyes for a long moment and swallowed before opening them to glance at my face. He set his jaw and shook his head briefly as he focused on the tiny paper. "I want to have Grim check my translation first. He's always been better with languages than me."

That might have been true, but I had a feeling he had a good idea what the note said.

"Let me take this home with me tonight and have him look at it. You should get some rest tonight, and I'll bring it by your shop whenever you want in the morning," he said.

I felt a little uneasy about letting it go. It was such a small scrap and easily lost. "I should probably take it to the Enforcement offices tomorrow." He could probably see the reluctance on my face.

"I'll take good care of it, I promise. I don't have any jobs tomorrow, so I'll go with you." He leaned forward and brushed a kiss against the side of my mouth.

After I stepped through the Gate, I sent a spectral for Sidney —to check on her and let her know about the note. Her return message was too garbled to make any sense of. Not for the first time, I wondered at just how sentient the spectrals were and what, if anything, they made of our messages to one another.

CHAPTER 13

I GOT to the shop early, wanting to get as many custom orders finished as I could to make up for all the time we'd been taking away from the shop. Since today was Friday and I'd be traveling back into Oar's Rest today, I might even need to work over the weekend, depending on how long it took.

I made it to the shop just after six a.m. and lost myself in my list of projects, completing several by the time Sidney wandered in at nine. She had dark circles under her eyes and one glance at her grumpy countenance told me to let her finish the coffee she was carrying before engaging her in conversation. I watched her slump into her chair and drop her head back so her mouth gaped open like a goof. Her hair was mostly loose today, and her braids looked like she'd slept on them.

My self-control was never my best feature. "You know, someday the spectrals are going to rise up against us, and when they do, their first victims are going to be the people who made them carry drunken gibberish."

Sidney cracked open one puffy eye and focused it on me. "You make it sound like they don't have a choice in whether or not they deliver messages. We pay them."

"Okay, well, I don't have any idea what your response was trying to say last night."

"That makes two of us." She dropped her head over the back

of the chair again, so I went back to work while she finished her coffee.

As I was finishing up an alchemist's string of worry beads, Sidney tossed her empty cup in the trash can and set to separating out sections of her hair and braiding it back from her face. "Josh decided he was going to join me at the bar last night, and I was dumb enough to let him."

Josh and Sidney were competitive in everything, and drinking was no exception. I bent back to labeling the worry beads when I lost the battle to contain my grin. The last thing we needed was Sidney grumping about me laughing at her self-inflicted hangover this morning.

"How's his leg?" I asked, changing the subject.

"He's fine. Good as new." Shifter healing was the envy of nearly every species. "He was as surprised as we were when I told him about the sprite."

"Mmm, do you remember my message about the note I found?"

"Vaguely." She tied off her braid and turned to face me. "Do you have it with you?"

I shook my head. "Levi wanted to have his roommate translate it. He said he'd bring it back this morning."

"Well, text him, already. Tell him to hurry up. I want to see it."

I handed her my finished project to complete the paperwork for and retrieved my phone. Levi's magic brushed up against me about an hour later, and I hurriedly finished setting the citrine stone in a hair ornament. I had the last clamp shut, and the stone powered up by the time the bell rang above the door.

I couldn't help being a little embarrassed about the excitement I felt when he stepped into the shop. Truly, I'd only seen him just a few hours ago, but when he met my eyes and gave a little smile, I felt it in my chest. How was it possible to feel this greedy for someone I'd known for so little time? My eyes skimmed over his form, taking in his damp, tousled hair and his slouchy, casual, athletic clothes. They took me back to the bliss of falling asleep in his arms the other night, and I felt a disappointed pang at the knowledge that we couldn't do it again any time soon.

If ever.

But then he pulled a plastic baggie with a paper in it out of his pocket and laid it on the countertop, one corner of his mouth turned down. "I didn't want to risk losing the tiny note, so I put it in here along with Grim's translation." His eyes bounced back and forth between Sidney and me.

I stood and thanked him, taking the bag and returning to my desk. I retrieved the larger piece of paper from the bag first, unfolding it to reveal neat, slashing print. Sidney leaned over and snatched the bag to look at the tiny note left inside while I read.

Golemancer-

As I write this, it has been eight days since the kelpies attacked our homes. It has been eight days since my husband and our daughter were killed beside me while trying to flee The Deep. Eight days of discussions and no action by the council that claims to protect us but does nothing. Every moment they waste means more danger to my people and less chance that my only remaining child will ever live to see adulthood or that we will have a chance to restore my city someday.

The mer are deaf to our cries, and so I come to you. My only hope is that you will create something for us that will step in where our current protectors fail. I will bring you the largest heartstone I can hope to carry through the Void. I know I can't return, but I have already died, eight days ago when my people fell. I do what I must to protect my son. Please don't let this decision be in vain.

SIGNED,
   Adonci Tyr

I FELT like I'd been punched in the gut as I slowly sank into my chair, reading through the translation a second time. Somehow my eyes found their way to Levi's, and I held the paper toward

Sidney for her to take. His deep blue eyes seemed to hold concern, but whether for the situation or for me, I wasn't sure.

Sidney gave a low curse. "Who *doesn't* want a golem from you?" She started at the top again as I watched her incredulous expression. "Lady straight-up martyred herself to make her point. What kind of bureaucratic bullsh—" Her eyes snapped to mine, and she cut herself off. I felt the burn starting behind my eyes again. "I mean, can we help them?" she asked.

My heart sank further. "Even if we could, I gave the heart-stone to the Enforcer." Levi was around the counter and had pulled me gently against his stomach before I even noticed my voice had been shaking.

Sidney frowned. "I'm not entirely sure that was the wrong thing to do, honestly. What if we'd been accused of stealing it? Or worse, murdering her to steal it? Are you going to turn this note in? It could light a fire under whatever council has been dragging their feet if they see people are going to these extreme measures." She chewed on her bottom lip, something she wasn't often prone to doing.

"I'd planned to, yes. That's why I came in early." I sighed and pulled my hand down my face, trying to tamp down my emotions. "Do you want to come with us, or would you rather stay here?" I asked.

"I'll hold down the fort." She rapped her knuckles on the counter next to her and handed the bag and paper back to me with a grimace. "Take your time. Silence will probably be good for my head anyway."

<hr />

Two hours later, I stood in front of a reception desk, staring at a diminutive redhead who had some kind of sleep or dream-related magic and liked to over-starch her shirts. "Who did you say sent you?" she asked for the second time. I heard Levi huff an impatient breath beside me and reached out to touch his arm lightly.

"Officer Balcorte," I answered. "He said he called ahead and that Ms. Ta'nith would be waiting." We'd gone first to the

Enforcement building in Oar's Rest, and been lucky enough to speak with Officer Balcorte, the original responding Enforcer from yesterday.

He was grateful for both the note and the translation, although he said he'd need to have it translated by someone in-office as well. He said he wouldn't be able to release the heartstone from the evidence locker, which I'd expected, but also said someone from the council that the sprite, Adonci, had referred to in her letter had made a note in the file that they wanted to speak with me. The council was based in a little city named Whitewave, up the coast from Oar's Rest, so we took the rail.

The receptionist's mouth turned down in a frown. "I don't see any notes that she's expecting you. I'm afraid I'm not allowed to—"

"Do you think you could possibly ask her yourself?" Levi asked, cutting her off and turning on the charm. "We've already traveled for an hour at her request, you see." His words were nothing out of the ordinary, but his voice became honeyed, and his lure was out in full force. The receptionist blinked slowly, looking a bit dazed.

"S-sure… sure, one moment. Just a moment." She rose and stared at his face for a beat with a hazy expression, before stumbling a step backward and darting into a hallway behind her.

I turned to look at Levi and stared at him when he didn't respond. "What?" he had the gall to ask. I sighed and rolled my eyes. That boy was dangerous.

I rubbed at the rings connected to my manacle. "I'm just glad I have my ward so you can't do that to me," I muttered.

"Not unless you ask me to," he said, and I shivered.

He was still smirking at me when the receptionist returned, followed by a beautiful middle-aged woman with inky black hair whose magic gave me impressions of slushy sea ice and the joy of chasing fish through dark underwater warrens. I blinked at her, trying to make sense of that. She didn't look like what I thought a mer would look like, but there was something animalistic about her magic. Still, she didn't feel quite like a shifter. Strange.

"Elara Hawthorne? So sorry to keep you waiting," the older lady said, smoothing the front of her grey silk blouse. "I got busy and forgot to let the front desk know to expect you. Thank you for coming! I'm Muriel Ta'nith, please follow me."

We followed Muriel into a richly appointed office with heavy tapestries and gilded paintings depicting ocean scenes, and a desk overflowing with papers and stacks of files. She heaved a sigh as she sank into the chair behind her desk and shoved a pile of papers out of the way so she could see us.

"Please, take a seat," she said, gesturing to a pair of oversized chairs situated in front of her desk. "The Enforcer I spoke to earlier said you were the ones who discovered the sprite in the Void, yes?" she asked as we took our seats. She pulled a sheet of paper from the top of a stack next to her and began to write.

"I did, yes," I answered as her eyes flicked up to Levi with a speculative quality, then focused on mine. "I found her outside my shop in Seattle, but we weren't able to get her back into the Boundlands fast enough."

Muriel's eyes softened slightly. "Thank you for your efforts, regardless." She focused on Levi. "I'm sorry, but I don't recall you being mentioned in the report. And you are?"

"Levi Navarre." He pressed his mouth into an unhappy line when she continued to stare at him with a slightly skeptical gaze. "Birth name, Leviathan Chansoneau. I'm just here for moral support." He leaned back in his chair and crossed an ankle over his knee, his arms lazily draping over the sides of his chair. He'd ratcheted back his lure, but it was still distinctly noticeable.

Muriel resumed her notes. "And you are… mer?" Her voice was politely disinterested, but I could see the curiosity in her eyes.

"Give or take." Her pen stilled at his response, and she raised her eyes to meet his, one eyebrow raised in confusion. "I'm land-locked," he clarified.

She blinked at him. "You don't have an aquatic form? But you have mer bloodlines?" Her question was clearly only meant for him, but she shifted her gaze between me and Levi.

"Basically." His enchantment held no lure this time, instead giving a slight rebuff. I wondered if he even noticed.

Muriel frowned and made another note. "Well, as I said I'm Muriel Ta'nith. I'm not sure how much the Enforcement office informed you about what I do." Her voice pitched up at the end of her statement, as if to make it a question.

I sank back into the oversized chair a bit when her focus landed on me again. "He said you were from the council that Adonci... that the sprite, referenced in her letter." I tried not to fidget, but I just couldn't get comfortable in a chair sized for an orc.

"Ah, yes. His spectral included a copy of that. That's a bit of an oversimplification, actually. I'm the Liaison for the Alliance of Oceanic Nation-States that have a presence here in Whitewave. The council is part of that, headed up mostly by mer." Her eyes flickered to Levi before returning to me. "But I'm not specifically a part of that."

I couldn't tell if she was uncomfortable discussing mer in front of Levi or suspicious of him, but her reactions to him put me on edge.

"The sprites have been protesting in front of the council building, and the sparks are showing signs of taking up their cause. Both the fairies and the council are petitioning the Alliance to try to straighten things out, but we're focused on trying to cope with the influx of refugees from The Deep and coordinating defensive measures between the sprites and a number of aquatic races and—" She took a deep breath and eyed her overflowing desk despondently. "Everything's just a big mess right now."

I nodded to show her that I understood, even though I categorically *did not*. It seemed like the polite thing to do, but she waved me off, probably tipped off by my expression.

"Don't worry about it. I pulled what I could find on record about you yesterday—I hope you don't mind—when I was notified that the sprite, Adonci, had passed in the Void and been returned to the Boundlands by you. Curiosity on my part, wanting to know why she entered the Void in the first place. It seems she knew she would never make it as far from the ocean as your home in Golden Laurel, so she decided to try her chances in the Void." Muriel slouched as she discussed Adonci's end, taking a moment to stare blankly at her file. But then she slapped on a tight smile and met my eyes again.

"I noticed that your focuses during your university studies were on amulet artifices and golemancy." It was impossible not to notice the excitement building in her voice, and dread began pooling in my gut.

"That's correct." I felt Levi's gaze on the side of my head. A quick glance told me he was fighting a grin for some reason.

Muriel lifted a file from the same stack and pulled out another sheet of paper, scanning a few lines near the top. "You received very high marks and several awards," she murmured. "Do you still trade in golems? I can only find records of a few golem sales right after your schooling was completed."

She set the paper down and focused her gaze on me. "I ask because the Alliance could use some golems to add to their defense capabilities, and with your skill level, and relationship to your father, who has a very impressive resumé, you might be a prime candidate. Is that something you or your father would be interested in? I haven't been able to find a way to get in contact with him."

I sighed—I couldn't help it—and squeezed my eyes shut briefly. My first reaction was to say 'no, thanks' and dust my hands of it. I didn't want to be involved because of the ethical issues with trading heartstones and because the last thing I wanted was for my creations to end up becoming war machines. This lady was plainly asking me to make this Alliance a weapon of war.

But wasn't that what Adonci had been after when she stepped into the Void? Would I have told her no to her face if she'd explained her situation and asked for my help? I wasn't sure anymore.

I decided to start with the easiest question, not that I'd actually remembered all of her rapid-fire inquiries. "My father is under private contract with the elven parliament and has signed a non-compete agreement with them, which remains in effect for... well, at least the next two years, last time he mentioned it."

Muriel frowned slightly. "More's the pity."

"For myself, I've taken a step back from golemancy in recent years because there are a number of ethical issues in building them that make me uncomfortable." I made an effort not to touch the wasp nestled in my jacket pocket. "I'm not saying I absolutely wouldn't be interested, but I've turned down a number of these requests in the past, and accepting one now would make things much more difficult for me in dealing with people I've previously said no to."

Her brow furrowed as I spoke until she appeared completely perplexed when I finished. "Ethical issues? I don't… I'm sorry, I'm afraid I don't understand what you mean. How is it any different than creating an amulet or any other magical object?"

In my peripheral vision, I saw Levi sit forward and brace his elbows on his knees, but I focused on Muriel. "I've encountered problems in the past with fairies asking for things as heartstone payment that were highly illegal and morally repugnant. Now I insist on customers providing certified documents that trace a heartstone to its origins, which can be hard to come by. That's not even getting into a construct's final purpose. Will I be creating something that bears no purpose other than violence, in the end? If I create something that causes suffering or ends a life, am I as much to blame for that suffering as the person wielding the object? I have zero desire to add to the arsenal of a conquering nation. What assurances do I have that my constructs won't find their way into such hands someday, even long after I've passed on?"

I made myself stop. I could continue this train of thought for a very long time, as it was something I'd expended a lot of mental energy on. To her credit, Muriel appeared contemplative instead of irritated as I'd expected.

"And unfortunately, I turned the heartstone Adonci provided over to Enforcement, and Officer Balcorte informed me this afternoon that it's been locked away until further notice."

She waved a hand dismissively. "I could submit a request for release, but the Alliance has several much larger heartstones readily available. I can tell you, from sitting in on hours upon hours' worth of meetings with Alliance groups bickering and arguing with one another, that no one intends to use golems to conquer anyone else's territory. These would be used strictly for defense, and defense is desperately needed for The Deep right now. My only real concern is how territorial the Alliance is being about the heartstones. I may have to convince them you're a mer," she joked, and then darted another glance at Levi.

"So how can I allay your other fears?" She visibly wilted as she cast her gaze around the paperwork overflowing her desk. "And how quickly can I do it?"

When I looked over at Levi, his eyes were intense, betraying some emotion I had a hard time reading. He studied me as if he found me fascinating but didn't know what to make of me. He looked as conflicted as I felt, and his eyes lingered on me for a long moment before turning to address Muriel.

"Do you mind if she takes some time to think? Maybe have some lunch and come back? She's had a long couple of days, and I know she hasn't eaten yet."

He was using his most persuasive voice again, his lure front and center, and I couldn't find it in me to feel anything but grateful. I hadn't realized how run down I was feeling and some time to regroup sounded really good. Plus, I regretted not having Sidney with me to talk this through with. She was usually my sounding board at times like this.

I looked to Muriel for her response, and she gave a sharp nod. "Of course. I will see if I can find out anything about the heartstones we have available and get in contact with some Alliance members who might be able to speak to your other concerns."

I thanked her and rose, turning toward the door, only to hesitate at the last second. "Do you happen to know where Adonci's remaining child is?" I asked Muriel before we left. "If he's being cared for?"

Muriel pasted on a sad smile. "I don't have that information unfortunately, but even if I did, I wouldn't be able to divulge anything about him."

I nodded. "I would like to speak to some of the sprite members of the Alliance." Muriel gave her assent before Levi wrapped a loose arm around my waist and guided me to the door, releasing me immediately once I complied.

He led me to a little out-of-the-way eatery a few streets down that specialized in all kinds of different seafood skewers wrapped in seaweed. We stood at the counter, and I chose the scallops. He frowned at me when I dug out my wallet and shook his head, looking mildly offended.

"This is one of my favorite little hole-in-the-wall joints in Whitewave," he said when we took our seats at a table in a lonely corner. "If the selkie can't get you in touch with the sprites, I have some connections who can."

"Selkie!" I bit out, suddenly making sense of Muriel's magic. "I thought she might be a shifter."

He chuckled and thanked the waiter who brought our plates. "Close enough, right?"

I just stared at him, trying not to smile. Sidney would probably beg to differ.

"What do you think you're going to do, though?" he asked before poking at his fish.

I heaved a cleansing breath. "I honestly… I don't know." My mind started spiraling out through all the 'what-ifs' and worst-case scenarios—all the ways this could go wrong—as I bit into my meal. By the time I finished, I realized I felt much better having put some food in my stomach, but I hadn't gotten anywhere productive in my head space. I didn't even remember eating most of it, and Levi was quietly watching me with concern etched into his features.

"You're doing some heavy thinking there." He took a sip of his water and leaned back in his chair. I felt his knee bump against my leg several times under the table like he was deliberately tapping me. "Do you think you could talk some of it through with me?" His eyes looked soft and maybe even a little bit vulnerable.

I swallowed. "There's just so much at stake here," I told him. "Aside from worst-case scenarios of golems being used for nefarious purposes, say an assassination, or some despot inheriting one of my creations a thousand years from now, I'm not actually sure how helpful a golem from me would be to The Deep. A construct like my wasps, with practice, I've managed to complete in a matter of hours. A larger golem? Those can take weeks. Months even. Some of the constructs my father builds take months *with* a team helping. What if I build them something and, by the time it's finished, the whole city is already plundered and gone? It just seems like this is a long-term project, when something is needed now, or a week ago.

"Not to mention, I still have a business to run during all this time I would spend building something I'm hesitant to unleash on the world at all. I would be fine taking the time off, but Sidney still needs an income, and I can't leave her high and dry, let alone all the customers who have already placed orders and are depending on me. I can't just shut my business down for a month or more and expect everything to be fine when I come back."

Levi chewed for a minute while staring blankly in thought. "Does it have to be all or nothing?"

"What do you mean?"

"Well, if building such a large object would take too long and cause too much strain on your business, what about creating a smaller one? Or several smaller ones over a period of time?"

I pondered that as an option. If the Alliance didn't have another golemancer in their rosters and I didn't give them a choice, they might have to accept a downgrade. Chances were high they didn't, but it wasn't impossible.

Levi interrupted my thoughts. "How do you control a golem? Can you tell it to only defend and not attack?"

"Kind of. I can give it a basic set of underlying guidelines that only another golemancer can change. When I hand it over to its final owner, I instruct it to allow them to give it basic instructions, but they can't modify its original intent. The problem is, any golemancer could modify a relatively small construct. It would have to be substantially large to keep most others from modifying it."

The sentries at my parents' estate had been passed down through my family for thousands of years. They were so large that, if no one was born with magical strength enough to modify the massive heartstones that controlled them, they sometimes went for a generation or two without anyone in our line being able to interact with them. Not that they needed it. They'd sat, silently guarding our estate, for longer than we could remember.

My hand froze on my glass as an idea began to take root in my mind. "I need to talk to my mom."

CHAPTER 14

MURIEL SEEMED MORE PERPLEXED than I'd expected. "You want to loan us your personal sentries?"

"They belong to my parents, but yes, my mother has given me permission to loan out two of them temporarily, for use in defense of The Deep. These are heirlooms, part of our family heritage, so as you can imagine, the terms of the loan would be quite strict. But they are formidable and supposedly quite useful in combat."

She gave a slow blink—perhaps trying to take everything in —and I shifted in my chair. "Supposedly?" she repeated.

I shrugged. "It's been a few hundred years since they've been roused. No one attacking our estate has made it past the dogs."

I heard Levi choke on a surprised laugh beside me and turned to catch him trying to turn it into a cough. His face was flushed slightly with his effort, but he couldn't hide the wicked amusement dancing in his eyes. "Excuse me," he wheezed.

Muriel was still staring at me, her eyes round in her face. "I see. What are these sentries, exactly?"

"Stone golems, humanoid… they basically look like very large statues. They're both just under two hundred hands high, one is a little shorter, but not significantly." They topped eighteen meters, by human measurement. "They'll be a little slower underwater than something specifically built for that purpose, but they will provide a good measure of defense in the short term."

"How short term are we talking?" She sat forward and spared a glance for Levi as he situated himself in the chair beside me. "And how soon would they be available?" she asked, returning her focus to me.

"The length of the loan would be at the discretion of my father, though my mom said theoretically they would allow them to remain in The Deep until I created something more permanent as a replacement. Or you find a suitable replacement if we can't come to an agreement.

"As for their delivery…" I winced. "I will need to hand deliver them from Golden Laurel, since they're too big for regular transport and too big to fit through the Gates." Not to mention I didn't think the government of Seattle would be too pleased to have them in the city. "My mother said she would try to contract over-sized transport, but she didn't think it would be possible on short notice."

"Yes, I would think not." Muriel gusted out a heavy breath. "Where does that leave us, then?"

I frowned. "With me trekking through the Bound's countryside for two weeks on the backs of some very, very large statues."

"Two weeks."

I nodded. "That's significantly quicker than I, or anyone else for that matter, would be able to build you a construct of any reasonable size. It gives the city protection, while I decide how much I want to contribute, and gives you breathing room to find other options. I can have my parents send you a copy of the contract as early as tonight."

Muriel stared at the desk in front of her for a few beats before visibly steeling herself and meeting my eyes. "Tonight." She gave a single, sharp nod. "I will contact the council immediately regarding the contract. Will your delivery fee be built into the contract?" she asked.

"I'm doing this as a personal favor to Adonci because she asked me for my help. The rest of the loan negotiation will be between you and my parents."

She pulled the drawer open in front of her and removed a

tiny pair of gold-colored scissors, snipped a tiny lock of hair off, and held it out to me. I held open an empty locket for her to place the hair in, closed it securely, and then reached for the scissors to repeat the ritual. We were in this together now, though to what degree, I couldn't say.

She pulled a small notebook from behind a stack of files and tore out the top page to pass to me. "I wrote down the names of the sprites who are members of the Alliance committee since you said you wanted to speak to them. They haven't returned my messages yet, but I'm certain we can arrange something."

We said our goodbyes and rose to leave, but as I made it to the door, Muriel spoke.

"Ms. Hawthorne?"

I paused with my hand on her office door and turned to face her.

"Thank you, and I just want you to know that I respect your desire for transparency."

I gave her a small smile. "You're welcome. We'll be in touch."

We stepped out onto the street and into the sunshine, and I felt a little lighter. Nothing I did would bring back Adonci or any of the lives lost in The Deep, but at least we had a plan to move forward, and in some small way, I was able to help.

I looked to Levi to find his blond hair rumpled like he'd been running his hands through it, and he had the side of his bottom lip caught between his teeth. He kept his eyes focused on where we were heading, even though I knew he could tell I was looking at him. He looked excited and mischievous, and it only increased the longer I watched him.

"What?" I asked him, but he just grinned to himself and shook his head, tucking his chin into his chest. When I gave him a droll look in return, he smiled wider, gestured to his mouth and throat, and shook his head again. His eyes were dancing with amusement, and I realized he hadn't spoken during my second meeting with Muriel. "You were awfully quiet in there that time," I pondered aloud.

Levi choked out another laugh. "You think?" he wheezed, still laughing, and his lure lashed out, strong and forceful. It struck against my ward so intensely that I stumbled and turned to face him with shocked, wide eyes.

He barked a sharp laugh at my reaction and turned his head away to try to pull himself together. "I'm sorry," he said, dragging his hand over his face to wipe away the smile. It didn't work.

"It was just kinda hot watching you dictate exactly how everything was going to go down. You were so fierce, and then the comment about 'nothing getting past the dogs' that came out of nowhere." His eyes were dancing with barely contained hilarity. "I just knew I wasn't going to be able to control this," he said, gesturing at his throat. Judging by the potency and insistence of his enchantments scrabbling against my ward, I assumed he was referring to that and not merely his laughter.

"Your magic?" I asked, feeling obtuse. I realized the only other time I'd felt it this strongly was the night I'd stayed at his apartment and he'd told me he was turned on…

Oh.

OH.

"Uh, *yeah*," he said, giving me a meaningful look as my cheeks grew hot. "Just, ah, give me a few minutes to shake it off, and I'll be good as new." He shot me a flirty grin. "Just a little awkward to have Ms. Ta'nith feel that and know I was all hot under the collar, or worse, derail your discussion completely with it." His cheeks flushed just slightly at his admission, even as his eyes dropped to my lips. "I could sit and listen to bossy Empress Elara dictate her business terms all day. I don't know what that says about me, but there it is."

He bent to give me a quick peck on the side of the mouth, and then, appearing unable to help himself, kissed the side of my jaw for good measure. That was frustrating, even though I knew more contact was risky for him in the Boundlands. Was it wrong of me to crave more when he'd made himself clear?

By the time we entered the railway station, he must have calmed down a bit, because his enchantment levels were much more normal as he dug out a calling chip and explained that he wanted to ask his dad about some of his sprite contacts. We spent the hour-long ride back discussing my upcoming trip with the constructs, and he surprised me with his desire to come with me.

"Of course," he said, like it was a given. "Is that really so surprising?"

I leaned back in my seat across from him and tried to make sense of him. "Don't you have jobs scheduled? Two weeks is a long time to step away from your life on such short notice."

He shrugged a single shoulder. "I can reschedule them." His eyes turned soft as he watched me. "Two weeks would be a long time to be away from you too, and I…" He trailed off and pressed his lips together for a second while he searched for his thoughts somewhere out the train window. "I wouldn't like that. And I don't like the thought of you traveling so long alone. Who knows what's lurking out there in the wilds? This way Sidney can stay with your shop, and I get to spend time with you."

I grinned at him, both pleased by his admission and amused by his concern for me. "I can't imagine anything wanting to attack me when I'll be accompanied by two constructs the size of six-story buildings, unless I were traveling in the mountains, but I'll be going around."

He shook his head. "I'd bring Eeyore too if he didn't need to be so close to the Void."

"Why would he *need* to be close to the Void?"

Levi gave a slight shrug. "That's his jurisdiction. He's assigned an area, and he gets a stipend for it. He brings our souls back into the Boundlands so they're not trapped in the Void."

Blinking repeatedly was the only response I could give. *There's so much to unpack in that statement I can't even spare the brain power to think about it right now.*

We decided to leave early Monday so I could have tonight and tomorrow to finish up all the projects I could at the shop, and still have time to pack and arrange to talk with some sprites on Sunday.

Discussing plans with Levi was enlightening. I warned him that, even though we'd try to stay at inns when we passed by a town, since we'd be traveling as the crow flies as much as possi- ble, we'd have to do a lot of camping. He just shrugged and seemed totally unconcerned. He said he'd spent much of his childhood escaping into the cliffs near his house to sleep on the jagged rocks overlooking the ocean. I had a feeling his idea of camping and mine (I felt more at home with the concept of 'glamping') were wholly disparate.

By the time we arrived in Oar's Rest, Levi was anxious and visibly agitated. "I've sent three spectrals and gotten no response from my dad," he grumbled. "That probably means I need to go over there."

CHAPTER 15

"Where does your father live?" I asked. "Is something wrong?"

Levi huffed, sounding irritated. "Probably nothing more than usual. He's here in Oar's Rest. This is where Grim and I grew up." *Oh.* I searched his eyes as the train pulled to a stop, but they looked guarded. "He's probably just drunk. I'm not particularly worried." I ignored the minuscule push-back I felt in his magic. Now that I was getting to know him better, it felt more like an extension of his emotional state and less like a personal rebuke.

As we exited the train, he wore an irritated scowl, and I was unsure whether he would prefer I come along or head back to the shop alone, so I asked.

He grunted and gave me a self-deprecating smile before sighing to himself. "Honestly, no, but not because I don't want *you* there."

I nodded, understanding his desire for privacy in what seemed like a delicate family situation. We walked outside, and he turned his glower to the horizon. But then he gave me one of those brittle smiles that didn't reach his eyes. "But you might as well, right? It's only fair you see the whole ugly package."

I flinched a bit at what felt like a retort. I started to explain that I didn't want to intrude and that he deserved his privacy with his family, but he just shook his head slightly and tugged me along.

"Not here."

We were heading toward the sea, and the smell of salt air wrapped around us, heavy and sultry. The buildings gave way to large juts of stone that dropped away into the ocean, with a smooth sandy beach carved out below, and he tugged me with him into a large crevice among the rocks.

"I think… I need this for me, for my own sense of security. Look, I just…" He paused for a second to gather himself, pulling his hand down his face in frustration. "Please tell me you can feel this between us too." His eyes were a little frantic, out of control and vulnerable, and I made myself focus on his words instead of his magic plucking at my emotions. "Because if it's just me, I don't know what I'm going to do, Elara."

He searched my eyes, and while I wasn't sure what he found, I nodded to show him I was with him, that I felt it. This connection to him was a tangible thing.

Levi heaved a breath, trying to calm his nerves, I thought. And when he spoke next, it was to the rock behind me, his eyes focusing just over my left shoulder. "There are moments when it almost feels like I *need* you already, and that scares me. Terrifies me. Should that be happening so soon?" His eyes flashed to mine briefly, still full of questions.

"And… Elara, my dad is a *mess*. He's always going to *be* a mess. I have to take care of him a lot. And one of my fears—one of many, mind you—is that you're going to see this part of my life and it's going to be too much. Too broken, too ugly. I'd much rather know that now, I think, than months from now, when I'm in too deep."

His gaze snapped to mine and held me fast, his eyes intense and wistful. Even with my ward, his enchanting words felt like a living thing, trailing seductive fingers just at the edges of my subconsciousness. His words brought me back to the weary expression he'd worn when I'd seen him on the bus in Dry Gulch, and his troubled eyes when he sold me the trinkets he kept locked away in his room.

"Levi…" My heart beat painfully as I watched his conflicted

expression. I didn't want to push him with physical contact here in the Boundlands, but I still needed to touch him, so I grabbed the hem of his T-shirt in my hands. I wrapped my fingers in it, anchoring him to me. I swallowed thickly, trying to find the words to put his heart at ease and explain my own.

The seconds ticked by, and his breathing didn't slow, so I reached up and grabbed the collar of his shirt, tugging him down toward me. The man was simply too tall, and I was going to have this conversation with his face, not his chest. *No matter how nice it is.* Confused amusement flickered over his features, but he acquiesced and hunched over until his face was only a few inches from mine.

"Levi." I waited until his expression sobered and I had his full attention before continuing. My voice was soft and calm, and I injected every ounce of sincerity I could muster. "I'm going to come with you, not to evaluate whether the difficult parts of your life are too much for me, but to support you the same way *you* supported *me* this morning, and last night. This is what it means to be together, is it not?"

I searched his eyes and found that some guardedness I hadn't noticed was there had dropped away completely, and he looked a little hesitant. A tiny bit lost. It broke my heart for him.

"You don't need to be afraid of showing yourself to me. Even the painful parts. Especially the painful parts. I want to see all the little details that make you who you are because I want to *know* you. I *care* for you. I think I need you too, and I'm okay with that."

He released a jagged breath, and then his mouth was on mine, soft and urgent, and I was breathing in the scent of his skin before I even realized he was moving. I knew even this much contact was probably pushing his luck, but I had no intention of stopping him or trying to be the responsible one. *He'd* kissed *me*, and all bets were off. I wanted this too much, and I accepted my selfishness for what it was.

My response to him surprised even me, my ragged gasp, the surging desire that jolted through me. My blood boiled in my lips where we connected, and instinctively, I opened my mouth to taste him. His lips were smooth and hungry against mine, and I tasted them hesitantly, unable to help myself from trying to connect with him even more since all I felt allowed to touch him with was my mouth, where he'd initiated the contact.

It was shocking when his tongue met mine, slick and intimate against my mouth. He hummed a response and his lure lashed out against me, all the more intense because of his feelings and that it was carried by something musical rather than mere words. I couldn't imagine what it would feel like without my protections. My fingers were like hooks in his shirt and the entire elven army couldn't have dragged me away from him.

It wasn't something I'd ever considered before, how it would feel being connected to someone with only our mouths. He pulled away and then kissed me again. And again. Kissing my mouth open and stroking my lips and my tongue so enticingly with his own.

I had to fight myself to keep from gripping his shoulders and arms, so I kept my fingers locked in his shirt, despite my building desire to rise up on my toes and climb higher. I didn't want to push him farther than he wanted to go, especially here in the Boundlands.

Some passerby whistled and cat-called in a language I didn't know, causing Levi to stiffen and break our kiss. He didn't respond but instead rested his forehead against mine while we struggled to catch our breath and rein ourselves in. His pupils were blown out as he stared at my face, and my cheeks felt crimson as I realized belatedly that if he'd responded to the man, his enchantment would have been excessive. *That could be embarrassing.*

He murmured low, just for me to hear, "You are always welcome where I go." I struggled to place what we'd been talking about until I remembered his dad. "Just please—" He paused and closed his eyes briefly. "—don't judge me too harshly."

Judge him? I just wanted his mouth back. My thoughts must have shown on my face because he chuckled and pressed one more quick kiss to my lips. I gave my own chuckle as I mentally wrenched myself back into the present moment.

"Let's go check on your dad," I sighed. His answering grin was dreamy and warm as he led me to a sandy path weaving gently along the side of the bluff. Grass swayed knee-high among rocks on the hill and waves lapped gently at the sand below. "Can I ask you a question?"

"Anything," he replied.

"Why did you change your name?" He'd mentioned during our meeting with Muriel that his birth name was different than the name he currently went by. Up ahead I could see clusters of small wooden houses, weathered and worn. Tiny bungalows with warped wood, paint long ago chipped and faded, peeked out from where they were nestled above the rocks.

"My first name is the same. Levi is just less of a mouthful than Leviathan. In merfolk culture the mother passes her name to her children, not the father. Chansoneau was my mother's surname. I didn't want her name though. She didn't raise me; my father did."

I glanced at his face as we walked, but found it devoid of emotion. My heart hurt for the little boy who had felt rejected by his mother.

"This is us." Levi directed me onto the porch of a shanty with bowed treads on the front porch and thorny white-apple blossoms climbing up into the eaves. Garlands of broken seashells hung from the rafters and swayed with the breeze. I wasn't sure what color the walls had originally been, but now they stood muted in browns and grays.

I followed hesitantly behind Levi as he unlocked the front door and pushed his way in. He called out in his native tongue, and there was no reply. "Dad?" he tried in English. I started to take my shoes off at the door, but thought better of it when I spied some broken bottles on the floor. Levi had already disappeared through a door in the back of the room, and I noticed he didn't flip on any lights as he moved through the house.

I heard him curse and begin speaking rapidly, but he was back to his native language again, so I couldn't understand him. I felt a spark of panic and hurried to catch up with him, stopping to flip on a light when I had trouble making out their shapes in the dark. I guess it would make sense that mer people wouldn't be bothered by low lighting. Light wasn't easy to come by underwater.

Levi was bent over his dad, who lay shirtless, sprawled on the wood floor in the hallway. The air smelled musty and rank, and Levi's face held more frustration than fear as he felt for a pulse under the larger man's jaw. His father appeared to have a similar amount of mer bloodlines as Levi, which told me Levi's mother probably wasn't entirely full-blooded either. He shared Levi's light-colored hair and swimmer's build, but his face was blockier and less sculpted than his son's. His nose appeared to have been broken in several places and healed incorrectly.

"Is he breathing?" I asked, and Levi nodded. I noticed his father had a large welt above his eye and bruising on his jaw and shoulder. "Did he get into a fight?" His knuckles looked pretty swollen, something I only knew to look for thanks to my friendship with Sidney.

"Probably," Levi grumbled, as he tried to turn his dad's torso to check for more injuries. "He may have just smacked his head when he passed out from drinking too much again. He's been in a bad place mentally for as long as I can remember."

"Should we send for a medic?" That's what I would do if I found one of my parents in this state.

But Levi shook his head. "He just needs to sleep it off. I'm gonna move him off the floor. I want you to stay back, because sometimes he wakes up swinging."

"Okay. I feel like I should probably give him some privacy if you don't need my help. Do you want me to wait out front?" I wanted to clean up some of that glass before we left.

"Sure." He was already trying to figure out how to get the prone man off the floor, so I made my way into the kitchen and eventually found a broom tucked into a storage closet.

I had managed to pile most of the larger pieces of broken glass into a small trash can when I heard raised voices at the back of the house. Trying to decide whether or not I should intervene, I realized I was gripping the neck of a broken bottle like a weapon and quickly dropped it in with the rest. *I might be getting a little too big for my britches.* I touched my wasps just to reassure myself they were still with me.

It was over as soon as it started though, and when I didn't

hear anything else concerning, I warily bent to finish the task of sweeping up the remaining glass.

Levi returned before I was finished and retrieved the broom from me. He shooed me off, speaking in low tones, saying he didn't want me to cut myself on his dad's mess. I stood aside and watched him carefully sweep up the remainder of the glass, noting his countenance and posture.

His shoulders were hunched and his jaw clenched, and I was startled to notice a scuff on his jawline. There was another red mark on his bicep, and my ire flared.

"Levi—"

"Let me finish this up and grab some bills and we'll go."

His enchantments were roiled—as if he didn't know whether to push or pull—and I bit my tongue as he dumped the dustpan and stepped outside to sort through some envelopes in the mailbox. He kept two and replaced the rest before locking the front door and turning to meet my gaze with hesitant eyes.

"I'm sorry. He's not been in the best state, but he hasn't done that in a while. It wasn't the best idea to bring you today."

I couldn't control my scowl. "He hurt you." I couldn't fathom my father ever leaving a mark on my body. The reddened skin on his arm was starting to fade, but the angry mark on his lower cheek looked like it was going to get worse. The longer I stared at it, the more incensed I felt.

In the back of my mind, I felt like maybe it was none of my business. Levi was a grown man, and his relationship with his parent wasn't my place to interfere. But in a larger, not entirely rational, and currently infuriated part of my mind, it was absolutely my business. Because Levi was *mine*. I didn't stop to wonder when that notion had settled in. I'd blown right past it and was trying to wrestle with confusing feelings of Mama Bear meets Righteous Anger.

He gave me a confused smile as he bent the envelopes in half and stuffed them in his back pocket. "What do you mean?" he asked.

"What happened to your face? And your arm? Why were you two yelling?"

Levi touched his cheek. "Did he get me?" He flinched.

"Yeah, I guess he did." He gave me a wry grin. "Shall I go tell him our Empress disapproves of his drunken flailing?" he teased. He bent to kiss my forehead and ushered me off the porch.

"This isn't funny, Levi. Why do you help him at all if he's going to treat you like that?"

He flashed me a sad smile. "He doesn't know I'm trying to help him. He doesn't even know who he is right now." His voice was soft but melancholy. "If I didn't help him, he'd be sleeping on the street somewhere. I don't want to enable his behavior, but I don't want to abandon him either. He took care of me when I was little and I needed it. I can't afford much, but I can at least keep him off the street."

I wasn't ready to take such a charitable view of the situation. "Isn't there some kind of medical help for him?"

Levi stooped to pluck a seashell from the sand at the edge of the path and absently rubbed at it with his thumb as we walked. "Sure, of course there is. But it doesn't do any good unless he wants the help. I've tried in the past to get him into some programs. But they cost money we don't really have, and he hasn't responded well to any of them anyway."

He paused on the path, looking out at the ocean below as it roared against a wave break farther out from shore, before eventually dropping his shell back into the sand at his feet. "I get frustrated with him all the time, but I think the broken bond he had to my mom is just too painful for him to bear."

And that, right there, was the crux of the matter. Why he made a home for himself in the Void, even though it would eventually shorten his lifespan by decades. Why he'd permanently marked his body with defensive runes. Why he kept me at arm's length, even though it didn't appear to be his desire.

Now that I could see it all, I didn't know what to do about any of it, except to be careful of his boundaries and hope we could figure it out together.

I stooped to pick up the shell he'd dropped.

CHAPTER 16

SATURDAY MORNING WAS SPENT FRANTICALLY PACKING for a two-week trip through the wilderness. Since our route would keep us away from most towns, I needed to bring our supplies with us from the start, so I did my best to pack practically: stout boots, warm clothing, easily washed blankets, and waterproof jackets.

I also refilled the venom compartments on my wasps and made sure I had all of my amulets in peak condition.

My mom was already tracking down dry rations and maps for us. I was looking forward to seeing her—however briefly—on Monday. I hadn't seen her since before she left to go spend time with my dad while he worked several months ago. She often spent time traveling back and forth between the estate and wherever my dad was located.

Admittedly, I was a little nervous for her to meet Levi. She'd seemed a little surprised to find out a 'boy' was accompanying me on the delivery trip instead of Sidney but didn't give her opinion about it either way.

Rafe was the only male she'd ever seen me interact with, and as implausible as it was, I think, deep down in her romantic heart, she'd always hoped I'd end up with him someday. How she thought that would work out biologically, I have no idea. The man was a sentient tree. I missed him terribly, but I'd never thought of him as anything more than a brother. *With lots of bark and thorns.*

By the time early afternoon rolled around, it was time to meet up with Levi. We were heading into Oar's Rest to meet with a group of sprites Muriel had arranged for us to speak with last minute. I appreciated that she seemed to be taking my requests seriously, but the tenor of her messages made me suspect the rest of the council might not be.

Levi met me at the Gate to Oar's Rest and his magic curled around me as I neared him, frothy seawater and warm sunshine. He was leaning against a brick column, wearing slightly dressier clothes than usual, with a long-sleeved button-down shirt cuffed up to just under his elbows. His dark blond hair was tousled, and he grinned when he saw me, making my heart give a happy little flutter.

"You look nice," I complimented him.

"It seemed respectful," he said, glancing down at his outfit. "I wasn't sure who you were meeting with, and I didn't want to risk rolling up on some feudal lord in sweatpants and a hoodie."

I gave him a small smile, which felt a little wistful because he always looked so snuggly in his comfortable t-shirts and sweats.

"My Empress deserves a better escort than some scrub in track clothes." He gave a tiny, self-deprecating smirk and pushed off the wall to head for the Gate.

"I like your track clothes," I said a little distractedly as I studied the painful looking bruise on his jaw. "It looks worse than it did last night," I said gently, feeling my smile dim a bit.

His smile turned a bit lopsided as I followed him to the guard and through the Gate. "Yeah," he finally replied once we were through to the other side. "It doesn't feel great." He raised a hand to touch the bruise and thought better of it at the last second.

"This is the entrance." He gestured to a courtyard gate to our left. It was a simple break in the stone wall, with an ancient looking gate that had ivy so deeply embedded in it that it would have been impossible to close it.

We were supposed to be meeting a sprite named Arvad at a fountain in front of the courthouse. I took a moment to focus myself and stepped into the courtyard. It was time to see what kind of situation I was working with.

"If you can't understand them, I can probably translate," Levi stated quietly as he followed me through the entrance.

That probably should have occurred to me to ask. Any time I'd dealt with sprites in the past, they'd been shore traders, so they'd spoken all the common languages. But that hadn't happened more than a small handful of times. They just didn't care to come to the surface very often.

"How many languages do you speak?" I asked, curious.

"Just three." He waved a hand dismissively. "Only common and the mer dialect fluently. My Abyssean is passable, since the mer language is related."

Abyssean was the commonly spoken language between most Oceanic races. Many had their own languages, and various dialects within those groups, but somehow Abyssean had become dominant. I didn't know enough of their history to know why, though.

We headed toward the multi-tiered fountain set in the courtyard, and I noticed the courthouse visitors were giving it a wide berth. As we got closer, I saw over a dozen fairies sitting on the edges or crouched in the water. Many of them held tiny signs I couldn't read, and even more bared their teeth and hurled copper coins from the bottom of the fountain at passersby who got too close. I wondered briefly if that would negatively affect the wish of the person who had deposited the coin in the first place.

"What are they saying?" I asked Levi, unable to understand the sprite's unorganized clamor. Granted, I couldn't have understood them even if it had only been one speaking, since none of it was in a language I recognized.

"They're angry," he murmured quietly, reaching out to toy with the ends of my hair as he explained. "They say they aren't being provided for after their evacuation. One is yelling that he thinks the Alliance provoked the kelpies into attacking. Another one is holding a sign that says the Alliance is just going to wait until The Deep is destroyed so it can secure all of their heartstones."

He paused for a minute, watching. "That guy over there"—
he nodded surreptitiously to another sprite standing on a park
bench—"is trying to convince two of the more aggressive ones
that their time would be better spent elsewhere. They're making
the rest of the group look bad."

The male Levi indicated appeared to be one of the oldest in
the group, if I could judge by his paunchy build and hazed-over
eyes. He was clearly worn thin by his peers but seemed to be
holding his own in his debate with the other two sprites, and he
was keeping a calm demeanor even while frustrated. He had an air
of authority about him, and I decided he was probably my contact.

I took a seat on another nearby bench to wait for a break in
his conversation, rather than risk being pelted with coppers by
the protesters in the fountain. The tiny man didn't make me wait
long, waving off his companions and lifting off the park bench to
drift over toward us.

Fairies didn't have wings quite the way most humans imagined them, but their magic allowed them to fly, even the sprites
who lived underwater. His path was lazy and a little wobbly, and
I suspected his energy was probably depleted.

It was surprising to see someone like him, whose magic felt
very sharp and strong—my reading said he could control ocean
currents on a whim—unable to keep a short flight path steady.
He'd probably spent at least a week on the surface, only heading
back to the water to recharge when he absolutely had to.

"Golemancer?" he asked wearily as he alighted on the bench
next to me. At my nod, he sighed deeply and introduced himself,
"I am Arvad Ren, one of the Elder... council from The Deep."
His words were slow and measured, as if he chose them carefully
as he spoke. It was obvious by his speech patterns that our tongue
wasn't native to him, but I was so touched he'd made such an
effort to communicate with me.

I inclined my head to him briefly, since trying to shake his
tiny hand would be awkward and strange, seeing as his entire
body could fit in my own hand.

"It's a great pleasure to meet you, Mr. Ren. My name is Elara
Hawthorne. This is Levi Navarre. He can act as a translator if

needed," I introduced. "Would it be more comfortable for us to speak at the tide pools?"

The luminescent markings his body bore seemed greatly faded compared to the other sprites I'd interacted with, though whether that was due to his age or separation from the ocean, I didn't know. Regardless, the least I could do was try to make sure the man was comfortable while I took up his time.

Arvad's eyes lit up at the suggestion, but then he hesitated, until Levi interjected, "My skin has been peeling lately, so I would love to spend some time at the tide pools."

I felt my eyebrows pull down in confusion because I'd never noticed any skin peeling on him before, and he could visit the pools any time he wanted. But then Arvad acquiesced and seemed relieved at the idea, and I realized Levi had spoken for the sprite's benefit.

When we arrived at the rocky section of beach, I found a dry piece of sun-bleached driftwood and settled in to wait as Arvad gratefully submerged himself in a craggy puddle. Levi quietly excused himself and made his way over to a large crop of thorny-looking succulent plants nestled in some sand back by the cliffs. I didn't have time to wonder as he bent toward one of the larger plants because Arvad floated to the edge of the pool closest to me, watching me with only his overly large eyes breaking the surface of the water.

"Thank you for taking the time to meet with me today, Mr. Ren," I said sincerely.

"You call me Arvad," he said slowly, lifting just enough that his toothy mouth rose out of the water before sinking back down to his eyes. "This is much better," he sighed, drifting slightly in the pool. He turned his head briefly to survey Levi before narrowing his gaze at me. "What is your relationship with the mer?"

Did he mean Levi? Or the mer in general? "Levi doesn't readily identify as a mer, but he's my…" I hesitated. I wasn't sure exactly what to call us. "Boyfriend?" That seemed as good a fit as any, even if it felt weird on my tongue. He was mine. That was what mattered. "Other than him, I've never met a mer in my life." I didn't count Levi's father. We hadn't really been introduced.

"He is a singer though, no?" he asked, lifting his face out of the water just enough to glance over at Levi. "I can feel his magic in his words." He seemed suspicious of Levi as he narrowed his eyes at him. It reminded me that Muriel Ta'nith, the liaison, had shown a similar reaction.

"He is a siren, yes," I confirmed. "You're welcome to ask him about his heritage yourself." What response he'd get, I couldn't guess. Levi was as touchy about his bloodlines as Jordan was about his vampirism.

"I'm sure you have many other things you need to be doing, so I'll try not to take too much of your time. I just wanted to speak with some people from your community so I could better understand what I've been asked to do and some of the dynamics at play with the Alliance."

Just then, Levi approached, holding several thick stalks of the spiky plant. He split the skin with his thumb, peeling the top layer back and revealing some dripping clear tissue inside. He dug a chunk out and bent down to offer some to Arvad, speaking to him quickly in Abyssean, and then demonstrated rubbing some of the liquid into his own skin.

Arvad climbed gingerly out of the little pool and took some of the goop, volleying questions at Levi in curious tones.

Finally, Levi looked up at me. "I'm just explaining that the plant will help with his—" He paused to search for a word. "—slime coat? The barrier on his skin that protects him. Being out of water is hard for them, and this will help. And he wanted to know about my affiliation with the mer. I've explained that I have nothing to do with the Alliance, nor do I want to."

Levi took a seat on a rock near the pool and began methodically stripping the tough outer skin off of the plant stalks. He had a large, wide leaf from another plant, which he laid out next to him and deposited the inner tissue of the thorny plant onto.

I turned my attention to Arvad, who was busily smearing the tiny chunk of plant all over his body. He lifted his eyes to Levi and watched him as he sat, quietly making himself useful, before speaking to me.

"Ask me questions. I will answer."

I smiled briefly. Something about his bluntness was endearing.

"Can you tell me about the Alliance?"

"Alliance… we all have war treaties, so we won't fight. All the ocean peoples have someone to stand for them in the council. Lots of talking. Too much talking. Mer are bossy—" He clicked his teeth shut and glanced at Levi, who nodded in agreement but didn't take his eyes off his work, until Arvad looked away, at least. Then he glanced at me with a playful leer and wiggled his eyebrows. The idea of him 'being bossy' made my face hot, and I quickly refocused on Arvad.

"Mer is biggest group on the council, so they decide all the things," Arvad continued. There was resentment in his tone, and suddenly things started clicking into place for me. No one liked to have an outside group making decisions for them, especially when that group didn't hold up their part of the bargain—like protection.

"What is it you want to do?" he asked. "You make a golem for the Alliance?" he guessed as he dipped to scoop seawater from the pool and massage it into his skin. As he did, the markings on his body began to glow just a little bit brighter.

"A sprite named Adonci Tyr came for me in the Void with a heartstone and a note asking me to provide a golem for defense of The Deep." Arvad nodded with a deep frown but didn't appear surprised, which told me he'd already heard about it. "Now the Alliance is requesting I make a golem for them, but I have some reservations about doing so. Why is this Alliance requesting the golem instead of the sprites? If the sprites own the heartstones, shouldn't you be requesting the service yourselves?"

Arvad looked to Levi and asked a few questions in Abyssean before answering me, "The mer took our largest heartstones because they said we couldn't keep them safe." His tone was bitter and held an ocean of resentment. Heartstones were a fairy resource. They were the only ones able to create them and survive the conditions to harvest them. It sounded like the mer were taking advantage of the sprite's distress to acquire them under the thinly veiled guise of being helpful.

I pursed my lips. I could see this group using a golem to defend the sprites and then holding onto it for "Alliance purposes" once the city was properly fortified. If I was going to make a golem, I wanted to supply it directly to the sprites—after all, it was their heartstone and their city—but if I took the contract with the Alliance, I had a feeling the mer wouldn't allow that.

My mind took a dozen pathways imagining all the ways this could go wrong. My gut told me my fears were well-founded, so I asked Arvad what his thoughts on it were and what his fears might be if I took their contract. He asked Levi for clarification on a few things and sunk back down into the pool with a frown to think for a moment.

We ended up talking for a while longer, discussing his concern that the golems would only serve to escalate the violence and destruction surrounding The Deep. Would relying on the Alliance for defense eventually mean economic enslavement of his city to pay for that defense? How would their culture and way of life change due to interference by these outsiders? Would they ever be able to rid themselves of the mer's interventions once they were firmly entrenched?

I had a lot to work through in my mind, and I knew that no matter what choices I made there were going to be unfortunate outcomes, but a plan began to take root as we talked. Eventually, we escorted Arvad back to his companions and Levi delivered the rest of his plant goop wrapped in a leaf with a slight bow and quick exchange of pleasantries.

Before leaving town, we followed Arvad's directions to a small grotto that had been set up as an emergency shelter, where he indicated Adonci's mother was caring for her last living grandchild. I felt a little better knowing her son was being cared for by his family and among his own people, but seeing all the displaced people, the despair and hopelessness written on their faces, pierced me through. I couldn't save them. But maybe I could give them some of the tools to save themselves.

CHAPTER 17

"STOP IT. You're annoying me. I can handle the shop for a few weeks," Sidney grumbled as she checked another name off her list. Her hair was pulled back into an easy ponytail, and she reached back to tighten the gathered strands as she leaned back in her chair.

I huffed at her. "I just feel guilty about leaving you here by yourself for so long. And I'm not going to be here to update any product or fill any orders—"

"Elara, stop. Chill."

I put the last clamp on the gem set I was placing in a sword hilt and set it down to take a breath. She'd taken the news with only a few questions after I'd returned to the shop Friday evening. When I told her I was planning to work last night and today to fill all the most important orders, she'd opted to come in with me, even though it was Sunday, so she could start placing calls to any customers that might happen to be in The Void. *"That way if anyone is angry about their orders being postponed, I can just hand the phone to you and let them yell at you and not me,"* she'd half-joked.

So far, no one had been angry, but I'd been scrambling all day to get every bit of work done I possibly could. Sidney had brought me lunch, Levi had stopped by with dinner for all of us, and I hadn't left my desk except for a few unavoidable bathroom breaks. We were both a little cranky.

"I'm sorry. I'm just stressed out about all this. There are going to be people coming in to pick up orders that aren't here, and I hate doing that to people." I focused on the gem set in front of me and pushed some of my energy into it, directing my intent toward speed and strength.

Sidney just shrugged. "We aren't Voiders, Elara. We're used to not having instant communication with everybody we've ever met and their mothers." She made a face like the thought was horrifying before continuing.

"And yes, this shop is important to the two of us. We've put a lot of work into it these last two years, but I get that it's not a baby on life support, ya know? These sprites are people. They're real, actual babies, and mothers and fathers and brothers and sisters. They matter more than people getting their orders on time."

She had her boots propped on the counter and crossed at the ankles, doodling large scrawling loops on her notepad as she talked. "Worst-case scenario: our shop goes under. We'll survive. We can always figure it out, right? But these people literally might not survive. You've basically got an entire city trying to hang on for the next two weeks, hoping you come through for them. You made the right choice."

She said it matter-of-factly, shrugging as she spoke, as if she didn't know her words were a balm to all my guilt and fear and second-guessing. Sometimes I loved my best friend so much I wondered how I'd gone most of my life not knowing her. "Thanks, Sid."

"I'm not saying you don't owe me. I'm so jealous that Levi gets to watch you animate those juggernauts I could peck his eyes out."

"Ugh, you're awful." I broke into a wide grin. "I'm sure you'll come up with some way for me to repay you."

"Yeah, like a paid vacation after this is all said and done." She kicked her feet off the counter and rapped her knuckles once on her desk as she stood. "Speaking of which, I'm going home. Am I going to see you before you leave? I'm not, am I?" She bent to loop her arms under mine and hauled me up out of my chair for a hug.

"Sidney, what—" She lifted me off the ground and squished me against her boobs like I was a toddler.

"I can't help it. You're just so *little*," she said when I protested. "Do you need anything before I go? You've got your wasps?"

I waved her off and locked the front door behind her—you'd think she was my mother sometimes. Uninterrupted time to work helped me focus and get more done, and three hours later, though my eyelids felt heavy, I scanned my list of orders and felt pretty good about how things were wrapping up. I was beginning to pack up for the night when someone's magic brushed over my awareness, and ice slid down my spine.

Two someones' magics. Just around the corner, out of view of the front window, I could feel the two men who had pulled knives and cornered me in Dry Gulch. I didn't need to question it. I recognized their magic immediately.

I dropped into a crouch and backed behind a counter, where I wouldn't be in view of the windows, and sent my wasps to the front door. I couldn't let them get inside. My brain tried to parse through my options, but it was hard to think over the pounding of my heart. I pulled out my phone and sent a short message to Levi. He was so close, but knew I couldn't rely on him being awake or seeing my message in time.

Within seconds, a man had his hands cupped to the front window, his face peering in through the glass. A loud BANG sounded as the second phantom shook the front door to try the lock.

I didn't even think.

I just reacted.

All six wasps scrambled through the mail slot in the door, metal legs clicking. I fought against a full body shudder, desperate to keep a mental grip on my weapons, only allowing two wasps to deliver their payload. The rest were to watch and wait. I didn't spend all that time devising a non-lethal defense only to screw up now and kill them in blind fear.

Screams erupted as the men became aware of my hunters, flailing and trying to fight back. Two thuds sounded dully as the screams cut off, and I sat in silence for several beats, trying to calm my racing heart. The view through the window wasn't low enough to see the sidewalk without creeping closer, so I crouched and drifted as quietly as I could to the door, quickly finding dark shapes sprawled on the ground. Fear tried to overwhelm me again, but I shoved it back, finding a root of anger instead, simmering and growing in the back of my mind, and I clutched onto it like a tiger by the tail.

I grabbed what I needed of my belongings, checked the men again for movement, pushed more energy into my little constructs, and unlocked the door. Time to get out.

The cold night air felt damp on my skin as my breaths shuddered out of me. I'd no sooner flipped my keys in the lock, wasps hovering at my shoulders, than I flinched at the sound of a horse moving at a fast canter. Hoofbeats rang out loudly, echoing and reverberating across the concrete and glass business fronts. I could feel Grim's power growing and speeding toward me at an alarming rate.

Oppressive darkness materialized for one instant under a streetlamp at the end of the block, flashing through the circle of light in the blink of an eye. His magic felt like an avalanche, a crushing python, heaving and constricting with every breath. He was a yawning abyss.

And he truly was on horseback... if you could call it that.

He rode a wraith—was himself a wraith—the cloak of shadow wrapping around him and whipping behind him as he drew near. Grim rode straight at me, looking for all the world as if he would trample me under the hooves of his steed. His cloak flared wide, and the horse disappeared—there one second and gone the next—depositing him neatly on his feet a dozen paces in front of me. He continued walking toward me without breaking his gait, twirling what appeared to be a war hammer made of shadow in one hand before tucking it... *somewhere*... and then it was gone.

While I wasn't afraid of Grim specifically, his magic was overwhelming and suffocating in its intensity, making my already frayed nerves stretch wildly. I wrestled through my racing thoughts and grabbed ahold of the most pressing one. "Did I kill them?" I choked out. Was that why he was here?

"Unfortunately not," muttered a voice over my shoulder. I shrieked and spun to find Jordan staring at the two men with a disdainful expression, before turning a more baffled expression on me.

"What is *wrong* with you morons?" Levi's magic was a hint of salt air and splashing waves under the onslaught that was Grim as he practically flew up the block.

I was still having a hard time deciding who required more of my attention: Grim and his writhing cloak of shadows or the two men lying on the pavement in front of my store. I felt Levi's strong arms close around my shoulders as he tucked my head against his neck, his chest heaving. His voice vibrated against the side of my face. "I asked you to *help* her, not scare the daylights out of her. She's already hyperventilating."

Am I? It was hard to tell with the ringing in my ears.

Levi pulled my head back enough to search my face. "Are you hurt?"

I shook my head.

"Okay. Try to calm down and tell me what happened. We're here now. You're safe."

"Doesn't look like she needed us in the first place," Jordan grumbled, leaning over the man closest to us. He bent at the waist and sniffed, crouching lower as he went and taking several short, shallow inhales before blowing a large puff of air out his nostrils like it offended him. "Heavy sedatives."

He flicked me a sideways glance before dropping to his knees and rooting through a small duffel bag lying on the pavement that I hadn't even noticed. "Long-stemmed lighters, tape, hunting knives, zip ties, old rags..." He stood and frowned at the men, sparing a long glance at a gasoline can lying on its side a few feet away. "It's quaint how much gear a normal person needs to commit arson and kidnapping."

Levi's breath came out in a wheeze, and he clutched me a little tighter. "Elara? What happened, honey?"

"I panicked." My voice sounded robotic to my own ears. I felt him nod against the top of my head. His jaw moved slightly like he was mouthing something at Grim. "I felt them coming, and when I saw them peeking in the windows, I reacted." I turned just enough to be able to watch Grim's response, but he was entirely impassive, his face giving nothing away.

"I've seen enough," Jordan fairly growled, stooping to grab the man closest to him by the upper arm and flipping him into a fireman's carry. "Totally lame. I was promised some fun tonight."

"Shut up, Jordan. I said no such thing. I told you Elara needed help." Levi sounded more tired than angry as he held me against his chest.

"I thought it would be more fun." His petulance struck me as hysterically funny in the moment, though I was still too out of it to react.

"I spend all my time trying not to scare people and the one chance I get to do it on purpose—ruined. What's the point of having this awesome party trick if I never get to use it?" He turned to face us with a sarcastic smirk, his irises turning blood red before glowing like hot embers.

"You idiot," Levi tried to push Jordan's face away, but Jordan dodged under him, laughing. "She's probably already going into shock," Levi said. "Keep your nightmare fuel to yourself."

Grim gave a quiet sigh, which I wouldn't have noticed except that I was so focused on him—the intensity of his magic hadn't abated at all. He stooped to grab the second man by the front of his shirt and then nonchalantly wrapped Jordan in a gentle head-lock, causing him to tip unsteadily with his shouldered burden and laugh even harder.

"I've seen these men," Grim said quietly to no one in particular. "I'll take care of it." He turned and walked off into the night with a protesting vampire under one arm and a dangling man clutched by the front of his shirt in another, as if it were the most normal thing in the world. Maybe it was. Jordan yelled for Levi to throw him the duffle, which he did, and then they were gone.

"Is Jordan going to eat them?" I finally asked into the silence.

"I don't think Jordan's the eating-people type," Levi responded. "Besides, I think your drugs would turn him off it anyhow."

"That's good."

"Mmm."

⥈⥏⥈

LEVI HAD WALKED me to the Gate and waited with me while I called Sidney. He'd offered to stay the night with me, but in my shaken state I knew I'd be too tempted to want to push his boundaries in my desire to be comforted. Sidney had seemed like a safer guard for the night.

Now, as she dropped me off at the rail into Upper Golden Laurel, where I was supposed to meet Levi, I felt incredibly guilty about how visibly tired she was.

"Promise me you'll sleep this week and only do the absolute minimum at the shop," I said as we entered the station.

"I'll sleep," she said, "but I'm also gonna do some scouting to figure out where those guys are working out of and what can be done about them."

We met Levi inside the station, and Sidney seemed edgy about leaving me with him. He shouldered his pack easily, while I'd brought a pack and a duffel that probably weighed as much as me. He laughed when he realized both bags we carried were mine.

"Give me that," he said, taking the duffle Sidney carried and setting the strap on his shoulder.

She squished me against her again, extracting a promise from Levi that he'd keep me safe before leaving. I thought I'd done pretty well with the wasps, if I said so myself, but I didn't ever want to be in that position again if I could help it.

"Did you pack your whole house?" Levi teased, balancing the bag Sidney had given him.

"Supplies," I said, rifling through my pockets. "I probably should have hired a porter," I muttered.

"No need, I've got it," he said with a small grin, watching me dig in my coat with curious eyes. He still seemed wary, but relieved to be getting started on our trip.

Found it! I pulled a small glass vial from among the assorted stones and amulets that usually made a home in my pocket, and presented it to Levi. "A gift."

He reached out and plucked it from my fingers. "What's this?" he asked, studying the iridescent, mauve-toned liquid inside.

"It's for your cheek." My neighbor, Bette, had stopped by last night after Sidney and I arrived to let me know she'd finally made some small progress on the bond-breaking potion I'd asked her to create for Levi's father. She was more confident it was going to be possible to make but ended up needing some drahk up front to secure some rare ingredients.

She smelled faintly of burnt hair and cinnamon, but I wasn't sure if it was related to the potion or not, so I didn't ask. While we were negotiating a final (and very high) price for the new potion, I'd arranged for the purchase of some healing draughts for the trip and a balm for his bruise. All the purchases together had been costly enough that I would be feeling the pinch for a while.

Healing draughts, in general, tended to be expensive because they had a very short shelf-life and very few alchemists or apothecaries had what it took to get them right. Most people didn't trust them because the majority of the ones in the markets were forgeries or expired products. Bette didn't personally make these, but she had a contact who did, and I trusted her to supply me properly.

Levi pulled the stopper on the bottle and gave it a hesitant sniff. "Is this going to turn me into a frog?"

"I thought you said you didn't have an aquatic form," I said with a smile. "No, it's not—Wait, stop." I snatched it from him as he raised it to his mouth and poured some into his palm. "You don't drink it. It's a balm. Rub it into your bruise, you goof."

"How am I supposed to know? Aren't these things usually expensive?" he asked, wrinkling his nose slightly at the smell. It just smelled slightly warm and nutty to me.

"Usually, yes." This one wasn't an exception, but he didn't need to know that. "I can get them from my neighbor sometimes when she has them in stock." I hefted my pack higher onto my shoulders while he cautiously raised his hand to his face and rubbed the liquid in.

I had to roll my eyes. "It's safe. I promise." People were so dramatic about medicine sometimes. Our train rolled in, so I followed him on and settled in for the short stretch to my parent's side of town. By the time we arrived, his bruise was a mere shadow of what it had been. Probably felt a lot better too.

My mother had arranged for her porter to meet us at the station, only instead of being a hired hand like most people used, this one was a small, personal golem. By small, I meant that he was just shorter than me, though still rather wide. He was made of stone and had no head, but rather, a crescent-shaped carving where a man's shoulders might be and a larger than necessary heartstone that levitated in the middle.

"Hello Ryo," I greeted the stone sculpture as I approached it, for no other reason than it made me happy. I pressed some of my magic into his heartstone and felt my father's familiar magic answer mine.

"Is it a person?" Levi asked as I took my duffle bag from him and slung the strap over one of the points of the crescent moon shape in Ryo's "shoulders".

I blinked at him, confused by his question.

"Does it think?" he tried again.

"Oh. No. He's just a construct. My father made him and named him. He's kind of our butler." I'd said 'kind of' because he had many uses throughout our home. His heartstone was large enough to power not only him but many other things as well, so he lent his magic to other purposes as needed throughout the day.

Levi's eyes were narrowed in suspicion at my father's creation, but he raised his hand as if to touch the heartstone suspended in the crescent.

"Don't touch that," I warned, grabbing his hand and pulling it back.

"Why?"

"He will defend himself." I led the way to the street where our transportation would be waiting.

CHAPTER 18

PRIVATE TRANSPORTATION like my family's was almost unheard of in the Boundlands. Most people took rails when they could and walked when they couldn't. Some people rode animals or rickshaws, but more often than not, we walked. The very, very rich drove private cars that hovered just off the ground using the same magical tech as our public rails.

My parents had something all their own.

"What is that?" Levi's voice was flat as I approached the door of my father's transport. It was a construct made of metal, stone, and glass, looking somewhat similar to human cars, though my dad had only briefly seen one himself. He didn't have enough human ancestry to make it long in the Void and found his few excursions there 'baffling overall.'

Inside was spacious and comfortable, with seats in the front facing backward so everyone could converse during a trip. I took my bag from Ryo and tossed it onto the floor inside. "It's a private transport. Ryo plugs into the front and powers it himself. Ryo, will you take us home, please?"

I climbed in first and turned around to see Levi hesitate just slightly before unslinging his pack and climbing in behind me. He sat heavily beside me, looking around with a slightly horrified expression. I reached across him and shut the door for him while

Ryo stepped into an indentation in the front that was built to hold him, and pushed some of his power into the transport.

The air around me hummed with my father's magic, reminding me of old-growth forests and springy ferns curling out from underfoot. The feeling was familiar and immediately calming, reminding me of hours spent playing in his workshop while he tinkered and built.

"What's wrong?" I asked Levi. He looked like he'd just had an adrenaline dump and was headed toward fight instead of flight, leaning forward in his seat as we levitated slightly and began drifting down the street. "You've ridden a bus. Haven't you ever ridden in a human car in the Void?"

"No," he hissed slightly. "Do I look like I hang out with Voiders all day?" He bared his slightly too-pointy teeth to make his point and glanced out the window before sinking back in his seat. The interior of the cabin caught his attention, and he stared at the leather seats and clean lines of the interior walls. "What kind of Narnia shenanigans have you dragged me into?" he whispered mock-aggressively.

"Put your safety harness on." I demonstrated, showing him how to click it into place across his lap. We weren't really in danger of getting into a wreck the way humans did on a daily basis. There was no traffic here like there was in the Void, but occasionally, an animal would run out in the road and Ryo would have to come to an abrupt stop, sending us tumbling to the floor.

"Seriously, Elara, I knew you came from money, but this is *crazy*."

I shrugged, realizing he felt uncomfortable and not knowing what to do about it. "It's not a big deal." He looked at me like I had two heads.

"It's not like it's *my* money, and they didn't even buy this, my dad made it." Kind of. He commissioned the transport and then created the heartstone sharing rig with Ryo by himself. That was the important part in my mind anyway.

Levi sighed and rubbed his face. "My anxiety about meeting your parents just quadrupled."

"Dad won't even be there today. My mom didn't come from money, and she's mostly human." I frowned slightly, wondering about his reaction to the estate. "I should probably warn you that the house is quite large."

"I figured." He slid farther down in his seat, loosely gripping the straps of his backpack, which rested between his feet. I knew the disparity between our economic situations had the potential to cause problems, but I'd hoped that since it didn't matter to me, it wouldn't matter to him.

I watched him as his eyes took in the details of the cabin around him and the archway of trees looming over the road—actually the beginning of the long driveway leading to the estate—above us. His face radiated stress in the slashing lines of his eyebrows and the twitching muscle as he clenched and released his jaw.

My gaze drifted to the muscular lines of his neck, his Adam's apple bobbing as he swallowed, and the indentation in the muscles above his collarbones. He caught me looking, and I felt my cheeks heat.

"I can't believe I took you to my dad's. What are you even doing with someone like me?" he asked despondently.

"Because I want you," I answered curtly, feeling irritated. I knew I was already a little in love with him, though it felt too early to admit such a thing, even to myself. Did he think money affected how I felt about a person? "What kind of question is that?"

Even as I asked it, I felt myself grow defensive about what kind of person he was accusing me of being—not to mention the category he placed himself in—and firmly shoved that line of thinking back. This was insecurity, plain and simple, and I wasn't going to allow it to be a wedge between us. "Don't answer that. We are not our families' financial stations. It doesn't matter to me, and I had hoped it wouldn't matter to you."

I reached out and squeezed his hand as Ryo brought our transport to a stop in front of the main gates to the estate house. He released a deep sigh as we pulled to a stop. This conversation would have to wait.

"That's… a lot of dogs," he said, and I looked up to see the bulk of my parent's pack of mastiffs jumping at the gate.

My answering grin stretched my face so hard it hurt. I loved these dogs so much. My family had been breeding them for generations, and my dad had always had a special interest in their training and pedigrees. He also liked having them as guard dogs for when my mom was home and he couldn't be.

"Don't touch them or talk to them, please. No eye contact."

Ryo opened my door and reached in for my bags, backing up to let me out once he had retrieved them. I stepped out and raised my closed right fist to my sternum, and as one, the dogs sat and the barking stopped. Until the youngest popped back up, all wiggle-butt puppy enthusiasm, and I sighed in spite of myself. He was the sweetest boy, but my father obviously hadn't been putting the time into him that he usually invested in them.

Ryo unlatched the gate, and I stepped through, pausing to place my hand on the exuberant puppy's rump and guide him into a sitting position again, before reaching back to take Levi's hand and leading him through the pack. The oldest dogs waited patiently, the younger ones quivering with energy and excitement as we made our way to the front steps. It gutted me a bit not to have the time today to spend with them like I normally did.

The manor was built of stone and was large for elven standards (we had notoriously low birth rates), complete with manicured gardens, a sweeping tower, and defensible parapets. It was, in essence, a small castle, set atop a craggy hill, surrounded on all sides by a wide, rolling meadow. The grass eventually gave way to deep forest, but off to the side and further back from the house sat the family crypt, which served as both the entrance to the catacombs and a place of residence for the sentries we'd come to retrieve.

But first I planned to raid the fridge and give my mom a hug.

One of the large wooden doors into the main keep swung open and there she was, looking younger than a full human would by at least two decades, all pale skin and dark-brown hair. The only thing that gave a hint at her age were the wisps of grey hair beginning to form at her temples.

People often remarked about how I took after my dad in features, but while my skin was closer to my father's darker elven grey, my small build and dark hair mirrored my mother's. Our taste in clothing had always been our most noticeable difference.

Where I preferred blouses that were loose fitting and billowy, or slouchy like the sweater I wore today, my mom always dressed in conservative, understated, high-necked affairs.

She had a quiet strength I'd admired my entire life, and she was gentle and tender-hearted. One time when I was eight, my father's favorite dog had given birth to her first litter of puppies, all stillborn. My father had been disappointed, of course, but the sounds of my mother weeping when she found them still ripped at my heart when I remembered it.

She was as loving as she was beautiful, so I was surprised at the spike in my nerves as she pulled me into a hug. I'd caught her suspicious glance over my shoulder toward Levi, and even though I knew she would respect my choices and I didn't need her approval of him, I *wanted* it.

She huffed a quiet laugh as her finger tangled on one of the tiny chains in my hair, and she drew away to extract it and fix my hair. "Elara, dear, did you mean to wear every amulet and charm you own?" Her smile was indulgent as she teased me, and my gaze fell to the single pendant she wore around her neck, a symbol of a bird, a gift from my father. He'd always called her his "little bird."

I'd made her some amulets in the past, but she never wore them anymore, claiming she disliked all the clutter. Clutter or not, my charms were a part of me. "I've never worked on a construct the size of the sentries. I wanted to make sure I would have all the power I needed." I fingered the moonstone power-well hanging from my right ear.

Levi shifted behind me, and my mother's gaze flicked over to him with acute interest. I turned to him to begin the introduction. "Levi, let me introduce my mom, Elish Hawthorne al' Einin." He took my mother's extended hand and gave a slight bow, all manners and chivalry, but kept conspicuously quiet. I was finally beginning to realize this was a thing he did when he didn't want his enchantments to affect anyone.

"Mom, this is Levi Navarre. He's my... my person. He's mine." I cringed. It hadn't occurred to me how strange saying the word 'boyfriend' to my mom would feel until the last second, and I'd panicked.

I felt Levi's fingers snake gently into my hair and rest possessively at the back of my neck. I didn't need to look at him to know his shoulders were shaking in silent laughter at my awkwardness. My mom's eyebrows raised slightly at my declaration, her eyes bouncing back and forth between us before coming to rest on the ward on my wrist. She didn't need to hear Levi speak to know he was a siren; I'd gotten my magical discernment abilities from her. She leveled me with a knowing look.

Beside me, Levi chuckled in spite of himself, and I felt his enchantment skitter over my protective ward, reminding me that my mom didn't have one. With all the packing, I hadn't thought to make her one. I felt defensive all of a sudden, imagining her accusing me of being brainwashed by his magic. *Ugh.* I probably shouldn't have sprung that on her.

To my great relief, my mom simply cocked an eyebrow at me and welcomed Levi graciously. A mention of honey cakes had me darting for the kitchen like an excited child. Unfortunately, they were all packaged up, along with the rest of our food for the trip.

My mom laid out a paper map on the table, and we used our calling chips to store it so we didn't have to deal with keeping it safe and dry. We discussed the best options for routes, where to find inns for an evening and where we'd have to camp. After everything was done and squared away, there was nothing left to do but call the sentries. My mother hugged me again and told me she was proud of me.

"You aren't going to come watch me call them?"

"Oh, no. Those things are terrifying. I'll stay and watch from the balcony if you don't mind. I know we've discussed this in detail, but please, *please* be careful. Remember what your father taught you." She cast a wary eye out the kitchen window toward the crypt. I kissed her cheeks, and she bid Levi farewell.

"It was lovely meeting you, Mr. Navarre." Her gaze flickered over him once more in curiosity, her sharp eyes cataloging every detail. Oh, the interrogation I was going to get later.

"And you, Mrs. Hawthorne." He seemed to be taking all of this better than he had the transport, or maybe he was keeping his freak-out internal this time. My mom blinked when his enchantment washed over us.

I led the way out of the back of the house and down the stone path to the sentries, Ryo following us with our bags.

"Your person?" Levi asked, now that we were alone, and I winced. I knew it was too much to hope he'd let that one go. He took my hand and squeezed my fingers lightly with gentle reassurance.

"Sorry, I panicked," I grumbled under my breath, making his grin spread further across his face.

"I like it," he said with gentle amusement, and my heart gave a pathetic thud, reflected in my smile.

We climbed the short staircase and stood under the large marble arch, looking into the chamber. It was a cavernous space with a high domed ceiling rising several stories above us. Sunlight streamed in through window cutouts set high in the stone walls and Raald, the largest construct, knelt against the back wall with his stone wings folded behind him. He contained a heartstone from the sparks, little fire fairies, and in one fist, he held aloft a lantern lit with an eternal flame. He looked like an exquisite carving of an angel of war but had actually been formed with lava instead.

To his right and left, two doors led down into the crypts, where my ancestors lay. My parents would be buried here, and so would I. It had been so for over a dozen generations.

Against the right wall, Leothen crouched—the ceiling would have needed to be at least six stories for him to stand at his full height. He was a true stone sculpture, wearing a stone crown, carrying a stone broadsword, and looking for all the world like a massive stone knight.

Domm squatted across from him, against the wall to the left. He was the shortest, at only five stories tall, and he was also the oldest. We didn't even know how old he actually was, other than that he'd been part of our family for several thousand years. He was humanoid, like the others, but didn't bear the likeness of a man like they did. His massive arms were much larger than his legs, giving him a build much closer to a gorilla than a man.

He had very large shoulders with immense jagged boulders

jutting out above them and his back. He was crudely cut, his face looking more like a protective mask for playing sports than a statue's face. His eyes were nothing more than two vertical slits, and he had a few other divots carved out of his face, but nothing more. He carried no weapon other than brute force, and something about him made the hairs on the back of my neck stand up a little.

Domm's magic wasn't quite the same as the other two and wasn't anything close to what we used these days. When I'd played in here as a child, I'd pressed into his magic several times out of curiosity and always gotten the impression that it was very primal, ancient in its nature. There was just something more to it than any other golem I'd ever seen. He and Leothen were the two I would be bringing with me today, and my discomfort with the unknown nature of Domm's magic hadn't abated.

I blew out a large breath, trying to release some of my unease. I could do this.

"Poseidon's ugly mother," Levi swore. I shot him a confused look, only to find him gazing at the constructs in awe. "These are what we're taking? You can control these things?"

"Uh, yes. In theory. That's the hope." I tried not to let my nerves into my voice and scrubbed my hands off on my jeans.

Levi was quiet for a beat, then came a flat, "What?"

"Well, I've never done this before," I admitted. "At least, not on this scale." No point in waiting around for my nerves to build. I raised my hands slightly to center myself and prodded at the magic in Leothen's heartstone. I'd start with him in case Domm gave me trouble. I eyed the more primitive structure to my left warily, imagining losing control of him, then returned my focus to Leothen.

He was already active, waking from over a century of slumber as I pushed my energy into him and tried to get a grip on his current directive. My ancestors had instructed the golems to "watch and defend", and so they sat, passively sending out magical feelers, waiting for any magic that didn't match our family and wasn't escorted onto our property by us. Anything that made it past a specific boundary would rouse the golems, and they would terminate it. With extreme prejudice.

Rousing them now made my skin prickle a little bit, partly due to how dangerous they were, but mostly because of the immense amount of magic flowing between us as I began to change Leothen's directive. *Come with me. Obey.*

Dust began to fall, followed by abandoned bird nests and other debris as Leothen began to right himself in what sounded like a slowly grinding avalanche. I skittered out of the archway, followed closely by Levi, who was sticking to my side like glue. His face wore a mixture of excitement, awe, and horror.

Leothen ducked low under the arch and stepped over the short row of stairs, straightening to his full height on the nearest open patch of grass to the crypt. I felt a little drained, almost winded, but that had come easier than I expected.

Now for the fun one, I thought wryly.

CHAPTER 19

⬦

Domm's magic almost seemed eager when I touched it this time. There was something tricksy in the undercurrent, though it was difficult to describe. It reminded me of the slippery playfulness of the fae, almost as if the stone itself had retained some of their magic as well as whatever distant ancestor had poured his or her power into Domm.

I narrowed my eyes at the construct and focused my magical grip more tightly on the heartstone. There was more going on here than just "watch and defend." It felt like he had other connections, similar to how Ryo was set up to interface with various magical objects around our house. Maybe that was where my father had gotten the idea?

Shrugging off the weird echoes resonating in the magic, and trying not to let my mind drift to the construct I'd powered up in college that had damaged the campus, I strained harder to feed more of my magic into his heartstone. Perspiration beaded on my skin as I fought to change the instructions imprinted on the golem. It felt like I was sitting atop a wild mustang, unsure if it would obey my commands or fling me from his back.

The two vertical slits in Domm's faceplate lit from within, glowing a deep ochre color as he began to animate and turned his head to face us. I startled, stepping back a bit, and noted Levi had done the same and was swearing a blue streak. When I glanced back, he had his hands raised slightly toward me, as if he were planning to grab me and run.

I pushed harder at his heartstone with my magic, suddenly nervous that maybe I wasn't strong enough to call him with us. I felt myself begin to pant slightly with the exertion and dipped into one of my power amplifiers to add more energy to my commands. As I did, though, I noticed there were places in his energy that felt immovable.

I could probably layer more commands on top of his previous ones, but removing his old directive felt impossible. I ground my teeth and pushed everything I had into weaving my will in around the currently placed instructions. They definitely had something to do with fae magic, but I couldn't pinpoint the specifics.

Come with me. Obey.

My skin crawled a little bit as I felt his power respond to mine, and more slits on his body began to light up from within. Some lit and some didn't, causing patterns that looked like runes to glow from his chest and arms, all with the same strange ochre cast as his 'eyes'.

I realized I had both my arms raised, and I was breathing heavily as if I had run a distance. And though I was suddenly exhausted and wanted nothing more than to take a breather, I had to scramble out of the way again instead.

Dust rained down amid the deafening roar of hundreds of boulders grinding against each other as Domm unfurled himself and crawled out of the room. The spiked protrusions on his back barely cleared the archway as he stepped over the staircase and onto the grass.

I half expected the ground to shake with the golem's move-ments, but other than the stones in their feet (and in Domm's case, his fists) most of their bodies were actually levitating. As they stretched to their full height the sounds of the stones clashing occurred less often, the gaps between them increasing to allow for better movement.

A glance at my mother on the balcony showed her fists both pressed to her mouth, in what I assumed was anxiety. But other than my unease with some of Domm's unknown previous programming—and my power exhaustion—I felt pretty good about my control over the golems and the trip ahead. I waved to show her all was well and got a tentative wave in return.

Levi had an entirely different reaction. I turned to find he had the backs of his fingers pressed over his mouth, only he was trying to hide a huge grin and his eyes were excited and sparking with heat.

"That—" He pointed at me. "—was *hot*. Why was that so hot? I'm pretty sure I just discovered a brand-new kink, and I don't really know how I feel about it."

"I… what?" His magic was so forceful that I just blinked repeatedly as my cheeks heated, and thanked my lucky stars my mother wasn't in ear-shot. Even with my ward, the enchantments felt seductive and sultry, and when paired with his sudden words I was left a little stunned. But… *pleased*.

I wondered what my face looked like and decided it was probably best not to know.

"I'm strangely aroused right now, and I don't think I could explain it if my life depended on it." My eyes started to drift down to see the evidence of his admission before I caught myself, and I jerked my gaze back up to meet his. His smirk looked like a dare.

We stared at each other in silence for a moment while I briefly fantasized about what it would feel like if he—*nope, Mom is totally staring at us from the balcony right now*. My glance toward the house served to remind Levi as well, and he shook himself out and braced a hand against the stone column next to him.

He glanced behind him toward the back of the crypt. "So, what's that one?" he asked, changing the subject. His enchantment hadn't lost much of its lure.

"That's Raald, a fire caster. Not much use underwater, which is why we're leaving him, but our records say he has a casting range of at least a kilometer." I barely made out Levi's low oath as he turned to stare at the fire golem, with its windswept hair and feathered wings, looking as if it had simply been frozen in stone.

"And these guys?" Levi gestured to the activated golems waiting for me on the lawn.

"These are juggernauts." I gestured to each as I spoke. "Leothen is purely melee. I thought Domm was as well, but he seems to have some fairy magic layered into his heartstone, and I can honestly say I have no idea what it's for. I can modify it, but I can't replace it, and I'm a little uneasy about that."

Levi's eyes narrowed at Domm. "Do you know what the runes say?"

"Nope. They're not elvish, or anything I recognize. You?"

He shook his head. "Could be a dead language, perhaps. I've never seen anything like it." He frowned and glanced between the three constructs. "These things could crush an entire army. Or, leading an army, could conquer an entire nation. And they're just sitting here, collecting dust at your family's estate."

"Guarding my family's estate," I corrected. "Still," I added, glancing between the imposing forms of the constructs, "I acknowledge it's a little overkill."

"Pretty sure just one of them is overkill," he muttered. "What happens if one gets hit by something big enough to break it? Like a cannon? Or a bomb?"

I shrugged and considered the golem. "Their magic would pull them back together. It would continue fighting until something shattered the heartstone. That's why their heartstones are embedded so deep inside," I explained. "Combat golems are built to protect the heartstone, so that it's hidden, while people who own a personal golem usually want the beauty of the stone on display."

He nodded and glanced at Ryo, with its heartstone floating in the air above its shoulders. "Well, now what?" He turned to me.

"Now..." I answered, opening one of my duffle bags and pulling out some rock climbing harnesses. "We put these on."

WE SPENT the day nestled in an oiled hammock suspended around Leothen's neck. Domm had too many moving parts for me to consider allowing him to carry us; I didn't relish the idea of getting squished between all the moving boulders. Leothen's torso and shoulders were a single piece, so they provided a stable surface for us to rest against.

Just above us, the construct's loosely curled, chiseled hair provided the perfect cubbies to store our bags and provisions. I'd needed to bundle up thoroughly against the chill, but other than that, I'd really enjoyed spending the hours talking with Levi, watching the scenery below as I listened to him sing, and playing with the cards and calling stones we'd packed for entertainment.

I loved his spirit. He was gregarious, mischievous, and easily amused, and he enjoyed teasing me gently and being teased in return. I quizzed him relentlessly about all the pranks he'd pulled on Grim and Jordan—everything from releasing a dozen fluffy baby bunnies in Grim's room to papering Jordan's room with Twilight posters and wearing a Team Jacob shirt whenever he was around.

He was far too curious about different ways he could startle Sidney into shifting unintentionally, and I wondered briefly if I should warn her before deciding it wouldn't do any good. She'd just be tense all the time, waiting for him to jump out at her like a jack-in-the-box. He'd seen the violence she was capable of. They would have to figure out their relationship with each other on their own.

When I asked him what had happened to the men who came to my shop last night, I assumed he was teasing me when he said he didn't know.

He gave a casual shrug. "No, I'm not joking. Sometimes it's better not to know. My best friend happens to be a reaper. No, not just happens to *be*—he *is* a reaper. It's who he is through and through. I learned a long time ago that sometimes I don't want answers to the questions I have. And even when I do want answers, he doesn't always feel obliged to give me them."

I probably looked like a gaping fish with the way my mouth was hanging open. "Maybe you don't want answers, but I do! Those guys came after me twice!" I should have called Enforcement regardless of the illicit sedatives.

Levi sighed and reached for me, quickly pressing a kiss to the top of my head before shifting his gaze between my eyes. "Grim might be a tight-lipped ass, but he's not going to let those men ever come near you again. If there's anyone in the world I can trust, it's him, and he knows how important you are to me. He'll make sure you're safe from them.

"I honestly don't know what happened, though. They were long gone after I got back from taking you to the Gate. Have you ever tried to catch up to a vampire when he starts running? Or a pretentious-ass reaper who can spawn a shadow horse out of nowhere? In the *dark*? I'll tell you how many times I've tried. *None*. I have to hang on to my dignity around those two when I can."

The absurdity of his description was just too much for me, and I burst out laughing. "All I can picture is a little kid on a tricycle trying to keep up with his big brothers on their cool-kid bikes." My chin trembled a little as I tried desperately to get a lock on my humor. His pride had already suffered enough.

"Welcome to my life, Empress. It's alright, you can laugh," he said indulgently as we swayed in the hammock.

We made camp deep in the Ruined Forests of Azyrdan. The name was a total misnomer; the towering trees were lush and verdant. A millennium and a half ago, dragons had burned the whole area to the ground, and the name had stuck. I cringed at the thought of all the trees we'd de-limbed on the way through. No matter how I tried, there just wasn't a good way to bush-whack with massive golems without some damage to the local flora.

We'd found a small meadow to park Leothen and Domm, then unpacked what we needed for the night. As dusk fell, Levi set about making a fire while I figured out what we were going to eat for dinner.

I dug through the supply rations, searching for the more perishable items since it made sense to go through those first, and was surprised to find some tiny foil packets tucked inside of one of the bundles. Pulling them out for closer inspection in the dim lighting, I tried to read the tiny print on the back but eventually flipped the connected row over and froze as I recognized the logo on the front.

Condoms.

Had Sidney...? No, she hadn't had access to any of the food

packs. That meant *my mom* had packed some condoms in with the food. And these were *human* condoms, which meant she'd made a special trip to the Void for them after I'd informed her I was bringing Levi along.

I. Could. Die.

"Elara?" Levi asked over my shoulder, and I realized I had made a choking sound. I whirled to face him, clutching the little packets to my chest like a squirrel. My face felt red-hot, and my heart was hammering in my chest a mile a minute. I knew I had nothing to be ashamed of, but I still felt caught.

I tried to answer, but only a squeak came out. Levi's eyes were trained on my hands, and to my horror, a length of five packets hung from my clutches. It was too dark for me to make out his expression, but I knew without a doubt he had no trouble making out what I held.

"Wow, Empress. Big night planned. I'm going to go ahead and get your disappointment out of the way by stating, for the record, that you're probably overestimating my stamina."

I knew I looked like a deer in the headlights, but I felt both shockingly amused by his words and intensely curious about the imagery he conjured. None of that came out, just an awkward squawk before I stuffed the condoms back where they came from in embarrassment.

"I didn't pack those," I stated emphatically, causing Levi to cackle with laughter. His amusement was catching, and I found myself fighting a grin. The combination of his enchantments and his contagious laughter was so delightfully attractive. "I didn't!"

He wiped a tear from his eye and bent to pull the strip from the bag for inspection. "I believe you, but what's the big deal? You're so shocked. It's just condoms."

"I just—" I froze for a moment, feeling like the gears in my head were stuck. "No, it's not *just* condoms. I was looking for *food* when all of a sudden I'm staring at a *massive amount* of condoms—"

"Yeah, it looks like a thirty-six pack." He was still pulling them out of the bag.

"—that were apparently packed by my *mother,* with the implication we would *use* them." There was so much there to unpack mentally that I didn't even know where to begin. Was she using this as a weird way to endorse our relationship? Was she vehemently stating she did not want me to have a child? Did she actually think I was going to need thirty-six condoms on a two-week delivery trip?

Levi chuckled and put them back. "Sure, it's odd, but she probably just wants to take care of you. I still don't understand your reaction." He gave me an oddly amused look as he began pulling mushrooms and greens from the bag, and I directed him to the tinned fish as well.

"I'm sorry, I was just—I was so flustered," I stammered. "I wasn't expecting condoms from my *mom* to be hidden in the *food*, and you've made it clear you want to take things slow, so I thought maybe it might look like I was expecting more from you, but obviously, I've never done that before, so clearly I'm fine waiting—" I snapped my teeth shut with a click to stem the torrent of words.

My skin felt hot, and I jerked my attention back to the food until Levi interrupted me with a flat, "What?"

I paused with a root vegetable in my hand to find his gaze locked on mine. "What do you mean, 'what'?"

"You said you've 'obviously never done that before'. What does that mean exactly?"

Oh. Well... Awkward. "I mean… I've never been with a guy." I knew I was well past the age most of my peers experienced physical intimacy, and I tried not to squirm under Levi's scrutiny.

Several heartbeats passed before he asked, "Ever?"

I shook my head, surprised by his surprise. I'd have figured it was completely obvious I had no experience with any of this.

"Do you just mean that you've… you've never had sex?" His eyes had an odd glint to them I didn't understand. This whole conversation was a reminder of how much I didn't know.

"No, I mean… I've never had a boyfriend, or any kind of relationship at all."

Levi blinked. "Oh. Well, neither have I." He went back to putting the mushrooms and fish in a pouch to warm over the fire and took a seat on a fallen log near my perch.

"Really?" I asked, a little surprised. "I guess that makes sense, not being able to touch girls, what with the whole bonding thing and all."

He turned and looked at me like I had two heads. "It doesn't work *that* fast," he chuckled. "I mean, I've... *been* with girls," he said diplomatically. "I just... didn't stay the night. Or ever see them again." He winced. "I realized after a few times that even that much left an unhealthy fixation, so eventually, I kept my distance altogether."

I fingered the vegetable in my hand for a moment as I thought about what this meant. He'd been with girls before me, which I knew logically was normal, though I was a little startled at the surge of jealousy I felt at the thought of it. Why had he risked being permanently bonded to someone like that? And why was he even risking it now, just spending time with me?

"What changed?" I asked hesitantly. "Why are you spending time with me?"

I couldn't help but worry that, if he thought about it too hard, maybe he would realize I wasn't worth the risk. Was anyone worth the risk? Being permanently bonded to someone for life, knowing they could walk away from him at any time?

Levi's eyes lifted to mine and warmed as he scanned my face, but his shrug was self-conscious. A small, self-deprecating grin claimed his mouth as he reached out to brush a lock of hair behind my ear with a finger. "I guess I'm pretty much already unhealthily fixated," he joked, but then his expression grew more serious as he studied my face.

I sank into the warmth in his countenance until I realized I'd probably given him the wrong idea about my experience level with... *physical* relationships. I was tempted to let it go, but it felt like a lie by omission. Not only that, but I frowned at the thought of how inexperienced I was with any kind of intimacy. He would figure it out eventually. Better to get it out now.

"I didn't just mean that I'd never... had a relationship." My frown deepened as I sliced the tuber into small, even rings. "I meant that I'd never been with any guy, at all."

His eyes snapped to mine with an intensity that confused me. "How is that possible?"

I shrugged slightly, feeling embarrassed, and sliced a second tuber before placing them in foil. I drew a deep breath and released it slowly. "I just haven't," I answered defensively. "I would say I haven't had the opportunity, but... Sidney says guys think I'm intimidating for whatever reason. I never wanted anyone... before."

When I peeked up at him from the corner of my eye, his eyes were hot and focused on my mouth. "I was really your first kiss?" he asked in a chuckle, sounding a little smug, his voice husky and caressing.

I didn't see why it would amuse him, but I caught myself beginning to lean into the sound of it. Before I could pull back, his fingers closed over mine, and he pulled me into his lap. Levi's palm pressed against my cheek, and he pulled me against him, brushing his lips against mine and wrapping his muscular arm around my back. He deepened his kiss, and I opened slightly to let him in, feeling his tongue slick against mine and enjoying the taste of him.

I gripped one rounded shoulder, marveling at the muscle and the feel of his collarbone, the cords of his neck. I pressed the other hand into his chest, gripping his shirt to keep him as close as I could. When I shifted my weight in his lap, I could feel his excitement, hard and insistent against my upper thigh.

The feel of his hardness pressing into me made me insane. I didn't try to understand it, but I needed more. I managed to turn just enough to slide my knee around his hip and settle deeper into his lap.

His lips felt like silk. The pleasure of his tongue teasing my mouth with promises of more, and the feeling of his body pressed into mine made me rock my hips, shifting against his erection with mindless need. The feeling it created made me gasp into his mouth, immediately craving more. Levi panted and clutched me tighter, kissing me harder and tensing his stomach muscles, arching to give me pressure back where I needed it.

I felt desperately empty as I rocked against him again, knowing this couldn't go anywhere and wanting it to anyway. How were we going to survive two entire weeks alone together? We couldn't. I needed him too desperately.

When he pressed against me again he groaned, wrapping me in ocean mist and sun-warmed sand. The magic of that sound nearly pulled me under as he clutched at me, and I fought against my need, trying to make the right choice to protect him.

"Siren," I gasped.

"Empress." His eyes were dark in the firelight, his pupils so blown out he looked drugged.

"Should we be doing this?" I whispered against his mouth.

"No." But he didn't stop immediately.

His movements slowed instead, and his hand moved to grip my rib cage, his thumb sliding down the side of my breast, feeling each rib on the way to my waist. He paused for a beat, wrapped both hands around my hips, and dragged my weight down his erection one last time before picking me up and setting me next to him.

He gripped the log on either side of him, his tendons standing out in stark relief against his arms, head hung low while he tried to catch his breath. I took a few steps back to seat myself on my rock, suddenly feeling chilled in the cold night air, and he turned his head slightly to watch me with a predatory gaze.

"Are you sure I'm the only siren in this camp?"

CHAPTER 20

THE MORNING RAIN was a fitting backdrop for my terrible mood.

Last night had proven to be an exercise in frustration as we finished dinner and set up camp. Levi had kept his distance from me throughout the evening after he'd kissed me, even going so far as to move his bedding up into the rocky ledges above the camp. He'd claimed that the heat from the fire was too much for him, and that he wanted to be able to see around us, but it was more than that.

Between being left wanting and falling asleep alone in a cold, strange place, I was feeling strangely morose. It wasn't his fault. I knew that. He'd been clear with me. I'd been the one to remind him he needed to stop last night.

But my heart wanted what it wanted. And my heart wanted Levi.

Even now, gazing at him through the constant drizzle and morning fog, I felt oddly alone. We were separated by a mere couple of feet, but the knowledge that he purposely kept that small distance between us made it feel like an impenetrable wall.

The rain had definitely affected my mood, though Levi seemed rather unaffected by it. It had started to fall during the night, and by the time we were harnessed and situated on Leothen, it had turned into a full-on deluge. I was bundled against the rain and the chill, but Levi looked entirely unconcerned, sprawled on his end of the hammock.

I let my eyes follow the long lines of him and marveled at his hardy nature. How could someone so beautiful be so masculine and sturdy at the same time? He sat forward and shook the water out of his hair, draping his arms across the tops of his knees, and I noticed a subtle mottled pattern of dull blues and greens had appeared over the tricep of his right arm.

"Maybe I was wrong about you turning into a frog," I teased him gently, wanting some of the levity back that we'd shared yesterday. I nodded at his arm and earned a crooked grin, which made my heart thud painfully.

Levi twisted his arm around to glance at it, hiking up his wet short sleeve to get a better look, and then shrugged. "If it goes beyond the patchy color-morph on my back and arms, I'll be as surprised as you. You'd think I could have gotten something useful, like water breathing, or fins, but no. Just some dorsal camouflaging."

I rolled my eyes at him, softening a little. "And the enchantments, the ability to see in the dark, and some serious cold tolerance."

He huffed. "Is the cold tolerance really a perk if I overheat easily, though? Kinda seems like a wash to me." His gaze slid to my building smile and turned a little heated. Eventually, he blew out a breath and turned to focus on the passing trees. The last of my sullen disposition slid away as I realized that he was frustrated too.

We were in this together.

"It's getting hard to see the ground here," Levi noted, peering down at the fog rolling through the trees and across the forest floor. "Should we take them to higher ground?"

That was probably a good idea. "There are some cave systems I'm trying to stay away from to the north. Let me dig out the chip with the maps on it." It would be worth it to spend a little longer going around them and avoid the possibility of a cave-in.

I stood carefully amid the rocking of the giant and readjusted my harness. Using what little upper body strength I had, I pulled myself up toward the rucksack containing the calling stones.

I felt Levi's hand on my leg helping to steady me and turned to give him a grateful smile. How I was going to get through the trip without constantly wanting to be plastered to him, I had no idea, but what I did know was that he was worth it. I loved his heart and his mind, and those alone would have to be enough for now. And they were.

With that thought, I boosted myself up into the cubby where we'd tied down our bags and dug through them until I found the pocket I was looking for. Before I could get it open, I heard a thunderous crash of splintering wood and felt my stomach lurch as the stone I was sitting on dropped out from underneath me.

My body pitched backward. I had no chance of grabbing a better hold on the rain-slicked golem as it swung forward, and I was launched with bone-jarring force from the golem's shoulder.

I only had time to turn my head and search for Levi, my terrified eyes locking with his shocked ones as I hit the end of my tether and heard the metal connections snap.

The trajectory of the golem had it down before I was, and I could see Leothen's prone form flattened below me as I was thrown through the trees.

Slashing pain lit my body as I splintered through tree limbs all the way down, finally plunging into icy water far below, full of downed trees. I couldn't see their submerged forms in the dark, murky-green water, but I felt their rotting masses as I slammed into them just feet below the surface.

Air exploded from my lungs on impact in a roar of bubbles. Frigid, icy water rushed down my throat to fill its absence. A few stunned heartbeats passed before darkness stole my thoughts, and the numbness in my limbs crept into the rest of my body.

I tried to struggle, shooting the last of my energy into the sentries, my wasps, anything I could reach in a desperate last-ditch plea for help, though I knew this was beyond their abilities. A heaviness settled in my lungs and silenced my mind. Something hard hit my chest and constricted around my upper body before everything went completely black.

PAIN.

I couldn't be dead yet. It hurt too much. In my ribs, the back of my skull, and multiple burning slashes along my skin. A surge of blinding pain in my chest forced bitter, fetid water up my throat and out of my mouth. Rough, wet sand scraped against my cheek as my body convulsed under a steady, crushing rhythm.

"Breathe!"

Levi.

My lungs. No matter how much I choked and gasped, I couldn't get air in them.

"Elara, *live.* Just... live! *Please, live.* I don't care about the bond. You can have it! I'm yours. Just breathe. Please."

His voice came from above me, the wild terror in it piercing through my pain like an arrow. I fought hard with my stunned body, trying desperately to obey, but I couldn't. The darkness clung to me, unrelenting and immensely heavy.

The sharp, crushing press against my chest and back continued to force water out of my nose and mouth, and every time it did, the pain was enough to send me under again. Flickers of memories flashed through my mind as Levi's voice continued to beg me to breathe.

Levi playing his guitar on the street and singing about a January wedding and needing a woman to protect him from the darkness all around him.

Flicker.

His mischievous smile as he clutched a locket with my hair inside against his chest.

Flicker.

The way his lips curved against mine as we crouched in a darkened alley.

Flicker.

Levi, looking out the train window as he admitted he didn't want to be away from me.

Until finally, the darkness took me.

EVERY BREATH WAS a labored pant that rattled, wet and thick. I coughed, then groaned because of the flare of pain it brought with it.

The constriction around my shoulders tightened slightly, and fear ricocheted through me. Trees were catching their limbs around me, wrapping around my throat, and dragging me back down to the bottom of the pond.

"Shhh, I've got you." A quiet murmur in my ear.

Levi.

"I've got you. You're safe now."

Everywhere was cold, except where my body pressed against his, where warm skin pressed against my face and torso, his arms cradling me gently against him. The pounding in my head kept me from opening my eyes, but I could hear the crackling of a small fire behind me.

My mind reeled, but exhaustion still entombed me, and I hurt in so many places. I felt my body shivering, but whether that was from the cold or from shock, I didn't know. I should probably be in a hospital.

"Potion," I whispered, remembering the healing potions I'd packed and trying to remind Levi. Thankfully, I'd gone over all the safety supplies on our first day. "The healing potions," I tried again, a little clearer.

I felt his hand caressing my back and noticed I was wrapped in my bedding, but my hair was damp. "I already got it and gave it to you over an hour ago, that's when the shaking started. I put the rest of the salve you gave me on your cuts but some of the lacerations are pretty deep. I'm hoping the potion is legit and takes care of those. Just rest now."

I wanted to stay with him, but the exhaustion was just too much. I had no choice but to follow his advice as the darkness took me again. My last conscious thought was that he probably shouldn't be holding me like this, but I couldn't make my mouth move to voice the words.

THE NEXT TIME I WOKE, the sky was dark, and the fire was down to nothing but coals. I was covered in blankets and draped across Levi's chest, and I immediately noticed how warm and flushed his skin felt.

"Levi?"

I shifted and tried to sit up, but his arms constricted slightly, holding me against him.

"How're you feeling?" he asked, sounding groggy. I felt surprisingly fine. Good, even. I stretched my limbs and took a deep breath experimentally, only to find I felt normal and rejuvenated. I didn't even feel the usual brain fog that was common upon waking.

"I feel… great, actually," I answered, starting to sit up, which allowed me to notice I was *naked* under my blankets. "Levi!" I quickly dropped back to his chest—before it occurred to me that pressing my naked body against him in an effort to hide my nudity didn't really make any sense. He pulled me closer to him and situated my arms under his. Trying to keep me warm?

"What are you doing?" My voice was breathless. I couldn't help but notice how soft his skin felt against my own. His muscles were taut and firm, but the skin under my fingers felt like satin.

"You were wet and cold." His voice was a dazed-sounding whisper. "I had to cut your clothes off when I pulled you out, to check for injuries. It was hard to get you warm again, and you just kept shivering… but I think that was the potion working." His enchantment wrapped me in an embrace as warm as his physical one, but his voice had a hazy, distant quality that concerned me, and his words were slurred.

Concern had me sitting up despite my nudity, pulling his face down so I could see him. His cheeks were obviously flushed, even by the light of the glowing coals, and his eyes had a thousand-yard stare I recognized from the night of the rave. His breath was coming in quick pants, and I remembered what he said about not being able to sweat.

"Are you overheating?" I cast my eyes around in the darkness, looking for water, finding a canteen within arm's reach and grabbing for it, trying to rip the cap off when he was slow to respond.

The blanket fell off my shoulders as I sat up, and just as I'd suspected, I was really, really naked.

I poured water on his damp shirt, which I found nearby, and wiped it down his face and chest, wringing water into his hair and then dribbling more water from the canteen into his mouth. His eyes drifted down to my chest, but his expression held no more than dazed delirium.

I needed to get him away from the fire. I got to my knees over him, doing my best to ignore my nudity—failing but trying not to care—and tried to figure out how I was going to move him when his hand smoothed down my forearm and closed gently around my wrist.

"Don't leave me." A murmured request.

"I'm not leaving you," I answered, confused by his reaction. "We need to get you away from the coals. Why are you so hot?" I hooked my arm under him and tried to haul him up, but —*surprise*—he barely budged.

"I didn't want you to be cold," he slurred. "You kept shivering."

I braced my feet on the ground and shoved at his torso. He slid a good foot on the blanket, and then, finally deciding to follow my lead, shuffled farther away from the heat. He collapsed in an exhausted slump and reached for me again, but I batted his hand away and wiped him down with cool water again.

"I understand that, but you're going to get heatstroke like this," I muttered. "Once I started to warm up, you should have cooled yourself down." At least his pants were still slightly damp. "Besides, we're in the Boundlands. You probably shouldn't be in contact with me that much here, right? The bonding problem?" I heard the panic in my voice.

"Too late."

My eyes shot to his in shock. "Too late for what?"

"The bond." He didn't move his head, but his eyes were locked on mine, sober and honest. "It's permanent."

His voice held no emotion. In fact, he almost sounded bored as matter-of-fact as he was. I felt my jaw drop open and tried to close it a few times without success as I struggled with a barrage of a million different emotions.

The two warring the hardest were guilt and joy. Joy because I loved him, and come hell or high water, he was mine now. And I *wanted* him. Guilt because it hadn't been something he wanted, and now he was trapped with me.

Guilt surged forward.

"I'm so sorry," I gasped.

"I'm not." His expression was still sober, and far calmer than I felt in that moment.

"Levi, you didn't want this. You saved my *life*, and now... now you're trapped with me, and you don't have any choice!" My eyes burned, and I felt hot tears spill over and make tracks down my cheeks.

His gaze followed their descent down my face.

"I've always had a choice, to an extent." His words were slow, but a little clearer this time. "I could have followed my instincts and stayed away from the mouthy little tinker who accused me of theft, but I think I fell in love with her the moment I laid eyes on her."

When he raised a knuckle to wipe a tear off my cheek, I leaned into his touch.

"You're only saying that because you're overheated and don't know any better yet." He rested his hand against my face, and I leaned hard into his palm, crouching on my knees before him, my tears becoming quiet sobs.

"Elara, my little Empress"—he gathered me against him as he spoke, tucking my head under his chin—"I just forced water out of your lungs and held you in my arms for hours as you shook. I thought I would lose you the whole time, and it destroyed me. I realized—bond or not—if I lost you, I would never be the same again. My choice was already made."

He stroked my skin and held me against him for a long time, while his body cooled and my heart calmed. When he finally spoke again, his voice was a whisper.

"I will never insist that you stay with me, though I'll always want it. Always." He swallowed thickly, and his enchantment pushed and pulled in the same sentence, as if he were focusing on it and trying to lessen its effects. "But I want *you* to have a choice. I won't demand anything from you."

There was a hint of desolation in his voice, as if he knew his worst fear was coming true but he was trying not to brace himself. It broke me.

"My choice is already made." I didn't hesitate at all as I leaned over him and took his mouth with mine.

CHAPTER 21

———⚜———

His response was immediate, parting his lips enough to meet my tongue with his own in a kiss that surprised me with its gentleness. In my periphery, I saw him raise his hands to embrace me, only to hesitate with them in the air for a few beats before he settled them on my back.

I didn't want his gentleness right now. The fire building in me burned too bright, was too consuming. I *loved* this man. And he was mine. If he didn't regret it, I wasn't going to either. I let joy win.

I deepened our kiss, wanting more of him, and smoothed my fingers from his jaw to the rounded caps of muscle on his shoulders. I reveled in how masculine he felt under my hands, his collarbones and chest substantial and strong under my smaller frame. He was sturdy and solid, and I loved it.

I trailed my fingers down his stomach, and he flinched and flexed his abs on reflex. His breath hitched. Fingers tangled in my hair. He brushed his lips along my jaw, kissing and nipping his way to the side of my neck, sucking gently as he scraped his nails along the back of my scalp.

I heard myself moan, and before I even knew I'd moved, I was in his lap again, straddling his hips. Needing to be closer to him. Right back where I'd been last night. But this time I was really, *really* naked, and he was *mine*.

Levi tensed underneath me, taking a few heaving breaths. "What are you doing, little Empress?" His voice was hoarse, and I grinned at the endearment as his enchantment rolled over me, tearing across my ward.

"I love you," I whispered against his cheek as I nuzzled closer, and the truth of those words settled deep in my bones. "And if the bond is already permanent, then I want to have you. Right now." I leaned forward against him to nip at his collarbone and felt his hands clutch at my back in response.

"But you're not touching me," I said.

I sat back in his lap to look at him and felt his hardness against my thigh, evidence that he wanted me too. At least… I hoped? I looked between his eyes, suddenly self-conscious of my impulsiveness, to find them dazed and so black his irises were just the slightest sliver of blue around the rim.

He groaned and flexed up against me once, panting to catch his breath. "I stripped you… because of your wounds. I didn't want… to take advantage." He kept his eyes fixed squarely on my face.

I narrowed my eyes at him in defiance and grabbed his arms, moving them until his hands were on the sides of my breasts where he'd put them last night. "You can touch me."

He surged up from under me, pressing into me and rolling me on to my back with a groan that sounded more like a growl. His mouth was on mine as he rocked against my center with a maddening friction that only made me crave him more.

He braced himself near my head, making me feel bracketed in and protected. He was everywhere. I'd never experienced what it felt like to lie underneath so much muscle and strength, but it made me feel protected and safe and I thrilled in it.

He finally, finally began to touch and caress me with his free hand, dragging it down my ribs to my waist, palming my breast and thumbing my nipple, cradling and stroking my flesh.

I gave in to my own curiosity, trailing my fingers down his abs and hesitating at the waistband of his pants to give him time to object. When he pressed himself against me, I dipped my fingers inside, sliding them along the intriguing hardness I found there. The skin felt different here, velvety and soft, utterly delicious.

Levi's breath shuddered out of him, and he pressed himself harder into my palm, trailing his mouth to my neck and giving me a nip with teeth so sharp it made me gasp. He soothed it with his tongue and brushed his hand down the back of my thigh, making me squirm. I needed more. He was teasing me. It left me feeling desperate, and a little unhinged.

I began pushing his pants down further when his fingers brushed around my thigh and dipped inside me. *Oh. That... was necessary.* He caressed me, stroked me, winding me tighter, pressing his palm against me hard enough to make me choke on a gasp.

"Oh—"

He kissed my neck, stroking me higher, but stilled as I clutched at him, struggling to get closer, gasping for breath.

"Oh. Please. Please, Levi. I need..." I didn't know what I needed, but I was desperate for more. I could scream for it.

"I know," he murmured against my jaw. "I've got you. I know what you need."

I wanted to sob with relief.

He began pressing harder with the palm of his hand, curling his finger inside of me, rubbing a place that had me stiffening and chasing his hand, working me higher until I felt like I was going to snap. I was panting with desperation.

It wasn't enough. "I need you. I need more. I want you inside me, please." I was begging. I didn't care. I was out of my mind with need for him. I squeezed his shaft harder, causing him to thrust toward me on a groan.

"I know," he whispered. "I just... It's probably going to hurt." He took a few panting breaths, never pausing in his rhythmic ministrations.

"I want to take care of you first because you probably won't orgasm your first time." His magic was stronger than any time I'd ever felt it, shaking my ward and reaching through with writhing tendrils.

The relentless rhythm he set pushed me over, and I gasped, bucking against his hand, one arm clutching at his torso hard, the other still in his pants.

"Yeah," he murmured as I came and finally began to quiet in his arms, "that's good. There she is."

He withdrew his hand and braced himself over me, kissing me sweetly on the lips. "Are you sure?" he asked and nuzzled my cheek. "We can wait, Elara."

I felt wrung out and supple, but I still wanted him.

I wanted this.

I nodded and kissed his mouth, still trying to catch my breath. "Please."

"Let me... get a..." He stood quickly, stepping over to a bag a few steps away. *Condom. Right.* I cringed inwardly, thinking about how they'd gotten there, but he was back before I had a chance to dwell on it.

He had it open and on before I could even think to try to watch, but he didn't press into me right away. Instead, he braced himself over me and took several deep breaths, placing kisses on my cheek and jaw.

He kissed my mouth, deep and covetous, his lips soft and pliant, his tongue teasing and caressing. His body melted into me, his arm reaching under the arch of my back to gather me against him, his tongue brushing against mine in a rhythm that mimicked what his finger had done.

Very quickly, I found myself panting, squirming against him again, feeling empty and aching, needing relief. Levi nestled down deeper between my legs and fitted his body against mine, but paused.

The hand under my back stroked me gently, and I realized he was drawing patterns on my skin. It took a moment for me to blink through the fog of desire he had created in me to realize he'd traced the letters "ok" on my skin.

My eyes locked with his and found a question there. He wanted to know if this was okay, if he had final permission to take me in this way. My heart melted, realizing that he wanted to be absolutely sure of my consent and found a way to ask me without letting his enchantment affect my response.

"Yes."

The first press was slow and caused him to hiss, his breath shuddering out of him as I gripped his shoulders. I couldn't help but tense and felt my mouth drop open from the pressure. The second press was painful, and he froze over me when I whimpered.

He whispered an apology, stroking my hair, brushing the back of his fingers down my cheek, placing gentle kisses on my lips and face. Slowly the pain faded back to pressure, and I rolled my hips toward him to encourage him forward, coaxing a groan from him as he settled deeper inside me.

Withdrawing and thrusting forward again caused me to tense, expecting more pain, but when none came, I relaxed, allowing him to cup the arch of my back again and pull me higher into his hips. The rolling, thrusting pressure still felt tender, but I could feel my body being pushed toward pleasure.

The intimacy of the act was enough to fill my heart with powerful longing and joy, desperate affection. Feeling his body join with mine was a heady rush that had me clutching at his shoulders, his neck, anything I could reach to try to get closer to him.

Levi's breathing sounded like he was in pain, but his eyes were lit with ecstasy. Watching his muscles flex and bunch as he filled me, stretched me, was a pleasure in itself. I wrapped a leg around his back, endeavoring to get closer as his movements became more forceful, stroking me higher and winding me tighter.

His name was a sigh on my lips as he slid a hand into my hair and gently gripped a handful at the back of my head, tilting my head back and exposing my throat to his mouth.

"Elara, tell me you're mine."

His words were broken, gasping things against my neck, made a thousand times more potent by the enchantments layered into each one. My ward was no match for his passion, but it wouldn't have mattered anyway, because I'd belonged to him for longer than I wanted to admit.

He was mine, and I was his. I wanted this man's heart more than anything I could imagine.

"I'm yours," I confessed. He gripped my body tightly against him and pressed into me forcefully as he came apart in my arms, shaking through his release.

He held me close and buried his face in my neck as he stilled, his breathing labored and uneven. I rained kisses on his cheekbone, his jaw, anywhere I could reach as I smoothed my hands down his back and across his ribs.

"I need you," he rasped.

"I'm yours," I answered.

———

I TRACED THE LONG, sinuous line of the kraken's arm in the tattoo on Levi's skin. The fire crackled behind me, burning low and only putting off a little warmth. Levi had bundled me in blankets and now held me loosely, brushing a finger against my skin occasionally as if to reassure himself that I was still here.

I still felt a little dazed as I thought back over everything that had happened today. So much had taken place that it almost felt like a dream or something that had happened to someone else. Still, one point of confusion remained.

"Levi?"

"Hm?"

"What happened to my golems?"

"Mm... I was more concerned with getting the water out of your lungs than I was with checking on the indestructible rock monsters." His voice was a drowsy mumble, his enchantments subdued well below the level my ward could handle. "But when I was searching for the bags to find that healing potion, it appeared your stony steed had fallen into a hole."

I felt my eyebrows draw down as I considered that. The cave systems I'd been skirting around must have stretched farther south than the maps showed. I dreaded the task of inspecting Leothen for damage in the morning.

"Also, the jagged looking one is glowing blue now, instead of that yellowish-orange. And it's kind of... pulsing."

"It... *what?*"

CHAPTER 22

LEVI'S initial assessment proved correct: Leothen had fallen in a hole.

Actually, the ground had caved in and swallowed him up to mid-thigh, thus causing my precious family heirloom to face plant unceremoniously and launch me into the swamp of sorrows. That wasn't its actual name; I'd made it up on account of the fact that at least half of my gem sets and power stones were now lying in the bottom of it.

I surveyed for damage and didn't find anything other than a rather large, watery cavern with newly uprooted trees sliding into it, and a *heinously* muddy golem. Leothen had managed to catch himself before he had completely flattened—which was fortunate for Levi, who'd been anchored to the golem's chest—and then straightened as best he could while waiting for further instructions.

Domm, meanwhile, was glowing with a pulsing, dusky blue light that caused different runes to light up on the faces of his boulders. We'd triggered some kind of signal, or maybe I had, when I'd sent that last panicky blast of energy out after I'd nearly drowned.

I had no way of knowing if the signal was doing something, or if it was telling me the golem was broken like some kind of primeval systems failure warning, because it was part of his ancient magic I didn't recognize. It didn't seem to be impeding my ability to control him—he responded to my attempts to interface with him just fine—but I couldn't turn it off either.

I sighed, feeling more than a little creeped out by the unknown, and turned to find Levi a few steps behind me. He offered me a hand up as I scaled back up an uprooted tree to get back to our campsite, helping me over limbs and holding back vegetation to make it easier for me to navigate. Whether it was the newly formed bond or the trauma of pulling my unconscious body from the water yesterday, I wasn't sure, but he'd been within arm's reach all morning. I didn't mind at all, but it took a little getting used to after his previous careful distance.

I blushed furiously at the memory of how thoroughly we'd erased that distance the night before and fought the urge to let my eyes linger on him overly long. I'd caught myself gazing, starry-eyed, at his mouth, his hands, the lines of his neck and shoulders all morning.

We have work to do, I reminded myself, scrubbing at the goosebumps on my arms.

I made my way back to our camp and stood on the muddy bank, staring out at the murky water with hard eyes. I knew I should be grateful simply for the fact that I was alive, but I was irritated about the magical gemstones I'd lost in the fall. I'd created most of them myself, spanning back years, and I didn't have replacements for some of them. I'd wanted to have them when I created the new golem for the sprites, and I doubted I would have time to recreate them.

I gritted my teeth and sent my magic out in little feelers, curious to see if I could find any of them beneath the water. I was pleasantly surprised to find that not only could I feel a few of the stones down in the depths, but that the two wasps I'd been wearing yesterday were there, as well, and responded to me. I called them to me, excited I could at least retrieve those.

"What are you doing?" Levi asked a few beats before my wasps broke the surface.

"Getting some of my things back."

He tensed beside me as the wasps came in, so I sent them to wait with their companions currently in our baggage.

"What all did you lose?" he asked distractedly.

"At least half of the amulets I equip daily, but at least I got my wasps."

He ripped off his shirt and handed it to me, toeing off his boots as I gaped at his suddenly naked chest.

"What are you doing?" I asked as he stripped off his pants. My eyes darted around awkwardly, unsure where to look. Years of ingrained modesty couldn't be erased in one night.

"Getting your stuff back. I don't let water take what's mine. Or yours." He rolled his eyes and dove beneath the surface. The water was a dark, muddy green. I wouldn't have been able to see my hand in front of my face, but he hadn't hesitated.

I waited a minute, possibly two, before I began to grow concerned. How long could a non-water-breathing part-mer hold his breath? This seemed excessive. What was living down there?

My pulse was hammering when Levi finally broke the surface a few feet in front of me and stood to walk to shore. He wiped the water from his face with one hand as it poured from him in rivulets and extended the other to me to drop his finds in my palm. My hair chains, several clips, multiple loose stones. A small thrill broke through my anxiety at having some of my amulets back, but only just.

"That scared me," I hissed at him. "What if something ate you? Do you actually have gills?"

He leaned to the side and shook his hair out. "No gills. There's nothing living in there that I saw, other than some fish and a few terrapins." His expression said I amused him. "I searched for more of your things, but I think anything else might have sunk into the mud at the bottom. I'm sorry."

He padded over to his backpack with as much concern for his nudity as a shifter and dug for a towel, pulling it out and beginning to dry himself.

"Thank you," I said, "this is far more than I expected to retrieve."

I studied the pattern changes on his wet skin, mottled shades of dull blues and greens across his back and shoulders, down the backs of his arms. There were darker grey striations across his spine, mostly concentrated around his lower back. The texture looked different too, as if he had a small ridge along his spine on his upper back. As he dried himself, the pattern dulled until I couldn't tell if it was there or I was just imagining it in places.

I started toward him to take him his clothing and dropped my head to focus on navigating the mud squishing under my feet. When I looked back up, Levi was frozen, staring into the woods with wide eyes. I followed his gaze and blinked a few times, confused.

Standing a short way off among the trees was a large white deer with antlers that held spectral flames curling up between the rack. Every time he moved, the world seemed to flicker out of existence for a blink where he'd just been, giving a dizzying effect that made him hard to look at.

"Levi?"

"… Yeah?"

"Is that a spectral stag?" My voice sounded hoarse.

"I think so."

My forehead drew down as I stared at it in confusion. Spectral stags were legendary, mythical. They were stories the dryads liked to tell occasionally to entertain their saplings. Legend had it they were always some kind of messenger or led children to safety if they were lost in the deep woods. This one just stood there, staring at us with eyes the same blueish white as the color of his flames. I swallowed thickly.

"What do you think it wants?" I asked. I wanted to look at Levi, to see his expression, but I was afraid that, if I did, the stag would be gone when I looked back.

"… I don't have any idea," he said, his voice hushed.

The deer lowered his head to sniff the ground, gave us one last glance, and wandered off back into the woods as if it were the most ordinary thing in the world. His footprints left behind a blueish spectral glow, but each one only lasted for a few seconds before it faded away to nothing.

I blinked rapidly, trying to clear my thoughts. "Do you think it wants us to follow it?" Wouldn't it have had a message of some kind? Did they just hang out randomly in the woods? *So many questions.*

"Uh…" I turned to find Levi staring back at the golem. "If it does, it's probably gonna take us a while to get going."

Right. Mud covered golem, broken equipment, a camp to pack up. I turned to see if the stag was waiting for us somewhere, but he was gone.

"You should probably… put some clothes on," I murmured to Levi as I hurried about packing up our gear.

⁂

EVEN THOUGH WE HUSTLED, it took much longer than usual to load up, on account of having to attempt to fix my harness and directing Leothen safely out of the pit he was waiting in without it caving in further.

Levi wanted to follow the stag, but we'd already lost a day in our delivery schedule. He argued it wouldn't hurt to head in the direction the stag had left, due to the potential for another cave in. It wasn't exactly the way I'd planned to travel, but I decided it was probably the area least likely to suffer another problem based on the locations of known mines and natural caves I had access to. We could veer back toward our projected route as the day progressed.

Domm shuffled along behind us with his gorilla-like gait, still pulsing with his strange blue glow, radiating ancient magic with each pulse. Every once in a while, I would think I'd caught a glimpse of the stag, far ahead of us, on a ridge or in a clearing, but on closer inspection, there was never anything there. Levi wasn't much help there because the midday sun was too bright for his sensitive eyes.

Eventually, I gave up looking and turned to something more productive, recreating some of the amulets I'd lost in the lake. They wouldn't be perfect, because I didn't have all my tools, and the extra stones I packed weren't exact matches for what I was making, but they would do. And if I was honest with myself, they would more than do—they would be great. I needed to relax my standards occasionally.

We sat closer to the middle of the hammock today, our legs tangling as I worked with my gems and Levi worked on his music. I asked him to tell me about his childhood, and he described growing up on the ocean cliffs with his dad, wishing he felt part of any community.

"The mer look down on landlocked people," he explained, "and even though I had friends around, and my dad, I always felt drawn to the sea in a way that no one else seemed to. Even Grim couldn't really fill that hole."

I frowned, imagining Levi's loneliness. "I would have thought your enchanted lure would have surrounded you with friends."

His laugh was bitter. "Growing up with that was a mind trip, having to learn to differentiate between friends and groupies. There were always people who wanted to hang out, but they made it feel like I had to be talking constantly or entertaining them somehow. There wasn't that give and take that a real friendship has, and in the end, their fascination with me just felt empty."

If he'd been part of mer society, he probably would have been insulated from that, since they were used to sirens and could have given him advice on how to handle it. It made me angry that he hadn't had help navigating those aspects of his life.

I thought of my father, a pure-blooded elf, and the resentment I would feel if his people rejected me, a child born of a mostly human mother. "How is it that the mer will breed with landlocked people, like your father, and yet shun them at the same time?" That part didn't make sense to me.

He shrugged as he took a moment to glance at the trees and gather his thoughts. "I think it's just the drive to procreate, honestly. They can come out on land to barter and trade, so it makes sense that, occasionally, they'd develop relationships with people they meet, even if the ocean always eventually calls them home. And mer birth rates are so low that, when they breed with races that are more prolific—like humans—you're going to see a rise in hybrid conceptions. But other than the desire to sow a few wild oats, we're not of any interest to them."

I scowled at that, feeling fiercely protective of Levi's feelings, but he moved the conversation along to happier memories of finding treasures washed up on the beach and exploring crevices and caves in the cliff walls with Grim.

I noticed something odd as I was powering up one of my gems. Levi was telling me a story about the time he'd changed Grim's auto-signature to "Prim-Reaper", and his words caused a strange kind of reverb in the stone as I pushed my energy into it. I wasn't sure what to make of it, but later, as he was working on his composition, I had to ask him to pause a moment. He'd been humming his tune as he wrote the notes, and the enchantment was so strong that it was interfering with the magic I was infusing into the stone.

All in all, it was a lovely way to spend the afternoon, working side by side on our projects and watching the forest drift by. It felt like we were able to exist in the moment for the first time together, ignoring outside pressures and what the future might hold. What else could be done? We were doing everything we could, and no amount of fretting was going to speed the trip along.

I loved having his company, just existing with each other and doing our own thing, and the way he absentmindedly touched me with the back of his hand, just because he could. I tried not to let my mind drift, because when it did, it inevitably wandered back to the night before and the way Levi had felt in my arms. The resulting ache and twinge in my body told me I needed some time to heal. I felt like my cheeks were permanently stained with pink, and to my surprise, his seemed to be too.

Instead, I studied him as he wrote, the way the wind tossed his dark blond hair and the way he crinkled his eyes against the sun. His mouth would purse just slightly when he pressed his pencil against the page, and his jaw would flex when he was frustrated. His dark eyebrows always came together when he had to erase.

It surprised me a little how comfortable I was with him, more than just enjoying his presence, but how completely natural our interactions and conversations felt. I'd never had this kind of ease outside of my friendships with Sidney or Rafe. I wanted to know everything about him—what made him tick, what wounds he carried, what brought him joy.

We ended our blissful day of chatting and working in a small glen where we could set up camp, instead of the inn I'd planned on, because we were still off course from our decision to follow the white stag. Tomorrow we would correct our course enough to make it to an inn the following night, and all would be back to plan.

⚬⚬✦⚬⚬

I WOKE TO A COLD, dark morning and Levi's arm curled around my waist. The fire pit was silent, which meant the coals had gone out, and I turned to burrow further into Levi for his warmth. He groaned and moved his arm to my shoulder, pulling me closer before I felt him stiffen.

"Elara," he breathed my name into my hair. "It's here."

I looked over my shoulder and was startled to find the white stag standing on the edge of our glen, staring up at Domm who was still pulsing his creepy blue light. I tensed as the ghostly apparition strode closer to us, pausing to inspect Leothen, then made its way to our fire pit.

His movements roiled my stomach, flickering in and out of existence as he did, and the long, proud antlers bracketing his spectral flames flickered the most. I recognized his magic as being similar to what Domm was sending out in little bursts, but other than that, it was like nothing I'd ever felt before.

Levi was holding his breath, and when the stag took a few more steps toward us, he was already moving, dragging me backward a few inches, away from the deer. It stopped and eyed us warily before leaning down to sniff my head. It took a step back, leading Levi to loosen his grip slightly, then turned and ambled into the trees, where it stood watching us for several minutes before disappearing into the forest again.

"What was *that?*" My voice came out in a croak, and I sat up to clear my throat.

"He sniffed your hair."

I shot him an incredulous look and opened my mouth to explain that I knew very well exactly what the enormous, flickering, transparent deer had done, considering I was right here when it happened—I just didn't *understand* it. But before I could get a word out, another thought crossed my mind.

"Can spectrals even smell things on our plane?"

Levi shrugged. "We should follow it."

I frowned at him, then looked back at where the stag had disappeared. "That isn't the direction we're going though. It'll take us farther off course."

Sure, nobody ever talked about a spectral stag outside of stories of it delivering messages or helping someone, but those were legends and who knew how much truth was in them. Maybe he just wandered around in the woods like a normal deer sometimes. I didn't know his life.

"Elara, it showed up at our camp two mornings in a row. Or is that common for an empress of your standing?" His voice was as wry as his grin.

I rolled my eyes and huffed. "I don't have any idea what that thing wants, but I do know that I have an *entire city* waiting on these golems as their *first* line of defense." I tried to explain more seriously. "We can't waste time on a wild goose chase on the off chance that a spectral *might* want us to follow it. We're not lost, we're not in danger, and we're already a day behind thanks to me being slung into the pond of pain."

Levi opened his mouth to argue, and then the gears got stuck. I probably should have kept a lid on the alliterative nonsense this early in the morning. He shook his head and scrubbed his hand through his hair. "I get that. I do. But that's a *spectral stag*," he groused. "When do those just show up and not have a reason?"

I started to interrupt, but he cut me off.

"Just—what if he knows something we don't? You almost died two days ago, Elara. I thought I'd lost you." His voice broke on the last sentence, and my eyes shot to his to find him imploring me with unshed tears that pierced my heart. "There could be anything in these woods," he continued firmly. "Hidden mine shafts, wyverns, basilisks… anything. Two days ago proved we're not invincible even with your golems. If he's trying to lead us around danger, and we ignore him, it could delay us further or worse."

I could tell by his expression and the stubborn set of his jaw how much of a battle he was prepared to wage if I fought him on this.

I sat for a moment, contemplating his words, feeling my guilt compound itself for scaring him with my injury. He was right about one thing, arriving with the golems a little late would be better than not arriving at all if something happened to us. I took a moment to weigh my options. "I guess we could start off in that direction and see what happens," I hedged.

Just for a little while. I could always course-correct later in the day.

After another rushed packing job and cold breakfast on the go, we were loaded up and back on the move. The morning's travel was relatively quiet, since most of it was across grassland, though there were still the occasional eruptions of birds from the high grass screaming their warning calls as they went.

Around midday, we found the stag standing on the edge of a clearing. He stood with his head held high, watching us approach until we were before him, then turned and headed into the trees. This direction was closer to my original plan, so though it was through hillier terrain than I'd originally aimed for, I directed Leothen to follow him. I flinched as we crashed through the overgrown wood, ripping limbs from trees and outright felling others, but the spectral stayed with us this time, waiting for us at the tops of rises when he got too far ahead.

Until he didn't.

Late in the day, he crested a rise ahead of us but was gone when we followed him over. Just blinked out of existence, back to wherever spectrals came from, I supposed. I couldn't even feel his magic, but I could feel a different magic. Powerful, soothing, familiar magic, reminding me of enormous primordial firs standing stalwart against year after year of raging storms. Of gentle sunshine coaxing tiny seeds open to reveal the fragile new life within. Of vast, complicated networks of hidden root systems relaying nutrients and messages across a dark forest floor.

I *knew* that magic. It felt like home. Why was it here?

"Rafe!"

CHAPTER 23

I WAS BOUNCING in the hammock, completely giddy with excitement, tearing at my harness clips and demanding for Leothen to put me down. Rafe was *here?* My mind was already racing ahead, trying to piece together why he was here, what his family group was doing on this side of the Ardacs, how much time I could potentially spend with him in all this mess.

I was clambering into Leothen's giant, stone hand from the hammock when I heard Levi choke out my name from behind me. I turned to find his face a mask of confusion, pupils narrowed into pinpricks of panic, his hands hesitating even as they reached for me, as if he could snatch me back to his side but was unsure of how he would be received.

My brain came to a screeching halt.

I wasn't sure if his fear or his hesitation was more painful to witness, but it brought me back into the moment with a resounding thud. Looking at it from his perspective—he couldn't feel my friend coming, didn't even know who my friend was, and here I was nearly five stories up, unharnessing myself with no explanation, after having been injured falling from this height just days before—made me realize I had been woefully naive. This bond between us I had so readily accepted in the moment was going to take *compromise* on my part.

"Come with me," I urged Levi, reaching out and taking his

hand in mine. I was simultaneously directing Leothen to halt the descent of his hand and tracking the incoming magic of the dryads below. I needed to learn to stop living in my head so much and start communicating with him the knowledge and senses I'd always taken for granted. "I can feel friends coming, down below. I'm desperate to see them. Come meet them with me."

Watching Levi's confusion clear and morph into curiosity made my heart swell. I couldn't wait for him to meet my childhood friend. I instructed Leothen to wait for us—verbally this time—and we rappelled down instead of using his hand as a lift. Levi was aware of my excitement and made as quick work of his harness as I did, finishing just in time for me to grab his arm and dash headlong into the trees, laughing at my own exuberance. The dryads would be on us at any second.

Levi kept pace with me as I leapt over nurse logs and scrambled through thickets of underbrush, untangling me from a briar patch and holding aside a dangling limb for me to dart under. After a few moments, though, the plants began to part for us of their own accord, leaning this way and that, vines tightening against tree trunks and brambles drawing in on themselves. I felt Rafe's specific magic blossoming around me as he encouraged the undergrowth to make way for me. He'd seen me, then.

And I spotted him too, among a few of his clan as they made their way swiftly and silently through the even larger trees of the woods. Even the oldest, Silas, could move like a ghost or a night cat when he wanted to. Rafe was near his mature height, standing well over a dozen feet tall, and he was built like a prizefighter, broad in the chest and thighs. It made him easy to pick out, even from a distance.

Dryads were humanoid, but that's where our similarities ended. Their bodies were made of sturdy wood, like a sculpture made of fallen logs or driftwood, their faces simple and placid, with eyes so green they glowed. Tiny wisps of chartreuse-colored vapor drifted from their eye cavities on humid days and both males and females had odd, antler-like protrusions from the backs of their heads.

I couldn't really blame six-year-old-me for confusing them with golems.

I met Rafe at a dead run, feeling like a little kid again as he knelt to catch me when I launched myself into the air, and he pulled me against his shoulder. "Hello, *aren*," he said, greeting me with the Elvish word for little sister. "What trouble have you wrought now?"

How do you hug a creature more than twice your height and made of bark and wood, with the occasional thorn? You do your best. He smelled of a strong mix of moss and oak, and two little chickadees scolded me fiercely for daring to intrude on their territory. A wistfulness for long summer days spent trying to coax them to take seed from my palm crept in amongst the nostalgia already buffeting me.

"I see Puff and Dust are still nesting in your shoulder," I laughed, holding back tears. I'd *missed* him.

"You know I could never refuse them." The tiny birds had excavated a cavity in his shoulder six years ago, and though he could have stopped them or healed it within a matter of days, he allowed it to remain and tolerated their constant brash chattering.

Sidney claimed he only put up with them because they kept his bark free of insects, but she had it out for Dust, and so I took her avian-flavored insight with a grain of salt. Rafe was simply too fond of the bouncy little birds for it to only be a symbiotic relationship. He spoiled their nestlings with foraged bugs and extra attention.

I introduced Levi to Rafe, thrilled to share him with my long-time friend. I took Levi's hand as I noted his wariness when the other handful of dryads gathered around us. They were reclusive enough that it wouldn't surprise me if he'd never met one. Their expressions could be hard to read; their interactions with humans were so rare that they didn't bother to use them that often. I'd learned to watch their posture, the tilt of their head, or even the movements of the trees around us.

"Rafe, I thought you were in the Ardac Mountains," I started. "What are you all doing here?"

He sighed, a sound not unlike wind rustling dry leaves. "The

Ardac are not so far from here." He gestured to the ridges standing on the horizon. "The rest stayed behind in the mountains, but I came with Silas when you called to him."

I frowned in confusion and turned to Silas, the eldest of all the dryads I'd ever known. His bark was chipped and scarred, missing entirely in large patches, and his posture spoke of a gnarled oak, withered and worn. "Silas? I haven't called Silas. How could I have called any of you?"

Calling chips were useless for dryads because they didn't have the types of magic needed to power them. Their cousins, the sylvans and the nymphs, could use them, but they didn't travel with Rafe's family because it was too dangerous for them in the Ardac—too many predators, too treacherous, too inhospitable.

"You did, child. You surely did." Silas's words were a sigh of wood creaking in the wind. I couldn't resent Silas for referring to me as a child. He was so old he considered my father a child too, and my father was nearly a hundred years old—though he looked no older than thirty or forty.

He gestured behind us, toward the golem. "With your stone man. I can feel it even now. Don't think we've been called on since... well, since the Sylvan War, at least..." He started off sounding proud, but then trailed off in thought the way he often did when telling stories. The Sylvan War was ancient, long before even Silas existed.

After a long moment, it became clear he wasn't going to continue. "I don't understand."

"Did something happen? Why are you traveling with your sentries?" Rafe was eyeing me with concern.

I explained the loan we were making to the sprites and how I'd fallen and nearly died, and the trees began quivering just slightly around me, betraying Rafe's deepening concern as I spoke. As I recounted the energy I'd pushed out before I blacked out, and how Domm had been pulsing magic when I woke, things began to fall into place. His pulsing magic was a distress signal.

Silas was nodding thoughtfully now, and the other three dryads behind him shifted forward to listen. I recognized one of them as a female named Chloē, and I gave her a little wave.

"That's about when a spectral stag started showing up. I think he led us here." I looked around for him, but couldn't see or feel him anywhere.

Silas waved a hand dismissively. "I sent him to see what was wrong. Just because we aren't physically present doesn't mean the pact is null. You've made an enormous mess of these woods." He stalked off through the trees toward the golem. I shot an incredulous look at Rafe before turning to follow Silas, trying to make sense of what he'd said and not trip over my own feet in the undergrowth. Levi reached out a hand to steady me but pulled back when I got my balance on my own.

"You *sent*... what pact... Silas, I'm so sorry, I don't have any idea what you're talking about."

He paused in front of Domm's foot and heaved a frustrated sigh. "Fleshlings have such short memories. Give them five generations and something is as good as forgotten." As creepy as the term 'fleshling' was, it beat being referred to as 'meat-people' which was Rafe's go-to. Silas pressed a hand to the side of Domm's foot, and I felt his magic swell. He gave a satisfied nod when the pulsing magic stopped, and his glow returned to its original ochre color.

"Your ancestors made a pact with my family. We sojourn on your lands whenever we need to rest or we have a sapling to raise. In exchange for that, we pledged to protect your property and your family from harm, to come when you called. Look at this mess," he muttered to himself, wandering off into the broken trees, pushing his magic into the ground and righting uprooted trees or sealing off broken limbs.

"So... you have three massive stone golems, one of which is a long-distance fire caster, and an army of dryad warriors at your disposal," Levi muttered dryly. "The title of Empress is becoming more fitting by the moment."

"Little good it will do the sprite city," Silas mused as he wandered to the next tree. "Saltwater would poison our roots."

"We could deliver the sentries," Rafe murmured.

"What—Rafe, no. That's crazy. I'm so sorry I called you out of the mountains on a false alarm. I had no idea—"

"It wasn't a false alarm, Elara. You were nearly killed," Rafe interrupted gently, and I felt Levi's hand close over my shoulder. "If we took these in your stead, we could deliver them in no more than four days. We don't sleep, we don't need daylight to know the terrain, and we can cut through the mountain passes with them."

"If you won't allow that," Silas continued, "we will at least accompany you to the shore—even though it will take much longer since you can't go through the mountains with us. If nothing else, your father would want his sapling protected... and perhaps we can mitigate some of this... *carnage.*"

I cringed at being referred to as a sapling, but also in acknowledgment of the swath of broken trees and churned earth we were leaving in our wake. I cursed inwardly that I couldn't cut through the mountains with them if they took that route—we'd never survive. But if I went the long way around with them, it would take the full two weeks, versus four days.

"I'll still need to install them with their orders for the sprite city." I chewed my lip, thinking hard.

"We'll meet you at Whitewave in four days' time," Silas replied, eyeing the sentries.

"And if you have trouble?" I couldn't help but ask.

"I'll send the stag."

If they had trouble in the mountain passes, I wasn't sure what I could do. It was risky.

I eyed the sentries, knowing the dryads' offer would be wise to take, and frowning when I realized my trip with Levi would be over. The selfish side of me mourned that our time alone would be over already. The private little bubble we'd created for ourselves would end.

While I was hesitant to give up control of the golem, I would be doing that when I handed them over in Whitewave anyway. And to be honest, Silas probably knew more about these sentries than even my father.

"Let me call my mother."

<hr/>

IT MADE SENSE, the dryad's proposal. And since time saved

equaled lives saved when delivering defenses to a city under attack, and my father knew *and trusted* Silas, my mother gratefully agreed to allow him to deliver the sentries on my behalf. She was just as baffled as I was about Silas's claim of a pact and the emergency beacon in Domm. As far as she'd known, the dryad people had always spent time in our forests and that's just the way things were.

I was already changing gears mentally. I thought I'd have more than another week before jumping into the next stage of the plan, but now that it was here, I found my brain skittering off in a million different directions, working through possible water golem builds and contingencies.

Rafe personally delivered Levi and me to the nearest town with our bags—after being admonished by Silas not to take too long or get lost—but not before making all kinds of delighted comments about how pleased he was that I'd "taken a mate" and wanting to know when I would have "new fledglings for him to spoil". I heard Levi make a choking noise as I simultaneously flushed bright red all the way to my toes and imagined Rafe offering fat little grubs to our hypothetical future baby.

Rather than fixate on that bizarre mental image, however, my brain latched on to the idea of a baby with Levi, *his* baby, a life together, and it took my breath away with how much I wanted that. I tried without success to shove those thoughts to the back of my mind.

That dazed feeling followed me throughout the rest of the evening, as we found an inn and I got a proper hot bath, ate dinner, and finally fell asleep, exhausted, clutched in Levi's arms. What would happen now that we weren't traveling together with the same purpose, insulated from the rest of the world? And now that I had a massive project looming ahead of me? A golem created for the defense of a city was going to be the biggest project of my life.

⤜⬥⤛

F RIDAY MORNING FOUND us at Muriel Ta'nith's office in Whitewave. She'd returned my spectral message about the sentries being delivered five days early with one of her own. The council was being difficult about my contract for the new golem creation, and she needed to speak with me in person as soon as possible.

We'd Gate hopped between the Boundlands and the Void until we made it back to Whitewave, then sent our bags ahead of us to Oar's Rest. I knew I should be grateful to the dryads for delivering our sentries early and for the benefit it gave to the sprites, but I couldn't help feeling slightly irked that I was here instead of nestled in a hammock with my favorite siren right now. He'd been twitchy all morning, flinching every time he thought I might step away from him, and I noticed it became worse the more people were around us. I couldn't even claim I didn't like his need for me, though I wished I could have removed his anxiety about it. We were a bit of a mess right now.

We weren't the only anxiety-ridden messes though. Muriel had dark circles under her eyes, and her desk was piled even higher with papers than the last time I'd seen it. It would be quite the headache to sort out if someone bumped a stack. She stood behind her desk, bent at the waist and staring down at it. I tried not to fidget in my oversized chair as I waited for her to gather her thoughts—she was obviously frustrated, her mouth pinched and her eyes hard.

"The council is… being exceedingly difficult," she started, with a growl in her voice I hadn't heard before. Her hands curled into claws on her desk. "Let me be honest here. It's not the whole council—it's the mer." She flashed a quick look at Levi, who sat sprawled in the chair next to mine, and he gave a quick shrug with a raised eyebrow.

"They decided two days ago that the contract should be awarded to a Seafolk, though it was thinly veiled that what they actually meant was to a *mer*."

Oh. Well, that made my life easier. "Well, that's okay. It would have been a massive undertaking for me anyway, and I understand if they want someone working on it that is more familiar with the issues."

"That's just the problem," Muriel bit out. "They don't actually *have* someone."

I felt my eyebrows pinch together and after a few beats of silence, I couldn't help myself. "I'm not sure I understand."

"I wish I didn't." Her tone was bitter, and she looked sick to her stomach. "I mean that, after two days of arguments back and forth among the other members of the council demanding that the leaders of the group who want a Seafolk provide alternative suggestions from *you*, they have none. The most they've come up with is a mer currently apprenticing as an artificer who has no discernible skill in golemancy but *just so happens* to be the nephew of one of the council members."

All I could do was blink. "So, do they not want a permanent golem anymore?"

"That's the part I can't understand." She threw her hands up. "They do! They've already begun amassing materials earmarked for use in its construction." Muriel huffed in agitation and began pacing behind her desk as she talked. "I don't know if it's sheer incompetence, which is a *distinct* possibility, or greed. Maybe they don't want to risk the heartstone falling outside of Seafolk hands, or maybe they just want to keep the money they would have paid you within the Seafolk community."

"It doesn't really matter why they want it," Levi interjected, "if they don't have someone available to fill the contract and don't have another plan for defense." His enchantment was an almost non-existent rebuff. He was displeased but trying to keep it under wraps. "This sounds like red tape that will leave The Deep without the protection it needs while they continue to squabble and make outrageous demands."

"If it's purely about the money, that's an easy fix." I turned to Muriel to address her. "I don't want any payment for this project. It's blood money as far as I'm concerned. Adonci personally asked me for protection, so that's what I'll provide."

Muriel stopped in her tracks and shot me an incredulous look. "You just said yourself this was going to be a massive undertaking. You deserve to be compensated for your time and efforts, Ms. Hawthorne. Especially when you consider how difficult some of these people are going to be to work for."

I shrugged. "I'm doing this purely for Adonci. I don't need a contract." More specifically, I didn't *want* a contract.

Levi noticed the dryness in my tone and gave me a side-eye. "I don't think this is just about the money. Money is well spent when it protects someone's reputation, which is clearly suffering with all the protests."

Muriel turned her tired gaze on Levi. "I'm not sure what you're getting at."

"I mean that if they want to hold their position of power in the Alliance, they need to protect their reputation. If they aren't going to pay to fix their reputation, it probably means they're wanting to do it themselves which would make them look even better. Hence the requirement that the golemancer be a mer. 'Look at us, we built you a golem ourselves and defended you.' Never mind that they don't have anyone to fulfill that role." Levi's enchantments gave a firm rebuff, betraying his irritation.

I felt skeptical. "Are these people really that petty?" I wondered if Levi's bad experiences were coloring his view of them.

"Yes," Muriel answered, her forehead resting on the palms of her hands. I hadn't noticed her take her seat again. "I do have an idea, but I recognize it might be a lot to ask."

Levi and I both grew quiet at the nervousness in her voice as she fingered a file in front of her.

"Would you two be willing to consider a paper marriage?"

CHAPTER 24

I HADN'T HEARD that term before. "A paper marriage?"

"Yes… a marriage on paper," she replied. A memory of her joking that she'd need to convince the council that I was mer surfaced in my mind. At least, I'd thought she had been joking. I glanced at Levi to find his face shocked and a little horrified, but Muriel wasn't looking at him. She had the file open and was pulling out papers.

"I have everything you would need to file it right here, and it's not like it would need to be permanent or anything. Mer never stay together anyway," she added dismissively. "It would probably make the most impact if you both took his birth name, Chansoneau, since it's more traditional, and that name itself holds some prestige in mer society." I flinched at her suggestion about his mother's surname, knowing he wouldn't take it well, but I was too stunned to respond immediately. I couldn't take my eyes off of Levi's changing expressions, which were heading through incredulity and anger toward rage. Muriel finally glanced up at me, then followed my gaze to Levi.

"I mean, I just thought… since they're demanding the person filling the contract be a Seafolk, and obviously marriage to a Seafolk would legally fulfill that requirement…"

"I will *not*." Levi was immediately on his feet, his magic seething with outraged energy and firm rebuff. "Absolutely not."

His finger stabbed toward the ground to underscore his words. "Are you—" He swallowed briefly, trying to rein in his temper and failing, his eyes still flashing at Muriel. "You're *not* joking. This is honestly how you're suggesting we deal with a greedy, incompetent government entity: capitulation. How *dare* you? And how dare *they* put us in this position in the first place?"

I'd never seen Levi so irate. On the surface, I agreed with him, but I could also see how, when placed between a rock and a hard place, Muriel had come up with what she probably considered a convenient loophole.

Honestly, I didn't hate the idea. Arranged marriage to the man I was already in love with and currently bonded to for life? I mean, twist my arm if you must. Obviously, Levi didn't agree, so it seemed like it was off the table. Which stung a bit, I admitted to myself.

Muriel's jaw dropped, and her head snapped back a bit at his response, but before she could even reply, Levi was slamming out of the room and down the hall, moving toward the front of the building. It was the farthest he'd been from me since I'd fallen in the lake. He was truly furious.

I felt him stop in front of the building, his magic pacing back and forth with him on the sidewalk in front of her office like a caged panther might. I didn't even consider that he would leave without me. His bond to me leashed him too tightly.

Was that how he felt about marriage? Even a "fake" one? Just another leash?

"I'm *so* sorry," Muriel whispered, her expression stunned. "I guess... I read that situation wrong."

I forced a small smile but it felt a little crooked. "Not necessarily. I think you just touched a few raw nerves."

She sighed and dropped her head into her hands.

"I'm going to go try to talk with him, and I'll contact you when I've figured something out. If you have any other ideas, maybe send them to me privately first, through a spectral?" I stood and eyed the stack of papers she'd pulled from her file. "May I take these?"

THE MORE I mulled on it, the more the idea appealed to me. What if it *wasn't* fake? What if we could just elope and skip all the nonsense of a drawn-out dating relationship and large public wedding and all the family drama? He was already bound to me, so I couldn't see what the big deal was other than the length of time social norms dictated was appropriate for a relationship before marriage. The length of acceptable courting time was different among every race and society, anyway. Was that naive of me?

Probably.

Okay, yes.

But it would also fix the contract situation, and I couldn't really find it in myself to be against the idea of a quick marriage to Levi... other than the fact that he clearly didn't want it. I just needed to figure out why. Was it me? I didn't think so, considering he said he didn't regret being bound to me. Was it marriage in general? That would be… unfortunate. Maybe it really was the timing issue.

I thought back to our conversation on the picnic table—what felt like so long ago—and remembered he'd said he wanted someone who was just as trapped with him as he was with her. He'd acted like he was furious with the idea, but some niggling little feeling in my gut brought to mind a quote from some long dead human playwright, "The lady doth protest too much, methinks." Could it be the idea of a *fake* marriage that made him so mad?

Obviously, no one would assume marriage between people who had known each other only as long as we had would be prudent. It was too sudden. Too permanent. *Foolish.* But a small voice in the back of my mind kept reminding me we were already, in our own way, permanent. He was bound to me physically through his bond, and he'd *said* he didn't regret it. Was he having second thoughts?

I watched his face as he stared out the window on the train to Oar's Rest, silently fuming. He hadn't spoken as I'd joined him on the sidewalk or as we'd walked to the train station. Instead, he'd simply fallen into step beside me, like my own personal storm cloud. I gave him space, content to wait until we had some true privacy to tackle his anger and the sprite's dilemma.

He ignored the waiters as they shuffled up and down the long aisles, pushing carts with food and drinks, his sullen expression twisting into a grimace as we pulled into the station. "Do you mind coming back to my house with me?" I asked, remembering what he'd said about his roommates' preternatural hearing abilities.

His answer was a brief shake of his head as he shouldered the duffle I'd picked up from the porter station. I belatedly realized he was probably trying to spare the general public the effects of his anger-laced magic. Lord have mercy, I was slow sometimes.

I arrived at my door to find no more than the usual amount of harpy feathers on my front stoop and let us into my unit with a sigh. If there was anywhere in the world better than a person's own space, I hadn't found it, and after days of sleeping on the ground, it felt like a relief to be in my own home. Levi drifted in behind me as I kicked my boots into the hall closet and dumped my bag on the floor.

He cast his gaze around with a reluctance that seemed to ease as he took in the multitude of pillows and throw blankets and the odd plants tucked here and there. The townhouse was clean and modern, but comfortable, and I could tell it was more to his liking than he had expected in his current mood.

"This is nice," he said, sounding a little surprised. "It fits you." The Crown District was new and affluent, but at least it didn't scream "old money" like my parent's estate. My house *was* nice, and I'd spent a lot of time making it cozy.

Levi carried my duffle up the stairs to my room for me, where I promptly breezed past him into my closet. I was wearing jeans today, which needed to be rectified immediately. Plus, I needed a minute away from his ire to clear my head. My closet was a generous sized walk-in perfect for housing my clothing addiction. I had planned to change into some simple loungewear, but as I stood there, an impish impulse had my hand hovering over a specific drawer in my highboy dresser.

I'd had a thing for negligees for the last few years. Not necessarily all lingerie per se—that was more of Sidney's wheelhouse. But in the same way I tended to hoard decorative pillows and drape throw blankets across every cushioned surface, I leaned toward nightwear that was luxurious with a nice drape, although perhaps a little scandalous. It didn't matter to me that I'd never dated or that it was just for me; I liked it, so I bought it and I wore it.

Sidney knew this about me, and one of her ways of teasing me was to buy me more and more frivolous 'nightwear' on every birthday. Not that I didn't reciprocate with more and more ridiculous lingerie—the last set had included a g-string that was basically nothing more than a giant bow for her rear with a few pieces of floss to hold it on—but I had a feeling her purchases for me probably got more actual use.

I plucked her latest gift from the back of the drawer and glanced over my shoulder toward where Levi was still grumbling in my bedroom about the audacity of the mer, his magic whipping out like driving rain. I tried to hide a small smirk threatening to take over my face. He had his weapon… I had mine.

Changing clothes felt a little bit like suiting up for battle. We were going to hash this out tonight. However… going in 'guns blazing' might derail the entire conversation. I eyed a short, silk robe hanging nearby and pulled it on over my 'sleepwear'. It fell to my upper thigh and covered my garment completely.

I took a steeling breath to gather myself and then padded silently from my closet. Levi was standing at my bedroom window, arms braced against the windowsill, his head hanging low as he scowled at something outside. His hair was a rumpled mess, like he'd had his hands in it just moments before, and backlit by the window as it was, it appeared like a glowing halo around his head.

"I'm going to assume you don't make a habit of chewing out frazzled selkies," I opened quietly.

He swung his angry glower toward me, but it disappeared in a moment of confusion as his eyes flickered over my robe before he shook off the distraction and focused on what I'd said. The anger didn't return, but his eyes stayed hard. He swallowed thickly and stared through me for a moment, until I wasn't entirely sure he was going to respond.

"She thinks she can use me."

I contemplated this for a moment. "Explain."

Levi ground his teeth and his eyes flashed as he worked to rein in his growing anger again. I felt a little bit like a mouse before a lion in the face of his burgeoning wrath, but I knew it wasn't directed at me.

"The audacity of these people… this *council*… and their self-centered disregard for people's lives… I can't even put into words my absolute *outrage*." He didn't need to. It was written clearly in the stiff way he held his body and the slashing, angry movements of his hands. "They want a mer name on their project, even at the possible detriment of the project itself, at the cost of people's *lives* if need be, so that they get the glory and the respect in the end. That they would use *you*, use me, use *us*—our *relationship*…"

He stopped for a moment to rein himself in again, his breath sawing out of him as his jaw clenched. "I can't stomach the thought that you would be trapped with me because of their meddling. It's bad enough that you're already forced into this… this *bond*, with me following you around like some starving mongrel."

"I don't feel forced—"

"That isn't the point. And I don't think it would even work. Do you think these people consider me to be a mer? They *don't*. I'm landlocked, so regardless of my parentage or my magic, I'm *just* a landwalker to them." His enchantment rose around us as he spoke, lashing about like a living thing, proving the falsehood in those accusations.

"I will *never* be 'mer' enough for them. I have *always* been and will *always* be an outsider. And then… *then* I'm supposed to go and let them use that part of me—that piece of me that was never good enough—to boost their reputation?"

His pain and resentment were palpable, tangible things, slicing through me and raising a fierce, blood-thirsty desire in me to protect him from the people who had cut him so deeply.

"Or to allow them to use you and your gifts, your empathy, your complete and utter perfection, for their own greed and pride? Yeah, I'm pissed. I want to help Adonci's people, but I *hate* that we have to benefit this council to do so."

I ignored the comment about my supposed perfection, but I agreed with him about my distaste for the council and was still mulling over that aspect of it. I watched him as he began pacing between the window and my bed. The next words out of my mouth tumbled out unprompted, vulnerable, before I could catch them, laying bare my insecurity and desire for him.

"So… this isn't actually about not wanting to be married to me?"

He stopped dead in his tracks and his eyes narrowed as he glared at me from across the room. I might have even flinched when he stalked toward me like a prowling lion, if I hadn't had years of training in proper composure and etiquette. Since I had, I held my head high and my shoulders back when he came to a stop just out of arm's reach in front of me.

"We *are* married as far as the mer are concerned. That's what a bond is, even though it's usually a temporary thing in their culture, it's as married as these people get. A legal marriage between us would serve no purpose to them but to bind you to me, and in effect, to them. *When I—*," he started, then paused to swallow before continuing. "*When* I marry you, Elara, it's going to be because you want me to, and not because some bureaucrats forced you into it."

Levi's eyes were hard again, determined, and his tone had an almost vicious certainty in it, but I couldn't suppress the spark of pleasure I knew my face showed.

That was all I needed to hear.

My mind made up, I circled a few steps past him, positioning myself so he was between me and my bed. I felt like, in that moment, our roles had reversed, and now I was the predator stalking my prey. I drifted toward him with a secretive smile threatening to curve the edge of my lips, wanting to back him into the bed. He must have seen the intent on my face because he blinked and took a step backwards, bumping into the mattress and startling momentarily, checking behind him before narrowing his eyes at me again.

"What are you doing?"

I allowed myself a small smile that felt positively wicked. "Sit down."

His answering smile held a fair amount of confusion as he slowly lowered himself onto my mattress.

"Back up. Against the pillows." I lifted my chin to indicate the area behind him and noted the imperious tone in my voice with hidden amusement. He wanted an empress? I'd show him one.

He slid back on the bed with his eyes narrowing further at me as he went, either in suspicion or at my tone. I set one knee up on the bed and prowled up after him, finally situating myself in his lap—my new favorite place—and settling the hem of my robes out around my thighs to keep things decent. For now, at least.

"Levi."

"... Yes?"

"You're already bound to me." I watched his face, scanning for any hint of a flinch or discomfort at my quiet announcement. Instead, I watched his jaw clench tightly as his gaze focused on mine with an intense quality that surprised me. It wasn't rebellious, as I had expected, but possessive, and I suppressed a shiver, biting into my lip as I considered my next move.

I lifted my hands slowly, hesitating slightly before settling them onto his chest. There was nothing I enjoyed more than feeling his body against mine. I gripped his shirt, wanting to pull it off before I changed my mind and went for the tie on my own robe. Sliding it open, I allowed the silken fabric to slide down my shoulders and pool at my waist. His eyes dropped to the ridiculously frothy lace confection I'd donned in my closet and widened slightly.

"Don't you want to bind me to you, too?" It was a breathy whisper that I almost didn't recognize as my own, and Levi made a choking noise. I smoothed my hands back up his abs to his chest, feeling the muscles underneath as he clenched his stomach before fisting my fingers in the smooth drape of his t-shirt.

I needed this off of him.

I wanted full access to everything underneath.

I should have demanded he strip first.

His hands wrapped around the backs of my arms, holding

me against him, and I leaned forward to nip at his jawline. "You said I could be your queen any time I wanted. Did you mean that?" I felt more powerful in this moment than I did commanding the massive stone juggernauts or creating juiced-up long swords. I might have been a little bit out of my mind.

When his breath shuddered out of him and his hands gripped me tighter, I couldn't help the smug grin that spread across my face. I busied myself with kisses and nips along the side of his neck to hide it. I must have looked like the cat who got the cream. Where had this man been all my life?

Focus.

"If you could marry me tomorrow, would you?" I asked.

"You know I would," he growled, flexing up against me and making my eyelids flutter. "But not because they demand it and not because it benefits them!"

"Forget about the council. I'm talking about you and me." My fingers were like claws in his shirt, and I tugged, causing him to lean forward and jerk his shirt off over his head. The motion of his hips beneath me distracted me, and my breath hitched at the feeling of his hardness outlined against me.

"I can't forget about them. They're why we're having this conversation right now." His chest and shoulders were heaving, and now I could see all of it. Long, sinewy lines of color snaking up his shoulder and over the mounds of his muscles, delicate golden skin dancing over flexing abs. I had the strangest urge to lick it.

"I know it's early by most people's standards, but I already want you to marry me," I whispered. "I want every part of you, and I don't care what the bureaucrats think."

"… What?"

I let my thoughts drift back to sinking in the pond, to the things I'd found most important at my end. "I nearly died, Levi —and I would have, if you hadn't worked so hard to save me— but of all the thoughts and regrets that crossed my mind while I was drowning, the one that pained me the most was that I'd never get to experience what it would be like to spend my life with you."

Levi's breathing stilled, and his mouth dropped open slightly, but I pushed on, needing him to understand how I felt.

"I find myself caring less about what society thinks regarding appropriate timelines, and more about what you and I want. If *you* want to wait and find some other way through the council's… *desires*, then I'm fine with that, and we'll do it together. But I don't want to make choices about our relationship based on spiting this council or appeasing social expectations."

"What exactly are you saying?" His voice was husky, and I had to close my eyes and concentrate because his lure was so potent it stole my breath away. I framed my thoughts carefully before I spoke.

"I'm saying that I would give you that commitment of binding myself to you, marrying you, and it would be real. Not a paper marriage. A real one. You already have my heart."

CHAPTER 25

Levi sat frozen for a moment underneath me, too stunned to respond. His heart hammered forcefully in his chest beneath my hands, and his mouth was parted just slightly, like it was ready for the torrent in his mind if the words could just break free. I leaned forward to take his mouth with mine—big, soft, open-mouth kisses that tasted of him and his decadent lips.

This seemed to jar him out of his stupor, and he clutched me against him as if I might flee. He broke the kiss, and his eyes dropped to my chest, taking in the sheer lace and ruffled fabric again as his breathing accelerated. One hand dropped to grip my hip, and he used it to drag me down against his erection as he flexed up against me again. I gasped for breath and rolled my hips, trying to encourage him as he leaned forward to brush his lips along the exposed skin of my upper breast.

"How did I get so lucky?" he breathed out quietly as he leaned back to look at me again.

"How did *I* get so lucky?" I repeated, giving in to my desire and leaning down to nip gently at his chest. He made that little choking sound again and tangled a hand in my hair, and I was already trying to unbutton his pants. He helped me slide back slightly so he could push them down and off.

Then he froze.

His whole body stiffened as he rested his forehead against my collarbone, and I thought I might scream as he panted for breath beneath me. "I don't have any rings."

What?

He raised his head to look at me when I didn't respond and must have seen that I was incapable of comprehension right now. "For a wedding. If we're gonna do this... I don't... I don't even have a ring yet." He swallowed thickly.

It took me several blinks to follow that train of thought. "I don't need a ring, Levi. I'd rather make my own anyway." This seemed to surprise him for a beat, though I couldn't imagine why. I made rings nearly every day, and I only had so much body real-estate—I couldn't waste space with non-functioning jewelry.

"Really? Does that mean you'll make me one too?"

"Yes." I tried to kiss him again, but he dodged away with a grin and a sparkle in his eye.

"Do I get a boost on it? What kind of boost can I get?" His excitement was adorable, but not what I wanted right now.

"Stop talking."

His response to my petulant demand was delighted laughter, and he indulged me with a kiss that started sweet and quickly became a desperate, wanting thing with a life of its own. I needed him more than I needed air. I loved him so much.

His mouth slanted against mine again and again, and when he dragged me more firmly against his hips, he gave a low curse as he realized I wasn't wearing underwear. My grin was uncontainable.

Levi's grip tightened on my hip. "Have you healed? You're not still tender?"

I had no idea what he was asking... or what year it was.

"From our first time," he clarified quietly.

Was I? "I'm fine." *Probably... Right?* I didn't care right then. I bit his neck, then kissed the mark, eliciting a groan.

"Should I get a—?" He moved like he was going to slide out from under me, and I gripped him tighter. "The condoms are in your bag," he said, laughing.

"Go," I whispered. "I'm not ready for babies," I joked.

Levi's pupils visibly contracted as a hint of fear flickered through his expression. Of all the reactions I could have anticipated, that wasn't one of them. I couldn't help a small, amused smile as he slid away and scrambled through the bag to dig a condom out.

"Was that a bad joke?" I asked when he returned, settling myself more firmly against his arousal with a slightly desperate wiggle.

His eyes shot to mine, and he blinked a few times before laying his head back on the pillows behind him. He swallowed twice and spoke to the ceiling when he finally answered me. "I know… it's not rational. I know you wouldn't leave me with a child."

It took me a moment to place his meaning, and his eyes dropped to watch me in silence as I did. His mother had left his father after she weaned him, as did many or most other mermaids with their partners and offspring. That was Levi's normal, the thing he'd permanently warded himself against with the runes hidden in his tattoos. The reason he lived in the Void even though it would shorten his lifespan in the long run. I pressed a kiss against his chin.

"I don't have those instincts, Levi." I kept my voice calm and rational… gentle. I wanted—*needed*—to reassure him that this thing he feared would never, ever happen. "I'm going to bind myself to you legally, but my love for you is what will keep me with you always." I pressed more kisses to his jawline, unable to help myself, and felt his hands slide around to my back, pulling me tighter against his chest. "I would destroy anyone who tried to separate me from my child. *Our* child."

Just the thought of someone trying to take away my hypothetical future child sparked a dark, primal rage deep in my soul. I would level nations using every golem on the planet. I knew he saw it in my eyes because he shivered.

"You could do it, too," he murmured and kissed me again. He crushed me to his chest, pressing the air from my lungs with the strength of his embrace. He released me quickly at the sound and smirked. "Sorry." Levi locked eyes with me and took my hand in his, comparing our hand sizes and studying the lines of my wrist. "So delicate, and yet, so powerful." His words were layered with his siren's call, so heavily saturated that my ward didn't stand a chance.

So why bother? I wondered. I turned my wrist toward him to reveal the clasp on the cuff. "Take it off."

His eyebrows drew together as he stared at my bracelet, and then his eyes flashed to mine with concern in them. I flipped open the latch on the clasp myself and explained, "Your magic is too strong right now for it to matter much anyway. I want all of you, and I trust you. Do you trust me?" I tugged the attached rings from my fingers and let the ward drop to the bed.

His answer was a nod, but that was still sparing me from his enchantment.

"Say something."

"You're my wife," he whispered.

I was wholly unprepared. His voice… I immediately felt my pupils dilate, everything around Levi growing hazy and distant. The strength of his magic pulled the breath from my lungs. My heart twisted, both from the statement itself and the crushing desire rising inside me.

If before I had wanted desperately to be close to him, now it was a deep, painful ache. My insides clenched with a strange emptiness, and I heard myself panting for air, like there wasn't quite enough.

My physical response was so strong, so frantic, that I felt a brief wave of panic before he placed his palm on my cheek and pulled me against him. "Shh, I've got you," he said, comforting me. I felt like I was drowning in my need for him.

"I've got you," he repeated as he lifted me slightly and lined our bodies up, pressing into me with deliberate slowness. The intrusion felt thick and hard, and we had to pause briefly to give me a moment to adjust before he was fully inside me. By the time I was seated on his pelvis again, his breathing was as ragged as mine.

Sharing my body with him like this took the edge off of some of my ache, but it wasn't enough. I needed more. I had a strange desire to consume him, to bottle him up and lock him away in my heart so he would always be mine.

"I'm here," he whispered, calming me. Gentling me. "I'm yours." It was exactly what I needed to hear.

I rocked my hips experimentally and gasped at the pleasure that shot through me. "That's right," he encouraged, placing one hand on my hip to guide my movements, the other on the back of my neck, sliding up into my hair.

I was lost in him. Gone. The only thing I could focus on was the feeling of him between my legs, building and growing, warming and twisting. My cheeks felt hot. Suddenly, his fingers clenched in my hair at the back of my head, making a fist and anchoring me.

I opened my eyes and found him staring into mine, his own gaze intense as the hand on my hip slid around to my rear, continuing to encourage my movements. My eyes drifted shut a few more times, but every time I opened them, I was met with stormy ocean blue looking deep into my soul.

"I love you," Levi murmured against my skin as I tipped over into the abyss, coming apart in his arms as he clenched me tighter.

I SPENT a long time on the edge of my bed holding the glass vials.

Bette had dropped by while Levi was still napping—worst timing ever—and knocked, much to my surprise. She said she'd seen me arrive with company and hadn't wanted to interrupt—while conspicuously darting glances around to try to get a better look at my company—but she wanted to bring me my mail and was simply too excited to wait to tell me she'd finished my potions.

She'd received the Apothecary Oversight Committee's approval for one-time distribution while they did more testing on it, but even that had been rushed through due to their excitement over a new potential 'elite potion' market. I'm sure it didn't hurt that she was a member of the board. She brought stacks of paperwork with her. Legal documents, ingredients lists, possible spell interactions, usage directions… it would need to be dosed out under a medical mage's supervision. I supplied the final payment and tried not to think about how much it cost me.

By the time she'd left, Levi was in the shower, and I'd been sitting there staring at them ever since.

When I'd made my negotiations before we'd left on our trip, I'd requested a second dose. Knowing Levi had the potential to bond with someone someday, even if that person was me—and that he might despise that bond—had driven me to make the extra purchase. But now that he had, even though he seemed content with it, would he take the potion and flee? My heart said no, but I couldn't help the brief flicker of fear. The thought of it sucked the breath from my lungs and created a pit of dread in my stomach.

He deserved the option. Everything in me demanded he be given the choice.

Still, my mouth was dry as I heard the water turn off in the bathroom.

I studied the potion as I heard him dress and pad into the room, little round vials wrapped in a thin but protective metal cage, with locking metal lids. The bottles themselves said these weren't some corner-market wares. The liquid was a deep, dark red, viscous, and vaguely luminous in places. It was a little unsettling to watch it roiling slowly behind the glass as I tilted my hand.

One bottle represented freedom for his father. The other, my potential heartbreak. Would he still love me without the bond? How much of his own need for me was this genetic curse? *I've seen for myself how much magic amplified that need*, I thought ruefully as I ran my gaze across the ward now locked securely around my wrist. Levi had replaced it on me himself before we'd even caught our breath.

Now he joined me on the bed again, sprawling loosely on his side with his head propped up on one elbow. "This isn't a bed; it's a nest," he said, referencing my multiple cream, beige, and grey blankets and the piles of pillows. *Maybe that's why Sidney likes it so much…*

I flashed a quick look at him, finding his hair mussed and still slightly damp. He hadn't donned a shirt yet, and I decided Levi wearing loose shorts and no top, still damp from the shower, was my favorite look on him. I gave him a quick smile, but it felt forced.

His eyes narrowed at me. "You're doing some heavy thinking again." Hot sun beating onto scorching sand and frothy, rolling water filtered into my subconscious as his magic washed over me. He'd ramped it up.

"I bought you something." My voice sounded hoarse to my own ears.

He was quiet, waiting for my explanation, but my focus was on the bottles as I clutched them a little tighter. "My next-door neighbor is an apothecary. She's an Overseeing member of the Apothecaries Committee and teaches her craft occasionally at the university level when they can convince her to make time for them. She's very good." I swallowed to stop myself from babbling.

"When you told me about your father's difficulties, I asked her if she knew of any potions that had the ability to break a long-standing enchantment bond." A quick glance told me I had his full attention. He was riveted. I forced myself to continue. "She didn't think one existed, but she thought she could potentially create one. She just stopped by to tell me they were finished." Not knowing what would come of this, it was easier to stare at the bottles, to watch the potion as it rolled about inside them. When I finally raised my eyes, Levi looked astonished.

He blinked several times, his mouth open slightly, before he reached out gingerly to take a vial. "You did this for us?"

I nodded.

"Elara," he breathed, his enchantment a living thing in that single utterance. He studied the bottle in silence for a long moment before reaching out for the second bottle, which I handed him. He seemed at a loss for words.

Eventually, his confusion won out. "Is it in two doses?"

"Yes, but… both doses are in the same bottle. The second one… that one's actually for you."

His silence stretched for a beat before, "*What?*" It was completely flat, spoken like a whip. He instantly held the second bottle a little farther away from him, as if it might bite him.

The movement made me realize I'd been staring at the bottles again instead of his face, and when I looked at him, I found him confused, alarmed, and maybe a little hurt.

"I didn't like… I don't want you to be trapped. I need for you to have a choice, to *choose* to want me instead of being compelled to want me," I explained, picking at my blanket to have something to do.

His eyes found mine and held, and everything in them was vulnerable and confused. Blue tide-pools of swirling questions. "You want me to take this?"

I thought for a moment before answering him honestly with a minute shake of my head. "No, I don't. I like you just the way you are. But I want you to have the *option* to take it—even if you never do—because it's important to me that you have a choice."

"I've made my choice." I couldn't help the conflict I knew shone through as he searched my face. "The bond I feel for you isn't the painful addiction that can never be sated that my father feels. The love we have makes it unique and powerful, and I *like* what we have together." The solemnity on his face faded as humor sparked deep within. "Besides, does it keep a bond from reforming?"

I shook my head. Bette said there were ways to slow them down, but her potion would only break a bond, not prevent it.

"Then what shall I do?" Levi asked. "Break our bond and run away?" He chuckled, as if the thought was laughable. "I love you, and my bond with you will remain, because I could never will myself to stay away."

I released my held breath, relief rushing through me even as it warred with my desire to do the right thing. "Then I want you to keep it, even if you never use it. Consider it a wedding present." I made myself hold his gaze, even as he studied mine.

⁂

"Y'ALL ARE *WILD*."

"I know." I'd decided I wanted to explain to Sidney in person, so we were sitting in the shop on Sunday morning while I worked on more back orders. Levi had peeled himself away from me for long enough to talk with his dad about the potion I'd procured and make him an appointment at a healer's clinic. He'd been agitated about leaving me, to say the least, but the fact that he *could* meant the bond was mellowing somewhat.

We were going to file for our marriage in the courts tomorrow morning, since they were closed for the weekend. Sidney was equal parts horrified and thrilled at this new development and still trying to process everything I'd told her.

"I mean, I know I said I wanted you to get married, but I didn't think you'd actually do it. So then, are you guys going to take his birth name?"

I shook my head, closed the clamp on a piece of obsidian embedded in an axe shaft, and pushed my magic into it. This one was destined for an orc who wanted increased strength. "No, he said he won't carry the name of someone who abandoned him, and I wouldn't ask him to. The whole topic is kind of painful for him anyway, and her suggestion about the names was just salt in the wound." I grimaced at the memory.

She nodded in understanding and took the axe from me when I was done with it. "Speaking of parents, have you told yours yet?" She flopped back into her chair and handed me my next project.

"No." I frowned because I was being a chicken and I knew it.

"Their feelings are probably going to be hurt."

I sighed. "I know. We can always do a bigger wedding later, if it's important to them," I said, knowing full well it would be. I was their only child, after all, and a daughter at that. Especially for my father, since elaborate weddings were expected in elvish culture, there would be some disappointment about my elopement.

"At this point though, I don't have time for anything more than just making it legal."

She stared into space, playing with the ends of her hair for a long time, lost in thought while I fashioned some hair pins for a little girl with an aptitude for illusion.

"I still can't believe you're doing this. I mean, don't get me wrong—I'm ecstatic about it—but… wow. I mean… *married*. Are you sure this is what you want?"

I was quiet for a moment, checking my feelings and my heart for the umpteenth time. I wanted to be absolutely positive I was giving her an honest answer.

And I was.

I wanted this. I would have been willing to wait, but now that the opportunity had presented itself and Levi was on board, I wanted it, and I told her so.

She sat quietly for a moment digesting my answer, and then muttered, "I guess you won't need all those condoms after all."

I blinked. "*What* did you say?"

"I said, I guess you won't ne—"

"I *heard* you. That was *you!?* What? How!?" I was on my feet before I'd realized I'd moved. "Sidney, I thought that was my *mom!*" I felt my horror on my face, remembering the embarrassment of thinking my buttoned-up mother had sent me along with a mega-pack of specially bought Voider condoms.

Sidney froze, and then was suddenly laughing so hard she had tears in her eyes. "You should see your face! I just packed them in with some food and posted it to your parent's house to be included with your travel rations." She gasped for breath and tried to collect herself but failed, collapsing into another fit of laughter.

"Did you, ya know, happen to need them at all?" she asked teasingly with her voice pitched high, wiggling her eyebrows and failing again to contain her laughter. "Because I have some questions about mer anatomy. I just want to know if he has a fish di— ow! Ack!" I smacked her with a stack of papers from my desk.

"I. Thought. Those. Were. From. My. Mom!"

And that was how Levi came in to find me angrily chasing a flapping, screeching magpie around our shop with a rolled-up stack of papers.

CHAPTER 26

Even though Sidney tried to pull rank with her "best friend card" and send Levi packing for the night so we could have one more sleep over, he couldn't handle more time away from me again so soon. His dad had confirmed that new bonds were much more forceful in the beginning and that it would mellow a little bit more as it, and we, matured. I couldn't really complain though, because curled up against Levi's chest was my favorite place to sleep. Somehow, I just had this feeling it wouldn't be Sidney's last chance to elbow me in the face all night.

Even so, she showed up late-morning and kicked him out "so we could get ready." While I was expecting this to be a very pragmatic paper-signing and get-this-show-on-the-road sort of endeavor, clearly my friend had other ideas. When she showed up with armloads of curlers and flowers and told my boyfriend to get out, I was so touched I almost started crying on the spot.

"No! Don't do that. You'll make your face all splotchy. I'll be super bummed if you don't throw some proper elvish hurrah at some point, but just in case you *don't*, I'm taking my maid-of-honor duties seriously *this* time," she said, dumping her armful of supplies and three bouquets on my bathroom counter.

"Where did you get all these flowers?" I marveled at the ranunculus, peonies, dahlias, and tulips all crammed in together.

"Pike Place in Seattle," she chirped. "Sit. Are we doing curls or braids, or curls and braids? What are you going to wear?"

By the time we were done, I was in a royal blue, lightly beaded maxi-dress with a half up-do of curls and braids. She redid my hair three times before she was satisfied with it. While I did our makeup, she pieced together bouquets for both of us that paired well with both my dress and her blush-colored one, then tucked a few extra flowers in my hair for good measure. A few quick little boutonnières, and we were ready to meet the boys. I had the *best* best-friend, and I told her so.

"I know. Let's do this!" Her excited clapping made me grin even more than her smugness.

I packed a small bag with a change of clothes—and some overnight things because Levi said he had evening plans for us—and then it was time to meet the boys at the courthouse in Oar's Rest. We arrived to find them in sharp, tailored suits that made Sidney's jaw drop.

Levi just chuckled at her and explained that he needed it for events sometimes before turning his happy smile back to me. I'd never seen his expression so warm and joyful as he took my hand and brought me closer to him.

Grim looked... well, less grim than usual. He seemed a bit curious, but his usual intensity was dialed back. When I'd asked Levi who he was bringing as his witness he'd said he would bring Grim, and mentioned, "For someone who always has something to say about my life choices, he's been surprisingly supportive about our relationship."

I couldn't have really explained it, but something about Grim in a suit for this made a lump form in my throat. Even though the gesture was small, and perhaps even expected, it made it feel like he took me seriously. Like he took this choice we were making together seriously.

Sidney—bless her—would go to battle for me no matter what, she'd proven that to me for years. Even if my ideas were silly and she disagreed with me, she'd back me up with guns blazing, and I loved her for it. I *knew* I could count on her support. But Grim was kind of a wild card to me. I knew Levi loved him, and they were childhood best friends, but he'd never said a word to me even though I couldn't deny he'd still managed to be gracious and polite. I'd heard him voice his displeasure to Levi the night I'd had to stay over, even though I didn't understand it, so I knew he wasn't the type to go along with just anything. Having his approval of this, like my own parents', wasn't something I *needed* but was something I desperately wanted.

Sidney's excited chatter broke through my train of thought as she dug out the little boutonnières and tucked them into Levi's and Grim's coat pockets. Levi thanked her, and Grim gave his flowers a tiny, bemused smile, which made me want to laugh and cry at the same time.

"Shall we?" Levi's voice was a murmur against my ear as he pulled me closer, and it made the butterflies in my stomach jump into overdrive. His lure and beaming smile weren't helping matters, but I couldn't help but return his grin. We were really going to do this, and frankly, I couldn't be happier about it.

The building was beautiful, old white stonework with massive columns and high arches, but I couldn't make myself look away from his handsome face and charming suit as he took my hand and we climbed the stairs. Inside was bustling with people coming and going. I tried to take in my surroundings as we were led to the officiant's office, to pay attention to the high windows letting light stream over the heavy desk, or to the stocky man with lightly greying hair who greeted us and confirmed our names. Magic buffeted me from every direction, but I barely noticed any of it.

I couldn't tell you the officiant's name or a word of what he said. I was too busy staring at my new husband—*my husband!* The roaring sound of my heart pounding in my ears made it impossible to concentrate. I watched his lips move as he repeated his vows and his magic blanketed me in his ocean mist and warm sand, drawing me in and promising me a forever I'd never known I needed.

It felt like *home*.

I managed to repeat the words the officiant directed me to speak, the binding promises and oaths of loyalty and commitment. His directions to place the rings made me blink a few times in confusion, but when I started to correct him that we didn't have any yet, Levi interrupted me.

"I brought us some place-holders," he said quietly, reaching into a pocket to pull out a box with two gold bands. "This way you can take as long as you need to make yours perfect." He plucked the smaller band from the box, and with a trembling hand, slipped it on my finger. My gaze darted to his to find his eyes glassy. He was fighting tears and his expression made my heart burst.

I handed my bouquet to Sidney, and it was all I could do to get his ring out of the box without dropping it and slide it onto his finger. When the officiant proclaimed us married, I dove at Levi. I needed him. I needed *this*. And when he scooped me up off the ground with one arm and cradled my face with his other hand to kiss me, everything was right in my world. My face was wet with my own tears, so my makeup was probably wrecked, but my heart was so full.

After a few long moments, Levi had to break the kiss. I couldn't do it.

Then we had a certificate to sign and forward ahead to Whitewave. The officiant was shaking our hands, Sidney was squeezing me tight and squealing in my ear, and then, suddenly, I was passed to Grim, who enveloped me in the gentlest hug that ever existed, as if I were made of the finest spun glass and he was terrified he might break me.

"Welcome, sister," he said to me, his first words to *me* since I'd known him. Then he switched to perfect Elvish. "*May your union be blessed, and your children be many, and may your seventh generation follow you home.*" It was a traditional Elvish wedding blessing, referring to when I would eventually greet my distant offspring in Paradise. There was no hope of me stopping my tears. I had silent tears streaming down my face as I clutched a slightly confused reaper's hands at my wedding.

I don't know why I hadn't expected our friends to take this seriously or be supportive of us, but the overwhelming emotion it caused felt momentarily crippling.

At least, until Sidney piped in with, "We're going out for drinks now, right?" Because that was familiar territory again. I choked out a laugh, but reached over to grip Levi's hand. Because bond or not, he was *mine* now.

⤞⟡⤝

WE ENDED up at a little pub in an older part of Oar's Rest, and because it was afternoon on a Monday, there were only a few patrons inside. The owner ran the bar and recognized the boys immediately.

"Levi! Victor! Long time, no see!" It took me a moment to realize he was speaking to Grim.

"*Victor?*" Sidney's expression held more than a hint of amusement. He slid her a mildly irked glower as we were led to our table, which immediately shut down any teasing she'd had in mind. I guess I wasn't the only one intimidated by Grim. Hopefully it would hold even after she got a few drinks in her. Probably not.

Introductions were made and explanations given for the dressy outfits, and soon we had a round of celebratory drinks on the way. We settled into a table in a candlelit corner of the pub, and I couldn't help but scoot closer to Levi as he draped an arm around me and chatted at Grim about the times they'd eaten here in their youth.

I watched him as he spoke, his face animated and cheerful, the sharp line of his jaw contrasting against the stubble on his skin, his lips pursing just slightly before he laughed. Sidney cleared her throat and shot me a knowing grin. I felt my face heat and ducked my head as she raised an eyebrow at me.

As he talked, Levi would reach out and touch me occasionally, as if to reassure himself that I was still close. Just little touches, trailing a finger down my arm or grazing a knuckle along my shoulder, until eventually he just gave in and pulled me firmly against his side. I noticed the barest hint of a smile—I might even call it a smirk—on Grim's face as Levi tucked me against him.

Luckily, I was saved from any ribbing by our friends as the barkeep returned with our food. He struck up a conversation with Levi and Sidney about the local goings-on, setting down our plates and rambling for a while about the fairy folk rioting in nearby towns. According to him, it wasn't just the sprites anymore, but other races of fae had begun protesting too.

It made me itchy to get the constructs delivered and get to work on the new defense system for The Deep. I had to remind myself that Rafe and Silas wouldn't be here until tomorrow night at the earliest, and I couldn't do anything about a new golem until the council approved my involvement. Levi must have sensed my restlessness because he started smoothing his hand down my arm again as he listened to the waiter talk. I melted into him a little bit, his gentle touches helping to ground me in that moment. It did no good to worry about the future right now. Today was our day, and I wanted to enjoy it for what it was.

I found myself watching Grim as we ate, though I tried to be surreptitious about it. He methodically picked through his food after it was placed in front of him, using his fork to remove any traces of meat and place them off to the side of his plate. I wondered why he hadn't just ordered it with no meat, but he didn't even seem perturbed, just like he was lost in his own head and doing something out of habit.

Levi reached over to Grim's plate and stabbed the discarded meat while he chatted with the bartender, popping it in his mouth without missing a beat. His action went completely unacknowledged by Grim, who simply continued piling tiny slices of meat on the side of his plate. It reminded me of the ease that Sidney shared with her siblings.

Sidney, however, watched them with outright fascination. She could be subtle when she wanted to be, but she simply chose not to be much of the time. You might have thought she was watching a soap opera with the amount of open curiosity she showed. I shared her fascination with Levi's silent friend to a degree, even though he intimidated me greatly, so I understood her interest.

That reminded me, though, that Levi had never given me an answer about what had happened to the men who showed up at my shop. I narrowed my eyes at Grim and swallowed. He might shrug off Levi's questions, but he couldn't escape me right now.

"Grim…" I started when the barkeep finally wandered off. I

had to steel myself when he raised his pale blue eyes to focus on me. "Will you please tell me what happened to the two guys who—"

"Tsst!" I glanced at Sidney when she interrupted my question to find her shaking her head minutely. I frowned at her. "Nope." She said it around a mouthful of steak, shaking her head harder.

I sat back, blinking at her, and turned to see Grim observing us with interest. He went back to eating while watching her carefully, but Levi was uncharacteristically absorbed in his food.

"What—"

"Huh-uh. Nope. You're good." She made a slicing motion with her hand, telling me to quit. "I don't think you have to worry about those guys anymore." Her voice was low, but at least she'd swallowed her food this time.

I narrowed my eyes at Sidney and frowned, then at Grim and Levi, who didn't notice anyway because Grim was watching Sidney and Levi was watching his food. It was clear all three of them knew something about the men from the Phantom Order, but how would Sidney have known anything, and why didn't I need to worry? And why couldn't I ask? There wasn't even anyone here within hearing range.

"What *exactly* do you mean?" I hissed at her under my breath.

"Just... they're gone, okay? All of them. Poof. Gone."

I glanced over to find both Grim and Levi watching her with curious eyes as she picked at her food.

"Gone, how?" I whispered.

"Judgment," Grim answered blandly.

Cold ice shot down my spine, and I shivered involuntarily. "What?" Levi tightened his arm around me.

Grim picked up his beer and took a long pull. "You should continue to guard your safety carefully," he said evenly, "but these men have been removed." His words, spoken entirely without emotion, were probably meant to reassure me, but they felt as comforting as a cold gravestone. The skin on the back of my neck prickled, and I was reminded of the fear I felt the first time I met Grim. Perhaps it would have been wise to hold on to that.

"What did you... do?" I asked when I found my voice, unable to tear my eyes away from him. I'd been lulled into complacency by his calm nature and his friendship with Levi, but as I remembered his mad dash upon the back of a wraith, I was reminded that this man... this being... was no tamed thing.

By contrast, he seemed completely at ease. "I submitted a witness statement and official paperwork all the way up the chain. You have nothing to fear for defending yourself."

"But did they... die? I didn't want them to die." I'd purposely armed myself with non-lethal weapons because I didn't want to kill people. What did *removed* mean in this context?

The smallest flicker of disdain was his only reaction before he answered. "All mortals die, Elara." He paused, watching me, as Levi's arm tightened around my shoulders, and then sighed, his countenance softening the smallest amount. "They were weighed and found wanting. Know that you're not the only person they intended to harm."

He met my eyes evenly, his face a mask of indifference. My shoulders dropped. Of course this was a bigger issue than just me.

"Thanks, Grim," Levi muttered and tapped Grim's beer glass with his own. Grim gave us both a small nod before excusing himself to return to the Void, looking bored as ever as he walked away.

Sidney's voice was low, unaffected, entirely matter-of-fact. "They're *super* dead."

I turned to stare at her, feeling like everyone around me was unhinged. She paid my crazy-eyed expression no mind, as usual, and continued with a shrug. "I did try to warn you to stop asking. The whole warehouse district in Dry Gulch got razed by rioting sparks, and that particular building is nothing but a pit now."

⁂

"I HAVE a hard time feeling pity for people who wanted to kidnap you or harm you and force you to make a golem for them," Levi responded flippantly when I asked him about the missing Phantoms later that night. He toyed with the ends of my hair as we lay tangled up in one another's limbs at the Bed and Breakfast he'd reserved for us in Whitewave. It was nice to have one last night to ourselves before the golems arrived and I started my new project. We'd spent the evening discussing our plans for the immediate future in between bouts of exploring each other in ways that made my face hot to think about.

"I don't feel pity for them," I grumbled. "But what do you think it means?" I asked, feeling unsettled by the whole situation and wanting to know if I'd been responsible for someone being killed. It wasn't about pity; it was about due process and the sanctity of life. I should have just called the police, illicit tranquilizer or no. I didn't want to seem ungrateful for Grim's—and Jordan and Levi's—desire to protect me. I truly was. I was just struggling with all that had happened.

Levi chuckled, though it sounded a little brittle as he tucked my head under his chin. "I think it means Grim helped them along," he said, his tone very mild. "I don't know!" he exclaimed when I tried to pull back to see his face. "He doesn't usually discuss this stuff with me. I was thoroughly shocked at how chatty he was with you today. Honestly, I don't really care as long as they're gone."

Levi held me tighter to keep me against him, not allowing any space between us. I couldn't help but feel a little betrayed by his friend.

"I think he didn't tell the whole story," he continued. "He's very good at that, and knowing what he does about so many things and people makes it kind of necessary sometimes. I think he knows exactly what happened to them, because that's not the kind of loose end he'd leave hanging. I suspect you're very safe from those specific men." He tightened his grip on me even more.

I tried to think back to our conversation about them the day after they'd shown up at my shop. "He said he knew them."

"He said he'd seen them," Levi corrected, "not that he knew them personally. Grim... sees things. Knows things. Not just about the afterlife and death, but things about the past and sometimes even about the future." I frowned into his neck, wondering what Grim knew about my past or future. "He isn't omniscient or anything," he continued, "but sometimes little glimpses just come to him. He doesn't always feel like other people need to be privy to that information, even if it directly involves them."

He was quiet for a long moment before he finally continued. "He wouldn't personally kill those guys, Elara. He's a reaper, not a murderer. But I'd say it's safe to assume he knows more than he lets on."

I considered that for a moment. "Do you?"

"Do I what?"

"Know more than you let on?"

I felt him smile against the top of my head. "Usually."

CHAPTER 27

"The contract was between the *council* and her *parents*," Côvon interjected angrily during my discussion with Muriel the following afternoon. I'd known the mer leader of the Alliance for less than an hour and already he was trying my patience.

Rafe and Silas had delivered the golems half an hour ago, meeting us in an open field to the north of Whitewave, and had beaten a hasty retreat back into the wilds. Too many people had insisted on joining us here, and between the amount of unwanted company and the distance from the rest of their family groups, they hadn't been able to return fast enough.

I was already frustrated about my friends feeling uncomfortable and overwhelmed, and now Côvon was demanding that he be in charge of the guardians looming at the edge of the meadow. They'd insisted on joining me for the delivery—Côvon, the leader of the mer, and two other mer military officers, Muriel, Arvad, the sprite we met at the courthouse fountain, and one other sprite. I was making a conscious effort not to dwell on how easily one of my golems could squish an annoying mer.

While still being taller than me, the mer that joined us were considerably smaller than Levi. Lanky and lean, they had an almost serpentine quality about them, with magic that echoed the hidden, craggy depths of the ocean. They walked on two legs, and were clothed with woven seaweed and seal pelts, something I wondered about Muriel's feelings on. Their skin was varying shades of mottled blues, greys, and greens, and they had a noticeable ridge down their backs. Another ridge formed a row of spines up the backs of their arms, and some long quills covered the tops of their heads in place of hair. I knew from pictures that, when they shifted to their aquatic form, the spines sprouted long fins. They also carried venom, though I didn't think it was actually lethal.

Either way, Levi didn't seem to want them to get too close to me. His jaw had been set the entire time, and even now his hand hovered behind me as if he wanted to snatch me against him and haul me away at any moment.

I sighed and kept my voice even, giving Côvon a slow blink as I answered his interruption. "Yes, and Arvad is a member of the council." Arvad stood off to the side, obviously unimpressed with Côvon's attitude but entirely unsurprised by it.

Côvon didn't even bother to acknowledge my response, addressing Muriel as he replied. "I'm the leader, the head of the council, therefore the golems should be assigned to me."

"Can you reach The Deep?" I asked him dubiously. I thought one of the main issues of their invasion was that no one was able to withstand the pressure that far below the surface to help. "How are you planning to deliver the guardians if you can't actually get to the city?"

The spines on the back of Côvon's head bristled and began to raise as he turned to look at me, and Levi let out a long, low hiss that one of the other mer returned. Levi's magic lashed out like a whip, causing Côvon to take a small step back. I was so startled by the sound coming out of him that I turned to glance at him before he subtly nudged me to direct my attention back to the others. I'd never heard him make a sound like that, and the low rattle the other mer included with it made my skin prickle with fear.

Côvon studied Levi for a long moment, the first time he'd paid him any attention since we'd arrived, before answering my questions. "I will take these guardians to the edge of our territory and then direct it to The Deep. It will follow my instructions, yes?"

I shook my head. "We insist that they be under the control of someone who will be present in their general location in case they need on-site instructions."

His spines bristled again as he considered this. "Then they will follow me to the edge of the sprite's waters, and I will pass them over to Arvad then." Côvon crossed his arms, and I couldn't help glancing at the spines lining his triceps before I turned to Muriel, who rolled her eyes slightly and shrugged.

"As you say," I lied, and pushed power into Domm first, making his glowing runes brighten slightly as I re-laid its instructional guidelines. It would follow Arvad, not Côvon, but would take some limited commands from Côvon if asked. It would defend The Deep from any kelpies within its radius for a maximum of two lunar cycles, unless relieved from duty by Arvad sooner.

It took less energy than the initial calling had a week ago, and so I was able to switch to Leothen almost immediately without needing to catch my breath. As soon as I was done, both golems stepped forward to await verbal commands, and everyone but Levi stepped back.

I used the distraction to bend quickly to Arvad's ear. "Stay close to Côvon until he hands you over the guardians," I whispered. His eyes met mine as I straightened. I hoped it wouldn't make a difference or even be noticed, but this power-play nonsense irked me.

Côvon was saying something to Muriel, and turned to leave with the other mer, heading toward the shore. Arvad stayed behind briefly, then flitted up to press something small into my hand before flying away with the other sprite to follow the mer. I watched my family's guardians pace obediently behind them, slowly disappearing into the night.

I didn't need to look at my hand to know a heartstone shard was nestled in my palm. Against my skin, they had a different kind of energy than any other stone.

Muriel sighed and dug in a bag she carried to pull out a thick stack of papers. "I have your contract for creating the new golem, along with your payment agreement. It wasn't as much as I asked for, but it was the best I could negotiate."

I thumbed through the contract, noting the payment amount was insultingly low for a project of this magnitude, but schooling my expression. It didn't matter, since I wouldn't be taking it anyway.

She continued, "They've requested that you meet them at the address provided on the first page there. It's a shipyard, with a warehouse where they've been hauling up materials for your construct."

That was news to me. They already had something planned?

"Oh yes," she said, answering the question clearly written on my face. "They found a behemoth skeleton sometime back, they said. A leviathan, I think?"

Well, isn't that just fantastic.

I must not have kept my distaste from showing because Muriel hesitated for a moment before stating softly, "I really do appreciate what you're doing for the sprites."

⁂

THE MER HAD BEEN INDUSTRIOUS. I had to wonder if they'd been collecting deadfall from the massive leviathan long before The Deep was ever attacked. Perhaps they had a dowser, someone like Val Harrington who specialized in locating hidden objects.

They'd even brought in some lorelei as contractors to do the heavy lifting. I'd never met a lorelei before, as they were a race of people even more rare than the mer—cousins that had interbred with orcs millennia ago. They shared some physical traits with the mer, but the size difference between them was staggering, making them look more like semi-aquatic orcs.

I'd spent the early morning surveying the shipyard, where the spinal column and the rib cage were being sorted and reconstructed. Leviathans were rather eel-like anyway so there wasn't really much more to them than that and a skull. Maybe some fin bones. Heavy fog made it impossible to see the project in full, but the workers seemed unbothered by the lack of visibility, calling out to each other in loud, ringing tones in a language that sounded almost song-like.

Levi and I were in the warehouse, where the massive skull

and some of the more fiddly bits were being kept. There were enormous bones stacked absolutely everywhere.

I was very much not over my aversion to using bones in a construct. Levi was doing his level-best not to smile every time I grumbled about it being *too close* to necromancy or that it was *disrespectful to the creature they came from.* However, there was a case to be made that these people had already put in a massive amount of physical effort amassing these materials, and it would also speed the process up considerably, having the beast constructed as it would have been in life. It was always better to mimic nature when possible, and not needing to 'reinvent the wheel' meant I would spend less time than it would take designing a new one. It didn't make me any happier to be using them, but I tried to remember this project wasn't about me, and that it would be going toward protection of people who needed it desperately. *Was this personal growth or decaying moral standards?*

It was difficult to ignore my personal feelings about it, though, when I was staring at the toothy maw of a four-ton skull. I grimaced and eyed one large razor-sharp tooth with a chip near the top. I felt myself slip into a full-blown frown as my gaze lifted to the gaping orbital sockets and I thought about how we were going to need to find a way to access the braincase without damaging its structural integrity.

I pushed that thought away for now and went back to the scraps of paper I'd assembled on a desk in a nearby corner, an "office" for myself, as it were, somewhere I could lay out my maps of The Deep and its surrounding areas, the anatomical layouts of several species of Leviathan, and a roster of everyone working on the project and their roles. I still needed to catalog all the materials I would need to begin magically linking the pieces of the skeleton together. *Maybe Sidney would know where to source this much iolite...*

Around midday the council leader, Côvon, stopped by to hover over my shoulder and ask questions about my plans and thoughts on the project. He introduced his nephew, Doldir, who I assumed was the one originally pegged to lead the project since the boy had some small artificer magic in him, and a lorelei named Khonlos, who was the project foreman and the man I'd be working most closely with to complete the golem. There was clearly no love lost between Côvon and Khonlos, and Côvon stormed out after a short exchange between the two of them. I'd have to ask Levi about that one later.

Khonlos, like the other lorelei I'd noticed in the shipyard, had magic with a murky feeling of water movement and increased strength—at least in short bursts—which was probably already impressive without the ability to boost it, considering how heavily muscled he was. I didn't even come up to his chest, and I had to focus on keeping my composure so as not to flinch away from him.

Lorelei didn't appear to have the ability to shift forms like the mer did, or at least not as much. They had a little bit of a water form and a little bit of a land form, so it just kind of seemed to meet in the middle. Khonlos had long, dark hair like an orc, gathered into clumps with tiny metal cuffs, similar to the ones my father wore in his own hair. His dark, mottled skin looked scaly in places, probably perfect for protection and camouflage under water. Like his mer cousins he had short spines projecting from the backs of his arms, but though his teeth were sharp and pointed, he had small, orcish tusks jutting slightly from his bottom jaw.

When he gave me a polite smile as he was introduced, I noticed his orange eyes had slitted pupils. His people were probably adapted as ambush predators. I suppressed a shiver and took a small step closer to Levi, who rested a reassuring hand on my back. It was silly, but 'instincts are instincts' as Sidney would say. I forced a smile and shook the foreman's hand, which he accepted briefly.

I wasn't sure what Côvon's nephew Doldir's job was on the project, but as soon as Côvon left, Doldir started sniping at Levi. Khonlos was knee deep in an explanation about which techniques he thought we might use to inlay amulets in bones of this size when we became aware of the conflict behind us.

"I'm here because I have every right to be," Levi said dryly, looking up at the mer from the notepad of music he'd been working on. I stiffened and turned to find Doldir posturing over Levi, who was giving him a droll look from his seat. Were they going to try to make Levi leave? The thought sent a shock of dread through me. He needed me because of his bond, and I realized I'd felt completely safe in this new environment because I'd trusted Levi to help me navigate.

Plus, I needed him for this project even if he didn't know it yet.

Doldir looked young, maybe just on the cusp of adulthood. He was lean and lanky, but his stance was cocky and his response to Levi sounded condescending, though it was spoken in Marée-san, so I couldn't be sure.

"Because the Law of Bonds says so. Now get out of my face," Levi responded, more forcefully this time. His enchantment snapped out, a telling sign that he wasn't playing around.

Doldir hissed at him and took a small step back to turn and look at me, his expression morphing into a mocking grin. "Bonded to a landwalker? Tough luck, man."

"I *am* a landwalker, you piss-breathing, Ken-doll-looking ass of a bottom-feeder." His magic gave a firm shove.

Doldir hissed at Levi again, baring dagger-like teeth, and this time Levi stood to his full height, towering over Doldir by head and shoulders. Levi hissed back, sounding *exactly* like a snake, making my skin prickle at the primal sound.

Fast as lightning, Khonlos darted between them, hissing and adding a deep thrumming growl—calling to mind some terrifying combination of a lion and a crocodile—at Doldir, who darted off into the stacks of bones on the far side of the warehouse.

I stood rooted to my spot while the guys returned to what they were doing, Khonlos muttering under his breath as he went.

"Do not worry, little one. He cannot make your mate leave," he said quietly when he reached my desk. Levi huffed in response but didn't look at him. "I will toss him into the harbor if he tries, and he can swim home to his daddy," Khonlos grumbled.

I frowned in the direction Doldir had run, then tried to remember what I'd been doing. "What does he do here?" I asked. *Did he really have some kind of job helping with the construct?*

Khonlos grunted. "Annoys everyone. Spies on us and reports

back to the boss. Distracts my workers with his chatter." Sounded pretty harmless, if not actually productive.

"What's a Ken doll?" I asked.

"He's got no genitals," Levi muttered. "No offense." He shot a glance at Khonlos before returning to his sheet music.

Khonlos barked a loud laugh. "He has genitals." He paused for a beat and chuckled. "Who wants their male parts to be swinging free on the outside, where anything can come along and snatch them off? So strange. Even landwalkers' male parts look like they belong on the inside. Don't you think they look like they belong inside?" He turned to see Levi's response, but Levi only smirked at his sheet music.

Khonlos shook his head, then bent to circle something on the drawing of the Leviathan's spine. "This would probably be the most structurally sound place to inlay the linking amulets," he said, returning us to our previous conversation.

I truly hoped this place wasn't the tinderbox it felt like.

CHAPTER 28

OVER THE NEXT FEW WEEKS, I sketched out where metal and amulets would be inlaid in the bones, and the mer, lorelei, and dozens of sprites worked to install them. It was an odd project for me, the first time I'd been directing others to do the physical work of building the construct instead of personally having my hands on the work myself.

The sprites worked tenaciously, bringing me each precious stone to modify, checking my drawings meticulously, and embedding every amulet with careful precision. It was clear they were working for the protection of their people, that this project was where they placed their hope for a future. Every day a few more would trickle in to join the fray, though more of the newer ones had scars and disfiguring injuries. An elder sprite named Rith mentioned they were kelpie injuries, and many more wanted to come help but were too wounded.

The mer spent most of their time in the shipyard, directing the lorelei on skeleton reconstruction and occasionally getting into scuffles with one another, though some of the larger men also helped haul bone. They spent the majority of their time in the water, and I was shocked by how long their tails and fins were. I'd learned to keep my distance after Levi carefully explained one day that, if one were to bond to me, he and they would instinctively fight to the death without hesitation.

Lorelei didn't bond like the mer did, so after getting to know them a little better, Levi seemed more at ease with me working around them. I was constantly in awe of the sheer strength they showed, both men and women, hauling massive bones around and twisting metal into shape with their bare hands.

The skeleton was so long now that, while most of the construct was built in the shipyard, the skull and neck were in the warehouse, with the two sections coming together on the drydock outside.

I was mostly comfortable in our routine, except for the occasions Côvon or Doldir would come over to talk to me, but Levi didn't usually tolerate them nearby for very long. They set my teeth on edge, anyway. Côvon filed away the contract I returned to him, without even a brief glance at it, and went back to yelling instructions to the workers. Doldir mostly just slunk around, looking shifty, but one time he'd snuck off with my construct drawings until I'd tracked him down and demanded them back. I didn't mind his curiosity, but I wasn't going to allow him to derail the project.

The work was exhausting, keeping track of every gem, plan change, and project update, not to mention the day in and day out energy spent modifying gems into amulets that would magically link the pieces of the construct together, making it a functioning golem. I hadn't even seen the heartstone yet. Khonlos said the Alliance was keeping it guarded and hidden until it was ready to be installed.

Levi helped where he could. He stepped in occasionally to mediate disputes between sprites and the rest of the workers when emotions ran hot or lent a hand puzzling tricky bones together when the lorelei were growing weary at the end of the day. I'd mentioned bringing in some orcs or trolls to help relieve some of the workload, and Côvon had shut me down immediately. No races without representation in the Alliance were allowed on the project.

Levi had kept busy with his own work, too—mostly writing music for a performance troupe based in Dry Gulch and others that purchased his original works—but I also knew he was paying close attention to the workers around us.

We worked most days at the warehouse, though he left occasionally to run errands or meet with his own clients or stop by my shop to help Sidney with something or other, and at night we'd taken up temporary residence together in a small apartment nearby. We spent our meager free time visiting nearby concerts or exploring, and he was teaching me to cook seafood. One night, after Levi had been gone longer than usual, I came back to the apartment to find he'd created a tiny reading nook for me with cozy blankets, pillows, and tea from home. Stolen moments learning about each other was our normal.

We even ventured home one weekend and tried to intermingle our friends by inviting Sidney to the guys' apartment to meet Jordan and have a movie night. It ended up being a *complete* disaster. Levi startled Sidney into shifting, and she attacked him, and then Jordan *ran away*. Apparently, he'd known Sidney from childhood. It had been over a week, and he *still* hadn't come home. She was still too grumpy to talk to me about it.

One evening, as Levi put the finishing touches on an elvish stew he'd found a recipe for somewhere, I sat at the small kitchen table, toying with a heartstone shard, pressing my energy into it this way and that. It was the one Arvad had slipped me the night I delivered the stone guardians.

"Levi, will you sing something for me?" I asked absently. I heard the stirring stop and glanced up to find him staring at me quizzically over his shoulder.

"Sing?"

"Yes, please. I have an idea that's been nagging me for weeks. Do you remember how I had to ask you to pause for a moment when I was rebuilding the amulets I'd lost in the pond? Your enchantments were interfering with the stones when I powered them up."

His eyebrows knit together in confusion, and he reached to turn off the heat for the stove. "You want to make an amulet with a lure in it?"

I shook my head. "The opposite, actually. Your enchantment doesn't always pull; sometimes it pushes. I've been thinking a lot about our older golem, Domm, and how the old magic was woven into its heartstone. It didn't just power the

construct; it also contacted the dryads and possibly that stag...
What if I could use your enchantments as a type of warning, or
deterrent, in the Leviathan construct? Then it wouldn't be
strictly melee, simply destroying whatever intruders it came
across. I could try to make it send out a wave of repulsive magic
first, and *then* it would attack if the intruder didn't heed the
warning."

Levi gave me a small grin as he set two bowls of stew on the
table and sat. "Only you would have compassion for the kelpies,
Empress."

"It's not *only* kelpies that could wander into the golem's exclu-
sion zone," I muttered with a frown, lost in the mental minutiae
of how I could potentially get this idea up and running. I'd
already spent weeks toying with the idea, but I hadn't been able
to pin down some of the smaller details.

His grin spread farther at my tone. "I think it's a great idea.
There are some old battle hymns that used to be sung by the mer
as war songs with a similar purpose. I think they could suit this
project quite well."

It took a few beats of silence before I realized I was staring at
him with a silly grin and made myself refocus. We spent some
time playing with the heartstone shard, and after several attempts
I was able to embed Levi's enchantment into it. It still felt like
something was missing, and I wondered for the hundredth time
if it was fae magic. Domm's extra magic had felt distinctly fae
when I'd tried to update his heartstone.

The short distance his enchantment could travel from the
shard was dissatisfying, but maybe that was simply because of the
tiny size of the stone? There were a lot of variables here, and this
wasn't something I'd done before, or knew of other golemancers
creating in recent times. But it did remind me that one of the
amulets Levi originally sold me was an enchantment amplifier, so
I sent a spectral message to Sidney to ask if it was still at the
shop. I couldn't imagine it would have sold already.

Instead of simply replying like a normal person, she just
showed up at the shipyard without any warning the next day,
landing clumsily on my desk in an awkward jumble of black and
white feathers. She startled Levi, who swore under his breath. I

glanced around to see if anyone else had seen her enter, but no one paid any attention to my corner of the warehouse.

"What are you doing here?" I whispered as she shook out her feathers and folded her wings back.

She made a gagging motion and then dropped a thumb-sized amulet on my desk with her beak. "Delivery." Her voice was higher pitched in this form and kind of tinny sounding.

"Gross," Levi muttered quietly.

"Shut up, it's a built-in pocket," she replied, miffed. "Figured I'd just bring it to you. Plus, I'm *super* nosy," she told me—like I didn't already know—eyeing the construct as she spoke. "Huh. Mecha-Leviathan. I wouldn't have seen that coming. You think they'd let me ride it?" Just then, one of the lorelei rounded the beast's skull, stepping into view. "Gotta go, I miss your face!" she called, launching herself off my desk and out a nearby window, up near the rafters.

I blew her a kiss as she left and earned myself an odd look from Khonlos as he approached my desk. At least it was only him. I knew the mer wanted much tighter security around the project. I held up the stone and explained its purpose to him—it boosted the effect of 'spoken' enchantments, a very niche amulet —and the best location for the sprites to embed it. He took the stone and left without any questions. I guess he didn't get paid enough to care about stray birds.

When he was gone, I turned to look at Levi, knowing how he felt about the items his mother had left him. But I didn't even need to voice my question. His expression was soft as his gaze traced my features before focusing beyond me to the skeleton. "I think it's a perfect use for it," he said. His magic was warm sand and gentle waves, and I adored him.

THE DAMP CHILL of the predawn air did more to help wake me up than the cup of coffee I clutched for warmth. Côvon had informed us last night that the heartstone was being delivered tomorrow, and there were still a billion things left to finish, so as much as I would have preferred to lounge in bed with Levi, another early morning was necessary. He groggily followed me to the warehouse, pausing to chat momentarily with one of the few lorelei already arriving for the day.

I took a small detour, bypassing the entrance to round the side of the building with the open bay doors where the spine of the great leviathan snaked out onto the dry-dock. Even these bones, much smaller vertebrae compared to the enormous skull housed within the building, dwarfed me by a foot or more. I tried to imagine what the animal had looked like in real life, coiled below in the murky depths, watching, waiting, feeling for prey in the water with the special sensory organs lining its skin. I shivered.

Try as we might to repurpose its bones, this construct would be a pale comparison to the savagery and predation of a real animal hunting its next meal. It would have its own special version of a sensory organ, at least. The heartstone would detect and locate the magic of other creatures, just like the sentries did on my parent's property.

I shook myself from my distraction and padded quietly alongside the spinal column to the open bay doors, vaguely inspecting each inlaid amulet and wrapped wire as I went. It was a neurotic habit mostly, because we'd been over each amulet and connection repeatedly at this point, until I came to an empty socket in a connection piece and stopped. I blinked, staring dumbly at the empty metal bracket where the connecting amulet should have been resting, and the skin prickled on the back of my neck.

Suspicion pulled my gaze to the enchantment amplifier that had belonged to Levi's mother, only to find that it too was gone. I bristled, outraged at the lack of protection Côvon had provided this project, and the heinous greed required to *steal* from it. I'd barely had time to process those emotions when I flinched, my heart suddenly pounding at the sound of wood creaking nearby and the soft whump of a lid closing. Doldir scurried around the front of the leviathan's skull with his arms full of iolite gems, his eyes widening when he saw me, clearly not expecting anyone to be at the worksite yet.

"You!" It was all I could get out before he shoved me hard, trying to barrel past me with his prizes.

My back cracked painfully against a stack of shipping containers, and the scalding coffee in my hands spilled out over my stomach and lap when my elbow slammed into the corner of the crate. I released the magical charge in my own amulets before he'd pulled his hand away, and Doldir gave a piercing, high-pitched scream and dropped to the floor. I'd decided after my conversation with Grim that I didn't *ever* want to use my wasps again if I could help it, so I'd reinforced my defensive amulets and made them stronger instead.

Levi came flying through the entrance on the other side of the room, leapt over me, and landed on Doldir's prone form, his fist connecting viciously over and over again.

"Levi, stop! Stop!" He was going to kill him! I realized Doldir's scream had been so high-pitched that Levi had probably thought it came from a woman, *from me.* "I'm *fine, stop!* He's already down!" Big arms reached past me as one of the lorelei workers pulled Levi off of Doldir. I looked past him to see Khonlos pushing through the entrance to take in the chaos around me.

His slitted orange irises snapped to me first, quickly cataloging my wild expression and the fact that I was half on the floor with coffee spilled all over me and surrounded by scattered amulets. He stomped through the maze of haphazardly stacked shipping crates to reach past the man who held back my husband, heaving for breath and with bloodied knuckles, and snatched up Doldir by the neck.

"Elara, what'd he do?" Khonlos asked in a low growl, not taking his eyes off of Doldir's bloodied face.

"He was taking iolite," I answered shakily. "And at least one connection stone is missing, and the enchantment booster I gave you."

"Where are the stones?" Khonlos demanded.

"I don't know!" Doldir screeched. "That bi—" Khonlos shook him by the neck like a ragdoll, thrashing him in the air like one of my father's dogs might savage a toy. "In my pocket!" he yelled.

One of the other lorelei reached into his hidden pouch and pulled out the missing stones, then patted him down to reveal three more. My stomach turned at the look of fury on Khonlos's face, but his voice was very quiet when he spoke.

"I want you to listen to me very carefully, little shark. If I ever see your face on this or any worksite of mine ever again, I will serve boiled mer soup to my crew that night for dinner." The look of sheer terror on Doldir's face as Khonlos hauled him off down the dry-dock by the neck made me wonder if maybe the rumors of the loreleis' past dietary predilection weren't just rumors.

Khonlos stopped at the edge of the dock and *hurled* Doldir into the harbor.

<hr />

THE NEXT DAY, when they brought in the heartstone, was the first time I ever had real doubts about my abilities as a golemancer. Even during school—when I wreaked havoc and accidentally summoned chaos—I had known it was just a matter of perfecting my skills, of finesse. My power level was never something I'd questioned or needed to think about.

It arrived in the middle of a large caravan of well-armed guards, packaged in a wooden crate over three meters high and wider still. I didn't need to have the crate opened to confirm it was as large as I feared. I could feel it. It beckoned to my magic, a blank slate ready to be used. But even touching it with my magic just briefly, opening myself up to feel the stone's own magic, caused a wave of dizziness I'd never experienced before.

Instead of pushing my magic into it, it felt like it was pulling my magic *from me*. I'd never even *heard* of a heartstone big enough to do that. Our bodies naturally buffered us from using too much magic, but I'd read stories of people who used more than they were capable of and were either permanently injured from it or died. Just the thought of this stone pulling me past my body's limits sent a primal kind of terror through me.

The sound of the side of the crate hitting the floor was loud in the warehouse, made more prominent by the collective hush of the crowd waiting to see the stone nestled within. It was the most beautiful heartstone I'd ever seen, a dark Prussian blue that reminded me of midnight storms. Deep, deep inside it, a small green light flickered, occasionally illuminating the stone from within, revealing tendrils of color even darker still as they wound through the structure. It almost felt as if one were looking down through the ocean into a kelp forest below at a flickering lantern buried in the sands.

Côvon let out a pealing, celebratory whoop, and I startled backward into Levi, not realizing he'd come up behind me. He steadied me, wrapping his hands around my upper arms, and a glance up at his face showed he was bristling at how close the mer were to us. They jostled each other in their excitement, puffing out their chests and talking loudly amongst themselves. I watched them for a moment, my gaze lingering on the glittering greed in Côvon's eyes before Levi gently squeezed my arm and directed my attention to the sprites with a tiny nod.

The contrast in reaction was staggering. They looked devastated. Mournful. One of the older sprites, the elder named Rith, looked like he would have been crying if that were something his species was physically capable of. They gazed at the stone with unconcealed heartbreak and despair.

"What's wrong?" I whispered to Levi. They'd been a part of this whole process. They clearly wanted this defense for their city. Why were they suddenly... *devastated* about it? They weren't making a scene or even any noise, but the heartache was clearly written on every feature of their small faces.

I glanced back again to see Levi grimacing at the mers' boisterous celebrating. He answered quietly, "It's probably their largest heartstone and the greatest wealth left to their people, and it's been confiscated by these buffoons. Sure, it will be used to defend them of course, for however long the council permits it, but it will still belong to the Alliance, because that's who you have to assign it to."

I slid my gaze back to Côvon, careful to keep my building hatred off my face. I didn't technically *have* to do anything. I didn't really want to get in trouble, but the circumstances of the operation didn't sit well with me either. It was hard to think with the heartstone's excessive magic filling the space around me, almost pulsing in time with my own heart. I needed some distance.

⋘⋙

I LAY COMFORTABLY NESTLED into the crook of Levi's arm, my head tucked into the dip in his shoulder with his hand beneath my hair, rubbing the muscles at the base of my skull. "You're a ball of nerves," he muttered quietly. "Why are you tense?"

I allowed myself a few moments to enjoy the blissed out feeling his fingers were creating in my scalp before I answered. We were curled up on the blankets of the bed in the apartment where I'd found him sprawled out with a book after dinner. "I'm horrified," I admitted, when I found the words.

I'd been sick to my stomach for most of the day, a queasiness and unease that refused to go away even when the sprites returned to work and I'd found familiar footing arguing with Côvon that, under no condition, was the heartstone to be mounted on the Leviathan's forehead, like some gaudy fashion statement. I'd made it clear to Khonlos that I would not stand for such a travesty of engineering, that the stone had to go *in the brain case* or there would be hell to pay.

I wasn't entirely sure how I'd back that threat up, but the relief I'd felt at his nodded acceptance and hidden sneer he directed at Côvon had settled my stomach just the tiniest amount. What was the point of having a weapon if you were going to place its most vulnerable component front and center? Côvon would enter the warehouse one morning to find the heartstone already mounted in the brain case, and it would be too late to do anything about it. He would rage and howl, but what could he do? Fire me?

But that brought me to my other concerns. Would he try to hurt me physically if he were very angry? Because I'd been shuffling through plans in my mind for a long while on this, and I had a feeling he would be *very* angry before the end of this. Today's defiance was only the beginning. Levi and I had discussed it *ad nauseam* over the past few weeks, and I was loath to bring it up again. It did nothing to calm my stomach.

Instead, with a sigh, I turned to the possible fallout. "How badly could it go if I *didn't* give the Leviathan to the Alliance?"

Levi's fingers stilled on my scalp. After a moment of silence, he resumed rubbing. "Between the Alliance and the sprites? The mer and the sprites? Possible legal repercussions for you? Retaliation toward you?" The gentle pull of his magic felt at odds with the seriousness of his words. I nestled deeper into his shoulder.

"Yes. That. All the above."

"Hm. I imagine there would be trouble between the sprites and the Alliance council, though that already seems to exist. It's just that the balance of power could shift. I can't say what the legal consequences of stealing a golem would be..."

I sputtered. "I *made* that golem! Well, kind of. But either way, it doesn't actually belong to them anyway!"

He tucked my head into his neck to quiet my interruption.

"You could argue that in court if they took it that far."

"I could just play dumb and say I slipped," I replied.

"You could," he answered, amused. The amusement faded as he continued. "As far as Côvon or the others retaliating in the moment, well, you still have your wasps. And a giant mer-crushing Leviathan."

"I'm not looking to add murder to my rap sheet," I muttered.

"Yeah, but they don't know that," he mused. "I can call in reinforcements..." he began, probably thinking of Grim, "but it would most likely make them suspicious."

"I don't even know if I'll still be standing when I get that thing powered up," I confessed.

"What do you mean?" he asked, pulling back to look at me with concern on his face.

"I've never experienced a stone of that size before," I admitted, trying to wriggle my way back into his side. I'd sent a spectral to my father to ask for his input—secretly, because of Côvon's demands that only sea-folk be involved—and his confidence in my abilities had buoyed me. His assertion that heartstones didn't pull magic from us had not. I knew what I had felt. Maybe he'd never seen one this big either? I was scared to drag him into this, knowing there would be consequences when I was done.

"I was dizzy just probing it today. I just hope I'm actually strong enough to power it up." This was going to be very anticlimactic if I couldn't do it. "I'm going to need every amplifier and power well I can get my hands on." I frowned, remembering the ones I'd lost at the bottom of the pond. "And the golem won't do me any good if I pass out unless I tell it to defend me, and then I won't be able to stop it from killing people." What a mess. Flashbacks from college plagued me.

Levi was quiet for a long moment. "I want you to focus on building your golem. Get the sprites what they need. No one else but you can do that right now. Don't worry about the mer," he said, and I was startled to hear a thread of amusement again in his voice in that last line. But then his voice grew serious again. "I won't let them touch you. You do what you need to do. I'll help you with whatever comes after."

CHAPTER 29

THE WEIGHT of my amulets felt reminiscent of armor, cuffed about my arms, draped in large swaths around my neck, bejeweling every finger until I felt as though I were wearing gauntlets. My head bore enough gemstones to furnish a heavy crown— power wells, magical amplifiers, focuses, and energy bolsters. The latent effect of so much magical feedback combined with the sheer power of the leviathan's newly embedded heartstone had me crackling with irritation and excess energy. The day had quickly come to power it up, and I felt simultaneously rooted in place by the sheer weight of it all, and ready to explode at any moment.

I caught Levi's eye for the barest second as he slipped in a door from outside of the warehouse. He nodded to let me know he'd finished discussing our plan with Rith, the elder sprite. Tuning Côvon's ranting out was becoming more difficult by the second, so I turned an irritated gaze back to him. He had to wear himself out eventually.

"It wouldn't do," I eventually interjected, "to have a weapon be so fragile." He'd been hissing and shrieking all morning about how this was *his* project, and *he* made the decisions about how the golem was going to be built. But that simply wasn't true. It wasn't his project, and I wasn't going to allow him to weaken the sprite's new defense system. I wouldn't explain again why the skull cavity was the proper place to lodge the heartstone; it was already done, and he wasn't going to be able to talk the lorelei into changing it. My goal now shifted to distraction.

"In fact, I have another way to make this construct even stronger and more... impressive." I'd been going to say effective, but had changed my mind and gone with what I knew Côvon was truly concerned with.

He swung his angry glower from Khonlos to me, so I knew I had his attention. Explaining the addition of Levi's battle hymn to the construct's defense abilities was necessary because it wasn't something I could hide or do in secret. So, I took the time to convince Côvon that this would make our leviathan golem much more formidable, adding greater flexibility and range to its defensive capabilities. It would already have crushing, slicing teeth, and the ability to weaponize the water around it, but now the addition of a siren's song would give it *range*. I'd thought I might have to sell the idea a little harder, but he practically choked on his satisfaction over having such a specifically mer trait become a central facet of the golem's arsenal.

I'd asked Levi before in private if it could be better to have a group of sirens instead of only him, thinking it would make the magic stronger, but he disagreed. "Female sirens have a much stronger lure than I have, but their ability to repel or instill fear with enchantment is nearly non-existent. Plus, there's the issue of the chaos it would cause having them on the job site," he'd answered with a look of subtle horror on his face. Mermaids were solitary or only spent time with other females when they weren't having babies.

My diversion finally worked, and Côvon eyed Levi when he took his place beside me, the pride over having what he clearly considered a larger claim now over the leviathan warring with the contempt he felt for my partner in his expression. I pushed energy into my defensive jewelry, wanting to blast his scales off, but I schooled my expression and held my head high as he thought it through. I had work to do and he was preventing it with his tantrums, but I took secret pleasure in the thought of how irate he would be when I was done.

Côvon eventually let us go back to work—watching us all as a hawk watches mice now that we'd defied him once—but I focused on my tasks. He wouldn't be able to see the important aspects of what I was doing anyway.

The laborers had finished assembling the skeleton, and I'd spent the last several days inspecting the build while Levi schemed with Rith. I'd walked the length of the beast over and over, carefully testing each connection and joint again, pushing my power into each bone's individual amulets and watching the movements of the joints to make sure they functioned properly and had full range of motion one final time. Khonlos would call out instructions to adjust pieces that needed it, and we retested again and again. By the time we reached the end of each day, I was exhausted and dragging, but Côvon had looked very pleased with the project as he shot Khonlos a smug grin and strutted past us. At least, he had been until this morning's heartstone disagreement.

The big lorelei paid him little notice, going about his work carefully and methodically. I could only hope he wouldn't get caught in the crosshairs during any dispute between the Alliance and me when the dust finally settled. Levi assured me Khonlos was fully on board and could handle himself, but I couldn't help but fret over how my choices might affect him as the foreman for our project. I hadn't personally witnessed their interaction directly after Khonlos had removed Doldir, but the tension between Khonlos and Côvon had strangely lessened somewhat. Côvon even seemed to keep a fraction more distance.

I surveyed the skull of the leviathan as it rested heavily on the floor of the warehouse, its great toothy maw front and center, with dark, cavernous sockets gazing sightlessly toward the gathered crowd of workers. It was a smaller group of us today, with most of the laborers finished and now absent. Khonlos stood to one side of me, with Levi on the other. Côvon and some of the mer were milling about, and *all* the sprites were there.

As far as I could tell, every sprite that had ever stopped by to assist with the project, and many that hadn't, were gathered to watch today. Côvon had tried to run them out, had sent his lackies after them multiple times, but they just flew back in the open windows or doors as soon as his back was turned. They gathered in the rafters and peeked out from behind empty crates. I'd even seen some peeking out over the rims of those gaping, eyeless sockets.

I was sure it wasn't just sprites in attendance either. Wisps, sparks, and other fae cluttered among the groups too. There was even a very suspicious flash of black and white feathers I'd glimpsed near one of the window ledges.

I wasn't used to working in front of so many people, and the butterflies I felt in my stomach weren't the good, sweet kind. My stomach churned with nerves, and I fairly rattled with pent up magic. It took all I could muster to pull my attention from the leviathan before me and the sprites surrounding us and focus my attention on Khonlos. He sighed deeply, scanning the crowd then the construct just as I had. A nod: everything was in order. *Time to begin.*

With every other stone I'd ever worked with, it was a matter of focusing on my intent and *pushing* my magic into the stone. This one pulled. At first it was a relief to simply release—if that was even the right word—some of my overflowing magic and allow the stone to pull it away, locking it inside, flickers of light beginning to glow through its orbital canals as it came online. But as its power stores grew, it became more difficult to keep a grip on my intent, my purposes for it, and feed it the correct amount of power without letting it take too much from me. A niggling fear told me this much power was reckless, but I felt that, if I controlled the flow and protected myself, it would be fine. I could spare no energy to focus on anything around me, only the stone. My trust was fully in Levi and Khonlos to deal with the mer and anything else around us.

I focused on feeding the stone power, attaching it to its construct, link by link, the images of The Deep—both provided by Rith the sprite and the maps of the city so far below—nestled in the black abyss where no sunlight ever reached. There were boundaries it would patrol, territories to guard, provisions for species allowed entry and species lists to repel. Unable to pull my attention from the task at hand, I reached toward Levi and brushed his fingers with mine.

"The battle hymn." My voice sounded far away, dissonant,

deeper. It took Levi a long moment to respond, and when he did, he sounded a little shaken. Seconds passed and his voice grew stronger, steadier, and with it... his magic. The ward around my wrist protected me from the brunt of his repellent effects, but the urge to run, to flee, still pressed on me. The stone echoed his enchantment as he sang, and I heard Khonlos grunt from beside me with the effort of remaining in place. Some scrambling at the edges of the warehouse told me others in attendance weren't so steadfast.

His song grew and changed, still simple in its construction but more forceful and rhythmic. I continued to feed power into the leviathan's heartstone, changing it in my own way. The golem was now pulsing blasts of magic, eye sockets glowing with blue light from the stone hidden behind them. Long shadows crawled across the floor of the warehouse behind stacks of crates and clusters of frightened mer.

"Rith," I called, my voice still sounding odd in my own ears. "Access your magic, please. Press some of it toward the stone, if you can." I couldn't turn to see if he'd heard me, but I felt it when his magic rose and began pouring into the heartstone. Not just him but nearly every fae in the room swelled with magic until the heartstone was thrumming with power.

If I'd feared before that I wouldn't know how to meld the fae magic with mine and Levi's, it proved unfounded. The heart-stone greedily accepted the sprite's magic, locking it around our own like iron bars I could only see in my mind's eye, could only feel. It fit perfectly into place, confirming my suspicion that it was the needed ingredient for combining and amplifying Levi's magic in the heartstone. Our magics weren't melded so much as woven together to create one whole, and for now, I was merely the conduit.

Slowly, terribly, that changed, as Levi's hymn drew to its natural conclusion. His enchanted words ended, and one by one the fae allowed their own magic to wink out, until eventually, suddenly, I was the only one left, and the leviathan's heartstone was far from finished. I drew more, fighting a flare of panic, pulling the remaining reserves from my power wells, reaching out into the aether to pull what I could from the raw magic of the

Bound's environment, reaching deep inside myself to surrender any last power I could find within to my burgeoning creation.

Specks of white swam in my vision, and I faltered. It was nearly done. Ringing in my ears made me hesitate a beat, because passing out before this was finished could cause unimaginable chaos. I had to remain in control. But the pounding continued until I followed the sound—not in my own head as I suspected—higher into the rafters, where distinct black and white feathers flickered back and forth, Sidney pecking and tugging at something metal up above.

I felt Levi's hands supporting my weight under my arms as I began to list lightly to one side, and I dismissed her distraction. The heartstone pulsed and pounded with our magics, a potent combination of mine, mer, and fae that I'd never felt before. It nearly matched Grim in its intensity. My whole body trembled with the effort of separating myself from the pull of the stone. Instinct warned me that any more magic leaving my body would have dire consequences, and the stone felt strong enough now to operate as its own entity.

One last final push, and I assigned it to The Deep—not a man, not an alliance, but the city itself and the people who lived there. The leviathan would patrol the boundaries I laid out in perpetuity, defending the people who truly owned its heartstone, the sprites.

Levi was fully supporting my weight now as I forcefully severed my connection to the heartstone. The room erupted in chaos as the leviathan began to move, intent on obeying its first directive—get to The Deep. Its heavy head lifted from the floor in a screech of clattering bones. Everyone scattered in terror, not expecting the sudden movement, except for the sprites who swarmed the construct. They clung to the skeleton with lips pulled back in tiny snarls, daring anyone to stop them as the leviathan reared up and out of the warehouse and suddenly plunged into the sea below.

Against my will, my gaze snapped to Côvon, reading his shock as it shifted to confusion, to suspicion, to anger, to rage. "That was mine!" he shrieked, before he lunged toward me across the open space. The last things I registered were the unabated hammering of beak on metal, the hot glow of sparks surging in through the warehouse windows, and the cold rush of water on my skin as Levi's arms lifted me and darkness swallowed me whole.

⁓◈⁓

CONSCIOUSNESS CAME SLOWLY. The bed was uncomfortably firm, and the brown stucco wall in front of my face wasn't familiar to me.

"Are you finally awake?" my father asked. I startled and rolled over, straight into Levi's hip.

"Whoa, easy. Take it slow," Levi soothed. His hand brushed the hair from my face, and he helped to prop me up a bit, offering me a cup of water. I shook my head. Thirst burned my throat, but I was more concerned about what my dad was doing here, wherever here was.

My father sat lounging in a high-backed chair in the corner of the stark, small room, with his boots crossed over one another and his jaw propped on his fist. I took in his familiar white hair— nearly as long as mine and hung loosely with tiny gold chains— and warm graphite colored skin. His finely featured face was decidedly disapproving. My mouth drew down into a frown to match his.

Levi stood carefully from the side of the narrow bed and bent to press a kiss to the top of my head. "I'm going to ask for some food," he murmured, before leaving the room.

My father's voice was dry. "You have... *so* much explaining to do."

I tried to shake the grogginess and rubbed at my eyes. "I don't even know where I am."

"Governor Nandine's personal ward. For three days! They wasted two healing draughts on you before I could explain that there was nothing physically wrong with you."

I guess that would explain why I didn't feel like a complete wreck after lying in one spot for three days. *Three days?* I gave my father a slow blink as I tried to process that.

"You powered up and programmed a heartstone that..." he

trailed off for a moment, his expression bewildered, "… I wouldn't even be able to *access* from the size Sidney describes. Started a small riot among the mer. Are apparently *married to one?*" He shot an incredulous look out the door Levi had left through, and I winced. Yeah, we were going to have to talk about that. "And then poured so much energy into the leviathan that you knocked yourself clean out for three days!"

"Hi, Daddy," I greeted him, completely ignoring his grousing and thrilled to have him with me even though I felt guilty he'd probably interrupted his project and rushed here. He'd had three days to stew in nerves, frustration, and whatever else, I was sure, but I was just waking up and tickled to see him. The look he shot me was all at once indulgent, chastising, and affectionate, before softening into something like exasperation.

A raucous caw from behind me drew our attention to Sidney's avian form, perched on the headboard, but she was only excited about the tray of food Levi carried.

My father narrowed his eyes and pointed at her. "And you know they don't allow animals in the ward. They'll chase you back out again if they see you. I don't understand why you don't just shift back?"

She gave a raspy chattering sound and dropped onto the bed as Levi set the mouthwatering tray of food on my lap. I was suddenly ravenous. Her voice was tinny sounding as she answered my father's question, "No clothes." I tore off part of a roll and passed it to her. Sidney didn't care about clothes. Sometimes she was just stubborn about wanting to be in her bird form, and I had a feeling this was one of those times. All the better to exasperate my father and spy on hospital staff probably.

"What were you doing there?" I asked her, remembering catching glimpses of her as I'd powered up the leviathan.

"I was gonna ride it." She fluffed out her feathers and snatched up another proffered piece of the roll, looking particularly hard done by.

"She was triggering the sprinklers," Levi answered for her, tendrils of sea foam magic brushing over me. "Or trying to. I think the sparks stepped in at the end." Sidney gave a trill of assent as Levi moved behind me and began gently gathering my hair out of my face as I ate, tying it back out of the way as he'd seen me do numerous times. My father watched the entire exchange with a gimlet eye.

"Why... sprinklers?" I asked around a mouthful of food, not even knowing exactly what I was trying to ask.

Sidney knew anyway. "They all grew big tails and fell on the floor!" she crowed delightedly, cackling in her own way.

The pieces fell into place. Sidney pounding on the metal piping in the rafters, sparks surging up to the ceiling, cold water on my skin. Côvon had rushed at us, but somehow, we'd gotten away just fine.

I felt my eyebrows pull together. "Do mer *always* shift into their aquatic form when they get wet?" I asked Levi.

"No," he answered, wrestling to keep his smug delight under wraps and clearly failing. "But it's a pretty strong reflex." There was no mistaking the laughter in his voice.

"And do you suppose," my father asked, his voice flat, "the mer are going to feel at all inclined to return my stone guardians?"

I blinked at him. "I built a failsafe into my orders before I passed them to the sprites. They'll return themselves to the field outside of Whitewave in another two weeks' time. I didn't know how long the new construct might take so I gave myself an extra buffer."

His relief was palpable, though he'd been less perturbed at the thought of losing them than I might have expected him to be. "And what of you, dear? How many lawyers am I going to need to hire to untangle your broken contract mess?" No anger, just tiredness.

I smothered a tiny spark of ire. He was tired and frustrated, and Sidney or Levi had called him off his project when I'd fainted. I knew my father well enough to know I would always be his little girl, even though I was grown and could take care of myself. "I can hire my own lawyers, thank you. And I never signed any contract or took a single drahk of payment. I doubt they'll have much legal ground to stand on if they want to fight with me." If they tried, I had no problem defending my choices.

My father settled more firmly back into his seat as he

watched me eat, a hint of a smile threatening to break through as Sidney pecked at my plate and Levi toyed with the ends of my hair. I beamed at him in return, thrilled with his obvious pride in me, until Sidney interrupted with, "She needs some guards though."

"Sidney!"

EPILOGUE
LEVI

———◇———

THE WORD SIREN has long been synonymous with seductress, enchantress, temptress. Ancient stories tell of beautiful mermaids coaxing travel-weary sailors from their boats with their songs, only to drag them to a watery grave. The thing is, in real life, nobody treats me like a murderous sea-hag, which might actually be preferable. Instead, they clamor around me with their dazed expressions, everyone wanting a piece of me for themselves. They crave more and more until there's nothing left to give.

The greatest irony of my life is that, by some genetic fluke, I inherited both the ability to snare and be ensnared, though it's so much worse than that. When a male is born both mer and human, some of us can be bound forever. It isn't a temporary thing like it is for a full-blooded mer. It's permanent, and so I've spent my entire life dodging that lure, refusing to let myself be caught by anyone.

Until her. Elara. The Empress of my heart.

I'd told Grim a long time ago that I would never be bonded, would never be owned. He'd disagreed, saying only that someday I would find someone worthy of crowning Queen of my heart. I'd laughed at him.

I can still remember what it felt like when I'd glanced up to find her standing in a crowd of magicless Voiders. A dainty wisp of a woman with hair the color of rich, dark earth and eyes like burnished chestnuts, dripping with jewelry and understated clothes. And then I smile as I remember the haughty glower she leveled on me as I sang my heart out for her, Grim's words ringing in my ears.

My curiosity about her had been insatiable, even as my instincts had told me to keep my distance. But how could I? Once I became aware of her deep intelligence, her gentle heart, her fierce desire to be courageous... No, 'queen' could never describe how I felt about this woman.

I take a deep breath, ignoring a twinge of guilt at leaving her to fend for herself for a moment among the crowd of well-wishers and watch her interact with them instead. I've borne the brunt of their attentions for most of the formal reception, and it's left me feeling utterly drained.

I'm grateful I don't need to keep as close an eye on her these days. Since the fairies have made it clear they're guarding her, I can afford to relax for a moment. Not that she can't defend herself; she can, and she has. For someone so tiny and ethereal, my wife has an immense amount of fight in her. But I can't help but worry. She'll always be a target for people who would use her, and she's just too precious to me not to stress a bit.

Even as I watch, a spark darts out to hiss at a guest who's ventured too close to Elara, and I let out a sigh of relief. We're not entirely sure when the fairies started showing up, stalking her quietly from the shadows, but ever since she handed the leviathan over to the sprites, she's spied their cousins hiding in her potted plants, or fireplace, or making themselves comfortable under the row house's eaves.

I know it makes her nervous that the sparks in particular seem to have taken a liking to her, since they aren't exactly known for their level-headedness. I probably have Jordan to thank for that. Fire elementals have always seemed pretty chummy with the spark community, and I doubt they'd begrudge his change to a vampire, the way the other races do.

Either way, their vigilance has taken out multiple Phantoms before she ever even caught a whiff of them. Even with their headquarters decimated—also thanks to Jordan, who seems quite excited about arson in general—they still tried to poke around. I grind my teeth at the thought, and again I'm grateful for the fairy-folk's fascination with my mate.

She is a vision as she drifts between diplomats and emissaries, rulers and governors—some family, some friends, all guests tonight at our formal wedding. My wife carries herself with a grace and dignity almost completely unknown in today's times. She looks every bit the powerful queen she might have been in another life, *especially* in that dress. Gauzy, draping, sheer, and white, it has an open back and gold details. Jeweled chains loop over her shoulders and down her back.

My body aches, craving the beauty and softness of her. The little sounds she makes.

A throat clearing beside me pulls me back into the moment, and I scowl at Grim.

"It's the debt," he says, just low enough for me to hear.

I give him a side eye and have to restrain myself from messing with him. We've been friends for so long I don't even bother trying to keep up with his jumpy train of thought. If I stare at him long enough, he'll explain himself.

Grim sighs, like I'm the one being unreasonable by not being able to read his mind. "It's a cultural thing," he says. "The fae can't abide being in another's debt, even if Elara would say she's owed no debt."

It irritates me to no end when he answers my thoughts as if he knows what I'm thinking. He doesn't. I'm pretty sure. I think. I cast a long look at him out of the corner of my eye. *'Dick,'* I call him in my mind, and he doesn't respond.

Grim always seems just on this side of omniscient, as if he doesn't have enough impressive magic. I'm super wound up tonight and trapped sitting here at our wedding party's dinner table, and he's all buttoned up in his prissy best-man's attire. It just makes me want to tweak his nipple or muss his hair and see what I can get away with.

Of course, he heads me off with a bored sounding, "Don't touch me," before I even realize I'm thinking about it. Fine.

He's wrong, though, about the fae's fascination with Elara. Sure, imagined debt undoubtedly played a role, to a point, but they've already repaid that many times over. Within a month of the leviathan's completion, the sprites had delivered *five* heart-stones as gifts for her. And we keep finding little piles of drahk hidden in her shoes or piled in the spice cabinet, though... maybe those are rent payments from the ones living in her plants... Either way, she funneled every red cent into a fund for Adonci Tyr's remaining son and other children left orphaned during the attacks.

If that weren't mortifying enough for her, the sparks once tried to refer to her as Empress. *To her face.* I feel my mouth turn up in an uncontainable grin as I remember her firmly explaining to them that she isn't any kind of empress, it's just my pet name for her. And the accusing glare she turned on me.

My smile softens as she turns and begins to make her way back to the raised dais where we sit. No, the fae's fascination with her has a much simpler explanation: gratitude, or perhaps the comfort of finding a friendly ally. Elara would never, ever consider herself to be a hero. In her own mind, all she did was right a wrong. Simple as that.

But Arvad has told me about the transformation her construct brought to his people, how they don't have to live in fear of the kelpies—or anything else, for that matter—anymore. How sprites that come from other cities to help rebuild The Deep often end up settling there instead. And how the dim glow of the leviathan's heartstone in the distance has become a source of great comfort to the sprites, his song—my song—keeping the nightmares at bay.

My grin returns... eventually she'll find out that sprites every-where have begun to name their new daughters 'Elara' and Sidney will have a field day.

Speaking of Sidney... "Where is Jordan? Is he hiding from Sidney?" I ask Grim. Jordan's more fun to pester than Grim anyway. Less predictable, at least.

"Ask him yourself," Grim murmurs. "He's cowering behind the third column." He flicks his gaze to the column in question and suppresses a hint of a smirk when we hear a low hiss. Oh, good, that means Jordan can hear us then.

"Jordan, it's safe to come out. Sidney's dancing with a dryad anyway," I call to him, knowing that's the opposite of what he wants. "Come sit with us."

He relents, slouching over to the table and slumping into the open chair beside me. His inky eyes search the milling crowd until he finds her, and he watches her spin through the crowd with Elara's friend Rafe.

"There's no need to hide from your best friends," I goad him lightly, trying to pull him from his distraction, lest he stew in his grumpiness all night. "Come engage in normal conversation like the common folk." He loves to remind me that I'm "marrying up" into the aristocracy and teases me that I'm supposedly above them now.

"Everything you say upsets me and knowing you is a burden," he answers gamely, and I grin. "To answer your question, yes, I'm hiding from Sidney."

I stand as Elara reaches the steps of the dais, stepping down to take her hand and help her up. The candles burning nearby don't do much to illuminate our little corner of this January night, and I know she isn't quite as adapted for night vision as the three of us. She specifically requested a night wedding so Grumpy McBite-face seated to my left here could join us.

"Is this where we're all hiding?" she asks as I retake my seat and pull her down into my lap, gathering armfuls of gauzy skirt layers as I turn her sideways and try to make her comfortable. It's been a long night, and now that the festivities are winding down, her tiredness is apparent. My fingers trace along the enchantment ward clasped around her wrist and I finger the latch, reminding me of her reaction to my voice when it's removed. I'm half tempted to haul her out of here so I can have her to myself. "Your dad seems better," she whispers, pulling me from my thoughts.

I search him out, finding him conversing with an orc. He still looks rough, but his eyes are clear and he's fresh out of rehab. I'm proud of the steps he's making, and I hold my wife a little tighter, reminded anew of her goodness and compassion. She's given me my dad back. "Yeah," I answer, and there's no missing the roughness in my voice. "He's having a good day."

"Oh, no. Sorry, guys. Gotta go," Jordan says as he stands. I'm surprised he's stuck around this long. The ceremony was hours ago, dinner long finished, cake cut, and dancing is winding down. I scan the crowd again, looking for blond hair, and just as I suspected, I find Sidney watching his progression with slitted eyes as he skitters away.

Grim sighs from across the table, and I cast a glance at him, noting the white haze beginning to creep over his irises. "I'm afraid I must make my goodbyes as well," he says, and I give him a nod, knowing he's got a 'job'. I'm so glad I wasn't born a reaper. *'Even if he does have all the best magic,'* I think to myself as he pulls a package from out of some shadowy unknown. Still not worth being on call for his *entire life* and dealing with dead people all the time. *No, thanks.*

He sets the package—a smallish white box with silver ribbon —on the table and slides it across with long fingers. Elara makes a grateful noise, picks it up and settles it in her lap. One tug at the end of the ribbon and the bow slides apart. She lifts the box top, and then I have no idea what I'm looking at. There's a little blanket, thin, with silver satin around the edges, two tiny, soft looking shoes, and a tiny gold bracelet (maybe?) that looks antique. Kind of a weird wedding gift, if you ask me, but what does Grim know about weddings? This might be the first wedding he's ever attended in his whole life, now that I think about it.

Elara is quiet for a long time, lifting each piece out and holding them for her own inspection. I open my mouth to thank him anyway, because he might be a weirdo but he's my weirdo and he tried, right? But she beats me to the punch.

"Grim? Am I pregnant?" The calm, quizzical tone of her voice somehow causes me to gloss over the question for half a beat, until it finally registers, and I'm left spinning. Because yeah, now that I look at them, I'm definitely looking at a gift for a baby. A little blanket people use to wrap them up in, some little bootie-things. I have no idea why a baby would wear a bracelet, but it's about the right size. But maybe... maybe he's just a dope and thinks people only get married for the purpose of having babies. That totally sounds like something he'd assume. For all his near-omniscience, Grim's got some weird ideas about life in general.

"Yes?" He says it like it's a question, and I feel like my head is about to explode. "You've... been pregnant for two whole weeks already." He casts me a bemused look, as if I'm somehow supposed to rescue him. As if he thinks I should also be aware of this obvious-to-him revelation. I don't even question how he knows it. If Grim says she's pregnant, then she's pregnant. He's never been wrong about something like this.

"I have?" Elara asks, her voice small.

"Do you... did you not know this?" Grim is quickly succumbing to panic, and I can honestly say I've never seen him so far out of his depth. I'd be laughing hysterically right now if he hadn't just rocked my world so thoroughly. I can't even feel my face, but I'm pretty sure I've got solid saucer eyes right now.

She sounds as confused as he does, but her voice is layered with patience and amusement as she asks, "How would I know that, Grim? Two weeks isn't long enough to even have missed a period yet. How would *you* know that?"

"I... can feel life?" he asks her, again like it's a question. "Can't you? It's *your* own body. *I don't know how this works!*" He throws me a frantic glance, but what am I supposed to do? I can barely follow this conversation, let alone try to patch the apparent gaping holes he has in his understanding of basic biology, because this bumbling doofus just *accidentally* informed us we're going to be parents.

A baby... with *Elara*... and it's already there. I feel my arms tighten around her, expecting all my embedded fears revolving around my mother's abandonment to come flying in, but they... don't. I'm reeling, sure, but the fear doesn't come, because I know my wife better than that, and she isn't the same as my mom. Elara chose to love me.

I realize I've missed part of the conversation as Elara thanks my best friend and he rises, shooting me a guilty look before retreating to the shadows. We're quiet for a few minutes, and then Elara dissolves into a fit of giggles. "His face," she gasps, and then she's hysterically laughing so hard that tears are rolling down her cheeks. I hold her while she quiets, which takes a while, but eventually she does and settles more deeply against my chest.

"Siren?"

"Yes, Empress?"

"Let's go home."

MAGPIES & MAYHEM

SIDNEY AND JORDAN'S STORY

———⟡———

HUMANS ALWAYS MAKE a big fuss about PMS, but you know what else sucks? Molting. Imagine being an angry, hormonal hot mess, losing most of your feathers, and then the prickly, itchy, bruising, painful process of growing them back. *For weeks.* Not to mention, the entire time you look like the bird equivalent of a hobo. That was me, folks.

At least I could escape some of it for a bit, when I was in my 'human' form. I was still an angry, hormonal hot mess, and my brain felt a little bit like it was on fire, but I could hide away the pin feathers and most of the desire to peck out the eyes of anyone who got too close. Somewhat.

Stomping up the stairwell to the nondescript third floor apartment wasn't enough to blow off my steam—I acknowledged that—but even though I probably wasn't fit for company, I still wanted to be there. For one, I hadn't spent any quality time with my best friend, Elara, in over a month. She'd been busy with an important project, which could literally save lives, and being newly married to a siren with an annoyingly seductive voice.

I liked her husband, Levi, but I couldn't help begrudging him all her time and attention he stole from me. I was working on it, okay? Maturity wasn't something that came naturally to me. I had to fight for every ounce of it, tooth and claw.

Which brought me to the other reason I'd accepted Elara's invitation for a movie night at his old apartment: curiosity. Levi lived with a grim reaper, and no one could have possibly expected me to be mature enough to pass up an opportunity to see a guy like that in his natural habitat, no matter how grumpy or irritable I felt.

The problem with my impulsivity was that I'd forgotten how nervous the reaper made me. Nervous was maybe a strong word. I wasn't scared of him—much. Something about his presence made me jittery, like I should strike first and ask questions later. That was entirely inappropriate, however, because the man had never been anything but politely disinterested in me.

It didn't stop me from glaring his front door down like it had offended my mother. Who knows how long I'd been standing there like a crazy person—I hadn't even knocked—when the front door slowly creeped open. Standing on the other side was seven-foot-whatever of otherworldly maleness, holding a bowl of popcorn and staring at me like I was the weird one. *How did he even know I was here?*

"Grim." I greeted him, standing there and pretending like I wasn't nearly quivering with tension. I couldn't feel people's magic the way Elara could—that wasn't in my wheelhouse—but I think it would have been impossible for anyone to be in this guy's space and not feel something menacing emanating out of him. His aura swallowed a whole room just by him existing in it.

He simply inclined his head toward me in greeting, then gestured toward the room with his bowl, stepping back to make way for me. So nonchalant. So normal. You'd never know he could spawn all kinds of things out of shadows and collect the souls of the dead. I wondered what he did with them. Did he eat them?

Grim's expression became more inscrutable the longer I stared at him, but I got the distinct impression he wanted to roll his eyes at me. I narrowed my own eyes at the dark-haired man and turned sideways to slide through the doorway, pretending like I wasn't trying to keep as much space between us as possible. Because I'm smooth like that.

It only took two small steps into the room to transport me

back in time to twelve-year-old Sidney, because seated in front of me, glowering at me, was my childhood day-dream. Jordan Houjin, my oldest brother's super-hot teammate and my pre-teen crush, was gripping the arms of his recliner like he wanted to destroy them. He still had those gorgeous cheekbones that looked like they could cut glass, those perfect, kissable-looking lips, and that glossy, raven-colored hair. Looking at him instantly took me back to days spent on the sidelines 'watching my brother's matches' as a gangly, gap-toothed child.

Jordan was different, too. His skin was all wrong, pallid and sickly looking. It caught the shadows in an odd way. Elara's words came back to me about Levi having a vampire roommate and my heart plummeted. What had happened to him?

Worse still, was how hard his eyes were as he stared at me. The playful, flirty, confident Jordan I'd watched growing up wasn't the same person I saw before me now.

But then, I guess I wasn't the same knock-kneed girl he'd known either.

"Hey! Sid's here—" Right over my shoulder, where I hadn't noticed his approach, Levi's exuberant voice sent me into a conniption fit. Between the hair-raising presence of the grim reaper on one side, and the dawning horror of discovering Jordan's fate, I had no mental space for anything else. My response to being startled was to shift—every time—and this time was no exception.

Before he could even complete his sentence, I'd collapsed in on myself with bone-crunching speed, flaring with heat and sprouting feathers. I tucked my arms-turned-wings against my body with a snap to pump me up out the neck hole of my shirt, flapping twice more before my clothes even hit the floor below me.

But—*CURSES!* I remembered too late. *My pin feathers!* Outrage flooded me. I don't consider myself terribly vain about my human form, but when it comes to my feathers? Yeah, I care what they looked like. Corvids in general are striking birds, and as a born-and-bred magpie shifter, I wear my black and white markings with pride. But right then, mid-molt, I looked like a buzzard with mange.

I had two choices here: I could remain an ugly-ass, mid-molt bird, with raging hormones and tender skin, or I could immediately shift back and be naked as the day I was born. My choice was made before my clothes had even touched the floor, but dang it, it *hurt*.

Shifting was always uncomfortable—calling magic forth and commanding a change to one's corporeal form was never a pleasant sensation. But twice? In less than a minute? The amount of magic required and physical exertion caused the second shift to be downright painful. And that did terrible things to my mood.

I was poised to strike the instant my body reshaped, my leg pulling up and releasing with a snap. It was an overreaction. I knew it before the kick even connected, so I changed course just enough to strike his chest and not his face. Levi took far too much pleasure from startling me into shifting for me to let it go completely.

"Oomph!" Over the back of the couch he went as I landed on my pile of discarded clothing. "I probably deserved that," he wheezed, sucking wind for a few seconds on the floor somewhere behind the couch. "Maybe not for this time, but definitely for one of the earlier ones."

Elara stood, frozen, a few steps from where he'd landed, holding two full drinks she'd begun to carry into the living area, exasperation written on every tiny elfin feature. I felt the tiniest spark of shame for punting her new husband across the room, but I ruthlessly stomped it into smithereens. I was standing here buck naked, in front of my childhood crush and a real-life-actual-grim-reaper, because he'd startled me *again*. My bones still ached from the rapid double shift.

"I told you she was molting," Elara muttered.

"You did mention that." I guess Levi had decided the floor behind the sofa was a comfortable spot, because he didn't seem to be in any hurry to get up. A soft crunching sound behind me told me that Grim was eating popcorn. That was my cue to extract myself from this ridiculous situation.

I unclenched my fists and my jaw, crouching to scoop up my

clothes, and careful not to give Mr. Reaper more of a free show than he was already getting.

"Levi's room is the—" Elara started, but I cut her off.

"I got it." I wasn't an idiot. I headed for the closest open bedroom with my clothes and shut the door. It had a large poster of the boy who played Jacob from the movie Twilight taped to the back, and the room didn't smell like Levi at all. It smelled like vampire.

To STAY up-to-date on release dates and more info please sign up for my newsletter at www.elsiewinters.com, follow me on Facebook at www.facebook.com/AuthorElsieWinters, or join my reader group, Elsie Winters Boundlands Babes!

NOTE FROM THE AUTHOR

Thank you *so much* for reading my story and taking a chance on a new author. It's hard to overstate how dependent new authors are on reader reviews and word-of-mouth recommendations, so if you enjoyed this and want to help others find it, please leave a review and tell others!

Do you want more? You can sign up for my newsletter to receive a FREE copy of Green-Eyed Monster, a short story about the day Elara met Sidney and Hyrak, aka 'The Great Golem Catastrophe'.

I'll also be providing updates and early chapters for Sidney's book, Magpies & Mayhem, and other related extras. Please make sure to check your promotions tab and verify your email address for the mailing list, otherwise it won't get added.

I hope you enjoyed the preview of Sidney and Jordan's story. Keep reading to learn more about Green-Eyed Monster.

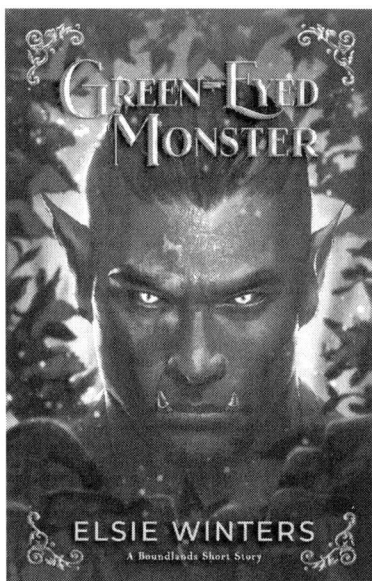

GREEN-EYED MONSTER

He's an orc studying for his accounting exam. She's a forest faerie trying to salvage her botany project. There's a magically animated stone sentry crashing through campus like a two-story tall wrecking ball.

The first time Hyrak lays eyes on Solandis, he's too immersed in the chaos around them to notice her soft beauty, but once she's in his arms, he's enchanted by the opinionated little fae's passion. Can gentle Hyrak control the fiery possession scorching through his veins? Does Solandis really want him to?

GREEN-EYED MONSTER is a short (10K word), fun Fantasy Romance with a guaranteed HEA. Content warnings include adult language and consenting adult romantic scenes.

Get a free copy when you sign up for my newsletter at elsiewinters.com!

ACKNOWLEDGMENTS

I could not have created this book without the help of so many people who are dear to my heart. I want to thank Susan R., Melissa M., and Lauren B. for all of their time, logistical help, and emotional support.

"Critiques with Katie" editor Kathleen Walker provided manuscript critique. Girleyne Costa illustrated my beautiful cover. Leigha Wolffe-Stoirm provided indispensable edits and guidance.

ABOUT THE AUTHOR

Elsie Winters lives in the deep, dark, woods of the Pacific Northwest with her husband, kids, a dog, and a random bobcat that hangs out in her yard. Her favorite pastimes are feeding Steller's jays who knock on her window for snacks and being yelled at by Douglas squirrels while gardening. She also reads paranormal romance books like they're going out of style and collects monster art that she has to hide from her kids.

Never miss a story! Check out my website to sign up for my newsletter or follow me on social media!
Contact info:
www.elsiewinters.com
elsie@elsiewinters.com

facebook.com/elsie.winters.1

twitter.com/elsiewinters15

instagram.com/author.elsie.winters

amazon.com/Elsie-Winters/e/B098KS326T

goodreads.com/elsiewinters

bookbub.com/authors/elsie-winters

Printed in Great Britain
by Amazon

85159202R00185